The Volunteer

Charles P Sharkey

Ringwood Publishing
Glasgow

First published in Great Britain in 2016

by

Ringwood Publishing

24 Duncan Avenue, Glasgow, G14 9HN

www.ringwoodpublishing.com

e-mail mail@ringwoodpublishing.com

ISBN 9-781-901514-36-0

British Library Cataloguing-in Publication Data

A catalogue record for this book is available from the British Library

Typeset in Times New Roman 11

Printed and bound in the UK

by

Lonsdale Print Solutions

About the Author

Charles P Sharkey has worked for 26 years as a criminal lawyer in Glasgow.

The Volunteer is his second novel after his successful debut novel, ***Dark Loch,*** was published by Ringwood Publishing in 2014. He is now working on his third novel, ***the Memoirs of Franz Sternberg***, a story of Berlin between the wars.

He has recently started a new career as a landscape gardener.

He is also singer songwriter who has had a number of his songs recorded by other artists. His first studio album 'Strange Hotel' has been well received. His follow up CD is due out next year.

Praise for *Dark Loch*

"*Dark Loch*, by Charles P. Sharkey is a deeply evocative book that transports the reader back to a world experienced by many Scots a century ago. The first chapter starts with the birth of Callum Macnair in 1895, but we already know from the prologue that whatever happens to him in the meantime, some of our characters are going to end up living out the nightmare of the trenches in France, two decades later ... The result is to draw out the contrasts in an impressive way and illustrate the tragedy and change being felt by every community across Scotland at the time." Review for Undiscovered Scotland

"*Dark Loch* is an intriguing story, entwining profound love and vivid horror as you drift between the glens of the Scottish highlands and the trenches of the 'Great' War. Tangible imagery and intricate characters make *Dark Loch* utterly believable and compelling."

Acknowledgements

In writing this novel I am grateful for the support and encouragement I have received from family and friends who have read early drafts and given valuable constructive criticism, in particular my partner, Lesley Walker.

My gratitude extends to everyone at Ringwood Publishing, in particular my editor, Philip Amey.

Dedication

This story is dedicated to all the victims of what became euphemistically known as The Troubles.

Book I

Chapter 1

Belfast 1960

Clouds smothered the hills to the west of the city as dawn broke over the tightly packed grids of redbrick terraced houses. Drifts of smoke were already rising from the chimneystacks, adding to the dreary palette. The morning quiet was broken by the sound of bottles rattling their familiar morning discord from a milk float that trundled along the cobblestones, before stopping with a jolt outside a corner house. After a glance at the grey skies, the milkman left two silver-top bottles on the doorstep and lifted the empties.

Marie Duffy heard the clatter of bottles at the front door and slowly raised her head. She rubbed the back of her neck and yawned before straining a glance at the alarm clock, which was ticking away incessantly; it was still only quarter past six. She lay back down on her pillow.

Soon the morning light lifted the darkness from the room. She carefully freed her arm from under her son's head, moving him gently back on to his pillow. He groaned for a moment, but did not waken. With her eyes still heavy with sleep, Marie blessed herself and said a short prayer, bowing her head towards a pained image of Jesus hanging on the wall opposite, above a cluttered chest of drawers. She confirmed her faith in the resurrection, ending the prayer in a hurried whisper. 'Sacred Heart of Jesus, pray for us sinners now … and please God, send Joe home. The children need their father. Amen.'

The codicil to her morning prayer had been the same for months, ever since the first of the men came home after signing the pledge. She had damned Joe more often than not for being a stubborn fool. *What the hell was he holding out for? Pride that's all, foolish pride! What did he have to be ashamed of?*

She blessed herself before getting up and putting on her dressing gown. The touch of the linoleum floor made her shiver.

Still a young woman in her mid-twenties, Marie did not consider herself to be beautiful, but she had a pretty face and a good figure that she was proud of. She brushed her long, dark hair and, after checking on the twins in the cot, went downstairs to fetch the milk from the doorstep.

Outside, a ginger cat sat on the windowsill, grooming itself in the early morning murk. Then a sudden flash of lightning split the dull skies, followed by a hollow clap of thunder that rumbled on to a growl. The cat had heard enough and scurried for shelter as the heavens opened up.

Lifting the two bottles, Marie quickly closed the door to keep out the flurry of rain, before going into the kitchen to put the kettle on. Still shivering, she warmed her hands over the gas hob, while the kettle gradually came to the boil. She made a cup of strong tea and went back upstairs.

Brendan groaned again when his mother slipped back in beside him. She pulled the heavy bedding from his hot body, hushing him quiet. The window frames rattled as the wind and rain lashed against them with menace. Another streak of lightning was followed by another deep rumble of thunder. Her mind was on Joe again. She anxiously lit the half smoked cigarette she had saved from the night before. The rush of nicotine calmed her a little. She wondered if the rumours were true; had he finally signed the damned thing? She took another long draw from the cigarette.

A Corporation trolleybus splashed along Divis Street,

before stopping on the Falls Road. A man, in his late twenties, got off with a parcel under his arm. He pulled his cap tightly over his head, and dodged the puddles as he ran across the road towards the maze of terraced houses. The conductor rang the bell and spat onto the road, cursing the weather as the bus continued onto Springfield Road.

When he reached Mill Street, Joe Duffy smiled to himself as he stood for a moment outside the corner house. He took a key from his coat pocket and opened the front door.

Once inside, he shook his wet cap, hanging it and his coat on a nail behind the door. He dipped his finger in the plastic font at the side of the door and blessed himself. He was not a religious man, but old habits die hard.

There was a framed photograph of his late father on the hall table. He picked it up and stared at it. He had the same sickening feeling he felt that morning when he signed the papers. He knew his father would rather have died in prison than taken any pledge to give up the struggle. He put the photograph back down; what was done was done. Careful not to waken the children, he took his boots off and went upstairs.

'Yer awake,' he said, opening the bedroom door to find Marie sitting up in bed.

'My God, Joe … I didn't even hear ye come in,' she said, nervously fixing her hair. 'I heard rumours that some of the men were going to sign it today. But I still didn't think ye would be one of them.' She made to get up.

'Stay where ye are,' he insisted, sitting down on the edge of the bed. 'What else was I goin' to do? There are only a few diehards left, like yer brother, and they'll never sign the bloody thing.'

'Ye know what Eugene's like. Me mammy said he was talking of going on hunger strike …'

'Going on hunger strike? What the hell for? All he has to

do is sign a bit of paper and they'll be glad to see the back of him.'

'I'm glad ye did, Joe. Ye've done yer bit and what good did it do?'

'It's finished, and that's an end to it. How's this wee fella?' he asked, putting his hand on Brendan's arm. 'He feels awful hot.'

'Aye, he's all right. He's got a wee temperature that's all. Look at yerself, yer soaking wet,' she said, carefully moving Brendan onto his side. Joe then noticed the twins in the cot. They were born only a few months after he was arrested and until now he had only ever seen pictures of his daughters. He got up to look at them for a moment. 'They're beautiful wee things,' he said, in a kind of absent trance, as he gently touched their heads. He looked out the window. 'Someday to be getting out,' he said, before turning to stare at his wife.

'Joe, ye better dry yer hair, ye'll catch yer death.'

'Och, stop worrying about nothing, will ye. Why don't ye take that off?'

'For God's sake, ye're only in the door.'

'Aye, but I've been in prison for the last twelve months. Take it off.'

'Ye don't have to speak like that. Put Brendan in his own bed,' she said reluctantly. 'And pull down the blinds.'

Under the covers, Marie took off her nightdress. She then watched Joe undress. Naked, he pulled the bed clothes from her and lay down on the bed. Breathing heavily, and with no attempt at being gentle, he forced himself between her legs. Marie closed her eyes and suffered every thrust in silence. It only took a few minutes for Joe to heave himself to a climax, his groans sounding more like cries of pain than pleasure.

With a deep sigh, he rolled over onto his back. He had thought about that moment for a long time; now, he felt cheated by its transience. He lit a cigarette. Bereft of the adrenaline that had fired his lust, Joe did not feel like speaking. He wanted to be alone, back in the solitude of his cell. He moved to the edge of the bed. The unbearable guilt at signing the pledge returned with a vengeance.

'I'm going down to put the kettle on. Will I bring ye up some breakfast?' Marie asked, struggling back into her nightdress.

'No, don't make me anything to eat; a cup of tea will do me fine.'

'But ye must be hungry.'

'We got something to eat this morning in the Crumlin, before they kicked us out. A cup of tea, that's all I want.'

Marie put on an unflattering green cardigan and a pair of old slippers. She went back downstairs where she washed herself in the kitchen sink. The water was cold and soon took the tiredness from her eyes. She then looked out into the backyard and saw one of Joe's pigeons, sitting drenched and forlorn on top of the old shed, where he used to keep them. After Joe was arrested, with money tight, Marie sold them to a fella on the Falls Road. It was only then she realised how hard it was to get rid of twenty homing pigeons. Every morning, for weeks, she had to shoo a dozen or so of them away; now only the occasional bird returned with a look of bewilderment at the empty roost. She opened the back door and waved a tea towel. The pigeon gave its wings a flutter and flew off.

Remembering why she had come downstairs, Marie put on the kettle, which was still warm to the touch. She sat for a moment in the gloom of the kitchen, afraid that prison had changed Joe; he seemed different, sullen. Lost in her thoughts, she did not notice the kettle boil until the lid began to rattle in a pique of vanity at being ignored. She made the tea and went back upstairs, only to find Joe fast asleep.

That was Joe Duffy's homecoming.

*

Unable to find employment, Joe signed on the dole. The twelve months he spent in prison had done little for his social standing within the Republican community of West Belfast, where signing the pledge was seen by many as a betrayal of those still inside.

The weeks soon turned into months, and he eventually gave up looking for work, spending most of his time in the Republican Workers' Club; a strange name, he thought, since the only people who went into it and had a job, were those serving behind the bar.

Nine months after Joe was released, Eugene Tierney walked free from the Crumlin Jail. He had still not signed the pledge, but the authorities no longer saw him or the IRA as a threat. There was no fanfare in the Ardoyne when he returned after nearly two years in prison. Eugene was now in his early thirties and as far as he was concerned, the war would never be over until the British were out of Ireland once and for all. The apathy of his neighbours infuriated him. 'Sing yer fucking songs, that's all yer good for,' he shouted one night as he was thrown out of a pub for berating the band for singing ***Kevin Barry***.

Marie was pregnant again. With little enough to live on and Joe on the dole, she began to fret about the future. She did not understand how her husband could get himself drunk with no money, but he did. At first she put up with his drinking, hoping that he would come to his senses and find a job. However, the whiskey had a hold on him and he continued to drink. No longer willing to endure his selfishness, Marie moved back to her mother's place with the children. Full of the drink and havering to himself, Joe did not even hear them leaving.

For a while, Joe made the most of his freedom and continued drinking until his dole money ran out and his cronies at the Republican Workers' Club were no longer willing to put up with him cadging drink and cigarettes. Left to mope at home for most of the time, he soon became miserable without Marie and the children in the house.

One morning, with a sober head, Joe got up and dressed before making his way to the Ardoyne to beg Marie to come home with the children. Even Marie's mother was impressed with her contrite son-in-law, the first time she had seen him in a suit since he got out of prison. Joe, now wearing a pioneer pin, promised he would get a job and never touch another drink. Marie relented and went home with the children.

Joe eventually found a job as a nightwatchman in a clothes factory in Ballymurphy, an area of Belfast where no one knew his past. It did not pay very well, but it was better than the dole. He gradually worked his way back into Marie's affections by handing in his unopened wage packet every week. Now he had work, Joe bought a few pigeons and began to race his birds again. Marie had her old Joe back.

Chapter 2

Marching Season July 1961

Jamie Morrison was a proud Ulsterman; British as his bowler hat and as Orange as the sash his late father wore. He was a large, stout man in his early thirties, with short, almost jet-black hair, and a neatly trimmed moustache under his pug nose. His chubby face was supported by a generous double chin, which almost nullified his short neck. At fifteen, he followed his father and two older brothers into the security of a lifetime job at the massive Harland and Wolff shipyards on the River Lagan. Although not from the wealthier Protestant middle class, he was still a member of a highly respected Presbyterian working class family and a staunch member of the local Shankill Orange Order. Like many of his family and friends, Jamie was also a Special Constable, and proud of his role in defeating the IRA in their recent inept Border Campaign. He would always be ready to defend Protestant rule in Ulster from the nationalists, no matter what it took. He believed in his religion as much as any man, and saw the right of the Protestant people to live and prosper in Ulster as a divine right. He also believed that the indigenous Irish Catholics were an inferior race and not worthy of the land they had once ruled. *We are the People* was his favoured chant when drunk. His politics were simple; Ulster was part of the union with Britain and would never be surrendered to the backward Republic, with its seditious nest of priests and peasants. *No Surrender. Never!*

'What a bloody day for it,' he grumbled, as he listened to the downpour outside, before looking up at his carefully pressed black suit, which hung over the open wardrobe door. He would have to wear his heavy black coat, even though it was the middle of summer. Today was a big day for him, and all Protestant Ulstermen, the Orange Passover: the twelfth of July. No amount of rain would stop him from doing his duty.

Unable to hold out any longer, he got up and went downstairs. He opened the back door in his vest and pyjama bottoms. He cursed, before rushing along the path to the outside toilet.

Once he finished his business, he hurried back indoors. 'Fucking hell,' he moaned, briskly wiping his face and chest with a towel. He sat at the kitchen table and lit a cigarette, trying to plan the day ahead, which was complicated with Liz being in the hospital for a second day with no sign of the baby coming.

He went upstairs to dress.

Before he had a chance to finish knotting his Lodge tie, there was a sharp knock at the front door. 'I'm coming,' he shouted, in a voice still hoarse from all the arguing he had done the night before in the Lodge. He put his shoes on and went down downstairs. It was his wife's sister, Irene.

'What about ye, Jamie?'

'Oh, it's yerself. Come in, I'm just about to put the kettle on.'

'I thought I'd better come 'round early to see if ye had any news,' she said, taking off her rain-mate and shaking the wet from it. 'This weather's awful, you wouldn't put a dog out in it … Well?' she asked as she took off her coat.

'What?'

'Jamie Morrison, ye've not forgot me sister already?'

'Ah, don't be silly, Irene,' said Jamie when the penny

finally dropped. 'She's on me mind every minute of the day. Sure, I was up seeing her yesterday and the matron told me it might be another week before she has the baby. They've only taken her in early on account of the last time. They have to be on the safe side, like.'

While Irene looked at herself in the hall mirror and fixed her hair, Jamie went back into the kitchen and put the kettle on the hob.

'She's not had it easy. I wish it was over with,' said Irene, once she was happy that her heavily lacquered hair had its shape back.

'My head's splitting,' said Jamie, rummaging through the kitchen cupboard for the aspirin bottle.

'Ye must have had a fair bucket full last night,' said Irene, taking a seat at the kitchen table, and lighting a cigarette.

'Oh, away Irene, I only had a couple of pints with the lads when I got back from the hospital.'

'Oh, don't be getting all defensive. It's none of my business what ye get up to. I see yer got the clobber on, anyway.'

'Aye, ye got to do yer duty,' he said, his chest pumped up with self-pride. 'Even in this miserable weather,' he added with a grunt.

'Aye, there must have been a few Hail Mary's said last night,' joked Irene, looking out at the foul weather. 'It could go off again, just as easy as it came on ...Thanks Jamie,' Irene added, taking the cup and saucer from his shaking hand.

'Maybe, here, have a biscuit. We've no' had any summer this year at all.'

'Och, it's the same every year. A couple of days are all ye can hope for,' she said, taking the biscuit and dunking it in her tea. 'Is there anything you want me to take up to Liz this afternoon?'

'Aye, I've got a few things in a bag, ye could take with ye.'

'Will ye be up later yerself?'

'Well, I'll see how things go. Of course if she has the baby today I'll be up before ye can say the Pope's a Catholic. We'd have no problem remembering *his* birthday if *he's* born today.'

'How do ye know it's going to be a boy?'

'Aye, it's going to be a boy, all right. Wait and see!'

'Aye, that would be a feather in yer cap.'

'It sure would.'

'Aye, I wouldn't need too many guesses to know what ye would be calling the baby. God, even if it's a girl ye could still call her Billie.'

'Away and don't talk daft.'

'I don't see why no'. Ye must have heard of Billie Holiday.'

'Ye're right. I never thought of that,' he said, his face lightening up.

'Anyway, I better get going.'

After Irene left, Jamie finished his tea with a smile on his face. *Billy Morrison*, it had a ring to it. *We are the People!*

Jamie got dressed and put on his father's sash, taking great care as he draped it neatly into place across his chest. The sash had been in the Morrison family for four generations. His grandfather, Walter Morrison, kept it under his tunic during the First World War, referring to it in letters back home as his silk shield. However, the shield had only limited powers, and Walter fell at Passchendaele in 1917; the German machine guns having no respect for tradition.

The blood stained sash arrived in the post with the rest of his personal belongings, and was passed to Jamie's father, the eldest son. A smile of satisfaction beamed across Jamie's face as he ran a proud hand down the intricately embossed needlework.

It stopped raining, and despite the grey skies, the Shankill Road was a blaze of colour. Bunting was draped between the rows of terraced houses, like Christmas decorations, blowing defiantly in the wind, while Union Flags hung from every other window. At the top of the Shankill, a flute band organised itself in the middle of the road. The drum major practised extravagant throws with his baton, expertly catching it with one hand and twirling it around his wrist, before hoisting it back up into the air and catching it behind his back. There were cheers of encouragement from the crowds that gathered along the pavement.

Eventually the band moved off behind the drum major; four rows of girls playing flutes, eight young boys with side drums, and a dozen men with accordions strapped to their chests. At the rear came the booming sound of the Lambeg drum, carried by the only man in the band with the build and arrogance to do it justice.

Other bands began to fall into line behind their lodge banners, mostly of King Billy astride his white charger. As each band marched off, the men and women of that lodge marched behind in strict formation. Many of the senior men wore bowler hats, white gloves, and of course the distinctive sash of the Orange Order. Jamie Morrison carried the banner of the West Belfast lodge along with his eldest brother, Robert. The pavements were now crowded with onlookers, enthusiastically cheering the parade down the road.

In the backyard, Marie Duffy pegged up her washing. She looked up at the sky as the sun began to break through the clouds. The clothes would be dry in no time, she thought, as she put another cotton sheet on the line. The backdoor was open and she hummed along to a Jim Reeves song on the wireless, *I hear the sound of distant drums*... She smiled to herself when she realised what she was singing along to. She was in a good mood; *in fact* she had been in a good mood for months. So much so, that she had thrown her last prescription of anti-depressants in the bin.

The wind caught one of the bed sheets and blew it into her face as she put the washing pole under the line. Finished, she lifted the empty washing basket and listened for a moment over the noise of the radio. They've started early, she thought, making out the dull sound of a Lambeg drum being thumped above the high pitched notes of the flutes.

Upstairs the twins began crying and Joe, who had been working all night, woke in a temper. 'Will the pair of ye be quiet for God's sake,' he groaned, but they cried all the more. 'Marie! Can ye come up here and shut them up or I'll never get any rest. I've got me work to go to tonight.'

'Ye don't have to shout, I'm coming,' she retorted, rushing upstairs.

'Take them down with ye.'

'Mammy's coming. Shush there,' she said, lifting Kathleen from the cot and putting a dummy in her mouth. The baby sucked for a moment and then started crying again as the dummy fell to the floor. Marie tried to wind her, but that only made her cry louder.

'Marie, will ye get them out of here,' pleaded Joe, pulling the covers over his head.

'Come with Mammy, grumpy Daddy has got to get some sleep,' said Marie, carrying Kathleen downstairs, and leaving Roisin, who was now quiet, in the meantime.

As Kathleen's screams descended the stairs, Joe glanced at the clock on the dresser. It was twenty to nine. He had only been sleeping for about half an hour. Exhausted, he started to doze off again, until the sound of drums and flutes began to fill his tired mind. 'Oh, for fuck's sake,' he cursed, while the noise of the bands crept closer. 'Orange bastards,' he shouted into his pillow. Roisin began giggling and threw her dummy out of the cot.

Unable to sleep, Joe got up and gave Roisin her dummy. He stood at the bedroom window and looked down the street towards Springfield Road, where he could see the parade passing.

'I thought ye might be up,' said Marie, coming back into the room to fetch Roisin. 'I don't think ye should stand at that window in case someone puts a brick through it. They all know what ye are.'

'Look at them. Ye would think they won the Battle of the Boyne yesterday, instead of nearly three hundred years ago … What's the matter?'

'Nothing, I just had another twinge. Oh!' groaned Marie, putting Roisin back into the cot and sitting on the side of the bed, holding her stomach. 'I think ye better go and get me brother to drive us to the hospital.'

Chapter 3

Labour Pains

Eugene Tierney could hear the bands getting louder. The traffic slowed to a snail's pace. In the back seats Joe was desperately urging Marie to hold on as she tried to control her breathing. The contractions continued and the pain was making her dig her nails into his arm. Eugene blasted his horn and cursed the cars in front, but there was little he could do about it.

Up ahead, a police car was parked in a lay-by, with two RUC officers sitting in the front seats, smoking. Eugene pulled up alongside. 'I've got a woman about to have a baby in the back seat. Will ye help us get through this lot?'

One of the officers looked into the back of the car and saw that Marie was clearly in distress. 'Follow us,' he said, activating the siren. The cars in front pulled into the side of the road and Eugene followed the police car along the Falls Road to Grosvenor Road. When they reached the tail end of the Orange parade, the police car edged itself through the following crowds, before finding a path on the other side of the road where it slowly drove past the marching bands. Stewards and police officers, shepherding the parade, waved the police car on as Eugene followed, unable to hide his utter contempt for the men in bowler hats and Orange sashes. 'Fucking dirty Orange bastards,' he muttered.

Marie felt the panic subside when they drove through the main gates of the hospital. The police had radioed ahead. Two orderlies and a nurse were waiting for her at the front door. She was helped into a wheelchair, and quickly taken into the maternity ward.

'Thanks,' said Joe to the police officers before they got back into their car and drove off.

'To hell with them,' muttered Eugene, under his breath, handing Joe a cigarette. 'I need a pint after that. I thought she was going have it in the bloody back seat.'

'Can ye drop me off at the house, Eugene?'

'Are ye no' coming wi' me for a pint?'

'No, I better no'. I promised yer sister.'

'Promises are made to be broken, come on, Joe. Ye can wet the baby's head wi' me.'

'Is the baby not supposed to be born first? Anyway, where are we going to get a pint at this time in the morning?'

'We'll get a pint in the Shamrock; a friend of mine runs the place. He'll let us in early.'

'I'm tired and need to get some sleep. I'm back on the nightshift at nine … no, just drop me off at the house.'

*

Within a couple of hours, Marie lay back exhausted, but happy it was over so quickly. The baby gave out a healthy scream when the midwife cut the umbilical cord before placing the child in a cot at the bottom of the bed. 'He's a fine, healthy looking boy.'

'When can I get to hold him?'

'Soon, the doctor will have to examine him first. The nurse will help ye out of that nightdress and clean ye up a bit. Sure it's been a busy morning. That's three babies born within twenty minutes of each other. The other two were much more of a handful. Yer wee boy came out like he was in a hurry to get to school.'

'Would ye like a cup of tea, Mrs Duffy?' asked the auxiliary nurse as she wheeled Marie's bed into the ward.

'Oh, that would be lovely.'

'Now rest awhile, ye'll have plenty of time to hold yer baby once he's been examined and weighed.'

Sipping the warm tea, Marie sat up in bed, thankful that she got to the hospital in the nick of time. She felt awful that her waters had broken in the back of her brother's car, but what could she do about it now?

Despite the initial drama, it was an easy birth and she felt well enough to go home. While she was combing her hair, the midwife came into the ward. 'Here we are,' she said, as she laid the baby in Marie's arms. 'He's almost eight pounds, that's a big boy ye have there.'

'Oh, he's beautiful,' said Marie, holding him against her face and kissing his puffy red cheeks.

'Ye don't know how lucky ye are,' said the midwife, nodding to the bed opposite. 'That poor soul's not got the strength to hold her baby and she gave birth almost three hours before ye. She had a terrible time of it.'

In the bed opposite, Liz Morrison was gradually recovering from the horrendous ordeal she had endured. The labour pains she feared came during the night and she was rushed into the delivery room before she woke up the whole ward. After hours of pain and fruitless attempts by a junior doctor and midwife to induce the birth, the baby remained in the breech position within the womb. Thankfully a more senior doctor came on duty before the lives of mother and baby were put in greater danger. He decided immediately to put Liz under a general anaesthetic and carry out an emergency caesarean section.

Feeling nauseous, Liz was still trying to recover from the effects of the ether, her memory of giving birth now a blur to her. She tried to sit up, but the pain of her stitches made her wince. 'Where's my baby?' she mouthed weakly, before resting back on her pillow. She watched the woman in the bed opposite breastfeeding, and felt a sudden panic. *Maybe there's something wrong ... Where's my baby?*

When she saw one of the nurses come into the ward, she forced herself to sit up in spite of the pain. 'Nurse, can I see my baby, now?'

'Sure ye can, Mrs Morrison; I'll bring him along in moment. Are ye feeling any better?'

'Yes, I just want my baby.'

'There's the midwife with yer wee fella now, Mrs Morrison.'

The nurse helped Liz to sit up properly and the midwife placed the baby in her arms. 'He's a fine wee boy, Mrs Morrison,' said the midwife. 'He has a wee eye infection, but nothing to worry about.'

'An eye infection?'

'The doctor's put some ointment on it. He'll be absolutely fine. It will clear up in a few days.'

'Oh, his poor wee eyes,' said Liz, nursing the baby in her arms, the pain now forgotten. 'Can I feed him now?'

'Sure ye can. Here, let me help ye with that,' said the midwife, undoing the top buttons on Liz's dressing gown. Once the baby found the nipple, it began feeding while the young nurse brushed Liz's hair. 'There! We want ye looking yer best for yer visitors. Are ye feeling any better?'

'I still feel a bit weak.'

'That will be away in an hour or so. Would ye like a cup of tea?'

'Yes, nurse, that would be lovely, so it would.'

'Ye carry on feeding. Remember if ye need me ring the bell above yer head. And don't be worrying about the baby's eyes. They'll be fine.'

'Thank ye, Nurse, ye've all been very kind,' said Liz, feeling a little better as she watched the baby suckle at her breast, burping bubbles of milk contentedly.

'Yer first?' asked Marie.

'Yes … and my last,' said Liz with a weak laugh, not wanting to mention the baby she had lost in labour a few years earlier. 'I couldn't go through that again.'

'Ye're only saying that now. This is my fourth. I have a boy and two little girls at home. Brendan is four and the twin girls will soon be two years old.'

'That's nice, a boy and two little girls. What did ye have this time?'

'Oh, another wee boy, we're going to call him Danny after me father.'

'That's what I had meself, a lovely wee boy. Ye wouldn't have a clue what the time is?'

'Aye, it's about twelve o'clock.'

'I'm wondering if me sister will be up this afternoon.'

'Sure she will.'

*

Joe lay on the couch in the front room, he was grateful

to Marie's mother, who had taken the children to let him get back to bed. He was not in the house much more than a couple of hours before she called back to let him know he had another son to bring up. There was no way he would get back to sleep now.

Once Betty had left, except for the faint ticking of the clock in the hall, the house seemed strangely quiet. He lit a cigarette and felt at a loose end. Maybe he should go up to the hospital, he thought, before convincing himself that she would want some rest to get over the birth. He would go up in the evening before going to work, he decided, suddenly itching for a drink.

Most of the Orange bands had long since made their way along Lisburn Road towards Finaghy Park; only if he strained himself could he hear the beat of drums. He sat up and looked at the picture of Pope John XXIII, which hung above the tiled fireplace, feeling a perverse sense of justice when he heard another rumble of thunder. He got up and sat by the window and watched the downpour batter off the street, washing the dirt from between the cobbled stones. For a moment he imagined the chaos that it would be causing the parade. 'Orange bastards, serves them right,' he muttered to himself. A sudden surge of adrenaline swept aside his tiredness. The seed sown by Eugene was now growing into a terrible thirst. He felt he deserved a drink. In fact, it would be failing in his duty if he didn't wet the baby's head with a few pints. *Damn it, I'm going for a drink! Haven't I been off it long enough? What Marie doesn't know won't hurt her. What harm will a couple of pints do?*

The pub had its usual afternoon feeling about it, busy but not as busy as the night before or, for that matter, the night to come. Afternoons were the preserve of the serious drinkers, men who had long since lost the grimace of their youth when knocking back the hard stuff. Everyone knew everyone else in the bar, and old friends sat together in huddles, under thick wafts of cigarette smoke. There were only two windows, draped with tatty green curtains at the front of the pub and very little daylight ever found its way through the grime, and onto the brown, linoleum floor. The only other light came from two bare light bulbs, dangling from long twisted wires in the middle of the nicotine stained ceiling. On the far wall there was a copy of the Irish Proclamation of Independence, with pictures of the 1916 Easter Uprising leaders around it. On another wall was a picture of the Glasgow Celtic legend, Charlie Tully. This was a Republican pub and proud of it.

A few regulars sat in the shadows at the back of the pub, speaking only occasionally until the last domino was placed on the crowded board and the tension lifted for a few minutes. They talked and laughed while the dominoes were turned on their spots. A noisy shuffle by eager hands ended the conversation and the next game began. Dominoes was an old man's game and most of the younger men preferred to stand, drinking at the bar, listening for the racing and football results on an old wireless, which crackled and whistled below the gantry.

Joe ordered a pint and offered a drink to Tam Reynolds, a regular, who was standing at the bar on his own. 'Cheers, I don't mind if I do,' said Tam, emptying what was left of the pint he was drinking. 'I thought that ye were off the drink, Duffy.'

'I was, but a fella deserves a drink after his wife gives him another son,' beamed Joe. 'He was only born a couple of hours ago, sure.'

'How's about ye then. A boy is it? Here, have me hand. Well done, a boy ye say. Do ye hear that, fellas? Joe's wife's had a baby boy this morning.'

Joe quickly became the centre of attention as the other regulars shook his hand in turn and offered words of congratulations. Joe knocked back a glass of whiskey that had been put in his hand. 'Aye, a man needs a drink sometimes. Women don't understand,' he said, more to himself than to anyone else. Tam nodded in agreement.

‘Aye, yer right there, Joe,’ said Tam, finishing his pint and looking at the empty glass as if it had swindled him. ‘I’d get ye a pint, but I’m a bit skint, like.’

‘That’s all right Tam, I’ll get them in. Two more pints, Patsy! And have one for yerself.’

*

By the late afternoon the speeches were over, and the drenched Shankill flute band marched back up the middle of Lisburn Road, playing their signature tune: “The Sash”. Cars and buses pulled up to let them pass. ‘*Fuck the Pope! No Pope here!*’ shouted some of the spectators following the parade along the crowded pavements. The band carried on up the main road back towards the Shankill.

Jamie Morrison and three other elders took a taxi back to the lodge to get things organised for the dinner dance planned for that night. Jamie was the chairman of the committee responsible for these annual functions, and there was no bigger function on the Orange calendar than the one commemorating the Battle of the Boyne.

The hall had been decorated the night before in red, white and blue bunting, and the top table looked resplendent under a picture of the Queen, in a fake gilded frame. Apart from King Billy, the young Queen was the only other human icon that adorned the lodge. She was the link to the dominance of Protestantism over Catholicism, Hanoverian over Jacobite, and British over Irish. She was revered, *almost*, in the same way the Catholics revered the Virgin Mary; a tangible link to the past and the Reformation that broke the stranglehold of the Church of Rome over Christianity.

'Jamie, it's Irene on the phone. She's at the hospital,' shouted Harry, the lodge's bar manager. Jamie got up and went into the back office to take the call, his voice nervous as he lifted the receiver and said hello. 'Aye, aye … that's wonderful. Tell her I'll be up later. Okay Irene, thanks for phoning.'

Jamie found it hard to keep the grin from his face when he hung up the phone. He took a deep breath, slightly drunk with the thought of it all as he looked at his watch again. He had enough time for a couple of pints. He marched back into the hall where the other committee members were busy setting up trestle tables.

'Well?' asked Colin MacKay, the lodge secretary, hanging up more bunting on the back wall. 'Has she?'

'Aye, it's a boy … Get that bar opened, Harry. The first round is on me.'

*

In the maternity ward, Liz was feeling much better now her sister had phoned Jamie with the news of his son. 'What did he say?' asked Liz when Irene returned.

'He didn't say much, dumbstruck I think he was. He'll be up shortly.'

'Oh, I can't wait to see his face,' said Liz, still nursing the baby, but beginning to feel a little sleepy again. 'Here, you better take him for a while, Irene. I need a wee rest.'

Once Irene took the baby, Liz lay back on her pillow and closed her eyes. Suddenly she felt a sharp pain in her lower abdomen, and sat up, taking deep breaths.

'Are you all right?' asked Irene, quickly putting the baby into the cot at the bottom of the bed before calling for one of the nurses.

'Where are you hurting, Mrs Morrison?' asked the nurse, before pulling back the bed clothes.

'It's away now, nurse, it's gone,' replied Liz, holding her stomach. 'It was just a pain where they cut me.'

'It will be sore for a few days. Don't touch it,' said the Nurse, looking at the scar on Liz's stomach, satisfied that the stitches were not too tight or coming loose. 'I'll get you some painkillers.'

While she waited for the nurse to return, Liz laid her head back down and closed her eyes. She began to think of Jamie, and how they met at the Shankill lodge, where he was already a well-known character. Liz only went to the dance at the insistence of one of her friends, Maggie Kirkwood, who had her eye on Jamie's brother, Robert. Maggie worked, at the time, with Liz in the offices of Windsor Insurance on Victoria Street in the heart of the city. She was a good-looking girl, and not shy coming forward either. Liz blushed, remembering how Maggie brazenly pursued Robert around the hall until she cornered him, before dragging him onto the dance floor. *Well they have three children now*, thought Liz as she took another sip of the lukewarm tea. She smiled when she remembered standing like a wallflower while Maggie danced the jive with Robert. It was then that Jamie made himself known. 'Haven't seen you in here before?'

'No, ye wouldn't have had. I've never been in before,' replied Liz, not in the least interested in his advances.

'Are ye here with Maggie Kirkwood?'

'Aye, and what's it to ye?'

'Just trying to be friendly … would ye like a drink?'

'I'll take an orange juice if yer buying.'

Liz smiled again, as she remembered how cheeky she

was to Jamie and how it only made him more interested in her.

Totally worn out, it wasn't long before she drifted off into a deep sleep.

It was late afternoon before Jamie entered the ward with a bunch of flowers that he had bought in the foyer. He looked a little embarrassed; quickly pecking a kiss on Liz's cheek and thrusting the flowers into her arms. 'Here, they're for you.'

'Oh Jamie, they're lovely.'

'I better get going,' said Irene, putting her coat on and kissing her sister on the forehead. 'I'll be up the same time tomorrow.'

'Well, look at this!' said Jamie, lifting the baby from the cot. 'He's a fine looking fella.'

'Aye, isn't he lovely,' said Liz, thrilled that Jamie was so taken with the baby. 'I think he got yer eyes.'

'Aye, he's got the Morrison nose as well,' said Jamie, his face flushed with pride and drink. 'I was thinking we should call him...'

'Oh, let me guess? It wouldn't be William by any chance?'

'I can't think of any better name. He'll no' forget his birthday anyway. What do ye think?'

'Aye, well, so long as ye don't buy him a white rocking-horse for Christmas,' said Irene as she turned to leave.

'Now there's an idea.'

*

Joe Duffy paid his fare and staggered to the back of the

bus. He had downed a few too many whiskies and he felt quite drunk. He lit a cigarette and looked out at the passing streets. The bus travelled along the Falls Road, before turning down Broadway. With the bands back at their lodges, the city streets were relatively quiet. Once out of the Falls, the streets were mainly Protestant strongholds and Union Jacks were flying defiantly on most corners. 'The butcher's fuckin' apron,' he mumbled to himself. He took another deep draw from the cigarette and tried to stop himself from falling asleep. He was deadbeat and had his work to go to in a few hours.

Marie was mortified when she saw Joe staggering into the ward. She clenched her fists tight and took a deep breath; the last thing she wanted was for him to make a scene. She bit her tongue as he walked sheepishly up to the bed. She strained a smile. 'So ye managed to get here?'

'I'm sorry. I missed the first bus…'

'Ye never missed the bloody pub,' snapped Marie, unable to keep her own promise. 'Ye better go and have a look at yer son. If ye can see him, that is.'

'Oh, I can see all right,' barked Joe, 'and don't ye be getting too bloody smart with that tongue of yers.'

'Why don't ye go,' said Marie in a strained whisper. 'I'll never speak to ye as long as I live, ye drunken pig.'

'Ah, shut up! Ye sound like yer bossy old mother.'

'Is everything ok?' asked Liz.

'Aye, why don't ye shut up and mind yer own business!' shouted Joe, the whiskey rising.

'Who the hell do ye think ye're talking to!' demanded Jamie, quickly getting up from the chair he was sitting on.

'Nurse!' shouted one of the other patients.

'Away and sit down, before I knock ye down,' taunted Joe, raising his fist.

'Joe! For God's sake,' pleaded Marie.

'What's going on here?' demanded the matron. 'Have ye no sense? Now, don't be causing any trouble.'

'Joe! Will ye please go home!'

Joe stood motionless, eyeing Jamie, who was still standing his ground. 'Yer no' worth it,' he said, pushing past the matron.

'Come near this hospital again and I'll get the police to ye,' shouted the matron, closing the ward door after him.

'I'm sorry, Nurse,' said Marie, her eyes full of tears.

'Nothing for ye to be sorry about, dear; ye only married him; it was God that created him.'

Joe went straight back to the pub and this time he did not give a damn how drunk he got. 'To hell with her,' he mumbled to himself. 'I'm having a fucking drink and she can go to hell!'

Joe woke up the next morning on the living room floor with Brendan pulling at him to get up. He tried to take hold of the child's hand to reassure him, but Brendan began crying. It was then he noticed Marie's mother sitting in the corner of the room staring at him. 'Leave the child alone, ye drunken pig,' she shouted in a temper, taking Brendan up in her arms. 'I suppose ye slept there all night like a tinker, and yer poor wife in hospital with the burden ye gave her. Do ye know ye left that front door lying open all night? Ye didn't even go to yer work either!'

'Ah Jesus, Betty, I only had a few drinks to wet the baby's head. Sure ye had the children last night … What's the harm?'

'Don't ye ah *Jesus* me! Ye haven't been to mass since ye got out of prison, and if it wasn't for Marie these children would be pagans like yerself.'

'Where are the twins?' Joe demanded, getting irritated

with Betty's tone.

'They're still at my house with Anna, ye don't think for a minute I'd leave them with ye to look after. Ye better get yerself smartened up before Marie gets home with the baby. I don't want her upset because of yer drunken antics.'

'Yer right, Betty, I'll have a shave and clean meself up a bit. Ye won't say anything to…'

'No, I'll say nothing, but not to save yer bloody skin, Joe Duffy! I don't want my daughter to rue the day she ever met ye, and her with four young children to bring up … Brendan hush, yer mammy will be home soon.'

Joe staggered into the kitchen. He stared at his bloodshot eyes in the shaving mirror, before stripping down to the waist. The shock of the freezing water on his face put some colour back into it before he lathered up. The razor blade was old, and he had to virtually scrape the growth from his chin. He heard the front door open.

Without finishing his shave, Joe went into the living room to find Marie standing with the baby, wrapped in a white crocheted shawl. She ignored Joe as she showed off the baby to her mother. Theresa, Marie's younger sister, then came in after paying the taxi driver. 'How's about ye, Joe?' she said, putting Marie's case on the floor. 'It's a fine looking boy ye've got there.'

'Thanks, Theresa.'

'Ah, he's a handsome devil,' said Betty, cooing over her grandson.

'He's a Duffy all right,' said Theresa.

'That's what we're worried about,' said Betty, casting a look of contempt at her son-in-law. 'Theresa, will ye put the kettle on before we all die of thirst in this house.'

*

It was almost a week before Liz was well enough to go home. In the meantime, Irene had cleaned the house from top to bottom, while Jamie turned the back room into a nursery. He bought a new cot, and papered the walls with light blue wallpaper covered in Walt Disney cartoon characters. Irene shook her head when he put up a picture of Glasgow Rangers above the cot.

Still fragile, Liz thanked the nurses and said goodbye, taking Irene's hand as Jamie carried the baby to the car. Jamie then drove them back to the Shankill with a grin on his face he found impossible to remove. He could not wait for Liz to see the nursery. *Billy Morrison, it had a ring to it all right.*

Once home, he took Liz by the arm and helped her to her favourite chair by the fire, while Irene went into the kitchen to make a pot of tea and a plate of ham sandwiches. Besotted, Jamie nursed the baby in his arms with a smile that lifted Liz's spirits.

'Hope ye still take milk?' asked Irene, handing her sister a cup of tea.

'Yes, thanks, Irene, but Jamie likes his black.'

'Ye still thinking of calling the little fella William?' asked Irene.

'Of course,' said Jamie, taking one of the sandwiches, which were cut into delicate triangles. 'What else could we call him?'

'I was thinking maybe we should call him Duncan, after my father,' said Liz, a faint smile of mischief on her lips.

'There're too many lads called Billy around these parts,' added Irene, sipping her tea and grinning at Liz from behind Jamie's back.

'But we agreed,' said Jamie, his face flushed. 'I've already told all the fellas at the lodge … Ah yer having a laugh, the pair of ye,' he said, more than a little relieved when he heard the two of them begin to snigger. 'Very funny.'

'Ye should have seen yer face,' said Liz, laughing even louder at Jamie's expense.

'I think ye better take King Billy,' said Jamie, handing the baby to Irene. 'I think he's just baptised his nappy.' They all laughed.

Chapter 4

The Misty Mountains

By the time Danny was five years old, Joe had been out of work for nearly a year after being sacked for missing too many days through the drink. To keep the wolf from the door, Marie took on a part-time job cleaning the big Protestant houses on the other side of the river. Even though it did not pay much, she liked her job. These middle-class Protestants had nice things to dust and polish, and she could clean their houses all day and not mind a bit. With her wages and Joe's dole money, Marie could scrape by, but only just. With very little in her purse to spend in the grocer's each day, the children often went to bed hungry for want of a decent dinner. Marie quickly grew to resent her husband's idleness.

Tired of Marie's constant nagging, Joe soon developed a hangdog look about him. With no money for the drink and only his pigeons to occupy his days, Joe had time on his hands during the winter months to fill Danny's head with stories and legends that his own father thrilled him with as a boy. The tale Danny liked best was about one grumpy little leprechaun, named Paddy Two-Shoes, who guarded the leprechaun king's pot of gold, high in the misty mountains. The only way to get the gold from Paddy Two-Shoes, without being bludgeoned to death with his shillelagh, was to use the magic fairy word that would turn the leprechaun into stone.

'Tell me, Daddy, what's the magic word?'

Joe smiled at Danny's pleading face, before whispering into the boy's eager ear, *Carrauntoohil.* 'Now don't be telling anyone.'

Every time Joe told the story, Danny would ask him to say the magic word again, and would repeat it under his breath, making sure his brother and sisters did not hear. With the magic word embedded in his mind, Danny often wondered why his father did not go to the mountain and steal the leprechaun's gold so they could have ice cream and sweets again like they did when he was working.

Joe eventually found work again. This time he managed to get a job in the linen mill on Conway Street. The hours were long, but the wages were decent, and he had his pride back. Now earning, he became boss in the house again, and, as long as he worked and stayed off the drink, Marie was happy to let him think he was.

Danny was now looking forward to the new school term, when he would be attending school for the first time with his big brother and sisters. With Joe working, Marie had enough money to buy Brendan a new school uniform and Danny was given his brother's old one. He was so excited about going to school that he did not care what he was wearing so long as it was a uniform with a badge on the jacket pocket. But when the day came and he stood on his own in the playground, some of the other children laughed at his baggy grey trousers, and at the holes in the sleeves of his jacket. The uniform and school badge immediately lost their appeal to him.

Sitting at the back of the class, he remembered what his father used to say when he had the whiskey in him. 'Son, always remember there's poor and there's poor, and even the poor like to mock those they think are worse off than themselves.' But at that moment, Danny was still too young to appreciate his father's philosophy on poverty. He was more concerned with the fact that he was the only one getting mocked and laughed at. By the end of the morning lesson he had enough of one boy who had been teasing him all morning about his 'hand-me-downs'. Once in the corridor, Danny landed a fist on the other boy's nose. They both ended up on the floor before one of the teachers pulled them apart. When Danny was dragged to his feet, his ill-fitting trousers fell around his ankles. The teasing only got worse and after school he had to endure another fight on the way home.

The next morning, he pretended to be sick. Marie could not get him out of his bed. She scolded him until he started crying through forced coughs. Thinking he may be coming down with the flu, she left him in his bed and told him to stay there until she got back from work. Danny had no intention of staying in his bed, he had other plans.

Forcing another few coughs, he listened to Brendan and the twins leaving for school. Marie then called up to him not to open the front door to anyone as she left to catch her bus. Once the front door was banged over, he got up and watched his mother from the bedroom window as she walked down the street. As soon as she turned the corner he dressed in his old clothes, kicking Brendan's baggy school uniform under the bed. He was never going to wear it again.

He went downstairs to look for something to eat. There was some bread and a pot of strawberry jam on the kitchen table. He made a jelly piece, before taking some milk from the bottle, which had been left in a bucket of water at the back door to keep fresh. He wondered if the golliwog was there to guard the jam and he whispered the magic word … 'Carrauntoohil,' before sticking a knife into the pot and spreading more thick jam on the half eaten crusty bread.

Once he had finished his breakfast, he went out the back door, which was always left unlocked, and hurried up the street to the corner of Springfield Road where he could see the mountains in the distance. The streets were busy with shoppers and he walked quickly with his hands in his pockets and gold on his mind, repeating the magic word to himself. He took a short cut through some backstreets and walked for about twenty minutes before he realised he was lost. He considered turning to go back home, but the allure of the gold was too great and he pulled up his socks and walked on until he reached a busy street which was awash with colour; flags were hanging from the windows and the kerbstones were painted red, white and blue. He thought he must be getting near the misty mountain and was wondering if there were any leprechauns in this magical-looking place buying their big bottles of Irish whiskey, which Joe said they had to drink every night to keep their magic powers. He then turned into another busy street that was more colourful than the one before. He stopped at the corner to tie his laces before turning to see the hills and mountains at the top of the wide thoroughfare.

The tops of the mountains were shrouded in a mist, and he hurried up to the main road that ran beneath the sloping fields at the foot of the lower hills. He was starting to feel hungry again and his stomach rumbled as he crossed the road and climbed over a stone dyke into a boggy field. His feet sank into the soggy ground and his shoes squelched each time he lifted his feet. Up ahead he saw some rocks sticking out of the heather and he squelched on through the moss, stopping every so often to look for the rainbow that would lead him to the gold. But there was none to be seen.

After a while, he felt tired, and sat for a minute on one of the boulders to look at his dirty shoes. His feet were already wet and his socks were now sticking to his skin. He watched some older boys carrying pieces of wood and stacking them at the bottom of the hill. They were building a gang hut, thought Danny, but *he* had better things to do. Rested, he walked on until finally reaching a well-worn path, which he was sure led to Paddy Two-Shoes. He repeated the magic word to himself, fearful that he might forget it. He then thought about all the nice things he would buy with the gold; top of his shopping list was a new school uniform.

The path was dry and he made his way up to a ridge where he hoped to be able to see if the rainbow was on the other side. His legs were now heavy and he struggled as far as he could go before having to sit down to take another rest. He was surprised when he looked back down the hillside how far he had come. Over the red brick buildings of West Belfast he could see the cranes on the docks where Joe told him all the Protestants worked. He remembered the story his father told him about the day he was desperate enough to apply for a job in one of the yards, and how the big fat foreman laughed at him when he told the foreman his name was Joseph Patrick Duffy. Needless to say, Joe didn't get the job. 'Why did the man laugh when ye told him yer name? That's not funny.'

'No, he wasn't being funny, son. He was making it clear that Catholics were not welcome on the docks … not in his yard anyway.'

'Why are Catholics not welcome?'

'Because the Protestants want all the jobs for themselves.'

'Why don't ye become a Protestant and then you'll get a job on the docks?'

'It's not that simple, son. You're branded in this country from the day you're born, and it doesn't matter if you're religious or not. A Catholic is always a Catholic and a Protestant is always a Protestant. Like a dog is always a dog and a cat is always a cat. It doesn't matter if the cat wants to be a dog, and barks like a dog. When the other dogs see it, they know it's a cat and treat it like a cat, but when the other cats see it acting like a dog they treat it like a dog, even though they know it's a cat.'

'What are we Daddy, cats or dogs?'

'We're second class citizens in our own country. That's what we are, son. Just like the blacks in America and South Africa.'

'But, Daddy, we're not black?'

'We might as well be, son.'

There was now a chill in the air and the mist on the mountain began to creep down the hillside. Danny picked up a heavy stick and tested it against a stone dyke. He might need it to knock out the leprechaun if the magic word failed to work. He wondered if the leprechaun was a Catholic or a Protestant as he made his way through the sways of heather and wet bog, hopping from one moss covered stone to another until he reached the next ridge. Turning back, he could now see across Belfast Lough. It began to rain.

With his feet now soaking wet, Danny was beginning to feel miserable as more foul weather swept in from the Irish Sea. He had not gone much further, but this time when he looked back down the hillside, a grey fog had smothered his view of the shipyards and most of the city.

'Where are ye going, young fella?' shouted a voice that seemed to come from the sky.

Danny took fright and looked around thinking the leprechaun had discovered him. There was no one to be seen.

'Over here!'

Danny turned again to see a silhouetted figure standing in the distance beside a thicket of gorse bushes. Whoever it was, he had something in his hand. Terrified, Danny tried to run, but he found himself trapped in the bog that sucked his feet into its mire. 'Carrauntoohil!' he shouted. But the grey figure kept coming.

*

It was after four when Joe got home from work and saw the anxious faces of his wife and children, their eyes almost pleading with him to do something. 'What the hell's the matter with ye?' he asked, taking his coat off and hanging it on the back of the door.

'It's Danny, Joe,' said Marie. 'He's missing!'

'What do ye mean, missing?'

'I left him in bed this morning when I went to work. When I got back this afternoon he was gone. I've been all over looking for him.'

'Why was he not at school today?'

'He wasn't feeling well. He had a cough and I thought it better to keep him off. Where the hell would he go in this weather,' she sobbed, her tears setting off the twins again. 'I've looked everywhere. We'll have to go to the police.'

'My God,' said Joe. 'What will they do?'

'They'll look for him and find him ... He's only a baby for God's sake!'

'Stop crying, that's not going to help. I'll get some of the neighbours to help me search for him. You can't rely on the police to do anything for us.'

'God, why would he run away?' pleaded Marie, getting on her knees in front of the plastic statue of the Virgin Mary that her sister brought back from Lourdes.

'I know,' said Brendan, almost reluctantly. 'He was crying in bed last night. When I asked him what was wrong he said that everybody at school was laughing at him because he was wearing my old clothes. They called him a tramp and a tinker. He said he was going to get gold and buy new ones and...'

'Get gold,' said Joe, putting his work bag on the table and rubbing his chin. 'I think I know where he might have gone...'

'Where?' demanded Marie, who stopped crying instantly and got off her knees 'Where, Joe?'

'I use to tell him stories about leprechauns and their pots of gold. He's gone up to the hills looking...'

'Up the hills! You and yer bloody old stories!' Marie snapped. 'Ye better get out there and find him!'

Joe went to a few neighbours' doors along the street, and soon had a dozen men following him as their wives went to the Duffy house to comfort Marie, who was now beside herself with worry. Brendan raced after his father.

The men stayed clear of the Shankill where they might be mistaken for a gang of Fenians looking for trouble. Brendan found it hard to keep up with his father's long strides, and had to run every so often not to be left behind. Through the drizzle he saw the hills up ahead, shrouded, like they often were, in the murk that had descended like a mantle.

Once they reached the bottom of the hills, the search party had doubled in size as men from neighbouring streets joined when they realised a young boy was missing. Joe leaped over a stone dyke at the bottom of the hill and turned to lift Brendan over. The rest of the men followed. Joe wiped the sweat from his face and shouted Danny's name with a hoarse cry in his voice. The other men spread out and began the desperate search.

Marie was back on her knees with her rosary beads in her hands, pounding her breast. Two of her neighbours were kneeling beside her to help her through the Stations of the Cross. Her mind was distraught with the idea that something terrible had happened to Danny. She looked up at the Virgin Mary and beseeched her to send him home safe and sound. *Holy Mary mother of God pray for us sinners now and at the hour of our death Amen...*

The twins sat at the foot of the stairs in the hall mouthing the prayers that were emanating from the front room. There was a rumble of thunder in the distance, quickly followed by a demanding knock at the front door that made Roisin jump. Kathleen got up quickly and opened the door.

'Is your mother in?' asked an elderly looking police

officer, holding Danny in his arms.

'Mammy, Mammy,' shouted Roisin. 'They've found Danny.'

Marie blessed herself and acknowledged the statue of the Immaculate Conception, her prayers had been answered. She quickly got up from her knees as Kathleen let the two RUC officers into the hall. 'He was found on the hills a few hours ago by a fella out shooting rabbits.'

'My God, thank you, thank you … is he alright?'

'He's fine. We had a doctor look at him. He's just a bit tired. We got him and his clothes dried off at the station. He'll be fine,' said the older-looking RUC officer, handing Danny to Marie, who held him like a baby. 'We would have brought him over sooner but he couldn't remember his address. We got a call half an hour ago to tell us that there was a search going on in the hills looking for a young boy. The woman was able to give us your address, and here we are.'

'I saw the leprechaun,' said Danny, wriggling out of his mother's arms. The twins laughed and the two officers smiled and shook their heads. 'You'll need to keep an eye on him in future,' warned the younger officer, his voice turning serious. 'There are fellas up there shooting rabbits; he could have got some buckshot in him.'

'He'll not be allowed out this door again. I can promise ye that,' said Marie, as Danny wiped the hair from his eye and sat between his two sisters on the stairs.

'He'd been searching for gold he tells us,' said the older officer. 'He's none the worse for his little adventure, but you better get him changed. His clothes and feet are still a little damp.'

'Thanks again, officers … me husband and some of the neighbours have gone up to the hills to look for him.'

'We'll take a run over and let them know he's at home.'

'I don't know how to thank ye,' said Marie.

'It's all part of the job … Cheerio, young fella,' said the older officer, ruffling Danny's hair, before following his colleague out the door.

As soon as the door closed, Marie went over to Danny and gave him a hard slap to the back of the head that set him off in a roar of tears, before running upstairs. 'The next time you lie about not being well enough to go to school, I'll take ye there myself by the scruff of the neck!'

Danny never found the grumpy little leprechaun or the pot of gold, but once his mother's wrath cooled, he did get a new school uniform. As the weeks passed he often thought about making another journey to the hills to see if he could find that pot of gold. This time he made the mistake of telling one of the boys in the class about the leprechaun. A crowd gathered around him in the corner of the playground demanding the magic word, but Danny refused to tell them. Patsy McGuire, the biggest boy in the class broke up the cabal of gold seekers and grabbed Danny by the throat. 'Everyone knows that leprechauns aren't real,' said Patsy.

'Yes they are,' said Danny, giving Patsy a punch on the nose that floored him.

Over the next few years, while Danny was fighting his way through his class, Brendan and the twins were busy passing class exams and getting good grades. At 7 years old, Marie knew Danny was still a bit young for her to be too judgemental on his progress, but when she got his first report card she could not help but smile. *'If he would spend less time fighting the other boys in his class then maybe he would have time to learn his tables. However, he does possess a vivid imagination and he has a natural aptitude for storytelling.' I wonder where he got that from*, pondered Marie as she put the report card in the kitchen drawer and looked at an old picture of Joe with his father.

Chapter 5

1968 Civil Rights

It was a fine morning as Nigel Brooke-Ramsey made his daily train journey through the Ulster countryside to Stormont Castle. He was from a military background, and most of his colleagues still referred to him as Captain Ramsey, which he did nothing to discourage. His years in the army left an indelible mark on his general appearance and manner, which civilian life did little to erode. Also a keen historian, he was proud of the fact that his family tree could be traced back to the English Civil War and the battle of Naseby, in which his ancestor, Sir Charles Ramsey, was killed on the battlefield fighting for the King.

Born in London, Ramsey was educated at Eton before graduating from Oxford with a first class honours degree in Medieval History. During the war, he served with distinction and was awarded the Military Cross for his actions during the D-Day landings.

After the war, Ramsey spent nearly twenty years in Whitehall as a middle ranking civil servant with the War Office. He was then suddenly transferred, without much notice, to Northern Ireland, where there was growing unrest in the nationalist community inspired by the civil rights movement in the USA, and the anti-apartheid movement in South Africa. The British government had become embarrassed with the unjust, bigoted system within its own borders and had ordered the Northern Ireland government to bring in reforms that would give Catholics the same social and political rights as Protestants and drag the province into the twentieth century.

Despite the pressure from Downing Street on Northern Ireland's Prime Minister, Terence O'Neill, to bring in these reforms, there had been little progress. O'Neill's own cabinet ministers showed a contemptuous unwillingness to support laws that would give the Catholic minority the same rights as the Protestant majority. Ramsey's brief was to assist O'Neill in persuading his ministers to carry out the wishes of the British government.

It did not take Ramsey long to realise that O'Neill was genuine in his attempts to bring reform to Northern Ireland, but he was thwarted at every turn by his own government and most of the Unionist population that had elected him. He just did not have the support to do what the British government and the nationalist community demanded.

Prior to his posting, Ramsey had a reasonable knowledge of the mired history of Ireland, but even he was shocked at the extent of the bigotry and unfairness he encountered within the Northern Irish civil service. In his first few weeks at Stormont Castle, he sought out government documents in relation to the voting rights, housing, employment and education. He soon found that the institutionalised discrimination against the Catholic minority was endemic.

Though his own ancestry had been Protestant for over three hundred years, Ramsey was not burdened with the prejudice of religion. After he entered the hell that was Dachau concentration camp at the end of the war, he developed a Darwinian approach to life and death. The horrors that he witnessed convinced him that there could not be a benevolent God, who cared about the welfare of mankind.

The train suddenly screeched as it crossed points just

outside Belfast, and the jolt caused an old lady opposite to drop her glove on to the carriage floor. Ramsey picked up the soft, leather glove and handed it to the woman. She smiled and nodded her appreciation.

The train slowly pulled into the station, and Ramsey folded away his newspaper. The Prime Minister's chauffeur was waiting patiently by the official car outside. Ramsey walked briskly to the immaculately polished Bentley. He would have been quite happy with a taxi for the journey to Stormont Castle, but O'Neill insisted he took advantage of the Bentley when it was available.

The car drove up the gravel path towards the baronial castle nestled in its own forest of elm and chestnut trees, O'Neill was standing at the front door beneath the haphazard nineteenth century turrets and gargoyles. The two men shook hands and Ramsey followed the Prime Minister into a boardroom, where the familiar faces of three senior cabinet ministers and the Chief Constable of the RUC were waiting.

Coffee was served, and the Prime Minister opened the meeting with his concerns about the growing violence surrounding recent civil rights marches. Ramsey listened and took the occasional note. O'Neill tried to persuade his ministers that there was now a greater need to implement sweeping reforms to the social and political situation in the province, but he was met with hostile dissent. Ramsey sipped his coffee as the meeting grew more heated and the arguments went around in circles.

After the meeting, Ramsey watched a defeated Prime Minister shuffle along the corridor like a wounded animal. Not only could he not get support for his reforms, he had been forced to concede to the majority view that a planned civil rights march in Derry should be banned on public safety grounds. Without the total support of his senior cabinet ministers and the constant pressure from Downing Street, Ramsey was sure that it was only a matter of time before O'Neill's position as Prime Minister became untenable. It gave him little pleasure to report his views back to Whitehall; getting little comfort from the personal letter he received a few days later form Harold Wilson, thanking him for the insight into the recent developments.

*

With both Joe and herself working, Marie felt she could afford the monthly rental on a new record player.

'Now, Mrs Duffy, ye'll have to keep the needle clean and I've a cleaner, which will stop the static and keep yer records in good condition.'

'How much more would that be?' asked Marie, anxiously counting the coins in her purse.

'Oh don't worry, I'll give ye it with the record player,' said the helpful assistant. 'Here, I'll even throw in a record. What kind of music do ye like?'

'Oh … anything by Jim Reeves or something like that.'

'I'm afraid, I don't have any of his music; I only keep a few records here for demonstration purposes. I have this by Chris Barber's Jazz Band. Would ye like that?'

'Never heard of him.'

'Ye would have heard of Josef Locke, no doubt.'

'Oh, I love him singing ***Hear my Song***.'

'I have the very record here,' said the shop assistant. 'You can take that with you. Ye'll get Jim Reeves records in Baxter's record shop in town. I'll have the record player delivered tomorrow morning.'

'That would be grand ... And after I pay this deposit, the rent will not be due until next week. Is that right?'

'Aye, Mrs Duffy, ye can come in and pay it next week, and every week thereafter as long as ye want the record player.'

The record player was delivered the following day when Joe was at work and the children had already left for school. Marie had the man set it up on the sideboard in the front room. When he left, Marie nervously placed the record on the turntable. She was over the moon when the magic of modern technology filled the room with music. Josef Locke sang his heart out for the rest of the day.

That evening, the whole family sat around the dining table and listened to the record a dozen times before the novelty began to wear off.

'Mammy, I'll go mad if ye play it again,' said Roisin, sitting with her hands pressed against her ears. 'Could ye not have bought something else?'

'I didn't buy it. The man in the shop gave it free with the record player.'

'No wonder,' said Kathleen. 'Turn it off, Mammy!'

'Just once more,' said Marie, lifting the needle carefully back on to the start of the record.

'Did ye know there was a B side?' said Brendan.

'Why did ye tell her that?' complained Roisin. 'Now we're going to have to listen to that side a dozen times as well.'

'Mammy, Father McFadden has just gone into Mrs Donnelly's house,' shouted Danny from upstairs.

'My God, look at the state of this place,' panicked Marie, clumsily taking the needle off the record. 'Oh, I think I've scratched it.'

Father McFadden hailed from County Sligo in the Republic and had been transferred to Saint Patrick's on account of his weakness for the drink. The Bishop thought it would give him back his sense of vocation and bring about his promised abstinence if he had a more challenging parish to occupy his mind. He was in his late fifties and a product of a family that had a tradition of sending the youngest son into the priesthood, whether they liked it or not. He had acquired a fierce reputation in the confessional box and many parishioners would forgo the chance to cleanse their souls and risk eternal damnation for another week when they knew he was in the confessional. Unlike Father Cunningham, who would soothe the sins out of his grateful flock's souls, Father McFadden would exorcise the demons out with his fire and brimstone approach, followed by a hefty penance on the contrite sinner.

In spite of his promise to the Bishop, it was well known that he still liked a drink, and the smell of whiskey was always on his breath; sometimes he even looked drunk saying mass. Marie was terrified of him. She dreaded his visits, and the children knew to warn her if they saw him around the place. 'Mammy, he's coming back out of Mrs Donnelly's house. I think we must be next,' shouted Kathleen, now watching the priest from the bedroom window with Danny. Father McFadden's knuckles had scarcely touched the door when Marie pulled it open. 'Hello, Father, come in.'

'Good afternoon to you, Mrs Duffy,' he said, even though it was early evening. 'Just a friendly visit to see how things are,' he added, taking off his black trilby hat.

'Come into the sitting room,' she said. 'Let me take yer coat?'

'Is it a sitting room we call it now,' he said mockingly. 'I think I'll keep me coat on, it's only a quick visit.'

'Will ye at least have a cup of tea?'

'Is it just the tea you have?' he asked. 'You don't have a drop of the Irish in the house?'

'Ye mean the whiskey, Father?'

'Yes, that's exactly what I mean,' he said, with a smile that made the wrinkles on his face creak open.

'I think Joe might have some in the kitchen,' said Marie, annoyed that the children had still not come downstairs. 'Brendan come down and say hello to Father McFadden … And bring down the ashtray,' she added, when the ash from the priest's cigarette began to fall onto the carpet.

Brendan looked at his sisters who were smiling at him, glad that it was neither of them that had been summoned. Danny hid under the bedclothes determined not to leave his place of sanctuary until the priest had had his drink and left for pastures new. Brendan went into his parents' room and lifted the heavy glass ashtray from under the bed, which was full of cigarette ends and ash. He went downstairs, handing it to the priest, who was about to let more ash fall onto the floor. 'Thank you, Brendan … but could you not have emptied it first?'

'Sorry, Father.'

'Now, Mrs Duffy, I still don't see that husband of yours at mass … Ah, that's a fine malt. Sometimes a Scotch is as good as an Irish,' he said, finishing the drink with a gasp of satisfaction, and with a face that looked ready for another.

'I don't know, Father, why he stopped going to mass. I can't even get him to talk about it,' said Marie, going back into the kitchen to empty the ashtray and get the priest another whisky. There was very little left in the bottle; hardy enough to do a glass justice. She added a little water, hoping the priest wouldn't notice.

'There, Father, I'm afraid that's the last in the house.'

'Ah, God be with you, Mrs Duffy, you're a fine woman and sure there'll be a place in heaven for you … unlike that husband of yours who's booking his place in hell's fire.'

'Oh. My God! Father, do ye think ye could have a word with him? I'm sure he will listen to ye. I would hate to think of him burning for all that time in hell and me up in heaven.'

'Aye, and for eternity, and that's a long, long time,' said the priest, with a nod of the head that confirmed the certainty of Joe's fate. 'He may not even listen to me. I think a donation to Saint Patrick's may be a worthwhile investment. What price to save a tormented soul from eternal damnation?'

'And what kind of donation would be reasonable, Father?'

'Oh, I'm sure half-a-crown would get him back on track and I'll keep him in me prayers.'

Desperate to save Joe's soul, Marie went in to the hall to get her handbag. She took a crisp ten-shilling note from her purse. She wouldn't tell Joe. What would be the point? He would only go off his head. He would thank her when he was with the angels and looking down at all the unfortunate husbands burning in hell's fire, who did not have a good wife to look after their souls.

'Father, that's all I've got,' she said, handing him the money. 'Do you have any change?'

'No, but what price a man's soul?' he said, tucking the ten-shilling note into the silk lining of his hat before putting it back on his head. 'I better be going; there're so many more poor souls to be saved in this parish. Goodnight, Mrs Duffy.'

After the priest left, Marie began making dinner, worrying about how she was going to get through the rest of the week without the ten shillings she gave to save Joe's soul. Glad to see Father McFadden disappear into a house further up the street, the children went out to play for a while. Brendan and Danny kicked a ball aimlessly against the gable end, while the twins played hopscotch on the pavement at the front of the house.

Just when the potatoes came to the boil, Joe arrived home. 'Can ye put the news on,' he shouted before even taking his jacket off. 'There's been trouble in Derry.'

'What's happened?'

'Just put the television on and we'll find out in a minute.'

'Put it on yerself, I've got the dinner to make,' retorted Marie, annoyed with Joe's tone, and still fretting about the ten shillings she gave the priest.

Joe threw off his boots in the hall and went into the living room. He switched on the television. The six o'clock news had just started. He held the aerial up to try and stop the storm of interference as the newsreader described the violence that had occurred that day in Derry. He watched grim-faced when the newsreel began to show dozens of policemen attacking unarmed civil rights marchers.

'What's happened?' asked Marie, when she came in from the kitchen.

'Paisley's loyalist mobs and the RUC attacked the civil rights marchers again. Gerry Fitt has been injured.'

'My God, that's terrible,' mouthed Marie as she watched three RUC officers knock one young man to the ground and ferociously batter into him with their batons. 'This country's going to hell. I wish those civil rights marchers would stop all this before it gets any worse.'

'Why? They have the right to march as much as those Orange bastards and more reason to.'

'But it's only causing trouble.'

Once the news report was over, Joe switched off the television and sat staring into the fire, clenching his fist and cursing under his breath. Marie went back into the kitchen to check on the mince and potatoes, but she had lost her appetite.

Chapter 6

We Are the People!

After spending Christmas with his mother in Stratford, Ramsey was at his London flat for the New Year, when he was ordered back to Belfast in early January. Before he left London, he was briefed by his office at Whitehall about the serious rioting that had taken place following further loyalist attacks on civil rights marchers in the province. He was greeted warmly by O'Neill at Stormont Castle, but he could see that the Prime Minister was under a great deal of stress. Ramsey offered what counsel he could. He had become one of the few people that O'Neill could turn to as his grip on power began to slip.

Over the next few months, the violence continued to escalate. The pressure mounted further when water and electricity installations were bombed across the province. Ramsey, under orders from Downing Street, urged O'Neill to rally what support he had left in his party and force through the political and social changes that would remove discrimination against the Catholic minority before the situation became critical. With many of the Prime Minister's own party now openly plotting against him, he did not have the support to offer the nationalists what they were demanding, or the authority to placate the majority of Unionists, who now saw him as a traitor. He had become politically redundant.

By the end of March, Ramsey informed his superiors in Whitehall of O'Neill's intention to resign as Prime Minister of Northern Ireland. As much as he liked the man, Ramsey saw no point in trying to dissuade him.

A few days after the resignation was made public, Ramsey was dismayed to read O'Neill's ill-judged parting statement in the Belfast Telegraph. *'It is frightfully hard to explain to Protestants that if you give Roman Catholics a good job and a good house, they will live like Protestants because they will see neighbours with cars and television sets; they will refuse to have eighteen children. But if a Roman Catholic is jobless, and lives in the most ghastly hovel, he will rear eighteen children on National Assistance. If you treat Roman Catholics with due consideration and kindness, they will live like Protestants in spite of the authoritative nature of their Church.'*

Disappointed with what he read, Ramsey closed the newspaper over and lit his pipe. He then heard a number of cars pulling up outside. He got up and went to the window. It was the new Prime Minister, James Chichester-Clark, arriving with his future Cabinet ministers.

To find out just what kind of man he would be dealing with, Ramsey studied a well-thumbed volume of Who's Who. He was not surprised to find that Chichester-Clark was from the landed, Protestant aristocracy. His ancestral home was in the county of Londonderry, where he had been the local Unionist MP since 'inheriting' his seat from his grandmother; such was the archaic nature of politics in the North. He had a similar educational background to O'Neill, having studied at Eton before joining the Irish Guards. Ramsey saw him as a mere compromise Prime Minister; a desperate attempt by the men in grey suits to hold the faltering Unionist government together after O'Neill's resignation.

The appointment of a new Prime Minister did nothing to stop the bloodshed. In August, unbridled violence erupted in Derry between the local Catholic community and the

RUC. Ramsey urged Chichester-Clark to withdraw the RUC from the Bogside and offer at least some concessions to the nationalist protestors. The Prime Minister summoned an emergency meeting of his Cabinet, and asked Ramsey to attend.

During the meeting, Ramsey watched with dismay as some ministers insisted the Prime Minister got tough with the Bogsiders. Ramsey was wondering how much tougher the RUC could be without carrying out a massacre. When the suggestion of withdrawing the RUC was made, the Cabinet meeting turned into a public school yard shouting match between red faced men in pinstriped suits. Chichester-Clark now realised just what his predecessor had had to endure; compromise was impossible. The meeting ended with resignation threats from some senior ministers.

Afterwards, the Prime Minister turned to Ramsey. 'You see what I have to deal with every day.'

'You have a difficult job, Prime Minister, not helped by your colleagues failing to grasp the bigger picture.'

'What do you think the bigger picture is?'

'If there is no movement towards a fairer and inclusive society, there will be civil war in this country. The Irish Republic will not stand by and watch the nationalist community being attacked by rampaging mobs of loyalists much longer. Their army is already erecting field hospitals along the border.'

'How does Mr Wilson see the threat from the Republic to intervene?'

'Wilson has little sympathy with your Unionist desire to be British, and would be happy for the Irish government to take over the North and get it off British taxpayers' hands. I'm sorry, but that's what I'm hearing, Prime Minister.'

'Thank you for your honesty, Captain Ramsey, will you dine with me tonight? I have a few things I would like to discuss with you. The walls here have ears.'

'Of course, Prime Minister, what time?'

'Let's say around seven-thirty, I'll send my driver to pick you up.'

*

After dinner, Ramsey lit his pipe, and sniffed at the rim of his brandy glass. During the meal Chichester-Clark steered clear of politics and the conversation had been mainly about matters of no real consequence. It was only when they moved into the library that the Prime Minister turned to what was clearly troubling him. 'I have decided, with some difficulty, to request Downing Street to deploy the army in the Bogside. Do you think this wise?'

Ramsey was taken aback with this unexpected question. He took another sip of brandy before answering. 'Do you think that's the only option you have left, Prime Minister?'

'The police have informed me that the situation in the Bogside is such that if law and order cannot be restored to the streets immediately, the fabric of society here will break down completely. Riots have already spread to the rest of the country.'

'But, there is always the risk that British soldiers on the streets could only add fuel to a fire that might otherwise burn itself out in time. If your government would only press ahead with the reforms that the civil rights protesters are demanding, then there would be no more need for protests. In time, the Protestant population will come to terms with what is only right in the twentieth century. The Catholics in the province have as much right to work and have decent housing as they have.'

'That's easier said than done.'

'With British troops on the streets, you might have more than civil unrest to deal with…' Ramsey paused for a moment and waited for a response, but he could see that Chichester-Clark was listening for something more encouraging, so he continued. 'However, the Irish government's threat to come to the aid of nationalists would be less likely if the British deploy a significant army presence in the province to protect Catholic areas from further attacks from the loyalists. But it's still a doubled-edged sword.'

Again, there was no reaction from the Prime Minister, who was now taking down notes. Ramsey took another sip of brandy to give him time to finish writing. 'It will be one thing getting the British troops into the province. It might be altogether more difficult to get them back out again. And there's the little matter of the IRA using the British presence as a recruiting sergeant, increasing their strength to wage a guerrilla war of resistance.'

'Our security forces will deal with the IRA the way they have in the past. It's the breakdown of civil order that's the problem.'

'The IRA will bring guns onto the streets if there are armed soldiers patrolling the province. Force through the reforms that the nationalists want and all this can be avoided.'

'I will not get the reforms through parliament without the support of the party, and I no longer seem to have that. I must first bring the violence to an end, and British troops will help get that done.'

'Maybe so, but Stormont would also be giving up control over its own internal security and that may lead to direct rule from Downing Street being introduced … I don't think you or your party would want that.'

'No, that's the last thing we want.' Chichester-Clark stopped his scribbling for a moment to contemplate his own downfall. 'No, we certainly don't want that.'

'Well, I should be going,' said Ramsey, emptying the brandy glass and putting his pipe away. 'I hope I have been of some help, Prime Minister.'

'You have been a great help, Ramsey. I can see why O'Neill put such trust in you.'

'You have to remember that my job is to keep the British government informed about the situation here, and remain in the shadows while doing so.'

'At least you are objective with your opinions, unlike most civil servants I have encountered. I value your views immensely.'

'Glad to be of some help, Prime Minister. Goodnight,' said Ramsey, putting his coat on and following the butler to the front door.

*

Marie was pregnant again and her nerves were shattered. Over the last few nights, in the more vulnerable areas of Belfast, Catholic homes were being burned-out by rampaging gangs of loyalists. She was now afraid to leave the house, and only crossed the doorstep to buy essentials from the corner shop.

When the children had gone to bed, haunted by the sound of police sirens in the street, she kneeled in the front room and said a decade of the Rosary. She was still on her knees when Joe came in from the backyard, where he had been feeding his pigeons. He looked at her as if she had lost her senses. 'There's no point praying, woman; as far as they're concerned, God's on their side.'

Upstairs, Brendan was sitting up in bed reading *To Kill a Mocking Bird*. He was now twelve years old, a quiet boy, but academically gifted. He regularly came top in his class in all subjects, with the exception of sports, which he disliked intensely. Distracted by the constant nattering of his two sisters in the other bed, he gave up reading and switched off the bedside lamp.

Except for the ethereal glow from the street lights casting long shadows on the bedroom walls, the room was now in darkness. Another police siren screamed in the distance. Danny got up and looked out the bedroom window; there was a yellow glow in the sky above the rooftops.

'The Protestants are burning the houses again,' he said, trying to see down to the barricade at the bottom of the street.

'They'll be coming to get ye if ye don't get back into bed,' said Brendan.

'But Brendan, why are the Protestants burning Catholic houses?'

'Because they don't like us going to mass ... Now shut up, Danny, and get to bed!'

'But why?' asked Danny, climbing back into bed beside Brendan.

'I don't know. They just don't.'

'It's because they don't want the Pope,' explained Kathleen, sitting up to make her point.

'The Prods don't like the Pope?' questioned Danny, who thought everybody liked the Pope.

'That's right,' agreed Brendan. 'The Prods don't believe in the Pope or...'

'Or the Virgin Mary,' interrupted Roisin.

'Aye, they don't believe in the things that Catholics believe in, and that's why they don't like us.'

'The Prods believe in God?' quizzed Danny.

'Aye, they believe in God, but they don't go to mass,' explained Kathleen. 'They have King Billy.'

'They go to Church and Sunday School,' interrupted Roisin. 'Maggie Murdoch's a Protestant, and she goes to Church every Sunday.'

'Aye, but it's not the same as going to mass,' said Brendan.

'But why are the Prods fighting wi' us now?' asked Danny.

'Because they don't want the Catholics to get anything; they want it all for themselves,' said Brendan, making a loud yawn. 'Right, that's enough. Get to sleep before the Prods come and get ye.'

'They want all what for themselves?'

'Shut up, Danny!' moaned Brendan.

'No, ye shut up!' shouted Danny, pushing Brendan.

'Ye better be quiet, there's Mammy coming up the stairs,' warned Kathleen.

The door opened and light from the hall flooded into the bedroom. 'If ye don't stop that noise!' scolded Marie. 'I'll take the belt to the lot of ye. Now get to sleep or I'll give ye what Paddy gave the drum! I hope ye've all said yer prayers?'

There were muffled giggles under covers when the door closed. Brendan and Danny continued to nudge and push each other. 'Mammy!' screamed Danny, after Brendan gave him a sharp elbow in the ribs.

'Shush,' pleaded Brendan.

'Ye two better stop fighting,' said Kathleen, sitting up to wag her finger at them.

'Shut up, freckle face,' shouted Danny.

'I'm telling Mammy what ye said.'

‘Tell her, see if I care.’

‘I’ll get him for ye, Kathleen,’ said Brendan, slapping Danny on the back of the head.

‘Ye big pig ...’

The bedroom door opened again.

‘Now will ye be quiet!’ shouted Joe, standing at the half open door. ‘Do ye want some of those hooligans out there to throw a brick through the window? Now to sleep, and don’t have me or yer mammy coming up here again!’

When the door closed, Danny pushed Brendan. ‘That was yer fault.’

‘I’m telling Daddy,’ said Roisin.

‘Oh shut up, ye tell tale,’ said Danny.

The room soon became silent. As the others gradually fell asleep, Danny lay awake; praying the barricade at the end of the street was big enough to keep the Protestants out.

There was a sharp knock at the front door. Joe went to see who was there. Marie’s mother, her face flushed, rushed past him as though she had been chased up the street by a swarm of banshees.

‘What’s going on, Betty?’ asked Joe, following her into the front room.

‘I don’t know what to make of it meself, but the way things are going it might be for the best.’

‘What are ye on about?’

‘Don’t tell me, Joe, ye haven’t heard?’

‘Heard what, for God’s sake?’

‘There was a news-flash a few hours ago. The British army is in Derry, would ye believe it?’

‘Thank God,’ sighed Marie, making the sign of the cross.

'I don't know what ye're thanking God about!' snapped Joe. 'There'll be civil war now.'

'Don't be daft,' said Betty, pleased with the effect her news was having. 'Ye're as well with the army than the bloody RUC and B-Specials. Those swine are the ones causing all the trouble.'

'Hold it a minute, Betty, there's the news on now,' said Joe, turning up the volume. They listened as the newscaster read the headlines: *'Today, after some of the worst violence since the present troubles in Northern Ireland began, British troops have been deployed in the Bogside district of Londonderry. The decision to use troops comes after a week of rioting in the province that has left five people killed and hundreds more injured. Although the Irish government has protested that the use of the British army was unacceptable, many of the ordinary Catholic population in the Bogside have welcomed the soldiers...'*

'There'll be plenty rioting in Belfast tonight,' said Betty. 'The British army in Derry, the IRA will not like that *craic*, ye know.'

'I don't care what they like,' said Marie. 'I'm glad, and I hope they're in Belfast soon. This madness has got to end, and if it takes soldiers to do it, I don't care if they're British or not. The Free State's not doing much to help us!'

Joe said nothing. He had a terrible thirst for the drink.

While they listened to the rest of the news, there was a sudden loud knock at the front door; Marie nervously turned the television down. 'Joe, don't answer it! I don't want ye going out tonight!'

'Don't be silly, woman. I'm not hiding in my own house for anyone.' Joe got up to answer the door.

Marie sat biting what was left of her nails, listening to the excited voices persuading Joe that he was needed to help man one of the barricades on the Falls Road. Joe did not say anything; he just got his coat from behind the door.

'Mammy, I don't want him to go,' sobbed Marie, wiping the tears running down her cheeks.

'I know, pet, but he'll have to. Ye know Joe; he'll not stand by and let people talk about him. He'll be all right.'

Joe said a quick goodbye to Marie and her mother, warning them not to open the door to anyone but him. He ignored Marie's pleas as she knew he would. He then made his way towards the bottom of the road, where the barricade was now over ten feet high. Groups of men stood around smoking and talking excitedly about what might happen now the British army was in Derry. There was even talk that the IRA would be out that night with guns! But no one was sure who the IRA was anymore. Not even Joe.

*

Dressed in his B-Special uniform, Jamie Morrison carefully carried his son upstairs. William was having nightmares again. The noise and smell of burning from the streets affected his nerves and the nightmares were becoming more regular as the riots became more frequent.

'He's sleeping,' said Jamie, when he came back into the living room. 'I better get going.'

'Aye, but ye'll try not to get involved in anything, will ye?'

'Don't worry. I'll be careful,' he said, putting his pistol in the holster.

'I wish ye didn't have to go out tonight.'

'The police can't be expected to put those Fenian bastards down on their own,' he said, kissing her on the cheek before closing the door behind him with his customary bang.

With the adrenaline rising, he walked briskly along the main road, nodding occasionally to passing acquaintances. Everyone in the Shankill knew yer man, Jamie Morrison, and he liked that. He bought an evening newspaper from the newsagents on the corner of Emerson Street, and spat in the gutter with a curse, when he read that a Protestant man from the Ardoyne had been killed that afternoon: shot in the face with a shotgun. He folded the paper under his arm and quickened his step. 'Fenian Bastards,' he muttered to himself, 'Fucking dirty Fenian bastards.'

When he reached Tucker Street, he could see a crowd gathered at the front door of the Orange Hall. Heads turned as Jamie came near. 'How's about ye, Jamie?' said one of the men at the door.

'How's yerself, Alec?' replied Jamie, as the group at the door moved aside to let him pass. Determined to get to the platform, he forced himself through the crowded corridor and into the hall. Space appeared in front of him as soon as he was recognised. He nodded and smiled his way up towards the rostrum. Half a dozen men of local importance sat behind a twelve-foot long, wooden table, which was draped with a Union Flag. There was a buzz of nervous chatter in the hall as Jamie was helped on to the stage. He shook hands with the local Grand Master of the lodge, Donald Hamilton, and took the seat that was offered to him at the end of the table. Men from outside the Shankill wanted to know who the big fella was. *Sure that's yer man, Jamie Morrison.* The mention of the name was enough.

With Jamie now present, the chairman of the meeting, the Reverend Andrew Watson, got to his feet. The Minister waited, while others on the rostrum gradually hushed the packed crowd to silence. 'Now that British troops are in Londonderry, it's only a matter of time before we see soldiers on the streets of Belfast. This meeting has been called to decide on how to deal with the threat from the Catholics in the meantime. It's ...'

'Burn the bastards out!' screamed someone from the back of the room. Others agreed less aggressively. The Reverend ignored the outburst and continued with his speech as if he had been merely interrupted by a cough. 'It's been a terrible week for Northern Ireland, and even today I've had to sit with the relatives of one of the victims and try to give them some reason for their loved one's murder. There is only one reason, and that's the disloyalty of the Catholics to the Crown and their murderous desire to join with the Papist Republic. If they want to join the Republic, then they can! There are buses leaving every day ...'

There were cheers of approval; the Reverend had touched the right nerve. It was near impossible for the next speaker, the local councillor, Brian Henderson, to be heard, and it took a few long minutes before his words became audible over the din of excited voices. 'We have to remember that not all Catholics are looking to leave the Union. Another night of violence will serve no purpose ...'

The local councillor's words for restraint were drowned out by the uproar of ridicule. He reluctantly sat down and was quickly followed by a speaker from the Ulster Unionist Party, but the men in the hall were not there to listen to pleas for restraint. Calls for revenge for the killing of the Protestant in the Ardoyne grew more and more aggressive. One of the speakers sat down mid-way through his first sentence. It was obvious they didn't want to listen to a middle-class schoolteacher from East Belfast. The crowd outside had grown as large as the one inside, and to make their feelings known to those in the hall, they began to sing The Sash. Those at the back of the hall joined in.

When Jamie got to his feet, most of the men at the front of the hall stopped talking, keen to listen to what the big man had to say. Jamie folded his arms and waited for quiet, but the singing at the back continued. 'Shut up!' he suddenly shouted, pounding the table with his fist. Within seconds the hall was silent. Jamie put his hands in his pockets and surveyed the packed room. 'Ye want to fight, do ye?' he said sneeringly.

'Aye,' shouted a young man, waving a stick. 'Aye, we want to fight! The Taigs burnt us out our house and stole everything we had.'

'Well ye might have a good reason to fight, but what are the rest of ye so keen to fight for?' There was silence until his fist banged the table again. 'If ye need a reason, I'll give ye one. Survival! Aye, that's the only reason I'm prepared to fight! We can't stand back and let the Republicans take our jobs, our houses and our way of life. We have to let them know whose country they're living in and if they don't like it then they can leave. Ye know, and I know that they'll not leave! And why? Because they know they can't live as well in the Republic as they can here! So they want us out! But if we're going to fight we have to be organised ...'

'The Catholics are rioting up at Divis Street,' shouted a young boy from the back of the hall; his face flushed, having run almost half a mile without stopping. 'They've shot two policemen.'

'Well, what are ye waiting for?' shouted Jamie, as the men at the back of the hall began to spill onto the street.

'Burn the bastards out!' shouted someone. 'Fuck the Pope!' shouted another.

Many of the more venerable members of the audience who had been hoping to persuade restraint, quietly slipped out the back door, fearing that they would be caught up in a riot.

While the mob from the hall swarmed down the Shankill Road, Jamie, with another dozen B-Special officers following him, turned down a side street, heading towards the RUC station on Hastings Street. The distinct sound of gunfire could be heard in the distance.

Chapter 7

Defending the Barricades

When night fell, the stench of burning rubber prevailed and a shroud of black smoke hung over the rows of houses along the Falls Road. The riots had been going on for hours. RUC reinforcements from other parts of the city arrived in the Lower Falls Road. Undeterred, the men defending the barricades continued to attack the police vehicles with stones and petrol bombs. Two of the RUC Land Rovers were soon engulfed in the flames.

Joe Duffy wiped the blood from the side of his face; he was still dazed and leaned against a gable end to keep his feet. He had not seen the blow, but he felt the wooden baton crack the side of his head as he struggled to keep the barricade from collapsing. He looked at the sticky, congealed blood on his fingers and wiped it on the side of his jacket. His eyes were stinging from the toxic fumes. He could hardly breathe.

Joe watched anxiously from the street corner as two Humbers made another attempt to break through the barricade, making reckless collisions into the mangled, burning junk. The defending Catholics moved in when one of the vehicles stalled under the weight of the collapsing barricade. Joe, with revenge on his mind, tightened his grip on the stick in his right hand.

But before he reached the barricade, there was a sudden burst of gunfire from one of the police vehicles. Most of the nationalists retreated into the side streets, but a few ignored the warning and attacked the trapped Humber. More petrol bombs scattered fire across the street. Joe was close enough to feel the heat of the flames on his bruised face, but he continued to move towards the Humber. Another burst of gun fire rattled out from the pillar-box slit of a Shorland armoured car that came to the rescue of the trapped Humber. This time two men were hit and the rest of the rioters ran into the doorways for cover. A huge section of the barricade suddenly collapsed allowing the police and a horde of Protestants, armed with pickaxes and clubs, to pile through the breach in pursuit of the fleeing Catholics. Joe dropped the stick and ran for his life.

'Get that big Fenian bastard!'

Howling like a pack of starving wolves, the mob quickly gained on Joe. His lungs struggled to keep up with his desperate gasps for breath. Dazed and disorientated from the blow to the head, he lost his footing and tripped. He tried desperately to get to his feet, but he was exhausted. Suddenly there was a screech of wheels. A car skidded onto the pavement. The back door swung open as a brick smashed off the bonnet. 'Get in!' shouted the backseat passenger, grabbing Joe by the jacket and pulling him into the car. Even in his confused state, Joe could hear the crackle of gunfire coming from the front passenger seat. 'That'll stop the bastards!' shouted the gunman as the car reversed at speed back down the street. The car then turned on a skid, and after a few more missiles smashed off the back window, the driver, with a howl of excitement, left the chasing mob shouting obscenities in his back mirror. 'Yer a lucky man, big fella,' said the driver over his shoulder. 'If that lot got their hands on ye, they'd have made mincemeat out of yer head.'

'It's more guns we need,' said the front seat passenger, holding up the pistol to make his point. 'The fucking Prods have them, and we'll need to get our hands on some … By the way, the names Fergal and that's Paddy,' he said nodding towards the driver, 'and that's me cousin Declan.'

'Thanks lads, ye saved me life … Yer not from around here?'

'No, the Ardoyne,' said Fergal, putting the pistol inside his jacket.

'Where is it ye live, big man?' asked Paddy.

'Mill Street, ye can let me out here,' said Joe, as the car turned into Springfield Road.

The battered Cortina pulled to a stop at the corner and Joe thanked the three young men again. 'It was nothing,' said Paddy, before warning him not to go near the hospital. 'The RUC are picking up people with injuries and charging them with rioting.'

'The Crumlin is full of daft bastards with bandages on their heads,' said Fergal. They all laughed.

'Here lads, there's the name on a grave up in Milltown Cemetery, it's over at the back wall. If ye dig down a couple of feet ye'll find a cache of weapons; a couple of pistols and a Thompson sub-machine gun,' said Joe, handing Fergal a piece of paper, which marked the plot. 'You young fellas may need them more than we did.'

'Are ye IRA?' asked Fergal.

'Aye, way back then, maybe,' said Joe, getting out of the car.

'Cheers, big fella,' said Fergal.

Marie was standing at the window, with the terror of the night in her eyes. She rushed to the front door when she saw Joe staggering down the middle of the road. 'Joe, are ye all right?' she asked desperately, running to his side. 'My God, yer covered in blood! What the hell happened to ye?'

'I'm all right, get in the house and don't be making a bloody fuss, or the neighbours will see ye,' he snapped. 'Ye can't trust anyone.'

Danny was still awake. He sat up when he heard the front door opening. There was panic in his mother's voice. His father sounded angry and was telling her to be quiet. He could smell the smoke that must have followed them into the house. He turned to look at his older brother for a moment, but Brendan was still fast sleep, as were the twins in the bed recess. A police siren passed in the distance.

Curious as to what was upsetting his mother; he got up and opened the bedroom door. The voices from downstairs became clearer.

'Och woman, there's no' point in ye telling me not to get involved. We're all bloody involved, whether we like it or not. Ye can't bury yer head in the sand any longer. There'll be a civil war before long.'

'Ye can stay in the house. Ye promised that ye would never get involved again. Look how they treated ye when ye got out of prison. None of yer so called Republican friends offered ye a job. Did they?'

'There's folk getting burned out their houses. The whole of Bombay Street is on fire tonight ... Ah, that's bloody sore!'

'Can't ye stop moving yer head until I get it cleaned?'

'This is not about the IRA or a united Ireland. We're fighting for our lives and there's no one in the Republic doing anything to help us. If we sit back and do nothing, then the whole of the Falls will be in flames. Where will we be then ... Ah!'

'I'm sorry, but I have to clean it. I still think ye should go to the hospital. Jesus, ye might have a fractured skull.'

'I can't, the RUC are arresting everyone that turns up at the hospital.'

'Well, ye better go and see Doctor Kelly first thing in the morning.'

'I'm not going to see any bloody doctor in the morning. I've got me work to go to.'

'Work ... Jesus, Mary and Joseph, are ye crazy? Ye can't go to work tomorrow! Not with a head like this.'

'And how are we going to feed ourselves if I lose me job? I have to go to work. I'll wear me cap.'

'Mammy, I can't get to sleep,' said Danny, tentatively opening the kitchen door.

'Get back up to bed! For God's sake,' snapped Marie.

'Keep quiet,' said Joe, getting up to listen to the sound of screeching brakes in the street. Not for the first time that night, Marie blessed herself as they listened to the sound of metal doors opening and banging closed. They all froze on hearing the demanding knock at the front door. 'Open up!'

'Joe, go out the back door. It's the police,' pleaded Marie.

'I'm not leaving ye and the children with those bastards in the house ... Danny get upstairs.'

'Police, open up or we'll put it in!'

Danny ran back upstairs and sat on the landing. The banging at the door became louder. Joe went into the hall. Marie rushed after him and grabbed his arm. 'Joe, please go out the back, for God's sake.'

'Away into the kitchen ... What do ye want here at this hour?'

'It's the police! Open the door or we'll kick it in!'

'What do ye want?' Joe shouted, putting on his cap to cover his head wound.

'Open the fucking door or we'll put it in!'

'All right, give me a minute!'

As soon as Joe unlocked the heavy lock, the door swung open, knocking him onto the hall floor. Half a dozen RUC officers and four B-Specials piled into the house brandishing their batons. 'That's the Fenian bastard,' shouted Jamie Morrison, bringing his baton down on Joe's head. 'Move again and I'll brain ye.'

'Leave him!' screamed Danny, running downstairs, punching out and kicking with his bare feet. 'Watch the brat or he might get hurt,' ordered the sergeant in charge of the raid, pushing Danny into his mother's outstretched arms.

'Leave me Daddy, or I'll ...'

'Shut him up! Or he'll get it as well,' shouted another officer.

Marie smothered Danny's anger, pulling him tight towards her as Brendan came downstairs and stood defiantly beside his crying mother. Joe lay on the floor, his face covered with fresh blood; the fight knocked out of him.

Some police officers began searching the house, kicking doors open and pulling the terrified twins from their bed and ordering them downstairs. Joe was pulled to his feet and handcuffed. Marie sat quietly in the living room with her arms around her distraught children, still holding Danny tightly by the arm as he wriggled to get free. The sergeant, satisfied that there was no one else in the house, began to read Joe his rights.

'What's he supposed to have done? For God's sake,' asked Marie.

'He was seen rioting and attacking police vehicles ... Get him out of here.'

'He's not been out the house all night,' said Marie. 'Ye can't arrest him for nothing,' she protested, as Joe was abruptly taken out by three officers.

Before leaving, Jamie Morrison smashed the plastic water font in the hall with a vicious blow of his baton. He turned and sneered at Marie with utter contempt. 'Fucking Papist bastards! Why don't ye fuck off to the Republic where ye belong?'

'This is our country and always will be,' Marie screamed back as she stood at the open door and watched in tears as Joe, handcuffed to the back, was pushed face down, into the back of the RUC Land Rover.

With his mother distracted, Danny broke free from her grip, and ran out after the police vehicle as it pulled away from the kerb. Lights had come on in virtually every house along the street and neighbours watched from their windows as Danny, wearing only his brother's long pullover, ran down the middle of the road screaming at the back of the Land Rover. Some of the officers laughed and mocked him, while Jamie Morrison spat through the half open back door and shouted. 'Get back to yer whore of a mother! Ye wee Fenian bastard.'

Unable to keep up, Danny stopped running and fell to his knees, screaming after the Land Rover as it sped through the dismantled barricade at the bottom of the road.

Chapter 8

Póg mo Thóin

The following morning, the sound of an ambulance passing in the street woke Liz Morrison from a deep sleep. She heard Jamie coughing downstairs, before he closed the front door and left for work. She glanced at the clock on the bedside table; it was ten past eight. It was not like Jamie to be late for work. With the morning slowly melting the night from the room, she lifted her tired body from the bed and went downstairs to make a cup of tea.

Still feeling worn-out, she sipped the milky tea and sat at the kitchen window, recalling Jamie's disturbing screams and shouts as he kicked and turned the bed clothes inside out. She remembered trying to wake him, but was unable to as he groaned and moaned, like a wounded animal. The kitchen was cold and she shivered under her dressing gown, warming her hands on the hot teacup. The clock above the mantelpiece was the only sound in the house, until she heard the postman at the letterbox. She placed her hand to her mouth to cover a yawn and went into the hall to collect the mail. It was then she noticed Jamie's truncheon lying on the floor. When she picked it up, there was blood and what appeared to be human hair on it. Horrified, she dropped it onto the floor. 'My God!' she gasped, rubbing her hands fervently on her dressing gown.

'Mum, what was that?' called William.

'It was nothing, son. Go back to sleep,' she said, picking up the truncheon and rushing into the kitchen where she washed it in a panicked frenzy. The blood was hard and she felt sick as she scraped it and strands of hair off with a nail brush. She did not know what to think, but she was glad she found it before William got up and came across it lying in the hall.

*

In the early morning mist, rivets were hammered into place and metal was welded to metal by men hardened and proud of their own labour. The smell of the gases used in the welding process spread inland with the wind coming off Belfast Lough. Those who lived near the docks had either got used to the stink and cacophony of noises or had lost their senses of smell and hearing because of them. Everything was big in the shipyards; the dry docks, the workshops, the cranes. Even the men looked like they were of another world when they stood on the decks and hammered and welded ships out of sheets of metal. Only one area of the yard was relatively quiet as the men of that section gathered around the gates of the workshops to hear what they already knew.

Jamie Morrison had been waiting for this day for years. Now that his uncle Alex had retired, the job of general foreman, which had been held by three generations of Morrisons, was passed to him almost by right. He took the workshop keys from Alex and embraced him. There was a lump in the older man's throat and a rare tear threatened to run down his face; a face that looked like it had been riveted together. Alex took a deep breath and stifled the emotion that was welling up inside him. 'Remember, Jamie, don't let these bastards grind ye down,' he shouted, turning to the assembled workforce of over a hundred men in cloth caps and dungarees, with a smile. They clapped and cheered the change of regime and the continuity of tradition in their section of the yard. When the euphoria began to subside,

Jamie cleared his throat and stood with his hands raised to hush the more boisterous, younger men. 'Today my Uncle Alex has handed me the baton that was once in the hands of my father and grandfather before him. This job is not just a means to an end but a sacred duty that fills me with pride and hope for the future. Although the orders are not what they were in the past, we will once again build great, ocean going ships that our forefathers astounded the world with. We are only one sector in this great shipyard, but you men are the beating heart of shipbuilding on the Lagan.' There was another outbreak of applause and cheering as Jamie loosened his tie and surveyed the welders, riveters, crane drivers, joiners, plumbers and general labourers in his charge. He had said all he wanted to say and ordered them to get back to work as if he had been in charge of them all his life. The men dispersed to their work places, some went back to the various workshops, while the bulk headed for the dry dock and the deck of a ship that was still only a shell of grey steel.

'They're all yours now,' said Alex as he followed Jamie into the office beside the main workshop. 'They're good men and if you're fair with them they'll be fair with you. It's the managers and the money men that you'll have most bother with. Things are not what they were.'

'I know the men are good men, I've worked with them for years,' replied Jamie, taking a bottle of whiskey from a side table and pouring Alex and himself a drink. 'I'll deal with the managers the same way you have all yer life … ignore them.'

'Cheers to ye Jamie, your father would be proud of ye today … if he was alive to see it.'

Jamie knocked back the whiskey, the mention of his father made him proud and sad at the same time. Even Alex looked up to Gordon Morrison, the best general foreman who ever set foot in the place. His death was still raw to Jamie, although it was nearly ten years since he was killed.

There was a plaque in the yard in his memory, and if the men had their way there would have been a bronze statue of him at the front gate. Everyone in the yard knew or knew of Gordon Morrison, who was decapitated in a freak accident when a chain, lifting a sheet of metal, snapped. His legend was welded into the men's minds when it was reported after the accident that he had sacrificed himself to push a young apprentice out of danger.

Jamie dismissed the temptation to sit at the desk that had been his uncle's up until that day. It was protocol to at least wait until the retiring foreman had left the yard before claiming what amounted to a family heirloom. The oak desk was a precious relic from the time when Jamie's grandfather was general foreman and no one but a Morrison had ever sat behind it.

'What are ye going to do with yer time now, Alex?'

'I've got yer Aunt Peggy to keep me busy and there are the grandchildren to keep me young. If that all gets a bit too much I can always hide myself away in the allotment.'

'You'll miss it,' said Jamie, seeing the sadness in his uncle's eyes.

'You've got to go when you've got to go,' said Alex, with a tinge of resentment in his voice that his days in the yards were over when he was still able to do the job as well as any man.

'To your health and a peaceful retirement,' said Jamie, patting the older man on the back.

'What happened to yer hand?' asked Alex, on seeing the cuts and bruises on Jamie's knuckles.

'I was on police duty last night. You know how it is; those Fenians fuckers have thick heads,' said Jamie, looking at his clenched fist, before taking another drink of whiskey. 'We are the people,' he shouted.

*

Joe Duffy had been in the cells all night before anyone, other than a police doctor, was allowed to see him. The doctor did not want to hear his allegations of police brutality and was out the cell as quickly as he could tie a bandage around Joe's head and give him a few painkillers. 'Tell your lawyer,' was as much as the doctor was prepared to say, banging on the cell door for the turnkey to let him out.

It was a couple of hours later before Joe was handed a copy of the charges against him. Mobbing and rioting, three police assaults, resisting arrest, and possession of an offensive weapon. Joe read the charges over and over again. *Jesus, I'm going to get a prison sentence with this lot. The bastards!*

As he sat pondering his bleak future, there was a clatter of keys at the cell door. 'Ye want to see yer lawyer?' asked the turnkey.

'Who?' asked Joe, still slightly deaf due to the dry blood in his ears.

'Yer man ... Yer lawyer.'

'I never asked for a lawyer. I can't pay for one of those fuckers ...'

'You won't have to,' said a voice over the shoulder of the turnkey. 'You'll probably get legal aid.'

Joe looked at the turnkey, who smiled back with amusement when the solicitor came into the cell. Joe looked at the smartly dressed, middle-aged man and smiled with nervous embarrassment.

'Och, don't worry yerself, being called a fucker at my age can just as easily be taken as a compliment. My name's John Dunn.'

'I'm sorry, Mr Dunn. I got this a few minutes ago,' said Joe, handing over the charge sheets.

'There's a table free in the interview room,' said the turnkey.

'All right, Harry,' replied the lawyer.

Joe took a deep breath and followed Mr Dunn along the corridor to the interview room. The white emulsion paint on the walls and ceiling had long since turned yellow with nicotine. There were another half dozen lawyers in the crowded room sitting opposite their respective clients, many of whom were more beaten up than Joe. The grey haired solicitor quietly read over the charges. Joe sat nervously rubbing his hands.

'These are pretty serious charges,' said the lawyer, after a cursory perusal of the court papers.

'What's going to happen to me?'

'Well, it depends on whether you admit to the charges against you or not?'

'I'm not admitting to anything. Look what the bastards did to me,' said Joe, turning the cut and bruised side of his face towards the lawyer and then lifting his shirt to show his badly bruised torso. 'They beat the shit out of me.'

'Well then, we'll have to see whether or not we can get you bail, pending your trial. At least you don't have any previous convictions. So there's a good chance that you'll get bail. What age are you?'

'Thirty-seven, thirty-eight next week,' said Joe, wondering why his twelve months interment was not with the lawyer's papers. He felt he should say something, but thought better of it.

'You're married with four kids.'

'Sure, how did ye know that?'

'It was your wife that asked me to take your case. I had a wee chat with her this morning.'

'Ye spoke to the wife? How is she taking this *craic*?'

'She's bearing up fine. Are you working?'

'Aye', but I don't know if they'll keep me on if they find out about this.'

'Well, you've got a job for now, and that's what matters.'

'Will I get bail, do ye think?'

'I don't see why not. You have four children and your wife's six months pregnant, she tells me.'

'Will that help with the bail?'

'Yes, that's another factor the court will have to take into account. I really don't think there'll be much of a problem getting you out.'

'When will I get taken up?'

'It depends when they call your case; it's a busy court today. It might be this afternoon.'

'This afternoon? I thought I'd be up this morning. I can't stand this place much longer. The cell stinks like nothing on earth. Ye have to get me out of this hellhole. I'll crack up if I have to spend another night in here.'

'I'm afraid it's not up to me when they call the cases. I'll do my best to get you out as soon as I can.'

'Can ye get me some cigarettes?'

'I'll ask your wife if she can get you some,' said the lawyer, getting to his feet.

Just as Mr Dunn was putting his papers in his briefcase one of the turnkeys came into the interview room and handed him an official looking document. After reading it for a second time, the lawyer sat down again. 'It seems you have spent some time in prison before, Mr Duffy.'

Marie sat at the back of the crowded courtroom, listening to case after case being called in front of a rather severe looking magistrate. She bowed her head every time he sentenced anyone to a term of prison or refused bail for those pleading not guilty. Occasionally, there would be gasps from the public benches whenever someone received an unusually heavy sentence. *The lawyer said he'd get bail,* she reassured herself. *He seemed like a nice man, and sure Johnny Kelly said he got him off with fiddling the electricity meter, and him as guilty as hell.* Her eyes went back to the purse, gripped tight in her hands. *What if the court wants more than ten pounds for his bail?* She began to fret again and said a prayer to St Jude under her breath.

'Six months,' said the magistrate, before quickly moving on to the next case, ignoring the gasps of disbelief from the shocked relatives and friends of the bewildered looking youth, as he was led away to the cells for throwing a few stones.

'Ye old Orange bastard!' someone shouted from the packed public gallery. The magistrate looked up and surveyed the public benches to see if he could detect whoever it was that had called his legitimacy into question. Heads bowed to avoid his watery eyes and their penetrating stare. Marie's heart was in her mouth when he looked in her direction for a moment. 'Another outburst and I'll clear the lot of you from the court!' threatened the magistrate as a boy, hardly out of school, was taken into the dock. By lunch time there was still no sign of Mr Dunn, and Marie had lost all hope of Joe getting bail after watching accused after accused being remanded to prison.

'Court will resume at two-o'clock,' the court usher declared as another accused was led away to the cells to face a lengthy prison sentence. As everyone stood up, the magistrate left the bench with a pronounced nod towards the lawyers. There was still no sign of Joe's lawyer.

Marie rushed out of the court building to catch the next

bus home to make sure the children had something to eat for their lunch break. She was glad to find her mother in the house when she got home and the children all tucking into spam, beetroot and mashed potatoes.

'Why didn't ye tell me that Joe was arrested last night?'

'I didn't have time, Mammy. He's in court this afternoon.'

'Will he get out?'

'Aye, sure he will, the lawyer said he'd get him bail,' assured Marie, her anxious smile enough for her mother to know not to ask anymore questions in front of the children.

'Here, take something to eat, ye look like a ghost. Danny, get up and give yer mother a chair.'

Marie could not eat anything, and was only home for about twenty minutes when she had to leave again to catch the bus back to the court. 'Mammy, can I come with ye?' asked Danny, following her to the door.

'No, son. Ye have to go back to school. I'll be back soon.'

'Is Daddy coming home?'

'Of course he is. Now, don't worry. Yer father will be home with me before ye all get back from school.'

'Marie!' shouted her mother from the backroom. 'Ye forgot Joe's cigarettes.'

'Oh, Danny, go and get yer father's cigarettes for me, there's a good boy.'

The courtroom was just as busy in the afternoon. Marie was dismayed to see the same magistrate come back on the bench; his face looking even more unsympathetic. There were still a number of lawyers sitting below the bench. Marie nervously raised her hand to her lips when she saw Mr Dunn standing talking to the prosecutor. He turned to see Marie's worried face and smiled reassuringly at her. The first case was called and a man, whom Marie knew from the Upper

Falls, was brought before the magistrate, still in handcuffs. He pled not guilty and he was refused bail without hesitation. The man was led away despite his protests of innocence. The same procedure was applied to the next five cases, with bail refused each time. Marie was beginning to feel ill; the courtroom was hot and stuffy and the confidence had long since left Mr Dunn' face.

'That old bastard would jail his own mother for not having a T.V. licence,' whispered a woman with bright red hair, sitting next to Marie.

'Joseph Duffy!' called the police sergeant.

Marie gripped the back of the bench in front of her as Joe's name echoed down the corridor at the side of the court towards the detention area.

'Yer husband?' asked the woman with the red hair. Marie was too distracted to answer and merely nodded without taking her eyes off Joe as his lawyer got to his feet to address the magistrate.

'My client pleads guilty to the amended charges under deletion of having possession of an offensive weapon. Yer Honour. The charges are as follows...'

Marie was horrified to hear the lawyer enter pleas of guilty to a variety of charges, while Joe confirmed each charge with an almost inaudible yes. The prosecutor then got to his feet. 'Yer Honour will see the serious nature of these offences. This man was also interned for twelve months in 1959 under the Special Powers Act.' The prosecutor continued to present a damning narration of the Crown case against Joe, detailing the injuries to a number of RUC officers with outrage in his voice. After only ten minutes of legal submissions by the defence lawyer, the magistrate looked at Joe in disgust. 'These charges are so serious that I have no hesitation in remitting your case to a higher court, where I have no doubt you will receive a sentence that will be much longer than any I can impose. In the meantime you will be remanded in custody … Take him away.'

Marie's heart was pounding out of control. She felt the courtroom closing in on her. 'Are ye all right, love?' asked the redhead. 'Do ye want to go outside for some fresh air?'

'What's all the commotion?' hissed the magistrate, as Joe was taken back to the cells.

'She's fainted, yer 'onour!' explained the redhead, while Marie was helped from the court by two police officers. Mr Dunn got back to his feet. 'Your Honour, perhaps I should have mentioned the fact that my client's wife is pregnant and she's the lady now being helped from the courtroom. Your Honour will see the distress remanding her husband to prison has caused her in her fragile state…'

'Although, Mr Dunn, I have sympathy for the poor woman, her husband is a danger to society and I have a duty to protect the public. Next case!'

The following morning, after a sleepless night, Joe was taken from his cell to an interview room where Mr Dunn was waiting with a young barrister.

'This is Mr Woodward, he will be pleading your case today,' said Mr Dunn.

'Good morning Mr Duffy, I'm afraid, having looked at what you have pled guilty to, there is little I can say that will stop you going to prison, but I will do my best to mitigate the length of that sentence…'

'Mr Dunn, you told me, if I got a deal and pled guilty I might not have to go to jail.'

'I'm sorry, Mr Duffy, but I did say *might* … The courts are taking a hard line on account of the riots that are still going on. You heard the magistrate yesterday, he showed no sympathy, and we don't expect you'll get much before Mr Justice Mulholland today.'

'Yes, I'm afraid we drew the short straw this morning.

Mulholland is not the best judge to have to go before. At least Mr Dunn has managed to get the offensive weapon charge dropped,' said the barrister. 'Your solicitor has given me all the information about your background - a pity about the previous prison sentence…'

'It wasn't a prison sentence. I was interned without trial.'

'Yes, but there was evidence from two police officers that your were a member of IRA, and that won't go down well here.'

'They had no evidence.'

'Well, I'm afraid they have plenty of evidence this time, and, you have pled guilty to it,' said the barrister, taking the wig that was on top of his papers and placing it on his head. 'I will do my best.'

'What about all my injuries? Those bastards beat me up,' said Joe, turning the side of his head towards the barrister.

'I'm aware of those, but the police statements insist you were resisting arrest. The judge will not see it any different.'

An hour later, handcuffed to two prison offers, Joe was taken through an underground tunnel that connected the Crumlin Road Prison to the Courthouse. He emerged in the dock slightly disorientated. The judge was already on the bench shifting through papers. The clerk called the case.

Marie, sitting in the public benches with her mother, listened once more to the crown case being put before the court. If anything, it sounded worse than what the prosecutor narrated before the magistrate yesterday. Her mother squeezed her hand.

After practically ignoring the barrister's rather timid plea in mitigation, the judge turned his attention to Joe for the first time. 'Joseph Patrick Duffy, you have pled guilty to a number of serious charges, and little of what Mr Woodward has said excuses your criminal conduct. You acted like a wild animal and badly injured a number of police officers, *who* were only trying to protect your own community … Your sentence, will be eighteen months imprisonment. Take him down.'

'You call this Justice!' shouted Joe. '*Póg mo thóin!*'

'What was that he said, Mr Woodward?' asked the Judge, as Joe disappeared in the bowels of the building.

'Hmm, *you call this justice*?'

'No, you fool, the other thing he shouted.'

'I think he asked Yer Lordship to kiss his arse,' interrupted the Clerk of Court.

'Mr Woodward, you better go down and take instructions from your client, I think he may regret his little outburst.'

On the bus home, it was difficult to say who looked angrier - Marie or her mother. 'The man has no sense, eighteen months was bad enough,' said Betty, clutching at her handbag and shaking her head. 'Why did he have to shout out anything and end up with another six months?'

'Two years,' mumbled Marie, touching her stomach. 'How am I going to manage on me own again?'

'You'll manage …'

Chapter 9

A Cuckoo in the Nest

A week after the British army moved into Belfast to keep the peace, Ramsey received an invitation to have a drink with the Prime Minister before he went home for the evening. He was sure that Chichester-Clark would be relieved at the response in the province to the deployment of the army. Even Ramsey was surprised at how well received the troops had been in the nationalist areas. Before going to the Prime Minister's office he read a recent intelligence report from MI5, which confirmed much of what was being broadcast on the BBC. With the army on the streets, the violence was replaced with an uneasy calm. Grateful Catholics were treating the British army as their saviours. At many of the check points, the locals kept the young soldiers' spirits up with endless cups of tea. However, he read, with some concern that there was strong intelligence that the IRA was re-arming.

'Would you like a sherry, old boy?'

'I don't mind if I do, Prime Minister,' replied Ramsey.

'What do you think about the situation now?'

'So far so good, but I have been informed by MI5 that there is a very real risk of a major IRA backlash if the troops remain on the streets beyond the end of the year.'

'I'm afraid that decision is now with Westminster. The ordinary Catholics are grateful for their presence; so why would the IRA want them removed after what has happened?'

'The IRA is still mainly dormant, but as I said, the

presence of British soldiers on the streets may change the nationalist focus from demanding civil rights to demanding a United Ireland.'

'Well, they can demand that if they like. They will not get it while I'm in office. In the meantime, I have ordered further changes to the voting system demanded by Downing Street. The nationalists' other grievances will be addressed as soon as possible.'

'It's a pity your predecessor was not allowed to make these same changes at the beginning of the year. The province may have been spared all this violence.'

'The benefit of hindsight is a wonderful thing, Captain Ramsey, but we have to deal with what has actually happened, not what should or should not have happened.'

'Quite so, Prime Minister, let's hope that we haven't left things too late, and that the nationalists are pacified with what's on offer. What about the Reverend Paisley and his lot?'

'Paisley will never be satisfied, no matter what we do. We could always put him back in prison for a while until this whole thing blows over.'

'I hardly think it will just blow over. Areas of Belfast are now being defined by the religion of the residents. Hundreds, if not thousands, of Catholics and Protestant have moved to new areas as a result of the violence. The religious intolerance in this country is downright medieval. That has to be tackled before you have any real chance of peace.'

'Medieval, is that how you see the people of this province?'

'That's how the world sees it, Prime Minister. Whole Catholic districts have been burned-out in West Belfast. It's a pogrom. How else can one see it? I better go. I have a train to catch.'

'Yes, I think you better. Goodnight, Ramsey. I know you

mean well, but these are my people.'

'Including the Catholics?'

Ramsey boarded the nine o'clock train to Bangor. He knew he had upset the Prime Minister, but he was sick of the hypocrisy. He was hoping that now the demands of the civil rights marchers were being treated seriously, and that the army was in control of the streets, he would be recalled to Whitehall. He was weary of Northern Ireland and its bigoted religious intolerance.

*

Dr David Wishaw was in his late fifties, with a thin wisp of silvery, grey hair on his balding head. He spoke with a soft, considered voice, at odds with most of his patients' broad, working class accents. His practice was in a side street, which ran from the Shankill through to the Falls Road. Before the troubles he had a reasonably mixed practice, but now that the street was divided by a barricade, even if they wanted to, his Catholic patients were now unable to come to the surgery. Most had already registered with other surgeries. There was a sharp knock at the door. 'Come in,' he responded, still washing his hands after dealing with the last patient, who had a bad case of inflamed haemorrhoids.

'That's Mrs Morrison in with her son.'

'Ask them to take a seat in the waiting room, Mrs Mooney. I'll see them in a few minutes.'

Liz took a seat away from the windows that were now protected with wire mesh after they were smashed during the riots. William was wrapped up in his new anorak, sucking a boiled sweet. While they waited, Liz read an old copy of Woman's Weekly to pass the time. She brushed the fringe of William's hair from his eyes as he flicked through his comic.

He smiled at her, his face pallid.

After only a few minutes, the waiting room door opened. The receptionist called them through to the surgery.

'Ah, Mrs Morrison, it's good to see you.'

'Hello Doctor.'

'And how are you, William?'

'I'm all right.'

'It's William I want to see ye about.'

'What's been the matter?'

'He hasn't been feeling well for the last few days, and ye can see how pale he is.'

'Aye, you're bit pale all right,' said the doctor, carefully looking into William's eyes. 'Have you noticed anything else?'

'He's very lethargic, and last night he woke up with stomach cramps.'

Dr Wishaw continued his examination, nodding at Liz's concerns. There was little doubt that the boy was anaemic, he noted, reasonably sure that it was simply an iron deficiency that was the problem. 'He should eat more food with iron in it, like liver,' he advised as William turned up his nose at the idea.

'I can hardly get him to eat mince, never mind liver.'

'There are other ways of getting iron into his diet, but I need to make sure there's no other reason for his symptoms.' He called the nurse in to take a blood sample, reassuring Liz that it was standard procedure and not to worry.

William was not so easily reassured. He hated needles and felt anxious when he saw the nurse bring in a silver tray with the needle and syringe. The little colour he still had, drained from his face and the room turned white as the nurse raised his arm and unbuttoned his cuff. 'It will be over in a few seconds,' she said, preparing the syringe. 'Ye'll be back at school before ye know it.' He turned away when she rolled up his sleeve, and clenched his teeth when the needle nipped into his skin. 'There, that wasn't too sore, was it?'

He stole a look at the syringe, which was still only half full. The nurse asked him about school, but William was unable to answer. She finally removed the needle from his arm. 'All over,' she said, wiping the blood from around the small hole with cotton wool. 'Ye'll feel better in a few minutes. Ye can sit by the window for some fresh air.'

William tried to stand, but his legs were too weak. The nurse saw that he was about to faint, and made him sit with his head down between his legs. When he bent down, he unintentionally broke wind, which made him giggle. 'Sorry, Nurse.'

'Ah, don't apologise to me, it's yer head that's down there, not mine.'

Jamie went back to bed when Liz and William left for the doctor's surgery; he had been on police duty until two in the morning. After telephoning the shipyard to let his boss know that he had up most of the night, he was given the morning off. He was worn out and needed the rest, but no matter how he tried, he could not get back to sleep. The adrenaline from the last few nights was making him restless. His hand was throbbing and he sat up to look at the bruising on his knuckles. He could not remember who or what he had hit his hand on.

He got dressed and went downstairs. The kettle had only started to boil when he heard keys rattling in the front door. It was Liz and William back from the doctor's surgery.

'How was it?' he asked, pulling his braces over his shoulder.

'The doctor thinks he may be anaemic and gave him some iron tablets.'

"Look, Dad, I got my blood taken. It was horrible,' said William, rolling up his sleeve to show the plaster on his arm.

'Och, don't be a big baby. It's only a wee nip. Nothing to it,' said Jamie. 'I give a pint of blood twice a year.'

'It was sore,' insisted William, gently pulling away the plaster.

Liz smiled, and went into the kitchen to make some lunch. Jamie got up from the settee and switched on the television to catch the midday news. Through a storm of interference, Mother's Time was coming to an end. He had to hold up the aerial to get the picture to settle down, as Andy Pandy told Little Ted that it was time for bed. The news programme came on a few minutes later with grim pictures of the previous night's rioting. Jamie cursed at the television as it flickered again during a street interview with Bernadette Devlin in the Bogside. 'Fenian whore,' he muttered to himself. 'Listen to that bloody bitch…'

'Jamie, there's no need for that language,' said Liz, nodding towards William, who was not even listening, too busy eating his lunch of sausage and beans, before washing it down with a glass of milk. 'Look, I'm finished.'

'That's good,' said Liz. 'Ye look well enough to go back to school this afternoon.'

'Och ma, I don't want to go back.'

'Aye, well, maybe not this afternoon. But if ye're feeling okay, ye'll have to go back tomorrow.'

'I better get off to work,' said Jamie. 'I might be a bit late getting home to make up for having the morning off.'

'Dad, can I go with ye?'

'Ye don't want to go to school, but ye want to go to work,' laughed Jamie.

'School's boring.'

'Well, I'll tell ye what, young fella. I'll go to school for ye and ye can take my place down at the shipyards. How's that for a deal?'

'All right.'

'Ye'll no' be saying that in a few years' time, when ye have to get up at six in the morning to go to work. Ye'll be like all the rest of us, wishing that we were back at school. Right! I need to be going, before I've no job to go to.'

'Can I walk with ye to the bus stop, Dad?'

'Aye, okay. Get yer jacket.'

The following week, when Liz took William back to the doctor's, she was glad to see the army on a roadblock at the bottom of the Shankill. The soldiers let them through without fuss. William was excited when he saw the soldiers and their rifles up close for the first time. He offered one of them a boiled sweet, which the young soldier took with a smile. 'Thanks, son,' said the soldier in a strange accent.

'Are ye Scottish?' asked William.

'No, son, I'm from Newcastle.'

'Come on, William, we'll be late for your appointment.'

Liz was dismayed to see that one of the windows in the surgery, despite the wire grid, was broken again. She could not understand why anyone would want to smash the windows of a doctor's surgery. Once in the waiting room, she looked through a pile of magazines to find something to read, while William was still thinking about the soldiers. He was looking much better now; the iron tablets seemed to be making a difference. Liz was sure the doctor would only be a few minutes with him.

'Mrs Morrison, the doctor will see you now. William can

wait here with me. The doctor would like to speak to you on your own first.'

'It's William I'm here about.'

'I know, but the doctor just wants to have a chat.'

'All right … You sit here William, while I speak to the doctor. I'll be back in a minute, son, read your comic. I won't be long.'

'I'll keep an eye on him,' said the receptionist, with a friendly smile.

Dr Wishaw got up to greet Liz as she entered the consulting room. 'How are you today, Mrs Morrison?'

'Oh I'm fine; I'm only here about William's blood test.'

'Yes, that's what I want to speak to you about.'

'Doctor, is there anything wrong?'

'Oh, no, the boy is absolutely fine. As I thought, he was deficient in iron and the tablets will take care of that. It's just that I didn't know he was adopted and I…'

'Adopted, what are you taking about? He's not adopted. You must be looking at the wrong file.'

'He's not adopted?'

'No, he certainly is not. Why on earth would you think he's been adopted? Sure he's been coming here since he was a baby.'

'When I got the results back from the lab, I checked both your and your husband's files for any family history of anaemia, just to see if there was a common cause. It was only then that I noticed that William has a different blood group from both of you…'

'Doctor, I don't understand what you're talking about!'

'You and your husband have different blood groups from William…'

'But how's that possible? I gave birth to him.'

'I don't know, there's probably been a mix up in the lab,' said Dr Wishaw, concerned with the obvious distress his comments had caused.

'I don't know why you're saying there's probably been a mix up; he's my son for God's sake!' insisted Liz, panic taking over her as she tightly gripped her handbag, and stared intently at the doctor.

'I'm sorry for upsetting you, Mrs Morrison. I'll contact the lab and see what's happened. I must have been given the wrong results. Come in tomorrow, I should know by then what's happened. I'm sure there's been a mistake.'

'There's no doubt about it. There has been a mistake!'

Liz was still numb as she stared out of the bus window. She took no notice of a convoy of army vehicles passing on the other side of the road until William pulled at her coat sleeve.

'Look, Mum, the army are heading into the Falls.'

'Aye, son,' she replied, as she watched a few bystanders waving at the truck loads of young soldiers.

'Are they going to shoot the taigs?'

'Where did you learn that language?'

'That's what everyone at school calls them.'

'Well, don't you be using it! The army is just here to keep the peace.'

Once the distraction of the convoy had passed, Liz's mind returned to what the doctor had said. She was positive there was some kind of mix up at the lab, but she could not stop her mind wandering back to the days of her pregnancy and the morning she gave birth. She was unable to stop herself from thinking the unthinkable. She tried to remember the moment she was given William to hold, but her recollection was vague. The lapse of over eight years, along with the medication she was given at the time, clouded her memory. She could feel her heart racing as the doubts began to taunt her mind. 'Oh, my God,' she muttered to herself.

'What's wrong, Mum?' William asked, tugging at her coat sleeve again. 'What's the matter?'

'Nothing … Nothing, son,' she finally answered, her mind coming back from the past as she gave William a hug and ruffled his hair, pushing her thoughts aside for the moment. 'We'll be at Aunty Irene's in a few minutes, read your comic and I'll get you a new one on the way home.'

When the bus crossed Albert Bridge to the east side of the river, over the wind-bruised waters of the Lagan, she looked across to the shipyards. She imagined Jamie at his work, unaware of her fears. Then, her mind turned back to the hospital ward again, and Jamie's confrontation with the drunk man, whose wife was breast-feeding a baby boy with black tuffs of hair. She looked again at William. She began to feel unwell as the bus pulled up at their stop. 'Mum, that's our stop,' shouted William. Liz got up and shouted at the driver to hold on. They got off and walked the short distance to Irene's house.

The next morning Liz got up shortly after Jamie left for work. She had not slept all night. After sitting in a trance for an hour or so, she got William up for school and sat watching him as he ate his breakfast in the kitchen. 'What's wrong, Mum, you look unhappy?'

'Nothing's wrong, son. Eat up your breakfast before you're late for school.'

*

The walls of the surgery seemed to close in around her

when Doctor Wishaw confirmed her worst fears. The blood tests were accurate. William was not her son. Liz had to stop herself from fainting as the doctor continued to explain that the mix up was not in the lab, but in the maternity ward. 'How could that happen?' she pleaded. 'You'll have to have another look at this, doctor … this can't be right!'

'I can assure you that I have checked and doubled checked the files. I have also spoken to the staff at the Hospital and they have given me the details, including the blood groups, of the four children born on the same morning as William. There were three baby girls and another boy; the child of Joseph Patrick Duffy and Marie Theresa Duffy from Mill Street, in the Falls. That child is your son, Mrs Morrison, there's no doubt. How it happened, I can't say. I'm sorry, but that's the situation.'

'They can't take William from me … can they?' asked Liz, becoming breathless, and on the verge of a panic attack.

'I will have to report what's happened, and then it will be up to the authorities to decide.'

'Oh, my God, I feel sick.'

'Would you like a glass of water, Mrs Morrison?'

'No … will they take William away from me?'

'I don't know what will happen. It will depend on the Welfare Board, and of course the other family.'

'They can't take William from me. I don't care if he's not the child I gave birth to. He's my son. I will kill meself if they take him. Why does anyone have to know, doctor? The children are eight years old. It will be cruel to have to tell them what's happened.'

'I have my responsibility to everyone involved, including your husband, Mrs Morrison, and …'

'You don't have to tell anyone anything,' said Liz, getting to her feet. 'How can telling anyone do anything other than destroy two families? It was the hospital's mistake in the first place … and should you not have noticed something was wrong long before now!'

'I don't think you can lay the blame at my door, Mrs Morrison … but perhaps you're right. Reporting this will do more harm than good to both families,' said the doctor, wishing now he had never checked the family's files in the first place. 'If I agree not to report this matter, then what I have discovered must be kept between the both of us.'

'Yes, of course. Thank you, Doctor … thank you,' said Liz, holding on tightly to the back of the chair, and smiling through her tears.

'You realise the risk I'm taking, and if that's the road we take then no one must ever be told what we have decided here … including your husband, Mrs Morrison. Is that clear?'

'Yes, Doctor, he's the last person on earth that I want to know about this. It would kill him.'

Chapter 10

The Coal Bunker

Joe had only served two months in the Crumlin Jail when Marie gave birth to their fifth child; a daughter they named Agnes. Struggling more than ever to make ends meet on National Assistance, she fell into a deep depression. With their mother unwell, the children helped around the house as much as possible. The twins shared most of the housework and looked after Agnes, changing and washing her dirty nappies, when they came home from school. Brendan took on a paper round, giving his mother the few shillings he made every week to help buy a little extra food. Danny had the impossible job of keeping the fire going. Every morning he would take an old pram and scour the neighbourhood for anything that would burn. Despite his efforts, the odd bits of wood he salvaged only gave a few hours of heat, before all that was left were white ashes. With washing hanging from the pulley every day, even when there was a fire on, the house always felt damp. There was a constant smell of poverty about the place.

With winter only around the corner, Dr Kelly put Marie back on anti-depressants, but instead of helping, they sapped the life from her. After the older children went off to school, she spent most of the day in bed, saving the firewood until the children returned in the evening. Often, it was only Agnes' cries to be fed or changed that would get her out of bed for a while.

Danny woke up early one morning, with the wind rattling the window frames. The room was freezing, but it was too early to get up. It was still dark outside. He rearranged his father's old duffle coat at the bottom of the bed to keep his feet warm, before pulling the blankets back over his shoulders. As he lay there he heard the sound of crying coming from the other bedroom. He raised his head to listen as the sobbing continued. Concerned, he struggled from under the weight of the bedding, trying not to disturb Brendan. He got up and quickly dressed. His teeth were chattering uncontrollably as he passed his sisters in the bed recess, and went into the other bedroom. 'Mammy, what's wrong?' he asked in an anxious whisper.

'Nothing, son, go back to bed, there's a good boy.'

'It's too cold to get back to sleep, do ye want a cup of tea?' he asked, trying to control his shivering body.

'That would be nice, son,' replied Marie, smiling at his overly concerned expression. 'I'm a wee bit tired that's all,' she said, wiping her swollen eyes with a crumpled paper tissue.

'Will I bring it up?'

'No, I'll be down in a minute.'

Before he made his way downstairs, Danny went over to the cot to look at the baby. She was beautiful he thought, but why did she have to smell so bad all the time? He picked up her dummy-tit that was lying on the pillow and put it in her mouth, but it fell back out with a bubble of spit. He gently patted her head and went down to make the tea.

Marie forced herself to get up and put on a thick woollen cardigan. She had become used to the cold, as though her body temperature had adjusted over the years, but today was colder than usual. She sat for a moment at her cluttered dressing table and combed the knots from her greying hair, wincing with every determined tug. She then got up to go downstairs, dipping her forefinger into a plastic font and blessing herself; even though the font had been dry of holy water for months. She looked into the other bedroom where

Brendan and the twins were asleep under a mountain of blankets and coats.

She heard the front door close with a bang. 'Danny!' she shouted, before rushing downstairs to see what he was up to.

In the kitchen she found a fire burning in the hearth, and a cup of tea on the kitchen table. She looked out to the backyard and saw that the old pram was gone. Sometimes it did not take much to make her smile.

In the early morning quiet, the streets were deserted. Danny pushed the battered pram with its buckled wheels along the road looking for a neighbourhood he had not already scavenged for wood. The streets were still littered with broken glass and stones from recent rioting; there was a strong smell of petrol from a burnt out bus that formed part of the street defences. He manoeuvred the pram around the barricade and crossed onto the Falls Road.

Not sure of the best way to go, he walked up one road and down another. There was an icy wind blowing, so he tucked his woolly grey jumper into the top of his loose fitting trousers, and buttoned up his jacket to the neck.

On Clonard Street, he saw a couple of army trucks and jeeps parked across the roadway. The soldiers were unrolling barbed wire and attaching it to concrete buttresses. An old woman came out of her house with a tray laden with cups and a teapot. One of the soldiers took the tray and thanked her. Danny turned up another side street; he was too busy to be passing the time of day with the British army. Using the pram as a wind barrier, he pushed it along, stopping every so often to pick up odd bits of wood.

His left foot was now hurting and he stopped next to a baker's shop to take off the shoe that had been bothering him. He rearranged a piece of cardboard he used to cover a hole in the sole, and picked out a small stone that had embedded itself in his foot. While he was examining the cut, a man, wearing white overalls, came out of the baker's shop and loaded a breadboard onto the back of a van parked outside. The man then went back into the shop, leaving the back doors of the van, lying open. The smell of warm rolls made Danny's empty stomach rumble. Pushing his shoe back on against the ground and pulling up his socks, he rolled the pram up to the side of the van and stared at the breadboard of freshly baked rolls and scones. He was just about to grab a few rolls, when he heard the baker's doorbell ring. He walked on past the van, his stomach rumbling again with disappointment.

Before he got to the corner of the road, he heard the doorbell ring again, and turned back towards the baker's shop. The deliveryman had gone back into the shop. On being presented with a second opportunity, he did not hesitate and pushed the pram up to the van again. The doors were still lying open, and he grabbed an armful of rolls, throwing them into the pram. The door bell rang.

'Hey, what are ye doing there?'

Danny put his head down and pushed the getaway pram down the street as fast as his legs and its buckled wheels would let him.

'Come back here, you thieving wee bastard!'

With the icy wind in his face, and the delivery driver chasing after him, Danny charged up the middle of the pavement without looking back. He almost overturned the pram when he turned down the next street. Regaining control, he ran, pushing the unruly contraption as if he had just stolen the Crown Jewels.

Exhausted, he took another corner before pushing the pram into a lane between two burnt out terraced houses. Afraid the deliveryman was just behind him; he abandoned the pram and climbed over a fence into a jungle of weeds and rubbish. There he lay beside some broken chairs and a discarded mattress, his heart pounding.

No one came, and after about five minutes, he started to

feel safe enough to have a look around the backyard. There was a strong smell of smoke coming from the abandoned house, although it must have been months since it had been set on fire. Getting up, he tentatively looked through the cracks in the fence, where he could see the pram lying upturned on its two front wheels. There was still no sign of the deliveryman. He climbed back over the fence, and put the pram back on its four wheels. He then counted the rolls, which were still warm to the touch. He had stolen a baker's dozen.

Before he could get the pram out of the lane, he heard a sound that had become familiar to him during the street riots; it was a RUC Humber. Pushing the pram back down the lane, he hid and watched as it moved slowly and deliberately along the road. When it reached the lane, the Humber roared into another gear and drove down the street at speed. Relieved, he climbed back over the fence with two rolls in his pocket. He found a corner to shelter from the wind where he devoured them.

His hunger tempered, he began to break a few, half burnt, wooden chairs against the back wall. They were rotten and broke easily, but the wood would still burn. He threw the broken bits of the chairs into the lane, beside the pram. While looking around for more wood, he noticed a coal bunker at the back of the yard covered in weeds. It was secured with a padlock as big as his fist, which gave him hope that it might still have coal in it. He looked for something strong enough to break the padlock from the bunker, but could find nothing. The screws holding the latch were rusty and he tried to pull it off with the padlock, but it remained steadfast. It was getting late; he would come back for it after school.

Still not sure where he was, he pushed the pram back out into the deserted road and looked at the name on the corner, Bombay Street. He picked up a few more pieces of wood as he walked along the street of terraced houses. It was only then that he realised that almost all the houses were abandoned, burned-out shells. On the gable end of one of the houses, someone had painted; *Fuck the Pope*, in thick white paint. Halfway along the street, he passed a barricade that was being guarded by a few British soldiers, who were facing down towards another row of houses, where he could see a Union Flag fluttering in the wind. He turned away and walked down the next street, where a corner house had been reduced to rubble. Two more army trucks arrived; the place looked like a war zone. Feeling uneasy, he quickly made his way home, passing more burned-out houses in neighbouring streets.

Marie did not ask him where he got the rolls, and sent Roisin out to the corner shop to buy a tin of spam to go with them for breakfast. They all had two rolls and spam each; the most any of them had eaten in the morning for a long time.

While his siblings went off to school, Danny put some of the wood he had collected into the fire. He then pushed his mother's seat closer to the heat, so she could get the full benefit of it. 'I'm fine, son, and thanks for looking after me,' she said, pulling him close and giving him a rare kiss. 'Now hurry up and get to school before ye're late again.'

Mr Cullen, the lollipop man, was about to go home when he saw Danny running along the pavement towards him. The old man raised his hand and ventured back into the slow moving traffic, which stopped to let Danny cross. 'You better hurry, young Duffy, the bell has already gone.'

Out of breath, Danny walked the last few hundred yards to the front gate. The playground was deserted and he could see the lights on in his classroom and the teacher writing on the blackboard. The janitor smiled and scratched the back of his head when he saw Danny rush past him and run up the stairs. *That boy will be late for his own funeral.*

His classmates all stopped what they were doing and laughed at him when he poked his head around the door and smiled at the teacher. Miss Ryan shook her head and told him to go to his desk. Before he got that far, the door suddenly reopened. 'What do we have here? The consistently late Mr

Duffy, no less,' mocked Mr Ward, the deputy headmaster, with cane in hand. 'What excuses do you have this time?'

To the amusement of the class, Danny began to rattle off one excuse after another, each lie bigger than the one before. 'There was an IRA ambush and the Brits began shooting at everyone and…'

'Be quiet!' demanded Mr Ward, who had heard enough, and pulled Danny by the scruff of the neck out to the corridor. 'Hands up, boy!'

After the third blow, Danny refused to offer his stinging hands for any more punishment. Trying instead to offer another explanation, which was truer than anything he had said before. 'Sir, me mother's not been well and the house was freezing and the baby…'

'Get your hand out! And stop telling lies or you'll get the cane on your bare backside!'

Reluctantly, Danny offered his least swollen palm again and took the stinging blow with tears threatening to escape his defiant eyes.

Miss Ryan was still trying to build up the courage to intervene, when the sixth and final blow caught the tips of Danny's numbed fingers. 'There,' said Mr Ward, 'taken like a man!'

'But I'm not a man,' Danny whispered to himself.

As soon as the Deputy left, Miss Ryan came out and stood with her arms around Danny, as he showed her his swollen hands. She ruffled his hair. 'Please promise me you won't be late again.'

'I don't think Mr Ward likes me because me dad's in the IRA.'

'Now Danny, will you stop that talk. Your father is not in the IRA.'

'But he is, Miss; me brother said he's one of the leaders.

That's why they put him in prison.'

'I don't want you speaking like this; you'll get your father into trouble with these silly stories. Now do you hear me?'

'But he is.'

'Now stop it, Danny, there's a good boy.'

'Yes, Miss.'

'Now go to your desk. I don't want to hear any more of this nonsense.'

*

After school, Brendan made himself and Danny something to eat.

'Where have they gone?'

'I don't know,' said Brendan, as he stirred a pot of mince and potatoes that Marie had left on the cooker for them.

'Maybe they've gone to see granny,' said Danny, as he pulled up his socks and investigated what was in the pot. 'Mince. I hate mince.'

'That's all there is, so eat it and stop moaning,' said Brendan as he plated the food.

Once they had eaten, Danny showed Brendan the marks the cane had left on his hands, but his brother was not impressed. 'Ye don't get caned unless ye deserve it. None of the rest of us has ever been caned. It's not something to be proud of...'

'I'm not proud, but I was only late because I had to look for wood for the fire.'

'Ye should get up earlier then,'

'I was up before ye this morning and I was still late. It's not fair.'

'What else were ye up to this morning?'

'Nothing, what are ye taking about?'

'Where did ye get the rolls?'

'What's it to ye?'

'Ye stole them, didn't ye?'

'What if I did, ye ate them like the rest of us.'

'But I didn't know ye stole them!'

'But ye didn't ask me before ye ate them.'

'No wonder ye got the cane,' said Brendan, his face turning red with the realisation of his own hypocrisy. He had suspected the rolls were stolen as soon as his mother told him that Danny had bought them. Where would Danny get any money to buy them? But he had said nothing, and was glad to eat them to quell his hunger. He knew there was no point in preaching to Danny that it was a sin to steal. His own sin was the greater, and at least Danny was honest to himself.

'I'll tell Father Cunningham when I go to confessions,' said Danny, aware of his brother's sensitivities in these matters since he became an altar boy and started talking to God every night.

'That's not the point! Is it?' replied Brendan, unable to help himself.

'Well, what *is* the point? There was nothing in the house to eat this morning. Are we supposed to starve?'

'Ye knew fine well that Mammy was getting her dole money today and was going to buy food. Anyway there's not much we can do about it now. Just remember and tell the priest when ye go to confessions.'

'Only if it's Father Cunningham, I wouldn't tell Father McFadden anything, he'd only tell the police.'

'He's not allowed to tell anyone what ye say in the confessional.'

'He might, if he's drunk.'

'Ye shouldn't say things like that, it's a sin.'

Danny was now beginning to doubt whether it was a good idea to tell Brendan about the coalbunker, but he needed him to try and get the padlock off and get the coal back home. 'Brendan, would it be stealing if ye took something that someone else no longer wanted?'

'What do ye mean?'

'Well, ye know how I go to the old houses for bits of wood for the fire. Is that stealing?'

Brendan sensed a trap in the question, and turned to look out the window to gather his thoughts. He could feel Danny's eyes staring at him as he looked across the street. Mrs Donnelly had turned on her Christmas tree, which was always the best one in the street. He watched the coloured lights flicker on and off for a moment.

'Well?'

'I'm thinking,' said Brendan, as he formed his answer in his mind, fully aware if he said it was stealing, then like the rolls, he got as much benefit from the fire as Danny had. 'No, it's not stealing; the bits of furniture have been abandoned and are going to waste anyway. Sure half the families around here go scrounging for firewood in the winter.'

'So it's not stealing if it's been abandoned?'

'No, if the owners don't want it anymore and have left it, then it's not stealing.'

'What if it's not just bits of broken furniture that's been

left behind? What if they left some coal?'

'What are ye getting at? Where's the coal?'

'I'm not telling ye until ye answer the question. Is it?'

Brendan turned back to look out the window. Now her lights were on, he could see into Mrs Donnelly's living room as she stood on a chair to hang a chain of decorations from one corner of the room to the other. He wiped his breath from the misted window pane before answering. 'If it's been abandoned then no, it's not stealing. Why?'

'I know where there's a burned-out house with a bunker that's probably full of coal.'

'What do ye mean probably full?'

'Well, I've not got into to it yet.'

'What makes ye think there's any coal in it?'

'It's got a padlock on it. Ye wouldn't put a padlock on it if there was nothing in it, would ye?'

The mention of the padlock made Brendan think long and hard. He considered whether this changed the status of the coal and whether it could be said to be abandoned when the owners had secured it with a padlock.

'Is it?' Danny asked impatiently.

'No,' said Brendan, not completely convinced with his own answer.

'Where is it then?'

'I'll tell ye if ye promise to help me get the padlock opened.'

'Okay.'

'It's in the yard behind one of the burned-out Prody houses on Bombay Street.'

'They're not Protestant houses, they're Catholic houses.'

'Does it matter?'

'No … How are we going to get it back?'

'The pram, but we'll have to do it tonight. Do ye know where Daddy's torch is?'

'It's in the hall cupboard. I'll get it.'

While Brendan went downstairs to look for the torch, Danny began to get excited about breaking open the padlock. Instead of lumps of coal, he fantasised about finding a lost treasure of gold and silver, with big diamonds like the ones in the book, *Treasure Island*. He was planning how to spend his fortune when Brendan came back in with the torch, a hammer and a large screwdriver. 'Let's go.'

As soon as he had given up all the information about the coalbunker, it was inevitable that Brendan would take over. He was the older and stronger of the two, and had the torch. Pushing the pram as only he knew how, Danny was relieved to see the baker's shop was closed as he followed Brendan to the top of the next street. Now that Brendan knew the name of the street, he seemed determined to get there before Danny, who had the pram to push up and down kerbs and around corners. Danny regained the initiative when he watched Brendan walk straight past the lane, saying nothing until he reached the lane himself. He whistled at his brother to come back.

They went into the lane, where Danny parked the pram up against the fence. Brendan tried to straighten the two front wheels, which were now pointing in opposite directions. Danny found a couple of loose planks in the fence and pulled them to the side to make it easier to get in and out of the backyard. He made a half whistle to Brendan, who was now frustratingly kicking one of the wheels into some kind of shape.

'Shush…' Danny mouthed, pointing over the fence to the occupied houses on the other side. Brendan pushed the pram aside and followed Danny, who had disappeared into the backyard. Danny let out a cry as he tripped over some rubbish, banging his head on a metal clothes pole that was lying in front of him.

'Are ye all right?' asked Brendan, switching on the torch to see his brother sitting up holding the side of his head.

'I'm okay,' replied Danny, gently touching the cut on his forehead. Slightly dazed but no less determined, he pointed towards the coalbunker.

They began to clear away the junk and weeds leading to the bunker, stopping every so often when they heard noises from over the fence. Once the bunker was cleared Danny knelt in front of it and blessed himself.

'What are ye doing?'

'I'm praying that there's coal in it,' said Danny, his hands clasped together and eyes closed.

'Ye can't pray for something like that … it's sinful.'

'Why not? People pray for things all the time … Amen.'

'Here, ye hold this,' said Brendan, handing Danny the torch when he saw the heavy-duty padlock. He took out the screwdriver from his coat sleeve. 'Hold it steady.'

Danny held the torch over the padlock, using his body to shield the beam from the few neighbours still living opposite. The screws were rusty and tightly embedded into the bunker, but one by one they yielded. 'What happened?' asked Brendan, exasperated, when the screwdriver slipped off the head of the last screw.

'I think the batteries are done,' said Danny, shaking the torch in the vain hope that it would come back on again.

'Shush, I think someone is coming.'

They moved back into the corner of yard and held on to each other, expecting the RUC to appear with wooden batons. Danny looked at his brother and smiled when he heard a girl's voice. 'Three pounds or I'm keeping me knickers on.'

'I'm not paying any more than two pounds,' said a man with a strong Scottish accent.

'Ye agreed three pounds in the pub.'

'All right, I'll give you another ten shillings. I should be getting this for nothing. We saved ye lot from those loyalists.'

'That's what the army is paying ye for, not for screwing the locals. Okay, another ten shillings, but you must wear one of these,' she said, handing him a condom.

'I'm not wearing a fucking johnny.'

'Well, I'm not doing it without one.'

'I thought you Catholics were not allowed to use these things.'

'I'm not using it, you are!'

With negotiations settled, their differences were soon replaced with moans, groans and curses, while the wooden fence bevelled back into the yard with the weight of their bodies pressed up against it. The heaving and groaning did not last very long. The fence straightened, and the condom came over the fence and landed next to the bunker. Danny picked it up with a stick and flicked it across the backyard.

'Where's me money?' demanded the girl, while fixing her clothes.

'A wee lesson to ye. If you're going to drop your knickers for a few pounds, then at least get the money up front.'

'Give us the money, ye Scottish bastard.'

'No, and you're an Irish whore.'

After some pushing and shouting, the soldier relented and gave the girl the money. 'Let that be a lesson to you. Get the money up front.'

'Are ye some kind of pimp back in Glasgow?'

'Piss off,' he slurred, now urinating up against the fence.

'Piss off yerself,' shouted the girl as she hurried out the lane.

After breaking wind and cursing the Irish, the off duty soldier staggered on to the desolation that was Bombay Street and headed back to his barracks.

When he was gone, the brothers put the distraction out of their minds and returned to the job in hand. With no torch to find the head of the last screw, Brendan used the claw hammer to gently pull the latch and the padlock free from the rotten bunker. He lifted the lid and reached down into what felt like a bottomless, empty pit. Once he had satisfied himself that there was only coal dross in the bottom, he let Danny have a look for himself. The bunker, which had offered so much, was empty. 'That's what ye get for praying. God works in mysterious ways, but he's not a coal merchant,' said Brendan.

In better spirits, Marie did not know whether to laugh or cry when she opened the door to see her two boys covered in coal dust. The twins laughed at the pair of dejected prospectors, their faces and hands black as any miner's after a day down the pit. Fearing they would blacken the whole house, Marie made them undress in the hall, leaving them shivering in their underpants while she and the twins filled the tin bath in the kitchen. The twins were once again uncontrollable with laughter as the two brothers were led into the kitchen for their bath. Brendan nudged Danny, nodding towards the roaring coal fire and the full scuttle of coal sitting beside the hearth. Marie ushered the giggling sisters into the front room, leaving two fresh towels over the back of a chair. 'And don't be making a bloody mess,' she ordered.

Brendan braved the soapy water first, even with the heat from the fire, he shivered uncontrollably. Waiting his turn,

Danny hovered near the fire rubbing the goose pimples on his arms. 'Hurry up,' he moaned.

'Shut up and get me a towel,' demanded Brendan, scrubbing his thin white body frantically to get the ordeal over with as quickly as possible.

When Brendan stepped out of the tub, Danny looked at the grey bath water he was supposed to clean himself in. 'Mammy, the water's filthy,' he shouted.

'Get into it, ye big baby,' said Brendan, quickly dressing.

'Brendan!' shouted Marie from the hall. 'There's another kettle boiling on the stove; pour that into the bath for Danny.'

The boiling water did not make much of a difference as Danny washed in a frantic few minutes, getting out of the tub a whole lot quicker than he got in it. He dressed, while Brendan took the tub into the backyard and emptied it down the drain. Once they were both dressed, Brendan and Danny went into the living room. Danny was the first to notice the Christmas tree in the corner. 'Mammy, where did ye get the tree?'

'Someone put an envelope through the door this morning with twenty pounds in it.'

'Why would anyone do that?' asked Brendan.

'I don't know, but God bless whoever it was.'

'God works in mysterious ways,' said Danny, giving Brendan a nudge. 'He delivers coal after all.'

Chapter 11

What's Your Name, Son?

On Christmas Eve, with her mother looking after the children, Marie took the nine-thirty bus to the Crumlin Road Prison. Since the army took control of the streets, traffic moved freely again, although there were still some areas that were best avoided. After visiting Joe, she was planning to go into town, to do some Christmas shopping. She checked her purse was safely tucked inside her bag as the bus turned onto the Crumlin Road. She got ready to get off when she saw the imposing Victorian building come into view.

Joe was already sitting in the visiting room when Marie and the other visitors were ushered through the security checks. After getting a nod from the prison officer standing at the main door, she sat at the table opposite Joe.

'How are ye?' asked Marie as she unbuttoned her coat and took off her head scarf.

'Been better, my appeal against sentence was refused.'

'That's terrible, Joe.'

'I didn't expect anything else.'

'So you'll have to do the full two years?'

'No, I might get out earlier, if I'm of good behaviour; whatever that means. Anyway, that's that, how are the kids? Are they not coming up to see their father?'

'Joe, I told ye before. I don't want them coming here. They might say things at school; ye know what kids are like.'

'What the hell can they say? Are ye ashamed of me?'

'Of course not, Joe, we're all proud of what you did. We know you were only protecting your own … like any man would … I handed some tobacco in for you, I wish you were at home tomorrow, for Christmas, like.'

'There no point thinking like that, I won't be, and that's a fact. Just keep your spirits up, Marie, and don't be using those pills that doctor keeps prescribing you. They're no good for you.'

'I feel much better, Joe. I think it was having the baby with you in prison that got to me. I didn't know if I could cope on me own again.'

'Ye look better than ye did the last time ye were up. So stop using those bloody tranquilisers.'

'I'm all right,' she said taking his hand, and about to tell him about the twenty pounds that was mysteriously put through the letter box.

'I'm not supposed to tell, but ye'd hear soon enough,' he said, before Marie got her chance to speak. 'There's been a split in the IRA that's changing everything. I've been asked to act as CO in my wing, and to recruit as many young fellas as possible.'

Marie pulled her hand away. 'If ye get involved with them again, then you'll never get out of here.'

'I've got no option; we're either in the one camp or the other. A lot of these young fellas in here are saying the Army Council in Dublin have let the people of the North down. They've joined Billy McKee's new Belfast Brigade. They're calling themselves the Provisionals. Fucking traitors, that's what they are…'

'Joe, why are ye getting involved in all this again, have ye not spent enough time in prison?'

'I'm only a recruiting sergeant, so stop worrying about

nothing. Most of the young fellas in here have already joined with the Provisionals, anyway. They see the rest of us as dinosaurs.'

'No whispering over there,' shouted one of the wardens.

Joe sat back and lit a cigarette. Marie became tearful.

'Everything will be all right, so don't start crying. What's done is done.'

'I better get going,' said Marie, wiping her eyes with a tissue, before putting her headscarf back on. 'I'll pray for you. Merry Christmas, Joe.'

'Visiting time is not over yet.'

'I can't sit here any longer. I need time to think.'

'What's there to think about? Will ye be up next week?'

'Of course I will. Bye, Joe.'

Still upset, Marie took the bus back into the town; she was sick of Joe and his IRA talk. It was the only time in years that she saw him excited about anything. It was almost like he was glad to be back in prison.

As the bus turned into the city centre, she put Joe out of her mind. She had other things to think about. She had still no idea who put the envelope with the twenty pounds through the letterbox. She had thought long and hard about it, but she didn't know anyone who would have that kind of money, never mind be able to part with it. But, with over ten pounds still left in her purse, she was looking forward to buying the children a few Christmas presents and getting a decent size turkey for a change.

Once she got off the bus on Castle Street, she hurried to Marks and Spencer, hoping to buy the turkey before they were sold out.

The shop was busy and there were only a few turkeys left. 'I'll take that one. It should be big enough.'

'It will take a good few hours to cook that bird,' said the shop assistant as she lifted the turkey onto the counter.

'I'm sorry, can ye hold on a minute,' said Marie, frantically rummaging through her bag. 'Oh, my God, it's not there. I've lost me purse.'

'Take yer time, have another look,' said the shop assistant.

'It's not there … it's not there.'

'Maybe ye left it at home. I can keep the turkey for ye.'

'No, I had it on the bus. I remember putting me ticket in it. I've lost it.'

'I'm sorry,' said the assistant reluctantly taking the turkey off the counter.'

Marie left the shop and walked back to the bus stop to see if she had dropped the purse. There was no sign of it. Feeling wretched and unable to stop the tears, she walked home, stopping every so often to forlornly search through her bag.

*

Danny woke on Christmas morning to discover Brendan and the twins had already abandoned their beds. He rubbed the sleep from his eyes, before jumping out of bed, and dressing from the heap of clothes lying on the floor. He rushed, barefoot, downstairs in to the relative warmth of the front room and the allure of the coal fire. Brendan was sitting quietly at the window trying to fix a broken strap on his school bag. 'Where's Mammy?' asked Danny.

'She's in bed, she's not feeling well,' said Brendan, 'and don't go up asking for presents, because there aren't any. There's no money in the house to waste on Christmas presents.'

'What's wrong with her?'

'She's not feeling well, so you'll have to help. You can start by putting some coal on the fire before it goes out.'

Marie gripped the side of the bed. She had tried to get up early, but all she could remember was Brendan helping her back upstairs. She thought about her lost purse again; it made her feel sick. She took a few more sleeping pills and gradually slipped into a deep sleep for the rest of the morning

*

In the Shankill, there was a big smile on Jamie Morrison's face as he watched William unwrap his presents. The model Spitfire was soon flying around the living room with William providing the energy and the sound effects to keep it in flight, much to Jamie's amusement. Then, there was the James Bond car with its array of gadgets, and soon the Spitfire and the Bond car were in some kind of imaginary dogfight.

As soon as William had tired of the toys Liz had bought him, Jamie went upstairs and returned with a big box wrapped clumsily in Christmas paper. 'Here son, this is from me.'

'What is it?' William asked, carefully peeling away the line of sticky tape from the top of the box.

'Open it and you'll find out, son.'

Once the wrapping was off, William pulled the cardboard box apart and lifted out a small accordion, its weight and ivory inlay showing it to be of great age. He looked back at his father as his fingers instinctively tested the keyboard.

'It was yer grandfather's when he was about your age

and played in the Lodge band. He gave it to me when I was a boy, but I never did get the hang of it.'

'What's this?' William asked, lifting a black velvet pouch from the bottom of the box.

'It's his brother's sash, he'd want ye to have it, son.'

William took out the sash from the velvet pouch and looked at the intricate detail of names and dates embossed on it. When he put it around his neck, Jamie called Liz to come in from the kitchen. She stood at the door shaking her head when she saw William sitting on the carpet with his legs crossed supporting the old accordion. The Orange sash draped around his neck.

'You'll turn him into King Billy yet.'

*

Christmas passed as quick as any other day, and the New Year brought only wind and sleet to the Belfast streets, but the bad weather didn't stop the local children along the Falls from braving the elements to show off their new toys. Danny looked on with envy as Gerry McCue demonstrated the array of weapons that his new toy gun could fire. Each time he fired it, the younger children would willingly run to retrieve the plastic bullets as they bounced harmlessly off the askew pyramid of rusty cans, which looked more likely to topple with the wind than anything the plastic gun could propel at them.

'Give us a shot,' demanded Danny.

'Okay, but just the one,' agreed Gerry, who was a little afraid of Danny.

'Watch this,' boasted Danny, as he pointed at the cans and fired. A direct hit and a gust of wind made the pyramid come clattering to the ground. Danny reloaded but Gerry wanted his gun back. Danny refused. A struggle began for possession of the weapon until the telescopic sight broke off and fell to the ground. Gerry let out a scream that echoed all the way up to his mother's window. 'What's the matter Gerry?' his mother shouted from the bedroom window.

'Danny Duffy broke me gun!'

Danny let go his grip and was off running as fast as he could, back up the street with Mrs McCue's roar bringing the rest of the neighbours to their windows. 'I'll tell yer mother, Duffy, ye bloody wee hooligan!'

For the rest of the morning Danny stayed out of the way, kicking a tennis ball against the gable end. The ball was difficult to keep under control and seemed to have a mind of its own. He pretended to be George Best and tried to dribble around himself before striking it against the wall for goal. By the time he had managed to score half a dozen times, one of his socks had wriggled its way off his foot and down to the toe of his Wellington boot. He sat on the kerb and took the boot off to fix his sock. It was then he noticed a woman looking at him from across the road. She approached him.

'What's your name, son?'

'What's it tae ye, missus?'

'I think I know your mother. Is she at home?'

'No, she's at me auntie's house,' said Danny, still sitting on the kerb and trying to wriggle his foot back into the twisted sock. 'If ye know me mother, what's her name?'

'Is it Marie … Marie Duffy?'

Danny nodded at the lady, who was looking at him very strangely. 'She'll be back in about an hour, my big brother's in if you want to speak to…'

'No! No … I'll come back some other time… And what's your name, son?"

'Me name's Danny … Why are ye crying, missus?' asked Danny, puzzled, as the woman wiped the tears running down her cheeks and smiled at him.

'Here, Danny, take this,' she said, before quickly turning away and crossing back over the road. He opened his clenched fist to see a ten-shilling note folded neatly into the palm of his dirty hand. 'What's that for, missus?'

'Christmas, it's for your Christmas.'

Chapter 12

The Curfew

With Northern Ireland restored to some semblance of normality, Ramsey returned home for the Christmas holidays. He missed London, and its cacophony of noises, permeating from busy city streets, brimming with double-decker buses and taxis. It started to snow. He flagged down a taxi.

The flat was a few blocks from Piccadilly Circus, and he took the four flights of stairs rather than the unreliable, noisy lift, smiling when he came to the familiar black door with his name embossed on a brass plate. Peace at last, he thought, while pushing the door open against the pile of mail that had built up over the months since he had last been home.

Ramsey shivered as he turned on the central heating, leaving the letters on the table in the hall to read later. He had bought some coffee and milk at the corner shop and put the kettle on the stove. He carefully removed a treasured record from its immaculate sleeve and placed it on the turntable, delicately lifting the needle to the second track, his favourite piano concerto by Mozart.

Gradually, he began to feel the benefit of the radiators warming up, and sat back on the leather settee, sipping the hot black coffee, and listening to his state-of-the-art stereo. He was glad to be home.

He had already decided to dine alone that evening at a local Italian restaurant, where he was known and could always get a table at short notice. He loved Italian food, and delighted in ordering from the menu in his near-perfect

Italian. A starter of melon and Parma ham was quickly followed by a pasta carbonara.

The waiter brought an espresso coffee. 'You enjoy your meal, Captain Ramsey?'

'It was wonderful, Antonio, and I can say without fear of contradiction, it was the best meal I have had since I was last here.'

After flattering the waiter, Ramsey peered out over the net curtains at the rather gloomy evening outside.

He left the restaurant and headed towards the place that had teased his mind ever since he arrived back in London; Bacchus Gentleman's Club in Soho.

It was nearly three years since he last paid a visit to the club, which at the time was operating on thin ice with regards to homosexuality. Since the recent changes in the law, Ramsey felt less uneasy about succumbing to the needs that drew him there. His pace quickened when he recalled the seedy basement bar, with its saxophone music and smoky corners.

It came as a shock to him when he reached the top of the stairs to hear a Beatles song, ***I am the Walrus*** blaring out from a jukebox, and, by the time he passed the doorman, he was in another world from the wood-panelled bar he remembered from a few years earlier. Lights of psychedelic weirdness now covered the walls, and young men in neatly tailored suits danced with mini-skirted girls.

Sitting at the bar, he felt totally out of place as he noticed the old man in the gantry mirror staring back at him through thick heavy rimmed glasses. He ordered a double whiskey and ice, as the Fleetwood Mac song, ***Oh Well***, filled the bar. *'...I can't help about the shape I'm in, I can't sing, I ain't pretty and my legs are thin. But don't ask me what I think of you, I might not give the answer that you want me to...'*

The heat of the whiskey settled his nerves, adding an

edge to the bottle of Chianti he had enjoyed earlier. With the flashing lights irritating his eyes, he was considering going home for an early night, when a young man with long curly black hair took a seat next to him and asked for a cigarette. Ramsey produced a silver cigarette case and carefully presented the contents to the young man with as much solemnity as a priest offering the Holy Eucharist.

The young man, who introduced himself as Mark, smiled, carefully removing one of the cigarettes, before slowly putting it between his lips. Aware that he was being blatantly propositioned in a way he had never experienced before, Ramsey nervously lit Mark's cigarette, noticing for the first time that the young man was wearing eyeliner.

*

The relative calm that had descended on Belfast with the arrival of British troops was short-lived and in the spring the riots retuned to the streets with a renewed intensity. Each night, before going to bed, Marie would say a decade of the rosary to the sound of gun battles and police sirens. She was thankful that the British army had at least kept the loyalists out of the Falls.

On a hot summer's day, Marie returned home after visiting Joe to find a large convoy of British vehicles parked along the lower Falls Road. She passed through the army checkpoint at the bottom of the road with only a cursory search of her bag, and a cheery smile from the young soldier, who looked like he had joined the army straight from school.

'What's going on, son?' she asked, pointing to the convoy.

'Haven't got a clue, they tell us nothing.'

Marie was only in the house ten minutes, and had just put the dinner on when Kathleen shouted from the front room,

'Mammy, the Brits are coming up the road!'

Marie hurried to the window and saw the soldiers in full riot gear, chasing a crowd of young men down the street.

'What's that, Mammy?' asked Danny, pointing to a canister that had landed in the middle of the road with a hollow clatter.

'I don't know, son, what the hell it is?'

As more canisters followed, the whole street quickly became engulfed in a slow moving, toxic fog. 'Get into the kitchen,' shouted Marie, grabbing Kathleen and Roisin by their arms. 'Danny, go upstairs and make sure the windows are all closed and bring Agnes down! Brendan, help me wet these towels.'

Danny brought Agnes downstairs and handed her to Roisin. Marie put the wet towels over the children's heads and they huddled on the kitchen floor together as the gas seeped through every crack in the house. Their eyes were soon streaming with hot, stinging tears.

Barely able to breathe, Kathleen clung to Roisin, who was trying to blow the gas away from the baby's face. 'I wish Daddy was here,' said Kathleen, holding on to her twin's arm tightly.

'Hush, hush, it will be all right in a few minutes,' said Marie.

*

Private Harry Mitchell had only arrived in Ireland three days before, and this was the first time he had been outside the safety of the barracks. The adrenaline was pumping through his body as he ran with the rest of his company towards the first address on the list to be searched for weapons.

The company lieutenant gave two sharp knocks on the door. Without waiting for an answer, he ordered it to be kicked in. The door flew open; its flimsy locks no match for heavy hobnailed boots. The armed soldiers piled into the tiny terraced house.

They came upon the terrified faces of the Duffy family. As the soldiers searched the house, the lieutenant read over a prepared statement to the family, and then demanded to know where the guns were hidden. Marie stared at him in silence. 'This whole area is under curfew, and will remain so until every weapon has been found. So tell us where the guns are and we will leave you in peace,' continued the Lieutenant, taking a more conciliatory tone.

'Aye, so ye will,' said Danny sarcastically. 'Ye have no right to be in this house.'

'Be quiet, Danny,' snapped Marie. 'You're wasting yer time, lieutenant, there are no weapons here.'

'We will see soon enough.'

Once the soldiers had left empty-handed, Marie picked up the broken ornaments and tidied up as best she could. The children sat by the window to watch the continued deployment of troops along the street. Some angry residents were being ordered back into their houses and told they would be shot if they ventured into the street again. It was clear the army was taking control of the area with an iron fist.

That evening, Eugene Tierney was ordered into the Falls to assist the beleaguered Officials, who were now in a desperate gunfight with the army. He took a young Provo with him, Fergal Gallagher, and the two of them slipped into the chaos with ease. They took up a sniper position in a derelict house at the corner of Clonard Street and the Falls Road.

Eugene opened the bedroom window and tried to pick out one of the soldiers standing behind a row of Saracens.

‘What the hell is that?’ said Fergal.

‘It sounds like a helicopter!’

‘If you can get a shot at that…’

‘Are ye mad? We can’t shoot down a fucking helicopter. It will crash into our own houses,’ said Eugene, as he listened to a clipped English accent giving out orders over a loudspeaker to the soldiers below. The helicopter then passed on; further into the Falls.

‘Keep yer head down, I’m going to take one of these bastards out,’ said Eugene as he focused his aim on a soldier, who had just fired a CS gas canister down the street at a gang of youths. Eugene held his breath, squeezed the trigger and fired! He missed.

The startled soldier dived for cover behind a personnel carrier, while Eugene pulled away from the window and waited for a return volley of fire. When none came, he peered back through the open window. He realised that the cowering soldiers were still trying to work out where the first shot came from. He took aim at the head of a corporal who was screaming orders at his men. This time the bullet narrowly missed its intended target, and ricocheted off the side of a Saracen. Instinctively, Eugene and Fergal rolled away from the window as a hail of bullets shattered the panes of glass above them. ‘Let’s get to hell out of here,’ shouted Eugene. ‘This old rifle isn’t worth a fuck.’

‘Maybe ye need glasses,’ shouted Fergal, as they rushed into the hall, almost knocking each other down the stairs, when another hail of bullets peppered the bedroom walls. The two of them ran into the backyard, with the gunfire still ripping through the front of the house. Eugene dropped the rifle. They climbed over the back wall. More gunfire rattled out over the sound of dustbin lids banging on the cobbled streets. They ran down one street and up another until they reached Springfield Road, where Fergal had parked the car. ‘Fuck!’ shouted Eugene when he saw a convoy of army vehicles heading towards them. They ran down the nearest alley and onto Mill Street only to find another army patrol blocking their escape at the top of the road. 'Over here,' shouted Bridget Donnelly, standing at her front door and waving frantically at them. The two Provos ran across the road and into the house. Mrs Donnelly had already opened the back door. 'Yer sound, missus,' shouted Fergal, as he and Eugene made good their escape through the backyard.

'Mammy,' shouted Danny, who was sitting at the front window. 'The Brits are after Uncle Eugene. He ran into Mrs Donnelly's house with another man.'

'Get away from that bloody window,' shouted Marie, who looked over to see Mrs Donnelly standing at her door berating a couple of young soldiers, who quickly carried on down the street despite her taunts.

The curfew continued for three days and hundreds of Catholic houses were ransacked, with only a handful of old guns seized. When Ramsey was informed of the curfew and the resulting hostility from the Catholic residents to the aggressive nature of the searches, he was sure that the British army had now lost its cloak of neutrality, and would be seen by many Catholics as another enemy to be feared.

Over the next few weeks the Duffy household returned to some sort of normality until Kathleen woke her mother one morning in a state of panic.

'What's the matter?'

'It's the baby; I think there's something wrong…'

'What? What's wrong?' demanded Marie, throwing the bed covers onto the floor and rushing to the silent cot beside the window. She touched Agnes's lifeless face. 'Me baby,' she mumbled, lifting the body from the cot. 'Me Baby!' she screamed, waking up everyone in the house.

The twins went to get the doctor, while Danny ran all the way to his grandmother's house in the Ardoyne to tell her what had happened. Ignoring his mother's protests that Agnes was not dead, Brendan went to fetch the priest.

*

After the funeral, the house was full of grieving relatives.

'Ah sure, the wee thing's in heaven with God,' said one woman, eating a ham sandwich and sipping a cup of tea.

'But why did God need to take the baby?' asked Kathleen, sobbing to her Aunt Theresa.

'Maybe it was for the best. Yer mother's not been well since she had the baby,' said Theresa, turning to look at Marie, who was sitting in a trance in front of the fire.

'But meself and Roisin were looking after her.'

'I know ye were pet, but the baby's gone and all we can do now is pray for her little soul and look after yer poor mother until she gets well again.'

'What's meningitis?' Danny asked Brendan.

'I don't know, do I? What does it matter! It killed wee Agnes, that's all that matters.'

'I think it was the gas that killed her,' said Danny. 'The Brits killed her.'

'Stop that, Danny,' said his grandmother. 'The doctor said it was meningitis, and that's the end of it. That child had never been well since the day she was born.'

'It was the Brits that killed her,' shouted Danny, running upstairs in tears.

A few days after the funeral, while Marie was upstairs staring at the empty cot, there was a sharp knock at the front door. She fixed her dishevelled hair and went downstairs.

It was her mother, carrying a bag of second hand clothes, which she dumped in the middle of the hall floor.

'Good God, Marie, have ye been in your bed all day?' asked Betty, shocked at the sight that greeted her from the shadows of the hall door. 'Jesus, come in to the kitchen till I have look at ye.'

'I'm tired, that's all. I can't get to sleep.'

'This house is freezing and there's a smell that would knock King Billy off his bloody white horse!'

Marie sat down at the kitchen table, her frail body shivering violently in her thin dressing-gown. Her tears of misery were frozen in her eyes. Betty went up to the bedroom and retched at the overwhelming stench of urine from the baby's cot. She lifted the bedding and mattress and took them down to the backyard.

Betty then turned her attention to her daughter. First, she made a pot of strong tea. 'What do ye mean yer tired, we're all bloody tired. You've got these children to think of. You have to stop taking those damn pills that old lazy doctor keeps prescribing you. They're turning you into a walking bloody zombie. Are ye listening?'

Marie nodded and pushed her bony fingers through her knotted hair. 'Poor wee Agnes is all alone in that grave,' she lamented, the frozen tears melting and running down her face.

'I know, pet, but you have the other children to think about ... I'll put a fire on; it's like Siberia in here.'

Betty got up and tried to get the fire going with the little coal she could find at the bottom of the coalbunker. After a few Hail Marys and as many curses, the fire took hold. She then looked at her coal-covered hands and smiled with satisfaction at the blue and yellow flames that were beginning their merry dance in the centre of the hearth. She then got up from her knees to see Marie staring at the bag of clothes.

'That's better; there nothing like a good fire.' smiled Betty, 'You shouldn't lie in bed all day. It will only sap the life away from you. Here! Try this on,' she added, holding up a white blouse. 'At least get yerself out of that old dressing gown.'

Betty went through the bag, pulling out clothes; pullovers, blouses, skirts. Every so often she would hold up something to tempt her daughter, but Marie showed little interest. Betty soon gave up and made another pot of tea, mouthing a prayer to St Jude, who she thought must be awfully busy these days.

Chapter 13

It's Only a Game

Liz sat by the window. The roads were icy and she was having second thoughts about travelling to Glasgow for Hogmanay, but she had no option; she could not trust her husband to look after William with the amount of drinking he would be doing. She got up and poked the dying embers of the fire, before putting the hot ashes in a bucket and leaving them at the back door to cool off.

She was just about to call on William to get out of his bed, when he came running downstairs with his Rangers top on.

'You're not wearing that!' she snapped at him.

'But Dad said I could.'

'William, will you go back upstairs and take that off. Your uncle will be here any minute.'

'But Mum!'

'Let him wear it for God's sake. He'll be all right,' said Jamie.

'I'm not leaving this house until he takes it off.'

'He'll be fine, he'll be amongst friends.'

'I don't care. It's Glasgow he's going to, and I don't want any trouble.'

'He can wear it under his coat.'

Liz knew that once Jamie's mind was made up there was

nothing she could say that would make any difference.

'There's Uncle Robert now,' said William, rushing to open the front door.

Jamie's brother, Robert, was a taxi driver and a fanatical Glasgow Rangers fan. He travelled every other week to Ibrox Park, staying with friends in the staunchly loyalist area of Bridgeton. The New Year's Old Firm game was a bit special, and tickets were hard to come by, but Robert always knew how to get his hands on a few.

The ferry trip took over three hours before they arrived in the port of Stranraer. Robert then drove through the winding roads towards Glasgow singing as many Rangers songs as he and Jamie could remember. William sang along, even if he did not know all the words to some of the songs.

The car pulled up outside a row of run-down tenements on London Road, a few hundred yards from Bridgeton Cross. Robert's friend, Mae Burns, a ruddy faced woman in her fifties, greeted them at the close and led them to a ground floor flat.

'Come in, come in. It's good to see you all. I've got a nice wee fire on in the living room. Here, let me take yer coats'

'Thanks, Mae. You've met me brother before and this is his wife, Liz and their son, William.'

'Nice tae meet ye both. I hope you'll feel at home. There's a pot of mince and potatoes on the stove, Liz. I'll leave you to it. I'm only a couple of closes up the road if you need anything.'

The following morning, Liz and William went to *The Barras*, a colourful flea market in the Carlton area of Glasgow. William had never seen such a vibrant place before, with its cacophony of noises and wafting smells of candyfloss, toffee-apples and whelks overwhelming the senses.

'Morning, missus, you can have a full set of bathroom towels for five-bob. Any colour ye like. Ye'll pay four times more in the High Street,' shouted a cigar-smoking trader. Liz smiled at the man, but shook her head and moved on to the next stall. While his mother looked through a collection of second-hand records, William watched an old man, who was sitting at the stall opposite feeding peanuts to a monkey perched on his shoulder. The man's stall was full of clocks and old pocket watches, none of which seemed to know the right time. They moved through the busy market that seemed to sell everything and anything, much of which William thought was just junk.

After nearly an hour of walking from stall to stall, the novelty had worn off for William and he became bored with his mother's endless quest for a bargain.

'Mum, are you not going to buy anything?'

'There're a few things I'd like to buy, but there's not much room in Robert's car.'

'So, what's the point, my feet are killing me.'

'Okay, son, we'll go and get something to eat in a minute. Do ye fancy a fish supper?'

'Anything, I just want to get out of this mad place.'

The minute lasted another hour until Liz finally bought a pair of second-hand candlesticks. 'Mum,' moaned William, as the man wrapped up the candlesticks.

'All right, William, we'll go and get something to eat.'

They crossed a busy road to a café where they had a fish and chip tea before going back to the Bridgeton flat.

That evening, Jamie and Robert decided to go the local lodge for a few pints. Liz knew they would be having more than just a few pints and had no desire to join them, even though Robert insisted Mrs Burns would be happy to look after William. Jamie decided there was no point trying to persuade her, Liz was never one for drinking or late nights.

'We'll be back for the bells,' said Jamie, as he put on his

coat.

'Don't be getting too drunk,' she said, more in hope than expectation.

When the men left, Liz washed the dinner plates and tidied up the flat as best she could. William settled down on the carpet in front of the fire to play with his collection of football cards. He arranged his Rangers players first; it was the only team that he had enough cards to make a full line-up. Once he had all his cards laid out, he began to pick the best players from various teams that he would play in his own Scotland team. Unlike his father, who always insisted on Willie Henderson, he put Celtic's Jimmy Johnstone on the wing.

Once she finished the housework, Liz sat looking into the fire, wishing she was back at home. She was dreading William going to Ibrox. She ruffled his hair and smiled at him.

'What's up, Mum?'

'Oh, nothing, I'm just a bit tired, that's all.'

'When will Dad and Robert be back?'

'Don't worry about them. You'll be in your bed long before they get back.'

The hall was heaving. The locals mixed easily with the supporters that had travelled from Northern Ireland for the big game. While Robert spoke to a couple of friends, Jamie got the pints in. It was a boisterous evening, and their first few pints were soon followed by the hard stuff. Fuelled by the endless flow of whiskey, Jamie staggered to his feet and began to sing at the top of his voice. *Sure I'm an Ulster Orangeman, from Erin's isle I came, to see my British brethren all of honour and of fame, and to tell them of my forefathers who fought in days of yore, that I might have the right to wear, the sash my father wore!*

Others in the hall began to join in.

...It's old but it is
beautiful, and its colours they
are fine,
it was worn at Derry,
Aughrim, Enniskillen and the
Boyne.
My father wore it as a youth
in bygone days of yore,
and on the Twelfth I love
to wear the sash my father
wore...

'We are the People!' he shouted, before slumping back into his chair.

Full drunk, it did not take much for Robert to persuade Jamie to see in the New Year at Mae Burns' flat. They bought a carry out from the off-sales and followed the exodus from the lodge to the tenement flat.

Liz sat up until midnight before she gave up waiting for them. So much for bringing in the New Year in Glasgow, she thought as she listened to the drunken singing coming from one of the flats opposite.

The following day, Jamie and Robert did not get out of their beds until well after midday. Liz was happy to leave them there. When he woke up, Jamie could not remember getting back to the flat. His head was thumping. He sat up and tried to think for a minute, the taste of whiskey still in his mouth. His temporary amnesia soon subsided when he suddenly recalled waking up in a strange flat in the early hours of the morning. He lay down again and pulled the bedclothes over his head.

With nothing much to do, New Year's Day passed slowly. Liz and William watched TV for most of the day, while the two men lay around nursing their hangovers. In the evening Robert took a bottle of whiskey from his suitcases and poured Jamie and himself, what he called *the cure*.

Liz shook her head as she listened to the brothers toasting Rangers, while bad-mouthing Celtic and their supporters.

The next morning, Liz was up early. She put a fire on to warm the flat. The foggy morning spread a thin smear of ice on the windows and Robert's car was covered in a coat of crystal white frost. She pulled the curtains closed and sighed.

It was almost nine o'clock before William got up. 'It's freezing,' he moaned, shivering and chittering in front of the fire.

'There's no point standing there in your pyjamas. Get dressed and see if you can get your father and uncle up, while I get the breakfast on.'

Jamie could smell the bacon cooking and gradually woke from his scattered dreams. He tried to get up, but was too weak to get his body to respond. 'I'll need to lay-off that bloody whiskey,' he moaned. 'We better get up, Robert.'

'In a minute,' his brother yawned.

'Look, Dad,' said William, dressed in his Rangers top. 'I've got me top on.'

'Aye, okay son. Give me and your uncle a wee minute to get up. Tell yer mum to put me clothes out.'

That afternoon, Robert drove through the busy Glasgow streets to drop Liz off in the city centre so she could spend some time shopping. He promised to pick her up around 5.30pm at the corner of Stockwell Street and Argyle Street. He then drove slowly along Paisley Road West towards Ibrox Park. The traffic slowed to a walking pace as tens of thousands of Rangers supporters thronged the pavements and spilled onto the road itself. Enjoying the singing and the banter, Robert drove the car with one hand, while he waved his blue and white scarf from the window and cheered on a group of supporters who were singing: *Follow, follow, we will follow Rangers, everywhere, anywhere, we will follow on, Dundee, Hamilton, fuck the Pope and The Vatican...*

William had never seen so many people wearing red, white and blue scarves and was beside himself with excitement. Cars tooted their horns in rhythm with the chants of Rangers! Rangers! Rangers!

'Where are the Celtic fans?' asked William.

'They're still on their knees praying for a result,' said Robert. 'We're going tae hammer them today,' he added emphatically. 'We Are The People!'

They found a parking place near to the Ibrox underground station and walked to the Rangers side of the ground on the Copland Road end of the stadium. William was freezing as he followed his father and uncle, who were pushing their way aggressively through the crowds of men all rushing to get into the ground before the kick-off. Jamie handed over the tickets for himself and Robert. He then lifted William over the turnstile just as the teams were coming on to the park. William was overwhelmed with the noise from the 80,000 supporters, who all seemed to be shouting and singing at once.

They had a great view of the park as the whistle blew to start the game. The massive crowd fascinated William as much as the teams on the park. He began to recognise some of the players, and pointed out the Rangers captain, John Greig, to his father, as Celtic's Jimmy Johnstone put the ball through his legs. The first half was more of a game of attrition than a football match, and William was beginning to lose interest when the referee blew the half-time whistle. The floodlights came on when the last of the daylight began to fade. William listened as his father and uncle discussed the tactics used in the first half, blaming this player and that player for not playing for the jersey. Robert decided to see if he could get some hot food before the second half kicked off. The novelty of having a hot pie and Bovril took William's mind off the cold for a while.

Liz had been in most of the shops along Argyle Street and decided to go into one of the department stores for some lunch and take the weight of her aching feet. She was loaded down with too many bags and needed to rest for a while before heading back along to Stockwell Street. She had bought more than she intended and was worrying that there might not be enough room in the car for all the shopping bags. The streets and shops were still garlanded in Christmas decorations and she stood for a while to look at the massive Christmas tree outside one of the department stores, before going to order a pot of tea and some scones.

As the Christmas songs played their trivial jingles in the background, she began to think of Danny and wondered if she would ever see him again. Her mind was still haunted by the thought that her own flesh and blood was being brought up by a family who had no idea that he was not their son. Although she often found herself standing for hours on the opposite corner of Mill Street, she only managed to see him a half dozen times, speaking to him only twice. On the second occasion she felt a strong urge to reach out and take him in her arms. Instead she patted him on the head as he took the few shillings she placed in his small, dirty hand.

'Who are ye missus, and what's that for?'

'I'm ... It doesn't matter. Don't be telling anyone who you got that from.'

'That would be hard, missus; I don't even know who ye are?'

With the escalation of violence Liz had found it increasingly difficult to continue her compulsive visits to Mill Street. On her last visit, she stood at the opposite corner for over an hour, but there was no sign of Danny. She was about to go home when two women crossed the road towards her.

'What ye doing? Yer not for around here,' said the older of the two.

'I was waiting for a friend,' said Liz, turning to walk away.

'What friend?' asked the other woman, grabbing Liz by the arm.

'It's none of your business who I am waiting for, let me go!' Liz shouted as she tried to pull her arm away. The woman tightened her hold.

'You're not waiting for any friend; you've been seen hanging around here before. Who the fuck are ye? Are ye here spying for the Brits?'

'Please let my arm go, I was doing nothing wrong.'

'Get to hell out of here and don't be coming back,' said the older woman, nodding to her friend, who released her grip on Liz's arm.

The memory of that day made her feel uneasy. She stirred her tea again and tried to think of something else.

With William moaning about the cold for the last fifteen minutes, the brothers agreed to leave ten minutes early. Jamie was happy to be going anyway, there had been no goals scored and the game had not been much to look at. They struggled through the heaving mass of supporters, stopping for a moment at the top of the stairs for a last look as Rangers surged forward and came close with a shot just wide of the Celtic goal. They walked briskly back to the car; glad to have beaten the rush.

While in the car they heard a massive roar as they stopped at a set of traffic lights at Paisley Road West. Robert began fumbling with the car radio and eventually found a station: Jimmy Johnstone had scored a late goal for Celtic. Robert turned the radio back off in disgust as he banged on the dashboard in anger. Jamie did not say anything. William was just glad to be going home.

After picking up Liz, they headed back to Stranraer to catch the 8.30pm boat back to Belfast. They were worn out and said very little during the long journey to the ferry port. A heavy fog had fallen over the west coast of Scotland, and Robert had to strain his eyes to keep the car on the road as the rest fell asleep.

When they reached the harbour, Robert switched on the radio to get the news headlines. He pulled the car over when he realised the report was referring to an incident at Ibrox Park. He nudged Jamie awake.

'...It's not certain how many supporters have been killed today in this awful tragedy. Police and ambulance crews have been overwhelmed by the number of casualties. It's believed that most of the victims were crushed to death when barriers collapsed on the stairs as Rangers supporters tried to leave the ground after losing a goal in the 89th minute to Celtic...'

'Fuck,' said Jamie, turning to look into the back of the car where both Liz and William were sleeping. He turned off the radio.

Rangers had not lost the game; Colin Stein had scored an equalising goal in the dying seconds of the game. A goal that triggered a disaster, in which sixty-six Rangers fans were crushed to death and hundreds of others injured. Jamie found it hard to think this happened at the boring game he had watched. William was now famous with the local boys; he had been at the Ibrox disaster and survived to tell the tale. The only problem for William is that he had to read the papers like everyone else to find out what had actually happened. He hadn't even seen any of the goals.

Chapter 14

Man Down

Ramsey watched patiently as Chichester-Clark's face turned ashen grey, while nodding in agreement to whoever was on the other end of the line. 'Bad news?' he asked, as the PM turned to look out of the window.

'That was the Chief Constable; a British soldier has been shot dead in the Ardoyne during a gun battle with the IRA.'

'It was bound to happen sooner or later, Prime Minister.'

'I don't think Edward Heath will see it that way. I better call him before he hears it on the morning news. I'd rather do this on my own, if you don't mind.'

'Of course, Prime Minister, I'll be in my office if you need me.' After a cursory glance at his pocket watch, Ramsey gathered his papers and quietly left the room, leaving the PM deep in thought.

Under pressure to respond to the soldier's killing, and against Ramsey's advice, that evening on national television Chichester-Clark declared war on the IRA.

The shootings only increased, and after the killing of three off-duty soldiers from the Highland Fusiliers, Ramsey could see that Chichester-Clark had had enough. He did not try to dissuade him from resigning.

Ramsey now found himself at the disposal of the province's new Unionist leader, Brian Faulkner; a man he had grown to dislike intensely due to his disloyalty to his two predecessors. Ramsey only offered his advice when he was called on to do so, which under the new regime was not very often. Over the next few months, as the killings continued unabated, he found himself excluded from important government meetings and now spent much of his time writing his own memoirs.

Faulkner had no sooner taken residence in the Prime Minister's office at Stormont, when the IRA began an intensive bombing campaign intended to cripple the centre of Belfast and cause economic devastation to the North. Most of the bombs were hurled into shop fronts in the dead of night to avoid civilian casualties. However, the security forces were not given the same courtesy, and the IRA now deemed all members of the British army and RUC as legitimate targets. The slogans Brits Out and Up the Provos began to appear on the walls in nationalist areas.

*

Sedated with valium, Marie Duffy sat nervously watching the latest new reports on the increasing street violence. She blessed herself while listening to a report that another civilian had been shot dead by the army. Although she wanted Joe home, in a strange sense she was glad he was safely locked up in prison. If she could move to the Republic, she would have done, but she could not bring herself to leave her daughter's grave for any length of time.

With the future also bleak for her children, Brendan became more and more withdrawn and seemed to be in a constant state of melancholy, while the twins were as anxious and nervous as each other. They had all lost touch with their Protestant friends and despaired at the constant sectarian violence that was now part of everyday life.

Now nine years old, Danny reacted differently, and revelled in the fact that his uncle Eugene was now well known in the streets as one of the leaders of the Provos. 'There're two Brits going up the road!' he shouted one day, taking aim with his imaginary gun and shooting both soldiers in his mind's eye.

'Get away from that window!' snapped Marie, worried that the soldiers might be drawn to the house again.

'He thinks he's a sniper for the IRA,' teased Kathleen, as she combed her sister's hair.

'Shut up,' moaned Danny, letting the curtain fall back into place.

'God, Kathleen! That hurt,' Roisin yelled. 'I didn't hurt you when I was combing your hair.'

'That's because my hair was not in knots like yours.'

'I'm bored,' groaned Danny, 'Mammy, can I go out for a while?'

'No! You'll stay in the house, until those soldiers are back in their barracks. They'll shoot you if you go anywhere near those streets! And don't go into the kitchen disturbing your brother either. You'll put him off his studies!' she scolded as Danny got up to go through to the kitchen anyway. 'That's all he ever does. I'm just going to get a glass of water.'

Surrounded by his school books, Brendan had always been the quiet, more studious member of the family, but it was still a shock to Marie when he told her that he wanted to become a priest. With straight 'A's in every subject, Marie was proud and disappointed at the same time, she hoped he would go to university and study medicine or law after one of his teachers had told her. 'Your son has the brains to become anything he wants, Mrs Duffy.'

After a number of visits from Father Cunningham, Marie eventually accepted Brendan's decision to enrol with the Catholic seminary in County Meath. She had decided to keep it from Joe as long as possible, now that he had completely turned his back on God and was talking like a Communist. She was not sure how he would react to his eldest son training to become a priest.

Brendan looked up from his books with a sigh when Danny sat beside him at the kitchen table. 'Don't be asking me a hundred and one questions.'

'What ye doing?'

'What do ye think I'm doing? I'm reading.'

'I know yer reading, but what are ye reading?'

'It's called *The Merchant of Venice.*'

'What's that?'

'It's a play by William Shakespeare.'

'But what's it about?'

'Danny, I've got to study this. I don't have time to tell you.'

'Aw, Brendan, I'm bored sitting in there with them. I want to go out, but Mammy won't let me. Tell me what it's about and I'll promise not to annoy ye.'

'All right,' said Brendan reluctantly, beginning his simplified version of Shylock's bizarre bargain over a pound of the merchant's flesh.

With an insatiable appetite to ask questions and ignore the answers, Danny managed to make Brendan's short synopsis last over half an hour, before he reluctantly went back into the front room to sit in utter boredom with his mother and two sisters. He still could not understand why anyone would want a pound of another person's flesh.

'Danny, stop scratching your head,' said Marie, who was starting to feel itchy herself. 'Kathleen, will ye get the fine comb for me, it's under the sink.'

Still scratching, Danny reluctantly knelt in front of Marie, who placed a newspaper on her lap and began to tug the metal comb through his thick hair.

'I thought so,' she said, as she crushed the first louse under her nail. 'Bloody nits again! Roisin, get the bottle of Lisol before we're all lousy.'

'Danny's got nits!' Roisin teased as she went into the kitchen.

'Shut up, you had them last time … So did Kathleen … Didn't they, Mammy?'

'What does it matter who had them?' Marie sighed, crushing another louse onto the paper. 'Here, give me that,' she said to Roisin and began to pour the nit poison on Danny's head. 'Stay bloody still or you'll have it all over the place.'

'But it's stinging me eyes and it stinks.'

'There, go over and sit at the window while I do your sisters' hair.'

'Och, Mammy I've not got them,' complained Roisin.

'If he's got them we'll all have them. Now hurry up before I run out of patience.'

'Roisin's got nits,' laughed Danny, still scratching his own head.

As the nit hunt continued, Danny took up his usual chair at the window to keep an eye on anything that may be happening outside. He watched Mrs Donnelly, who was standing outside her front door with her arms crossed, shouting abuse at a young soldier, who was nervously kneeling at a lamppost waiting for a signal to follow his patrol, which was edging its way up the street. She then disappeared back into her house, only to reappear with a chamber pot. Danny watched open mouthed as she threw the contents of the pot at the soldier, which splashed down the back of his legs.

'Mammy, Mrs Donnelly has just thrown a pot of piss at a soldier,' laughed Danny.

'What the hell are ye taking about?'

'She has,' confirmed Kathleen.

They all watched as the soldier confronted Mrs Donnelly, who continued to shout abuse at him. Another woman joined in with the tirade. The soldier decided he was on a hiding to nothing and turned to rejoin his unit, who had already disappeared around the corner at the top of the street. At that moment he slipped on the road and fell heavily back towards the pavement, banging his head off the kerb. His helmet had saved him from serious injury as he lay slightly dazed on the ground.

As the soldier tried to get to his feet, Mairead Coogan, a sixteen year old who lived in the next house to Mrs Donnelly, ran up to the frightened looking soldier and picked up the rifle he had dropped. As the verbal abuse continued, other doors in the street opened and more women appeared and surrounded the terrified soldier.

'My God, he's only a few years older than our Brendan,' gasped Marie as one of the women pulled the soldier's helmet from his sweat soaked head of blond hair.

'Mammy, what are they going to do to him?' asked Roisin, nervously pulling at her hair.

'They're going to take him prisoner,' said Danny emphatically.

'Come away from the window,' demanded Marie as she pulled Danny by the scruff of the neck. 'Get into the kitchen the three of you!' she ordered.

'Och, Mammy,' moaned Danny.

'Don't make me lose me temper, do as yer told.'

Feeling sorry for the soldier, Marie watched as more of her neighbours from further up the road appeared on the street. A middle-aged woman began punching and kicking the cowering soldier, while two others ripped the top of his uniform open. He began pleading to be let go and started crying when he was hit on the head with the butt of his own rifle. There was little sympathy shown by most of the women, but a few tried their best to stop the abuse going too far.

'What's the matter, Mammy?' Brendan asked, joining her at the window.

'Oh, son, look what they're doing to that young boy. I hope the army come back soon or they'll end up killing him.'

'I'm going to go out and try and stop it!'

'God, no! Stay in the house or they'll turn on you!' she pleaded, grabbing his arm. 'Your duty is to your own brother and sisters. Stay here with me.'

'Okay, okay Mammy, but let go of my arm.'

'You promise you won't go out there!'

'You're hurting me! I promise.'

'Good,' she sighed, releasing her grip on his forearm. They continued to watch in silence as some of the women began exorcising much of the hatred that had built up over the months towards anyone wearing a British uniform. The soldier's pleas were being ignored as he was hit with sticks and stones, and another pot of fresh urine was poured over what remained of his blood-stained uniform. Then as quickly as it began, the women melted back in to the shadows, satisfied for the moment, that this symbol of British brutality had tasted some of its own medicine.

Marie suddenly screamed when she saw Brendan crossing the road towards the badly beaten soldier. She ran out after him. Her initial intention was to pull him back into the house, but her mind changed when she looked down at the battered face of the young soldier. Brendan was already wiping away the blood and mucus with a tissue. 'You're going to be all right,' said Brendan as he gently cleaned the soldier's face, 'What's yer name?'

'Alan … Wilson.'

'The army will be back for you soon. You'll be all right.'

Marie watched her son comfort the soldier, partly in awe and partly in anger at the danger he put them in. She looked around nervously and saw Mrs Donnelly staring at them from her bedroom window.

Not long after getting back to the barracks the corporal in charge of the unit realised he was a soldier down. The soldiers all looked at each other; no one had noticed Private Wilson's absence until then.

'How the hell did this happen?' The battalion captain demanded.

'Don't know, sir. We didn't have any trouble. He must have simply got lost.'

'You and yer boys will need to go back in and get him…'

'Captain!' Interrupted another soldier, 'We've just got a radio message from the helicopter that we have a man down.'

'Do we have a position?'

'It's Mill Street, just off the Falls Road.'

'Right let's get back in there … Corporal, make sure we have a medic with us.'

Private Mitchell grabbed his gear and climbed back into the personnel carrier. There was the deafening sound of metal crunching against metal while orders were being shouted frantically as more information was being relayed back to the barracks. Live ammunition was distributed, and terms of engagement were being barked at the soldiers. The diesel engines roared into life and the steel gates slowly opened as the convoy of four armoured vehicles ventured out into the hostile streets.

Danny was back at the front window watching Brendan defying his mother's pleas to get into the house. There was a sudden screech of car wheels coming furiously around the corner. A green Volvo pulled up and the man Danny had seen running into Mrs Donnelly's house with his uncle Eugene got out of the car and stood looking down at the soldier for a few seconds. The man then motioned to Brendan to move away, before pulling out a handgun from inside his black leather jacket and bending over the frightened soldier. 'You should've stayed in your own fuckin' country, son.' Brendan recoiled in horror, as two shots rang out in quick succession, taking the top of the soldiers head off. The killer then turned and jumped back into the passenger side of the waiting car.

With all her strength, Marie grabbed Brendan by the arm and pulled him onto his feet, his bewildered face now covered in blood. The car drove off at speed as a helicopter circled overhead like an angry wasp.

Marie helped Brendan back towards the house; he was in a state of utter shock as his mother tried to wipe the blood and specks of the soldier's brains from his frozen white face. As they stopped to open the front door, there was a sudden clatter of dustbin lids from further down the street. *The Brits are coming!*

The first army vehicles came roaring around the corner. Marie stood in the hallway with her back against the front door; still tightly holding her bewildered son. They could hear the screeching of tyres and the abrupt opening and banging of metal doors. Then the shouts and screams quickly followed.

Still in shock, Marie went into the kitchen, gathering her children around her, and waited in sheer terror for the front door to be smashed open. One of the terrified twins wet herself, but the family stayed huddled together as the urine formed a puddle on the worn linoleum. Marie began saying the rosary, with the children all mouthing the words with her.

Outside the soldiers took up positions, all the while fearing a sniper's bullet. In the distance, the sound of an ambulance siren neared. 'Oh for fuck's sake,' cursed one soldier, taking another look at his fallen comrade. 'They're fucking animals!'

'We shouldn't have left him at the rear. This was his first time on patrol,' said Mitchell, as the ambulance turned into the street. 'Why was he put at the fucking back?'

'You got a problem, Private?'

'No, Corporal!'

'Then help them get the stretcher into the ambulance, before we come under sniper fire. This is one of their tricks,' barked the corporal, before turning to yell at two other soldiers. 'You two keep that corner covered!'

On the way back to the barracks the soldiers were in a subdued mood. They could not understand why they were not ordered to ransack the whole area and at least get some revenge for the killing. They were not to know that internment without trial was to be reintroduced to crush the Provos. Plans were already being drawn up at headquarters for a full-scale raid in which every house in the immediate vicinity of the shooting would be searched and anyone with even a hint of IRA allegiance was to be arrested.

Chapter 15

Uncle Eugene's Visit

Jamie Morrison had already turned down a request to join the part-time Ulster Defence Regiment, which had replaced the B-Specials, feeling at the time they lacked the ruthless determination needed to take on the Provisional IRA. A few weeks later, he did not hesitate when asked to head the intelligence wing of the Shankill UVF. His manager at the yard initially refused to give Jamie any time off during working hours to fulfil his UVF duties, flatly telling him that he should do it on his own time and not the company's. The office manager's reasonable stance resulted in two men in balaclavas paying a late night visit to his home in North Belfast. The following day Jamie was told to take whatever time off he needed. Over the next few months Jamie spent less and less of his working day in the yard. His first task was to track down the gunmen responsible for the execution of the rookie soldier. He was given the authority to order the assassination of anyone involved, but his intelligence network was still in its infancy and he had no idea of the identities of the men he was looking for.

For the time being, much of his work was a combination of administration and frustration as the IRA continued their bombing campaign against the security forces and the commercial heart of Belfast. With the surge in bombings, demands grew within the UVF ranks for some form of retaliation, and the procurement of weapons became a priority for Jamie. He arranged for guns to be smuggled in from Scotland and further afield, but it would take time to build up an arsenal to take on the Provisionals, who, with the help of American money, had become better armed than the loyalist paramilitaries.

In a relatively short time, Jamie built up a web of connections within the security forces. Although the UDR was part of the British army, it recruited almost exclusively from the Ulster Protestants; many of whom were former B-Specials or members of one of the main paramilitary organisations. This gave Jamie access to a great deal of information about the Provos from his many contacts within the regiment and the local RUC. He soon gathered substantial intelligence of the known IRA leadership in Belfast, but his problem was tracking these men down as most of them had retreated into the Irish Republic as soon as internment was introduced.

Jamie operated out of a building off the Shankill Road, which was once a furniture showroom. He used an office at the back, guarded by two UVF men armed with Browning 9mm semi-automatic pistols, dressed in full combat gear and balaclavas. There was a Union Flag hanging behind his desk to enhance his own feelings of self-importance. He had six men directly under his command and they, in turn, had other foot soldiers to help with the constant need to gather intelligence. Billy 'Bulldog' Brown was his right-hand man and conveyed Jamie's orders to the other men. Bulldog was an ex-boxer, and was once a contender for the British heavyweight crown until he broke his hand in a pub brawl only a few weeks before he was due to fight for the title. That was ten years earlier and since then he had been working in the docks as a welder. Even with his labouring work in the shipyards, Bulldog was now out of shape. The muscle had turned to fat over the years, but he remained just as intimidating, with his shaved head and thick arms covered in loyalist tattoos. His broken nose and cauliflower ears showed anyone who looked at him just how much punishment he was able to take, and very few had ever tried to test his boxing skills outside the ring.

The two men would often drink together in the Claymore,

an illegal drinking den in the Shankill run by the UVF. The drink was cheap and the surroundings sparse, but the heavy iron door and wire meshed windows gave some security from the constant threat of IRA bombs. Not everyone who drank in the club was in the UVF, and many of the local civilian Protestants drank there for the same sense of security.

One Saturday afternoon, while Bulldog was at the bar, Jamie began banging his fists on the table as he thought about the two Protestants killed that morning in a bomb attack in the heart of the Shankill. He recalled driving back from a meeting with his RUC contact, when he heard the thunderous explosion in the distance. To Jamie, it seemed as if the IRA were able to strike anywhere and at anytime with impunity. The security forces were clearly unable to stop them. At the last Army Council meeting, he argued for some form of retaliation to take place and was assured that plans were afoot to take the war to both the IRA and the wider nationalist population. That was nearly a month ago and the IRA bombing campaign had continued unabated with little or no response from the loyalist paramilitaries. The only loyalists on the offensive were the Tartan gangs who roamed the streets at night looking for Catholics to beat up. At least they were doing something, thought Jamie, as Bulldog returned with the drinks.

At home, Liz was making dinner, while William was finishing his maths homework on the kitchen table. The news of the bombing had frightened her and she was glad when Jamie phoned that morning to say that he was safe. The news reports referred to the killings as sectarian and it seemed to Liz that there was no reason for the IRA to target the bar other than to kill innocent Protestants, who had simply been in the wrong place at the wrong time. While she washed the potatoes, she continued to listen to the latest radio bulletin, and only stopped what she was doing for a moment, when a local Unionist politician was being interviewed, venting his anger at the IRA for what he called, *this outrageous atrocity against innocent Protestant citizens*, while at the same time urging the security forces to come down hard on those in the nationalist community who gave succour to them. The reporter then pointed out to the politician that the IRA had not claimed responsibility for the bombing. 'Who else would commit a cowardly act of this kind of carnage against innocent Protestant people if it wasn't the Provisional IRA?'

'Mum, when will Dad be home?' William asked, unable to concentrate on his homework with the radio blaring in the background.

'He'll be home in a wee while. Take those books upstairs and help me set the table, there's a good boy.'

'Iain Campbell is coming round at half past. We're going to the hall tonight to play football...'

'No, not tonight, there's too much trouble in the streets and there'll be rioting after what happened today.'

'But Mum, it's only up the road...'

'No! Not tonight. I'd be surprised if Iain's mum lets him over the doorstep.'

'Can Dad no' take us?'

'Your father has been working all day.'

'Dad never watches me play football anymore. He doesn't even go to the school games,' sulked William, gathering up his school books.

'Your father has to work all week to put food on the table. He's too busy!'

'But Mum,' moaned William.

'There's your father now,' said Liz as the front door opened.

Jamie hung his coat behind the door. William went to meet him. 'Dad, will ye take me to the club tonight? We're playing football and...'

'Of course I will, son, once I've had me dinner.'

'I don't want him going out!' shouted Liz from the kitchen. 'There'll be too much trouble tonight after what happened today.'

'He'll be fine, I'll take him down.'

'I don't want either of you going out. It's too dangerous with all these bombings and shootings.'

'There're boys his age manning barricades down the street. He'll be fine. What's for dinner?'

'I've made some beef stew. It will be ready in a couple of minutes. How was work today?'

'Ah the usual,' replied Jamie, who had not told Liz about his role in the UVF, leaving her to believe that he was now having to work extra shifts at the docks. The less she knew the better, he had decided. She was a worrier.

'What did ye make of the bombing, isn't it dreadful, two men killed and all those injured?'

'IRA cowards! They'll get what's coming to them. Wait and see.'

'I wish it would all stop. You can't walk down the street now without men in balaclavas and guns stopping you to look through your shopping bags.'

'You tell them whose wife you are and they'll not stop ye again ... That looks lovely,' he said as Liz placed the dinner on the table.

'William, hurry up!' she called.

William came downstairs with the ball in hand and his Glasgow Rangers football strip on. 'Look!' said Jamie. 'It's wee Willie Henderson on the wing.'

Liz looked at the two of them and shook her head.

*

Joe Duffy had lost all his remission when prison officers found papers in his cell that proved he had been recruiting other prisoners to the IRA. He served his full two year sentence and was finally released only to be immediately rearrested and interned. He was expecting this to happen, and had warned Marie not to build up her hopes that he would be home any time soon. The children had grown used to their father being in prison, and with internment in place, they were not the only ones without a breadwinner in the house.

Joe was transferred to Long Kesh Prison, where hundreds of men were now interned. The prison was located on an abandoned RAF airfield some ten miles south-west of Belfast. The perimeter was surrounded by barbed wire fences and lookout towers, enclosing dozens of Nissan huts. It looked like a Second World War POW camp. The men were allowed to wear their own clothes and to assemble and organise themselves as they saw fit. The authorities turned a blind eye to the morning drills and general military nature of the prisoners' daily lives. The Provisional IRA now had its own recruitment and training camp supplied with food and board by the British government and with the constant arrival of new internees every day, the Provos' ranks grew. Joe refused to join and continued to try and recruit young men into the ranks of the Officials. He found very few interested.

In response to his father's continued imprisonment, Brendan became active in the local Civil Rights movement that was now calling for an end to the Stormont government's excessive use of detention without trial. Danny would rather throw stones at the British soldiers. At least *he* could see the point of that.

Marie hated the long bus journey to Long Kesh, but

this time Kathleen was there to keep her company. After the recent bombings, the police and the army were out in force, and both Marie and Kathleen had their bags searched twice before they were safely on the bus and heading out of Belfast. The bus journey took them away from the oppressive atmosphere of the city and into the Irish countryside, with its rolling green fields and farmhouses scattered along the hillsides. As they passed farmhouse after farmhouse, Kathleen could not help wondering, if they were owned by Protestants or Catholics, recalling what her mother had said, *if it's a big two storey house then it's Protestant and if it's not then it's likely to be Catholic.* She wondered if the sheep and cows knew they were Catholic or Protestant.

After undergoing the rather relaxed security procedure at Long Kesh, Marie and Kathleen were taken through to the main visiting hall where Joe was waiting for them. Marie felt anxious as she sat down, having made up her mind to tell him about Brendan's decision to enter the seminary. She waited until visiting time was almost over before dropping her bombshell into the conversation.

'A priest?' responded Joe, holding his head in his hands for a moment. 'A priest!' He repeated, lowering his voice to a low angry whisper. 'Have you put him up to this? With all your praying to this saint and that bloody saint. Bring him up with you the next time, and I'll knock some sense into his head.'

'I won't bring him up unless you speak to him civilly.'

'I'll tell you about the Catholic Church, will I? It's a self-serving bunch of hypocrites who want to steal your kids and then turn them into servants of a God that doesn't exist!'

'Joe! Not in front of Kathleen.'

'She's my daughter; you're not going to tell me she's taking holy vows?'

'No, Daddy,' Kathleen laughed. 'I'm going to become a teacher.'

'At least you'll be useful to the living ... So what do you think about all this?'

'If that's what he wants to do then let him ... He doesn't seem to like girls anyway,' added Kathleen, turning to her mother, who gave her a stern look of disbelief.

'Oh, God, you're not going to tell me he's a bloody poofter!'

'Damn you, Joe Duffy! Let's go, Kathleen, say goodbye to your father. I'll wait for you at the door.' With that Marie got up without another word. Her mind was made up; Brendan would go to the seminary next week as planned. Joe would have to get used to the idea that there would be two fathers in the Duffy family.

While their mother and sister were at Long Kesh, Brendan and Danny walked home from St Patrick's after another funeral service resulted in nothing but a thank-you from the grieving widow. Since becoming an altar boy, Danny had not received any tips, and was losing faith in the whole religion thing as a source of income.

While he was considering his future, Brendan suddenly froze when he saw a squad of British soldiers searching three men they had pinned against a wall. 'It's only the Brits trying it on,' said Danny as he walked past his brother with his hands in his pockets, whistling "A Soldier's Song". Brendan shook his head and reluctantly followed Danny, who had stopped to lecture the sergeant in charge of the operation. 'You Brits shouldn't be here; this is not your country!'

'Who the fuck're you?' laughed the sergeant. The other soldiers turned to look at the source of his humour and joined in with the laughter. Even the men getting searched saw the funny side, as Danny stood defiantly staring at the sergeant with his hands on his hips. 'It doesn't matter who I am,' said Danny as Brendan tried to pull him away, 'You shouldn't be searching people...'

'If that cheeky wee runt's your brother, you better get

him out of here before he gets a size nine up his arse,' said the sergeant, nodding towards Brendan to get going. Danny did not get a chance to say another word as a bullet suddenly exploded above his head, ricocheting off the wall. Everyone ducked for cover. The soldiers hid behind their jeep, too frightened to return fire as the three men they were searching made off down the street. Brendan grabbed Danny by the arm and ran across the road as another shot pierced the side of the jeep.

By the time they arrived home, the brothers were out of breath and still in a state of shock. They were surprised to find their Uncle Eugene sitting in the kitchen, drinking tea and chatting away to Roisin, who was glad to leave when her brothers arrived. Eugene rarely came to the house, but when he did there was always an air of intrigue about him. 'Yer back from mass, are ye? You should go to ten o'clock mass like meself. That way the day's not wasted,' said Eugene.

'We were there for a funeral,' said Brendan, not sure if he should tell his uncle what had happened a few minutes earlier.

'I forgot you two were altar boys. I used to be one myself.'

'Uncle Eugene, someone shot at the Brits up the road,' said Danny, drawing a look from his brother.

'Well, if they stayed in their own country then nobody would be shooting at them.'

'Are you waiting for Mammy?' asked Brendan.

'Danny, why don't you go out and play with your friends, I want to talk to your brother for awhile.'

Danny stared at Brendan for a moment before reluctantly going out to the backyard. He left the door ajar to hear what his uncle wanted to talk about, but Eugene got up and closed it. Danny sat on the step in a sulk.

Brendan poured himself a mug of tea and topped up Eugene's cup. He sat opposite his uncle who began to talk about the recent bombings. Brendan was beginning to feel uneasy as Eugene questioned him about his views on the Troubles. Brendan agreed that he wanted to see Ireland united as one country with Catholics and Protestants living in peace with one another as equal citizens. However, he made it clear that he did not believe that shooting and bombings were the way to achieve this. Brendan was almost too eloquent and knowledgeable for his uncle when he explained his own views in intelligent detail. Eugene was having none of it; he stood up and doused the fire with the dregs of tea in his cup. 'You're just like yer father, all talk and no bloody action!'

'My father's in prison, you're not!'

'Aye, but he's refused to join the Provos. And now you're talking like some middle class Protestant.'

Before Brendan could retaliate and ask his uncle exactly why he was there, his mother and Kathleen arrived home. 'Hello, Eugene, yer a bloody stranger in this house,' said Marie as she came into the kitchen with a bag of groceries.

'How was Joe?' asked Eugene, still trying to size up Brendan.

'He's been better … How are things in the Ardoyne? Are Susan and the kids all right? Nothing's happened?'

'No, everybody's fine.'

'We never see ye these days. I'll go up and get changed. You'll stay and have a cup of tea.'

'He's already had one,' said Brendan curtly.

'No, Sis, I'll have tae be getting back.'

'Nonsense, I'll be down in a few minutes. Kathleen put on the kettle, there's a good girl,' called out Marie as she went upstairs to get changed. 'There're some biscuits in the shopping bag.'

Eugene sat down again as Kathleen put the kettle on the gas stove, before taking out a packet of biscuits from her mother's bag. 'Do you take milk and sugar, Uncle Eugene?'

'Kathleen, I'll get that ... Can you give me five minutes to speak with your brother? I'll keep an eye on the kettle.'

'All right, I need to get changed anyway. Brendan can you make the tea?'

Brendan did not answer and Eugene waited until Kathleen left before speaking again. 'Sorry, son,' he said eventually. 'I came here to ask you to consider joining the *Fianna Eireann*. I'm looking for someone I can trust to carry messages from the Ardoyne to the Falls. I thought you'd be ideal and I mentioned you to some very important people. But with your views it doesn't sound like the *Fianna Eireann* would have you even if you wanted to join. But if ye kept these ideas to yerself I could still arrange...'

'I don't want to join. Some of them go around at night with nothing better to do than look for Protestants to beat up.'

'Well that's that then.'

'Eugene ... yer not leaving already,' said Marie, now dressed in her everyday clothes.

'Yes, I need to go,' said Eugene putting on his jacket. 'There's a car outside waiting for me...'

'Has Brendan told ye the news?'

'No, what news?'

'He's been accepted into the seminary at Maynooth in County Meath, he's going to be a priest. Isn't that something? The first priest in the family...'

'Well I'm not surprised,' said Eugene, turning to look at Brendan. 'I'm sure he'll make a fine priest. I'd better go.'

The car waiting for Eugene was idling at the kerbside. In the driver's seat Fergal Gallagher was listening to Johnny Cash signing "Folsom Prison". He turned down the tape player. ‘How did it go?’ Will he do it?’

‘Will he hell! We’ll have to get someone else to do it. He’s going to be a fucking priest!’ The noise of the engine drowned out the laughter inside the car, as it turned back up towards the IRA roadblock at the top of the street, where they were waved through without stopping.

Chapter 16

Bloody Sunday

By the end of 1971, with no let up to the bombings and increasing lawlessness in the province, Ramsey found himself called back to England to a high level security meeting with representatives of the Heath government, MI6, MI5 and Military Intelligence. His knowledge of the Irish problem was such that an RAF Puma helicopter was sent to bring him to the secret location. He took as much information as he could, sure that he would be questioned on how the Stormont government was mishandling the security situation, expecting that the ministers would be looking for some ideas from him on how to improve the ever-worsening crisis. Ramsey was determined to express his opinion that the recent introduction of internment was a mistake, and he had carefully prepared a report to justify his position.

The helicopter landed on a frost-covered back lawn of a large country estate some twenty miles from London. He could clearly see the city skyline in the distance as they came into land and he assumed that they must be somewhere in the Berkshire countryside. The RAF pilot declined to clarify their whereabouts with a mimed zip across his lips. Ramsey was greeted by a very stiff looking butler whose face looked as though it had been starched along with his shirt collar. 'Allow me, sir,' said the butler, taking Ramsey's suitcase. 'Follow me, Sir.'

Once out of the reach and noise of the rotor blades Ramsey straightened himself and walked across the lawn and in through the French doors at the back of the house. He closed the door behind him and followed the butler up three flights of a spiral staircase that was clearly not the main stairway in such a grand house. Ramsey surmised that it must be the staff quarters he was being billeted in. He was shown into a well furnished room with its own en-suite bathroom; a rather impressive room for what he thought was at one time servant quarters. 'This was once Mr Keats's room. He was the head of the household for over fifty years until he passed away a few years ago. It's been vacant ever since,' said the butler, placing Ramsey's suitcase on top of a huge engraved ottoman at the foot of the brass bedstead. 'Lunch will be served in the main board room at twelve-thirty. I'll send the boy along to fetch you about ten minutes beforehand. I'm sure you will wish some time to freshen up.'

On entering the conference room, Ramsey was met by Reginald Maudling, the Home Secretary, and a group of six other men, all heads of their respective departments within the British intelligence agencies. Formal introductions over, they sat down to a light lunch of consommé soup, followed by poached salmon. The general conversation at the table was on the United Kingdom's negotiations to enter the European Common Market. Ramsey found it strange that no one seemed to be in much of a hurry to discuss what they were really there for.

While coffee was being served, the Home Secretary got to his feet and shook hands with the head of MI6, before bidding the others in the room a good day. Then with a casual doff of his trilby he was gone. It was clear to Ramsey that this was not going to be a routine briefing and he waited patiently while the room filled up with cigarette and cigar smoke, which added to the clandestine nature of things. The housekeeper opened one of the bay-windows to let some air into the room. There was then a gentle tap on a coffee cup with a delicate Georgian silver spoon. All heads turned towards the smiling face of a middle aged man, immaculately dressed in a three piece pinstriped suit, white shirt and a narrow blue and red Oxford tie. 'Well, gentlemen, let's get down to business,' he said, nodding at the waiter to leave the room. 'The Minister has left us as you can see. This is not a discussion he wants to be party to, but instead, he has left it to me to report back any conclusions we reach today. Firstly, we are honoured to have Captain Ramsey here to give us an up-to-date picture from Northern Ireland, and to share his views on how internment has been working. In your own good time, Captain Ramsey, please begin.'

Ramsey was not prepared for such a sudden introduction to speak and his papers were still in his briefcase under the table. He decided it might look a bit too clumsy to start looking for them and began to speak as best he could from memory. 'Good morning to you all … It's my view that the situation in Northern Ireland has deteriorated since the introduction of internment and it will only get worse. It was clear from the reports coming into my office at Stormont that anyone with even a hint of an IRA connection, and many with none, has been rounded up in Gestapo-like raids on Catholic homes across the North. The British forces have become a brutal army of occupation to most nationalists.'

'Mr Ramsey,' interrupted the officer from Military Intelligence, 'I object to your use of the words Gestapo and brutal when you are referring to Her Majesty's Armed Forces.'

'I am only giving an opinion on what I see happening. If something is being carried out brutally, then those doing it must be referred as brutal. If it's an honest account you wish, then I may have to say some things that you do not like, or agree with, but they have to be said … I do however apologise for the use of the word Gestapo.'

'Carry on, Captain Ramsey. We will listen without further interruption,' said the MI6 officer, who was chairing the meeting.

'The whole process has simply played into the IRA's hands,' continued Ramsey with more confidence. 'The tactics of the army has turned moderate Catholic youths into hardened Republicans, and the IRA's numbers have increased dramatically over the last few months. The internment of so many nationalists in Long Kesh has allowed the hard line Provisional IRA men to persuade other internees to join their cause. That prison is now effectively the main centre of IRA recruiting and training activities in the whole of Ireland. The British government should recognise the folly of this policy being used by the Stormont regime. In my opinion, the riots and bombing will not only continue, but will dramatically increase.'

'What do you believe would be a better way of dealing with this situation?' asked the MI6 officer, before sipping what was left of his coffee.

'Bring internment to an end. It not only gives the IRA more potential recruits for the future, but it has failed to catch many of the more experienced men. The IRA leadership is living outside the North altogether. These men only cross back over the border to carry out bombing and shooting operations. Also, there would be less rallies and protests by civil rights marchers, which give an excuse for hard-line Unionists to attack them, keeping the cauldron of hatred and violence at boiling point.'

'But that doesn't provide us with any alternative tactic to deal with the IRA,' interrupted the officer from Military Intelligence. 'What about arming the loyalists to take on the IRA?'

'All you would be doing is pushing the situation nearer to civil war. There would also be more weapons on the streets, and I dread to think what kind of carnage would engulf the province. We tried the same thing in Kenya in the fifties and in Aden only a few years ago. It didn't work then, and I fail to see how it can work now.'

'Are there any more questions for Captain Ramsey?' the Chairman interrupted. 'Okay, that was very helpful and we appreciate your inside knowledge on these matters. There will be a helicopter waiting for you to take you back to Belfast, and once again, thank you for coming.'

Stopped in full flight, Ramsey was effectively censored from expressing the very opinions he thought he was invited to the meeting to convey. He had much more to say, but felt ostracised by an atmosphere of hostility and secrecy in the room. He lifted his briefcase from the floor and removed a black folder which contained his detailed report and left it on the table. 'Gentlemen, if you take the time to read this then I'm sure you will have a better understanding of the situation the security forces are facing in the North. I implore you not to make matters worse by arming the loyalist paramilitaries, their loyalty is not to the British government or even the Crown, but to their own perceived right to remain superior to their Catholic neighbours. I hope I have been of some assistance.'

Still a little hot under the collar, Ramsey was walked to the door by the grey-haired Chairman who seemed quite glad to see him go. After a curt shake of hands, the door closed with a heavy thud and he followed the butler back to Mr Keats's room to collect his overcoat and suitcase before heading out to the back lawn where the helicopter was sitting waiting for him. So much for a weekend in the countryside, he thought as he climbed aboard the Puma.

*

It was a cold morning, but Brendan was up early to travel to Derry. He had decided to join an anti-internment rally in the Bogside.

Marie apprehensively watched her eldest son board one of the three buses leaving from West Belfast. Most of those travelling to the march that day had husbands, brothers or sons in prison, and hoped that their peaceful protest would help bring internment to an end. Danny's demands to join his brother on the bus were quickly stifled with an angry slap across his face. Marie was in no mood for his nonsense. Having one son in harm's way was enough for her to bear.

While Brendan travelled through to Derry, Danny marked the day with his own protest against the British army and internment, by throwing a stone at a passing Saracen on the Falls Road. 'Dirty Brits, get out of Ireland!'

*

To his surprise, Ramsey was asked by Whitehall to monitor Stormont's planned operation to deal with the civil rights march, and their determination to bring the nationalist areas in Derry back under the control of the security forces. Before leaving, Ramsey read up on Derry and noted that the two main areas which made up the nationalist stronghold were the Bogside, a warren of dilapidated Victorian terraced houses beneath the ancient walls, and the Creggan, a bleak post-war concrete estate that overlooked the River Foyle. These two areas were essentially Catholic ghettos.

When Ramsey arrived at Ebrington Barracks, he was met by Major General Robert Ford and Brigadier Pat MacLellan. They were in overall charge of the planned operation. General Ford explained to Ramsey that the area now known as *Free Derry* was a nest of insurrection against the local army garrison. He pointed to a huge ordnance survey map on the wall, striking the top of his cane on the circled area of William Street and Rossville Street, known locally as *Aggro Corner.* He explained that this marked the start of *Free Derry* and was the place where the local soldiers regularly fought running battles with nationalist rioters. 'What are those?' asked Ramsey pointing to black marker lines on the map.

'Those, I'm told, are containment lines, but after today they will be removed and the Queen's writ will no longer stop at them. We are intent in bringing British law and order to the nationalists behind those lines whether they like it or not!'

The operations room was a hive of activity as Ramsey listened to the General explain their objectives. The marchers will not be allowed to reach their intended destination at the Guildhall in the city centre. The General emphasised his comment by using his cane to tap on another area on the map, circled by a red marker, with the words '1 PARA' clearly printed in the middle.

'I didn't know the parachute regiment was in Derry,' said Ramsey.

'They are now! Lieutenant Colonel Derek Wilford is in command, a good soldier, who knows how to lead his men. I will introduce you to him later today.'

Ramsey was then asked to wait in the corridor while the General and the Brigadier held an operational meeting in the officers' muster. Throughout the course of the morning, various ranks came and went, while the tension built with the increased activity. At one stage he noticed the obvious excited reaction of the other soldiers in the HQ as the commander of 1 PARA entered the building.

The tension in the building increased as the hours passed and Ramsey was suddenly beckoned to join the General and the Brigadier in the muster. He was introduced to Lieutenant Colonel Wilford, who then left the room with a casual nod of the head to his superiors.

'Fine soldier,' said the general. 'If we had more like him then we would soon have the Provos on the run. As I told you earlier, Ramsey, I am only here, like yourself, as an observer on behalf of the top brass back home. I have orders to accommodate you as a representative of Her Majesty's Government and Major Moorcroft will accompany you to our observation post on those ancient walls which have caused us so much bloody trouble over the years.'

After lunch, Ramsey followed the Major onto the city walls, which overlooked the Bogside. He was handed a pair of heavy duty army binoculars, and, following the Major's instructions focused in on what was obviously the start of the no-go area, clearly marked in thick white paint, *'Free Derry'*. He had seen many derelict streets in Belfast, but even they had not prepared him for the utter destruction he viewed through the powerfully magnified binoculars. The shops and public houses were gutted shells of dereliction, their windows and doors boarded up with ugly, battered, corrugated sheets. Every wall was smeared with Republican graffiti. Even the pavements had been ripped up during the last three years of rioting and used to create missiles to throw at the local troops, who, until now, had failed to venture beyond this ferociously defended frontier.

While Ramsey surveyed the layout of the area, he listened to the coded messages constantly coming in over the radio. Handing the binoculars back to Major Moorcroft, he took a casual look around the walls and ramparts, which were covered in sandbags. There were dozens of soldiers milling around in full combat gear, many carrying high velocity rifles over their shoulders. It was now almost two o'clock. He watched two Sioux military helicopters hover above *Free Derry Corner*, where the Royal Green Jackets had already erected a barricade to stop the march reaching its intended destination in the city centre.

The radio operator suddenly called out to one of his senior officers standing nearby. 'An important message from HQ, sir, one of the demo organisers has been in contact to say that the IRA has agreed to stay off the streets while the march is in progress.'

'Tell them we do not take the word of murderers. Find out if 1 PARA are in position yet.'

Using his binoculars, Ramsey noticed for the first time what looked like a biblical flood of demonstrators coming down William Street following a coal lorry draped with a huge 'Civil Rights' banner, while many of those that followed carried placards calling for the end of internment. Ramsey watched as the sea of people gradually made their way to Rossville Street where they split into distinct groups. The lorry and the main body of marchers diverted away from the army barricades at the bottom of William Street, while hundreds, of mainly young men, turned towards the line of British soldiers. Some protestors pushed through the helpless stewards to confront the army units who were blocking their progress into the city centre. The regular soldiers, batons at the ready, closed rank behind their shields and stood their ground as they came under a torrent of verbal abuse: *Brits Out! Up the Provos!* Stones and bottles battered off their vehicles and riot shields as the demonstration organisers tried in vain to pull the ring leaders away before the soldiers reacted.

Concerned at what he was witnessing, Ramsey turned to speak to Moorcroft, who, to his surprise, was no longer there. He looked around the ramparts and saw that a number of soldiers were now at the ready. He turned back to survey the buildings surrounding Free Derry Corner, and observed at least three army sniper positions on rooftops looking down to the maze of Bogside streets below. The radio was now crackling a flood of coded messages between the commanders on the ground and HQ.

The situation on William Street was beginning to look critical as the embattled soldiers began to fire rubber bullets and CS gas into the protestors. The gas only added to the overall picture of chaos when the smoking canisters were hurled back at the soldiers by the defiant youths.

Over the nearby radio, Ramsey could hear repeated references to the code name Neptune, just as a rather cumbersome looking army vehicle trundled around the corner and began to spray the rioters with purple jets of water. He ducked below the parapet when he heard the noise of a high velocity rifle being fired nearby. He regained his composure and looked around to see who might have fired the shot, but he could not tell whether it came from the positions on the wall or from one of the other sniper posts he had seen earlier. He scanned the streets below and it was clear that the shot had caused the rioters, and the other more peaceful protestors, to retreat in chaotic panic. He could now see that the Parachute Regiment were in hot pursuit of the fleeing Bogsiders, who were running in every direction. There was another loud echoing shot, quickly followed by more sporadic gunfire. Ramsey tried to focus on the confusion below, noticing for the first time that there were a number of men lying on the ground. Some looked as though they had been shot.

More shots! He wiped the sweat from his brow, and began to focus on the Parachute Regiment moving in scattered units around the concrete forecourts of the Rossville high-rise flats. He could see a number of the soldiers taking up firing positions, some behind walls, others kneeling to fire in the open. He turned his binoculars to the fleeing civilians and noticed that there were at least two other lifeless bodies lying prostrate on the ground.

More shots, but this time he was sure that they came from further down the wall rampart, and he could see that the soldiers seemed pleased with the result. He was now concerned that mass murder was taking place before his very eyes and that it was far from finished. He focused back towards the carnage around the tower blocks and observed a group of civilians, one wearing a priest's dog collar and waving a white handkerchief above his head. He could no longer focus on what was happening because the wind had blown the gas as far as the City Walls. His eyes were now stinging and he began to feel burning sensations in his chest. He moved away from the walls and found a corner to be sick in.

*

Fearing he was going to be shot, Brendan ran like everyone else. He followed two men in front of him, running towards the shelter of the Rossville flats. More shots rang out, echoing all around the concrete buildings. Brendan was too frightened to look back as he heard the roars and screeching of army vehicles enter the car park behind him. He ran as fast as his shaking legs would carry him across the open area between the flats. He panicked when he found himself on his own, engulfed in a sea of gas. His eyes were stinging as he looked for somewhere to hide. He then heard English accents, ordering him to stop. More gunshots exploded around his head. He tripped on some rough ground and fell beside a brick wall covered in IRA graffiti. He lay terrified beside the wall, his throat on fire, and struggling to catch his breath. Then, as the gas lifted, he could see two men on the ground to his left, one trying to reach the other. The wounded man was calling out for help as blood poured out from under his coat onto the ground. More shots rang out and CS gas canisters exploded onto the concrete concourse. Chaos reigned.

Begging God to keep him safe, Brendan looked for somewhere to run to, but he was too frightened to make a move in all the confusion. People were screaming and shouting all around him as 1 PARA advanced through the drifting gas.

Suddenly a soldier ran, screaming, towards him. Brendan held up his hands in submission, but it made no difference; he was immediately knocked unconscious with the butt of a rifle.

It was almost two hours later, before Brendan regained consciousness in hospital on the other side of the River Foyle. When he was finally able to sit up in bed and watch the televised reports of the march, he was shocked to hear what had actually happened. There was an outcry of indignation being expressed around the world as the death toll was put at thirteen dead, and a further seventeen wounded. It was no surprise to him to read in the papers the next morning that the IRA had issued a statement that they would now kill as many British soldiers as possible in retaliation.

After a few more days recovering in hospital, Brendan was glad to be back home, where he was seen as something of a returning hero; one of the wounded from what was now being universally referred to as 'Bloody Sunday'. Danny asked him if he would be joining the IRA to get the soldiers that killed all those people and smashed his head with a rifle. Brendan, with the solemnity of someone twice his age, smiled at Danny's zeal for vengeance and simply said, 'God will punish those soldiers who killed and wounded…'

'I bet the IRA gets them first!'

*

Ramsey got a jaundiced feeling in his stomach when he thought about what he had witnessed. The political fallout was still reverberating around Westminster and Stormont, where some politicians did not know whether to congratulate the British army or denounce it. The Irish government had no such qualms and roundly condemned the massacre of innocent civilians. Anti-British riots in Dublin resulted in the British embassy being burnt to the ground. A few weeks later the Official IRA made their blundered response when two stolen cars, loaded with two fifty-pound bombs, were left outside the barracks of the 16th Parachute Regiment in Aldershot; killing one army captain, a gardener, a Catholic priest and five female domestic workers.

The pressure was now on the Stormont government. Whitehall demanded they relinquish the control of all Northern Ireland's security powers to the British government. Ramsey found himself excluded from a number of high level crisis meetings between the Northern Ireland Prime Minister and his inner circle of ministers and political advisors. It was clear he was now seen as the enemy within and he conveyed those concerns to his superiors in Whitehall. He was given a two week leave of absence, and told to report back to his desk at the end of March. By then, he was told, there would be a significant change to the situation and whatever Faulkner and his ministers were discussing would be irrelevant.

Chapter 17

Direct Rule

After the political fallout following 'Bloody Sunday', the British government brought in Direct Rule and abolished the Stormont government, which resulted in uproar in the Unionist ranks and triumphant celebrations in the nationalist areas. Ramsey was immediately transferred to the Northern Ireland Office as a personal advisor to Willie Whitelaw, who had been appointed to the hastily created post of Secretary of State for Northern Ireland.

It was not long, in spite of the political rhetoric to the contrary, before Whitelaw made overtures to the IRA leadership through clandestine channels of communication opened up by Ramsey. MI6 agents were instructed to inform the IRA that government officials were willing to meet with their leadership with proposals for peace. The Provisional IRA response to a ceasefire was positive, but conditional on the release of Gerry Adams, who was in Long Kesh Prison, and the granting of 'political status' for all IRA prisoners. When Ramsey passed on these demands to Whitelaw, he was surprised to receive an internal communiqué from London conceding to both conditions demanded by the IRA.

With some apprehension, Ramsey travelled to Derry to agree to the terms of the ceasefire and the logistics of getting the parties around the negotiating table without the media finding out. The initial agreement brought about a declaration from the IRA leadership that ordered a suspension of all offensive operations. In response, the British army were taken off the streets, and an uneasy calm settled over the

North.

Ramsey met a delegation of six prominent IRA negotiators at an RAF airfield, a few miles outside Belfast. The flight to London was a tense experience with both parties suspicious of the other's motives and intentions. Arrangements had been put in place and the Northern Ireland Secretary was already waiting nervously at a secret location in Chelsea. Initial introductions were awkward with both sides keen to get down to the business that brought them there. The IRA Chief of Staff, Seán Mac Stiofáin, read out a prepared list of demands as though he had just taken the surrender of the British army from Whitelaw, and was now giving him the unconditional terms of the armistice. Ramsey noted down the IRA's unrealistic demands: *The British government should recognise publicly that it is the people of Ireland acting as a unit that should decide the future of Ireland as a unit. They should withdraw all British forces from Irish soil; such withdrawal to be completed on or before January 1975. Internment must be ended and there should be a general amnesty for all political prisoners, internees, detainees and wanted persons.*

As the British delegation entered into debate over the demands, they soon found out that this was not the starting point for the IRA to negotiate from; these were the terms they demanded in exchange for peace. Ramsey became more and more despondent as the various voices across the table retained their intransigent positions. Such an agreement would never be accepted by the British parliament, never mind the Protestant people of the North. After the meeting, both sides agreed to continue with the status quo until further discussions could take place. But within a couple of days the IRA ceasefire collapsed and the Grim Reaper once again turned his attention to the streets of Northern Ireland.

*

With the marching season in full swing, Jamie was busy arranging the lodge's annual dinner-dance. There were a number of important guest speakers invited from Scotland, including an ex Rangers player and a well-known Scottish comedian.

The fact that this was his son's birthday made the day all the more special, and this year Jamie decided it was time to get William involved in the lodge band now he had learned some basic tunes on the accordion. William tried to keep his promise to his father and practised every day as best he could. Still he found that he had no aptitude for the accordion, which to him, was the antithesis of what he thought of as music.

That summer, when William was accepted into the lodge band, Jamie insisted in paying for a professional photograph to be taken of his reluctant son, sitting with the accordion on his lap and wearing his new blue and white band uniform. The coloured image was displayed on the hall dresser with the black and white photographs of the previous three generations of Morrisons in similar poses. William did not like the photograph, he thought it made him look silly, and would periodically turn it facedown as he passed it in the morning only to see it standing back up in its former position when he returned home from school.

*

In response to the breakdown of the IRA ceasefire, the army, using tanks fitted with bulldozer blades, swept away nationalist barricades and entered the no-go areas to arrest suspected members of the IRA still at large. The top secret operation had been leaked, and the IRA leadership had already disappeared over the border. While Operation Motorman was underway, Ramsey was asked to provide a report to the Secretary of State on the effectiveness of these dawn raids.

He spent the first few days of the operation with the army, mainly in the Falls Road area. He was shocked at the level of squalor and deprivation he witnessed. He was amazed to find one family, of nine children, living in a pitifully small house that had no inside toilet facilities. The poverty was acute, yet the younger children often laughed and giggled at each other as though they had not a care in the world. But it was in the ravaged faces of the parents, struggling from one dole cheque to another, and the despondent sad eyes of the older children that he saw the true cost of British support for Stormont.

After the second day, Ramsey was approached by a nervous-looking lieutenant. The soldier produced a copy of the local evening newspaper, which reported the discovery of a mutilated Catholic body found in an alleyway near the Springfield Road the previous night. The soldier revealed to Ramsey that every time his squad was confined to barracks, another body would be found the next morning. When pressed by Ramsey, the lieutenant told of his concerns in seeing army officers in the company of loyalist paramilitaries when off duty. He had also noted that some of the UVF men were now armed with SLRs; a standard British army weapon.

Ramsey already suspected that Military Intelligence was training loyalists at the Palace Barracks, but now he had independent confirmation. Training and arming the loyalist paramilitaries against the IRA was one thing, but Ramsey now had the unnerving evidence that the British army was allowing loyalist death squads a free rein to terrorise the Catholic community.

Concerned with what he had seen and heard, Ramsey wrote his report on Operation Motorman. He was aware that his views had to be tempered with an element of detachment in case the more right-wing elements at the Northern Ireland

Office accused him of going native. After giving a detailed report of the army's operation, he went on to give his own opinion and conclusions: *This massive army operation may have regained control of the no-go areas, but it has not stopped the escalating violence in both communities. The violence has now taken a more sinister turn with the abduction and murder of Catholics with no known link to the IRA. I hate to use the term sectarian, but I can find no other word to describe such random and brutal murders. With each killing the violence inflicted on the unfortunate victim has become more brutal and the IRA is now retaliating in kind. There are rumours, and at least one unsubstantiated report that the British army may be involved in the training and arming of loyalist paramilitary groups. If this is true then we risk being dragged in to a sectarian war that could just as easily spread to the mainland. Unless the army are seen as impartial, and are able to offer more protection to the people living in these Catholic ghettos, then I can only see disaster and civil war ahead. I hope what I have managed to ascertain from my visits to these unfortunate areas of our country is of some use to Her Majesty's Government. If I could be of further assistance, I am at your service.*

A few days after submitting his report, Ramsey received a telephone call from the Secretary of State's office informing him that Mr Whitelaw wished to invite him for lunch. Ramsey was pleased. He had always found Whitelaw a very amenable character. Unfortunately, the recent negotiations in London with the IRA were now common knowledge and Mr Whitelaw had become a political leper to the more extreme Unionist politicians. Ramsey felt a little guilty for urging so strongly for the talks to take place. With their failure and details subsequently leaked to the press, he was well aware how much political damage they had done to the Secretary of State.

Lunch was to be a rather informal affair in Whitelaw's own private quarters. Ramsey was met by a smartly dressed man in a tweed jacket and brown corduroys. 'Good morning,

Mr Ramsey, nice to see you again. The Secretary of State is unable to be here and has asked me to convey his apologies.'

'Good morning,' replied Ramsey. 'Have we met before?'

'Yes, I do believe we have … Londonderry, I was the officer who escorted you on to the walls to observe the civil rights march that day.'

'Yes,' replied Ramsey, suddenly remembering the major. 'A uniform changes a man's appearance.'

'It's not often I get the opportunity to dine in such salubrious surroundings,' said the major, inviting Ramsey to take a seat at the unnecessarily large oval table, set out with the finest of silver on an immaculate, white linen table cloth. 'As Mr Whitelaw said, there is no point letting good food to go to waste.'

Ramsey smiled at the major in polite agreement and took the seat opposite as the waiter began to serve the starter of quails' eggs and asparagus. Ramsey tucked the linen napkin into his shirt collar, curious as to why a major in Military Intelligence would be acting on behalf of Whitelaw. It did not make sense. As they ate and chatted, the major seemed distracted and not very interested in the conversation they were having about the quality of Irish cuisine. 'Well, there's no point continuing with this charade,' said Moorcroft abruptly. 'Whitelaw is not even aware of this meeting, and even if he was he would not wish to be here. He is still in London; his return was delayed due to the recent resignation of the Home Secretary. This meeting was suggested by our superiors in Whitehall. I have read your report in which you suggest that there may be some collusion between British Intelligence and the loyalist paramilitary organisations.'

'That's what I believe, having spoken to a number of different sources including one British officer, who obviously wishes to remain nameless. The officer mentioned his disquiet at the sight of loyalists running amok in Catholic areas, while his unit is confined to barracks. Each time he has received such an order there are subsequent reports of loyalist bombings, shootings and abductions in the area. There was also one soldier who confirmed that he had seen paramilitaries in British Land Rovers wearing full combat gear. It sounds to me as if we are using the same tactic we used in Kenya.'

'What tactic is that Mr … or is it Captain Ramsey?'

'It's Mr Ramsey now, and I think you know fine well the tactic to which I refer: Use your enemy's enemy to kill your enemy! Or as the Romans put it, divide and conquer.'

'I don't think we have to divide the nationalists and the loyalists, do we? They could not hate each any more, even if they tried. No, Mr Ramsey, all we are doing is helping the loyal British subjects defend themselves against the IRA, who are trying to bomb them into a united Ireland and destroy the United Kingdom in the process.'

Ramsey dabbed his lips with his napkin and waited for the major to continue.

'Mr Ramsey, you were a military man once, and you of all people should know that war is an ugly business. The IRA doesn't play fair, does it? It's not like they agree to meet us on the battlefield and fight it out like soldiers.'

'Well, they're not fools. They are using the same tactics they used against us in the twenties and the same tactics the French resistance used against the Nazis.'

'Come, Mr Ramsey, you are not trying to tell me that you think of the IRA as a resistance organisation. My God, next you will be telling me that we are the bad guys.'

'I might not think that, but there are thousands of Irishmen who think that way. If you took a walk down the Falls Road and into some of the miserable hovels they are forced to live in then you would soon understand why.'

'You are starting to sound like you have changed sides, Mr Ramsey,' said the Major sarcastically, taking Ramsey's report from his brown leather briefcase and placing it on the table.

'I take it that's my report to the Secretary of State. Has he even seen it?'

'You have to understand, we have a job to do and if that means intercepting mail to politicians in the national interest then that's what we have to do.'

'He is not just a politician. He's the Secretary of State for Northern Ireland!'

'He is still a politician and they come and go on the whim of a Prime Minister or the ignorance of the British electorate. We are the ones who perpetuate and are charged with keeping our country safe from those who seek to destroy it. If you wish, you can phone Whitehall and receive confirmation, but either way you will have to amend your report where it refers to any collusion between the British army and the loyalist paramilitaries. The rest of the report can be on the Secretary of States desk for his return tomorrow.'

'What if I refuse?' asked Ramsey.

'I don't think you want to do that,' said the Major, taking out two photographs from his briefcase and placing them in front of Ramsey.

'Good God, what's this about?' he asked, staring at the photographs of himself and a young man he met a few weeks earlier.

'We know you took him to a room in the Europa Hotel and had sex with him.'

'It's not illegal…'

'I'm afraid it still is in Northern Ireland. I'm sorry, but you should be grateful that we have not passed this on to the RUC. We know what most of them think about homosexuality.'

Now under pressure, Ramsey could feel the beads of

sweat on his forehead and he turned away from the major, before taking the document back without a further word.

'I will send someone along in a couple of hours to uplift the report and I'm sorry that I have embarrassed you in this way. Sometimes war makes it necessary to be unpleasant.'

Ramsey was still looking out at the manicured lawn when he heard the door close with military assuredness. He was now being blackmailed by his own government; the men in grey suits who pulled the strings, while sipping port in gentlemen's clubs like they were still running the British Empire. He thought about the poverty and misery he had seen only days before in the Falls Road and remembered the major's parting words. *Sometimes war makes it necessary to be unpleasant.* Unable to bear his own weakness, Ramsey turned away from his reflection in the window.

*

When Joe was eventually released from prison, Marie and the children went to meet him at the bus station in the city centre. Although the children were glad to see their father, there were no great shows of emotion. They went to a cheap café and had some tea and sandwiches. As Marie counted the coins in her purse to pay for lunch, Joe noticed that the children had the mark of poverty on them. He was determined to put things right and over the next few months he tried his best to find work, but there was no work to be found anywhere.

Chapter 18

Ambush

When Major Moorcroft read the intelligence report, he ordered his secretary to bring him the files on Eugene Tierney and Fergal Gallagher. The major was now in possession of information that he was sure would lead to the elimination of two of the Provisionals' most feared gunmen. He read the list of operations that they were both suspected of being involved in, including a booby-trapped bomb that killed five off duty British soldiers only a few days earlier. 'I've got the bastards,' he said, as he got to his feet and made his way to the Belfast barracks where the intelligence had turned up.

The lust for revenge was palatable as Captain Bill Travers briefed his squad. The intelligence had been checked out and Operation Congo was given the green light. The ambush was to take place in the village of Kyle, twenty miles south of Belfast. An informer had confirmed that an IRA unit intended to target a vulnerable RUC barracks, which was manned by only a couple of officers at any given time. The fact that the IRA unit was commanded by Eugene Tierney made the intelligence all the more valuable.

With the briefing over, the code came over the radio with instructions for the operation to go ahead immediately. The men raced out to the waiting vehicles, which were soon revving up with the drivers keen to get underway. The soldiers forced themselves into the limited space in the back of the vehicles as the high metal gates of the compound screeched slowly open. The men were tense, but pumped-up to carry out the mission after it was confirmed to them that the targets were Tierney and Gallagher.

Harry Mitchell looked out through the gun slits in the back door of the Land Rover. He could see the other two vehicles following behind as the metal gates, topped with rolls of razor wire, closed with a hollow bang. They were on their own now and they knew they were heading to an area where the IRA was strong enough to carry out its own ambush.

It was always risky to rely on external intelligence, and most feared that they might be the ones being set up. When the Land Rover slowed down to negotiate speed bumps, Harry Mitchell could see as much of Belfast's night life as he wanted to encounter. The smell of burning rubber hung in the air, the periodic noise of police and ambulance sirens adding to the heady mix of smouldering violence. They turned one corner where a gang of feral youths began shouting abuse and throwing stones at the convoy. The Land Rovers roared on through the city's hostile streets.

Once out of Belfast, the convoy turned onto a narrow country road and headed south. The blackness of the night engulfed the men's thoughts, and the fear of a roadside bomb was on everyone's mind. The radio in the Land Rover crackled and whistled with the occasional metallic-sounding voice issuing updates to the officers in the front. Each time they bumped over a pothole or a dip in the road, a gripping silence was followed by a collective sound of nervous exhaling.

Harry was not religious, but he remembered the words of some prayers he learned as a young boy at Sunday school, and repeated them in his mind. He had not killed another human being but tonight he had a foreboding that he might have to. He gripped the barrel of his rifle tightly. The Land Rover hit a dip in the road with such speed that it bounced six inches in the air, briefly skidding on the road before the driver pulled it under control. The enraged officers in the front hollered some colourful expletives to the driver, who reined in his excitement and slowed down to let the other two vehicles catch up.

The village of Kyle was so far off the beaten track that it was virtually trouble free and its RUC barracks looked more like an old couple's retirement home than a police station. The officers who manned the barracks were part-time and spent less than a couple of hours in the station each day. Tonight however, a unit of six heavily armed SAS soldiers took up positions at various vantage points and waited in silent anticipation. The RUC officers were ordered to remain at home and stand by their telephones in case they were needed for any reason.

The village was deserted when Fergal drove down the main street. 'Eugene, I don't like this. Something's no' right,' he said, pulling up at the side of the kerb.

'What do you mean?'

'The place is like a ghost town, for fuck's sake.'

'These wee villages are always deserted at night. You're just getting a bit paranoid.'

'Paranoid nothing, I was right the last time.'

'The other boys will be waiting .We can't just pull out and leave them.'

'I don't know why they need us, anyway.'

'The top brass want it done right. These local lads don't have the guts for it. They're only here as back up.'

'Something doesn't feel right…'

'You're no' getting scared on me, son.'

'No, no way. I just don't like it,' said Fergal, putting the car into gear and pulling slowly back onto the road. They drove cautiously through the village. Even Eugene began to get anxious. He primed the weapons and looked at the line of closed shops on the main street. They could now see the police barracks a few hundred yards up ahead. Fergal stopped the car to see if there was any sign of life. The station had one front light on and they assumed at least one of the RUC officers was on duty. They knew that the shift change took place at ten o'clock and if they were lucky they might get a few more officers. Fergal noticed a Ford Escort, parked further up the road, flashing its headlights. 'That must be them,' he said, flashing his own lights in response.

One of the men in the other car got out and approached cautiously. He threw away the cigarette he had been smoking and bent down to speak through the open driver's window. 'How's about ye. We think it's Moore that's in at the minute. Johnston should be along shortly, he's the main target.'

'What's he driving?' asked Eugene.

'A Ford Granada, he parks it at the side of the station.'

'Get back to yer car and signal us if ye see him coming,' ordered Eugene, lighting up a cigarette, while looking back over at the police station.

The minutes seemed to last forever as they waited for the signal. Fergal was still anxious that something was amiss, aware that not a single car had passed them from either direction since they reached the outskirts of the village. It was now over five minutes since the change of shift should have taken place and there had been no sign of the other officer arriving. 'I'm goin' for a piss,' said Eugene, getting out and urinating in the bushes at the side of the road.

'Why don't ye go and find out what's up!' said Fergal impatiently.

Eugene pulled up his trouser zip and took another suspicious look back down at the main road towards the centre of the village. He then approached the other car, deciding to call off the operation. Two men in parkas got out the Escort to meet him; their faces looked concerned, if not a little frightened.

Fergal was still watching the police station when he noticed what he thought was a rifle barrel sticking out of one of the upstairs' windows. He turned on the ignition and began to flash the car's headlights frantically trying to warn the others. As soon as Eugene realised it was a trap, a rapid hail of bullets began to rip into the men standing at the other car. Eugene tried to run back to the Volvo, but was gunned down by semi-automatic fire coming from at least three different directions. In a frantic panic, Fergal pushed the gears into reverse and put his foot hard down on the accelerator. He pulled the steering wheel around, crashing onto the pavement while turning the car at speed as the back window was riddled with bullets.

Before the SAS unit opened fire, the army was already in place and the road in and out of the village was cut off by heavily armed road blocks on either side. On the northern side, under the command of Captain Travers, a dozen soldiers lay on the grass verge concentrating their aim on the headlights speeding towards them. Their orders were clear; to open fire as soon as the car came within three hundred yards, which was essentially as soon as it came over the blind summit just up ahead. The men followed the headlights in their rifle sights as they beamed over the black sky, before dipping back behind a row of trees. Captain Travers was anxiously following the car's progress on the undulating country road with his field binoculars when the headlights suddenly disappeared.

As the radio crackled out congratulations from Army Headquarters to Major Moorcroft in the police station, the men at the road block all stared up ahead waiting for the headlights to reappear. The captain turned anxiously to his corporal, who shrugged his shoulders. The seconds became minutes. The men turned their eyes from the road up ahead as they waited for fresh orders. It was clear to every one that the car had either crashed or the driver had turned off his headlights and took the car across the fields. Captain Travers had no orders to abandon the road block and take up pursuit and he dithered before radioing the situation back to the police station. Major Moorcroft's angry response was overheard by every man on the road block, 'Get after it, you fucking idiot!'

The first soldiers on the scene shone their torches on the gaping hole in the hedge where the car had forced its way into the fields. They found the abandoned car at the bottom of a steep slope where it had crashed into a stone dyke. The driver was gone.

While the bulk of the soldiers took up pursuit, the captain ordered the vehicle to be searched. Two rifles; three hand grenades, a couple of boxes of ammunition and a Hank Williams cassette were recovered. There were no blood stains and it seemed that the driver had miraculously escaped without serious injury.

The celebrations back at Headquarters became subdued when Captain Travers radioed back that they had found the car, but there was no sign of the driver. After an hour or so, he was ordered to call off the search. The SAS took over.

Only a few miles away from the abandoned car, Fergal lay in a thicket of thorny bushes. He had cracked his ribs against the steering wheel when he crashed into the dyke. He grimaced with every breath as he loosened the bullet proof vest that saved his life. Despite the pain, he forced himself to his feet and staggered through the moonlit fields, stopping every so often to get his bearings. He could hear the barks of pursuing dogs and the sound of helicopters overhead. He forced himself to keep going. There was no time to think of Eugene and the other men he left behind. He climbed another dyke and ran for the cover of a wooded area up ahead.

By daybreak it became clear that the one man the security forces top brass wanted more than any other was dead, Major Moorcroft tore down Eugene's photograph from his operations board. He looked at the other photograph on the board of Fergal Gallagher. He stuck a drawing pin into forehead. 'I'll get you, you fucking bastard.'

It took Fergal the best part of six hours to get back to the outskirts of Belfast, before he risked leaving the back roads to find a public phone. He waited another twenty minutes before Mickey Flynn arrived and drove him to a safe house in the Ardoyne. Fergal was in too much pain to say very much, other than they had been set up and Eugene and the others were dead.

'Eugene Tierney dead, my God, I never thought the Brits would get him.'

'Even he couldn't survive all those bullets. I told him there was something no' right. They were waiting for us … I need to lie down.'

Mickey helped Fergal onto the bed in the recess, before leaving to report the ambush to Northern Command.

*

Eugene's funeral had one of the biggest turnouts seen in Belfast for any IRA man. The Duffys followed close behind Eugene's own distraught family as the coffin, draped in the tricolour, was carried into the chapel. Father McFadden eulogised about the unselfish sacrifice he had made for his country.

The security forces were out in force, but stayed back as the huge procession made its way down the Falls Road towards Milltown Cemetery. Overhead two helicopters carried out observations, photographing those attending that interested them. Undercover army intelligence officers mingled with mourners to gather intelligence.

At the graveside, while others cried, Danny felt a sense of pride as the coffin was lowered into the ground and three volleys were fired over it.

Chapter 19

Wedding Bells

Ramsey, feeling his age, despaired at the ongoing situation in Northern Ireland and the inertia of the politicians to find some compromise that would end the killings. With the decline of the British economy in the mid seventies, Harold Wilson had had enough and resigned. The sectarian division in Northern Ireland had become so entrenched with each new tit-for-tat atrocity that the idea of a peaceful resolution seemed hopeless. A further three years of Labour under Jim Callaghan, brought nothing new to the table. With no progress being made to bring peace, the bombing and sectarian killings continued unabated.

In May 1979, the Conservatives won a landslide election victory, resulting in the United Kingdom's first woman prime minister. Ramsey watched the news reel of Margaret Thatcher, in her Tory blue suit, arriving at Number 10 Downing Street. He smiled when she quoted a prayer from St Francis. *Where there is discord, may we bring harmony. Where there is error, may we bring truth. Where there is doubt, may we bring faith. And where there is despair, may we bring hope.* For the first time, Ramsey believed that the country had elected a Prime Minister who had the will to do the one thing that her predecessors failed to do so miserably: bring peace to Ireland.

However, the hope she promised faded fast and it soon became clear that Thatcher was determined to bring the IRA to heel. Instead of looking to resolve the conflict, she immediately increased the security forces on the ground.

As Ramsey prepared to meet the new Secretary of State for Northern Ireland, Humphrey Atkins, he listened with incredulity to a newsflash on the radio: *It is with great sadness that we have to announce that this morning, the Queen's cousin; Earl Mountbatten of Burma was killed in a bomb explosion aboard his fishing boat in Sligo in the Irish Republic...*

Later that day, the news that the Provisional IRA had also killed eighteen soldiers at Warrenpoint, County Down, caused further outrage among the politicians from the whole spectrum of the British establishment. That evening, Ramsey watched the Prime Minister incandescent with anger, publicly condemning the IRA as cowards. Ramsey believed that these killings would only harden her hatred for the Provisionals and be another obstacle to any possible progress in trying to find a settlement to the endless violence. He switched the television set off and removed his glasses, considering it might now be a good time to retire.

*

Polishing the sideboard, Marie stopped for a moment to look at the children's school photographs. She lifted Brendan's and gave it a wipe with her duster, still finding it hard to believe that her eldest son would soon be a priest. She then looked at the photograph of the twins, always together, and both now studying at Saint Mary's Teacher Training College on the Falls Road. She would soon have a priest and two teachers in the family; now that made Marie proud. Then there was Danny, who left school with no qualifications, and could only find work in a record shop in town.

Danny spent most of his free time listening to music or

trying to play a few chords on a cheap guitar he bought from a work mate. Like most of his friends, he was a Clash fan, and now he had a guitar of his own, was desperate to learn at least one of their songs. The whole Punk, anti-establishment ideology seemed to fit in with Danny's rebellious nature and the existing anarchy in Belfast. With his spiky dyed hair and clothes covered in safety pins, Marie did not know what to make of him anymore.

A few days later, it was not Danny, but Kathleen who sent Marie running for the priest when she woke early one morning to find her daughter being violently sick into a bucket.

'How long have ye been pregnant?'

'I'm not, Mammy…'

'Don't lie to me, Kathleen. I heard ye being sick yesterday morning. I knew there was something not right with ye this last wee while. How long have ye known?'

'I'm sorry, Mammy, I'm so sorry.'

'There's no point in being sorry now. How long has it been?'

'I only found out a few weeks ago,' said Kathleen, wiping her mouth with a tissue.

'And is it Michael's?'

'Of course, of course it's Michael's.'

'What's he going to do about it?'

'What do you think? We're going to get married; we were going to tell you and Daddy at the weekend.'

'Jesus, Mary and Joseph, I thought ye had more sense, Kathleen. I'll tell yer father tonight that yer getting married; he likes Michael, and doesn't have to know yer pregnant. He'll find out soon enough. You better get dressed, and I'll go and speak to Father Cunningham.'

After college, Kathleen took the bus to Michael's bedsit in Ballymurphy and sat on the steps outside until he came home from work. She had been trying to make plans all day, but her mind was all over the place.

Michael knew there was something wrong as soon as he saw her sitting there. 'What are ye doing here at this time, Katie?'

She got up and walked towards him as though she was carrying the sins of the world on her shoulders. 'Michael, me Mammy knows.'

'Knows what?'

'What do ye think? She knows I'm pregnant.'

'Shit … Ah, don't start crying, Katie.' He put his arms around her and kissed her forehead.

'I didn't tell her, she saw me being sick this morning.'

'Fuck, what about yer da? He'll kill me.'

'She's not going to tell him until after we're married.'

'Well, come up and have cup of tea. What's done is done.'

Kathleen looked and him and smiled, 'You do love me Michael, don't you?'

'Don't be silly, of course, Katie.'

'Well say it. Can't ye?'

'For God's sake Katie, what are ye on about? I love ye … there, I said it.'

'What are we going to do, Michael?'

'We'll get married and move to England like we planned. Sure, I can easily find work there.'

Marie lost no time in making arrangements. The last thing she wanted was for Kathleen to start showing before the wedding. Her daughter being pregnant was one thing; everybody knowing about it was another matter. Joe was no fool, and he knew fine well that this was no planned wedding, but he said nothing.

Money was tight and Kathleen had to do with her mother's wedding dress, which she took into town to be altered. It was now ready for a fitting.

'It's a beautiful dress,' said the dressmaker, taking another pin from her lips to mark an adjustment to the length. 'Not like some of the dresses I see these days. There, that will do it,' she grunted, getting up from her knees. 'It will be ready on Tuesday.'

'I'll pay you just now,' said Marie, taking her purse from her handbag and handing over a twenty pound note that her sister Grace had given her to pay for the alterations. *Funny,* she thought, *it cost more to alter the dress than it did to buy it in the first place.*

They had both become accustomed to the bag searching and the various obstacles they had to deal with just to get from one shop to another. The centre of Belfast was now in a constant state of fear of bombings and many shops were scarred with the damage from earlier explosions. Some shops were closed altogether and boarded-up waiting for better times. At least Marks and Spencer stayed open. 'Mammy, why don't you get this one?' pleaded Kathleen, holding up a white blouse.

'Oh no, that's far too expensive,' replied Marie, looking at the price tag before she even felt the quality of the material. 'I can't afford it.'

'Oh, you can. It would look wonderful with your blue suit.'

'I guess, I could always try it on.'

Marie went into the cubicle and put on the blouse. She looked at herself in the mirror and then again at the price tag. She could afford to pay for it, but she felt it was awfully expensive and she was not used to buying expensive things for herself.

On the way home, Marie was still smiling to herself about the blouse as they walked along Divis Street and on towards the Falls Road. She could not wait to get upstairs and try it on again. Kathleen stopped to look at one of the new murals recently painted on a gable end; although impressed at the quality of the artwork, she would much rather they left the gable ends as they were. She was proud of her Republican identity but rather embarrassed that she lived in what many saw as a Catholic ghetto.

When they reached the top of Cavendish Street they stopped to watch an ambulance and two police vehicles driving at speed through another army checkpoint. 'My God, something's happened,' said Marie, taking Kathleen by the arm and hurrying home.

The ambulance and police vehicles that had just passed them were now parked at the corner of Mill Street. Marie put her hand to her mouth in horror; there was a young woman tied to a lamppost covered in tar and feathers. There was a cardboard plaque tied around her neck with the words *'British Whore'* smeared on it in a bold red lipstick. 'It's Sadie McGuire,' said Kathleen. 'She lives just up the road … My God, why would someone do that to her?'

Marie did not answer. She had heard gossip for weeks that one of the McGuire girls was pregnant to a soldier. As the ambulance crew untied the sobbing girl, Marie noticed Mrs Donnelly standing at her front door. Marie could see her fingers were black with tar.

*

The night before the wedding neither Kathleen nor Roisin could sleep. Instead, they sat chatting and giggling until nearly three in the morning. In the last few weeks, Kathleen spent most of her evenings with Michael, planning their marriage and their new life in England away from the Troubles. Roisin would miss her desperately and could not even think about how she would cope without her twin. Although she promised that she would visit often, Roisin knew she did not have the money to travel to England.

On the morning of the wedding the house was a hive of activity. Roisin was doing her sister's hair and make-up in the back room while their mother rushed from one room to another, making sure everything was ready. Joe decided he was only in the way and walked down to the workman's club for a few whiskies. It was his first drink for months and the whiskey hit home straight away. He ordered another.

'Ah, she's beautiful,' said Marie when Kathleen stepped into the front room to show off her wedding dress. Kathleen began to blush with all the compliments she was receiving and held her sister's hand tightly to steady her nerves. The house had not seen such a bright and happy morning for a long time, and the spring sunshine was streaming in through the front windows to add to the sense of occasion. Marie's mother and sisters were already in the chapel hall preparing the food for the reception, making the most out of what little they had to work with.

Father Cunningham had negotiated with the local IRA and the British army garrison to ensure that there would be no trouble in the streets that day, at least until the wedding party got into the chapel hall for the reception. The army agreed to back off and allow the cars through freely without the usual searches. In return, the priest confirmed that the IRA would step down and not carry out any operations in the area. However, as Kathleen sat in the car outside the chapel, a British helicopter hovered above. Joe looked up angrily, before it circled and headed off into the distance.

Kathleen took her father's arm for the long, nerve-wracking walk down the aisle to the altar where Michael was standing with his best man, his younger brother Denis. Father Cunningham was smiling warmly at her, while her brother Brendan stood by his side; a novice with his neatly ironed white cassock on. The congregation turned to watch her as she made her way to the altar. Michael turned to see her for the first time in her white dress and smiled, before turning back toward the priest. The chapel echoed to the sound of the organ as it played Mendelssohn's *Bridal March* until Kathleen found herself standing beside her soon-to-be husband. Joe placed her hand into the groom's nervous hand and then took his seat beside his tearful wife. Marie could smell the whiskey on his breath and frowned at him, but said nothing.

Father Cunningham tried to steady the bridal party's nerves, making jokes about how long they had been waiting for Kathleen, and how poor Michael was starting to think that he had been stood up. There was nervous laughter from the bride and groom, which spread throughout the congregation. The priest then took a moment to welcome everyone to the wedding and to say how pleased he was to be asked to conduct the service. Marie noticed Father McFadden sitting at the side of the altar; he looked like he had had a few whiskies the night before and was struggling not to nod off.

After their vows were exchanged, Michael gave his new wife a rather tentative kiss as one of Kathleen's cousins began to sing *Ave Maria* from the balcony at the back of the chapel. Marie sat crying throughout most of the service. She was happy Kathleen was married and that she would soon be away from the Troubles. She would miss her of course, but it was one less child to worry about.

After the service Danny waited to speak to Brendan. They laughed and joked about nothing in particular, before Brendan went into the vestry to change. Curious, Danny followed him in. 'You still want to be a priest?'

'Of course, it's what I intend to be,' said Brendan with

a smile, cleaning the hot frankincense ashes from the gold plated censer.

'Well I think you're crazy. It looks like the most boring job in the world. You can't even get married.'

'It's only boring if you don't understand it. Anyway, not everyone wants to get married.'

'But even a shag's not allowed…'

'Danny, I'll have your mother wash that dirty talk out of your mouth!' said Father Cunningham, admonishing Danny with a stern look as he entered the vestry. 'Not everyone allows sex to rule their lives.'

'Sorry, Father. I was only asking Brendan…' mumbled Danny, feeling his cheeks redden.

'God will look after your brother. He has chosen him the same way I was chosen to help other people. Now let's go and join your family next door before we miss anything and your face gets any redder,' said Father Cunningham, playfully slapping Danny on the back of the head.

It was almost nine o'clock before Kathleen and Michael took to the floor for the first waltz. The band played Kathleen's favourite song, Eric Clapton's *Wonderful Tonight*. The floor began to fill up as other members of the bridal party joined the happy couple. Brendan sat quietly beside Father Cunningham for most of the evening before the priest returned to the chapel house to make preparations for morning mass. Brendan was thinking about the letter he had received from the bishop a few days earlier informing him he had been selected to finish his studies in Rome. It made him nervous to even think of it.

Danny spent much of the evening talking to one of Kathleen's friends, Helen McCabe, whom he had taken a fancy to. She went to the same collage as Kathleen and Roisin, and had a pretty face. 'Do ye like working in a record shop?' she asked.

'It's okay for now. I think I might emigrate to America,' he said boastfully; knowing fine well he had neither the means nor the desire to leave Belfast.

'Do you have any family there?' asked Helen, who was sipping a soft drink and admiring Danny's ambition.

'I've got a cousin who lives in Queens. I'm sure I'd get a job. Sure there's plenty of Irish living and working in New York. It's just getting the money to get over there, that's all.'

'Do you want to dance?' asked Helen.

'Ach no,' said Danny. 'I've never really danced before.'

'Come on, I love this song,' said Helen, putting her glass down and grabbing Danny by the hand, before dragging him reluctantly onto the dance floor.

During the course of the evening, Marie and Joe sat together at the top table. Apart from the first dance, they had showed little interest in each other. Marie found it difficult to talk to Joe when he was drinking, and she was content just to watch her children enjoying themselves. It felt like the day had flown by as the band began to play "A Soldier's Song", to bring the night to an end.

The next morning, while Kathleen packed their bags, Michael diligently fixed a roof rack to the dilapidated Ford Escort he had borrowed from his brother.

In the kitchen, Roisin made breakfast for anyone with the stomach to eat it. Marie went upstairs to waken Joe. 'Are ye not getting up, your daughter's about to leave,' moaned Marie, picking up his suit from the bedroom floor. 'Look at the state of this!' she complained, hanging the suit in the wardrobe.

'I'll get up in a minute, for God's sake!'

'Ha! I thought you didn't believe in God,' she sniped at him.

'Close the door! I'll be down in a minute.'

Marie slammed the door and suppressed her anger for the sake of her daughter. The front room was full of relatives and well wishers, many of whom had been up all night drinking. Kathleen was dressed in her new trouser suit and was struggling to stop crying as she said her emotional goodbyes to her family and friends. Michael stood awkwardly at the door, holding his wife's suitcase and nodding at everyone who looked at him.

'Where's Daddy?' asked Kathleen, wiping away a tear that had escaped down her cheek.

'He'll be down in a minute; he's just getting ready,' said Marie, taking her daughter's hand and giving her a tearful hug. 'Roisin, go up and get yer father. Tell him she's leaving in a few minutes.'

'Daddy!' shouted Roisin, rushing upstairs.

'Stop all the shouting, will ye!' said Joe, as he came down to meet all the noise.

'Daddy, we have to go in a minute,' said Kathleen, smiling at his dishevelled hair and haggard appearance. 'Michael's got the car outside.'

'So you're stealing me beautiful daughter. Well ye better look after her,' joked Joe, as he gave Kathleen a hug.

'We'll be back in a couple of weeks, sure,' said Michael, eager to get out the door.

'Here take that with ye,' said Joe. 'I only wish it was more.'

'But Daddy, I can't take that,' protested Kathleen, opening the envelope crammed with five pound notes.

'Take it, and not another word. You're worth a lot more than money to me.'

'Thanks Dad,' she said, giving him another kiss on his unshaven cheek.

'We'll have to get going,' said Michael, struggling past all the junk in the narrow hall.

The whole street seemed to be standing around the car while Danny and one of his friends were still tying balloons and empty cans to the rear bumper. All the neighbours, many of whom had known Kathleen since she was a child, were clapping and shouting their best wishes. Danny helped Michael lift the heavy suitcases onto the roof rack. 'I think they've stolen the kitchen sink,' laughed Danny, as they finally got the second case on top.

Michael managed to get the car into the stiff second gear as it drove past the cheering crowd and onto the Falls Road. Many that watched the lopsided car splutter its way along the road wondered if it would get out of Belfast, never mind all the way to Donegal. Marie was silently looking at Joe's tearful face as he stood waving until the car turned the corner at the top of the road. For the first time in years she felt some of the love she had long since lost for him. She now realised where all his prized pigeons had gone.

Chapter 20

The Honeymoon

Kathleen stood with the cool Atlantic breeze in her face; the sea wild with huge waves crashing into the granite rocks. Michael took another photograph of her against the ever-changing sky, her hair blowing wildly as she defied the growing tempest.

'Isn't it beautiful?' she sighed, turning to Michael, who pretended to take a photograph of the brooding sea. 'Are you taking pictures of me?'

'No, why would I want to do that?'

'You know I hate getting my picture taken.'

'Methinks the lady doth protest too much,' mocked Michael, this time taking a series of shots of her as she feigned annoyance.

The morning was quickly changing. Streaks of grey and purple appeared on the horizon as a strong wind began to sweep in off the Atlantic. The beach was now completely deserted, and the footprints they had left that morning were now washed away in the surf. They watched a fishing boat struggling through the high waves, trying to reach shelter before the storm took hold. Kathleen felt a sense of panic every time the boat disappeared in the swell before bouncing back into view.

'That's a hard job,' said Michael, trying to focus on the boat. 'It's too far away to get a decent picture.'

'I hope they'll be all right,' said Kathleen, tightening her

Arranmore shawl around her head and shoulders. 'It looks so tiny out there.'

'They'll be all right; this will be nothing to them. Anyway they'll soon be in port.'

'Where's the port?'

'It's only a mile or so down the coast, the place we had lunch the other day, what's it called?'

'That was Burtonport. My God, that's miles away.'

'It's not that far. Anyway, we better get back before that lot comes in,' he said, pointing to the overcast horizon in the distance.

Kathleen had already gathered up what was left of their picnic, and was putting it in the boot of the car when a gust of wet wind nearly blew her off her feet. Michael caught her struggle on camera. *One to show the grandchildren,* he thought to himself.

They travelled back to Annagry along the coast road; the radio blasting out ***Pretty Vacant*** by the Sex Pistols. They both sang along at the top of their voices until the car almost ran into a few haggard sheep grazing on the grass verge.

'Slow down, Michael,' shouted Kathleen. 'You'll have us over the edge.'

'Sorry, Katie,' he said, slowing down to a speed that the car could cope with.

'Look! Michael. Look!'

'What?' He followed her gaze to the amazing deep coloured rainbow that dipped its colours into the sea and reached all the way inland, beyond the hills in the distance. The storm had passed over as quickly as it appeared, and the spring sun was making a tentative reappearance through the broken clouds.

'Go on, Michael, make a wish,' insisted Kathleen, who

had already made her own.

'Ah, away ye go. That's for kids.'

'You better make a wish before it disappears, please!'

'All right, there I've done it,' he lied.

By the time they turned off the main road and drove up the winding path to the cottage, the sun was shining brightly, and the thatch was gently steaming itself dry. A funnel of smoke was rising from the whitewashed chimneystack on the gable end; the smell of turf hung heavy in the air. One of the neighbours' dogs chased the rear wheels of the car up the dirt track, barking insanely until they stopped at the front of the cottage.

'Get away, ye mad bastard,' shouted Michael, throwing a stick for the dog to run after. Before he could get the picnic things out of the boot, the dog returned and dropped the stick at his feet.

'Here, give him this,' said Kathleen, handing Michael a half-eaten ham sandwich. Michael then threw the sandwich up in the air for the dog to catch. 'God, he's hungry,' he gasped, watching the dog devour the bread and ham without even chewing it.

'Do you want a cup of tea?' asked Kathleen, as she opened the door.

'Aye, go on then. Are there any biscuits left?'

'Yes, unless you ate them all this morning.'

The rented cottage was idyllic. Kathleen had gathered bunches of beautiful flowers from the wild garden at the back of the house and filled every vase and jar she could lay her hands on. The stack of turf at the side of the house was a godsend and the fire was on constantly, even when the sun was splitting the trees outside. Although they ate out most days, there was an old turf range fitted in the corner, which allowed them to cook a meal whenever they wanted.

That evening they had planned to go back to one of the village pubs they had been in a few nights before; a favourite with the locals. The bar staff had been very friendly and eager to tell them all the best places to visit during their holiday. Kathleen put on a cotton dress she had borrowed from her sister, and brushed out the curls in her hair. She touched her stomach and smiled at Michael.

The collie whined, watching them as they walked down the road towards the village. The weather had settled down to a calm evening with only a gentle breeze to ruffle Kathleen's hair. They crossed a stone bridge that spanned a peaty river, which flowed into the sprawling strand. Michael took another photograph of Kathleen with the Derryveagh Mountains in the background.

The pub was quiet. There were only a few customers sitting at the bar, smoking and taking about the changeable weather they were having. Michael ordered a couple of drinks while Kathleen looked at the old photographs that covered the walls. She laughed at the before and after pictures of the local royal constabulary barracks which was blown up during the war of independence. Many of the photographs were of long dead villagers, digging turf in the bog or gathering the harvest in times of great hardship in Ireland. Some of the poorer looking children were posing for their photograph unshod, but happy. She called over to Michael, who was coming back from the bar with the drinks, and pointed to an old photograph of a thatched cottage, which looked like the one they were now staying in.

Michael lit a cigarette for Kathleen, who took a tentative puff before passing it back to him. She liked the idea of smoking but still hated the way it made her head spin. The pub was slowly getting busy and a band began setting up their amps and microphones in the corner. They both loved the music they had heard since they arrived in Donegal, and were surprised how many contemporary songs these guys could play. The only constant was "A Soldier's Song", which was always played at the end of the night.

'Where ye from, young fella?' asked an old man, who just taken a seat beside them.

'Belfast, we're here on our honeymoon.'

'Well, aren't you the lucky fella?' said the old man, winking and giving a nod towards Kathleen, who began to blush.

'Och Dermot, stop your old nonsense, yer embarrassing the girl,' said a grey haired woman who was taking her seat beside her husband.

'Well, it's good to see a girl that still gets bashful these days,' said Dermot, knocking his pipe empty on the table, before sweeping the dry ash onto the floor. 'Ye must be glad to be away from all the troubles.'

'It's not that bad,' said Kathleen, recovering her composure after a sip of her drink and a quick puff of Michael's cigarette. 'You can get used to anything.'

'Aye, I'm sure you can, but it's terrible all the same.'

'Why don't you leave them alone, I'm sure they don't want to be talking to a couple of old folk like us when they're here on their honeymoon.'

'No, yer fine,' said Michael. 'It's good to talk to people, but we'd rather forget about Belfast for a while.'

'Aye you're right. You've left that behind ye for the time being. I'll shut up and let ye be,' said Dermot, lifting his pint of Guinness, signalling the end of the conversation.

The next morning, Michael woke with a thumping headache. Carefully freeing himself from Kathleen's embrace, he got up and dressed before putting on the turf fire. It was still early, but the morning light was beginning to seep into the cottage. He poured a cup of water from a china jug and stole a glance at Kathleen, who was still fast asleep. The yellow peaty water was ice cold and quickly quenched his thirst. There was no running water in the cottage and all their water came from an overgrown well at the back. After washing himself, he put a pot on the stove for Kathleen to use when she freed herself from her dreams. He then went outside and threw the soapy water in a ditch.

The grass and bushes were slowly shaking off the morning dew as the dawn began to rise above the canopy of trees that sheltered the cottage from the worst of the Donegal weather. The sweet tang of honeysuckle drifted in the morning breeze with the smell of burning turf. 'Morning,' said Kathleen, appearing behind Michael, who was still taking in the views of the strand in the distance as the tide was slowly rolling in. 'Morning, so you're up! I put some water on the stove for you.'

'I know… it was the pot boiling over that woke me up. What are you doing out here, its freezing.'

'It's not that bad. Look at the view. I think it's going to be a nice day. Maybe we should hire a couple of bikes.'

'God, how can you think about that at this time in the morning? I'm going to make something to eat. What do ye want?'

'Just some toast.'

After breakfast, Kathleen washed the dishes in a plastic basin of lukewarm water, while Michael went out to look for the dog to give it the leftovers. The church bells were ringing for ten o'clock mass and Kathleen stood at the front door and watched the faithful walking towards the chapel, the top of which she could make out over the row of rowan trees at the top of the road.

The Donegal honeymoon was over too soon, and, on the morning of their departure, Michael made a feast of leftover food for the dog, who quickly disposed of the raw bacon, eggs and bread. The collie then lay quietly at the front door, watching as Michael and Kathleen packed their things into the boot of the car. The view over the bay was breath-taking as the blue sky melted into the hazy hues on the horizon, while the tide was slowly retreating back over the strand. 'I wish we could stay here for ever,' said Kathleen, stopping to take in the rugged scenery that made her heart beat fast.

'We'll come back here next year,' said Michael, taking her hand and gently kissing her cheek. 'C'mon, we better get going.'

Michael put the front door key under the plant pot at the side of the door, while Kathleen threw a coin into the well at the back of the house and made a wish, hurrying into the car, afraid that she would cry if she said goodbye to the dog. They drove back down the winding hillside while the forlorn looking dog followed them until they reached the main road, where it stood and watched the car disappear over a dip in the road.

The smell of burning turf filled them with the scent of Donegal as they passed a few clusters of houses and shops along the main road towards the parish of Gweedore, where they turned onto the back road and the moors and hills of the Glenveagh National Park. It was an hour or so before they reached Letterkenny, the last main town before they approached the border. Michael stopped at a garage to fill the tank, while Kathleen spent the Irish change she had left on a newspaper and some sweets. The morning sky was beginning to cloud over, and a brisk breeze caused Kathleen to put on a warm cardigan. The weather was on the turn, and with every mile the grey clouds swallowed up the horizon.

By the time thcy approached the border on the outskirts of Derry, the metamorphosis was complete and the sunny Donegal morning of a few hours ago seemed more like a distant memory. The first specks of rain appeared on the windscreen. 'It will probably be snowing by the time we get to Belfast,' said Michael, turning on the windscreen wipers.

Michael felt uneasy approaching the border checkpoint. He pulled in behind a line of slow moving cars. Some were simply being waved through while others were pulled to the side of the road to be searched. Michael rolled down the window as a soldier carrying an automatic rifle to his chest approached his side of the car.

'Where are you going to?'

'Belfast.'

'Just the two of you in the car?' asked the soldier, trying to peer over Michael's shoulder into the back of the car.

'Yes.'

'Where are you coming from?'

'Annagry, on the west coast…'

'We were on our honeymoon, if it's any of your bloody business!' interrupted Kathleen.

'Pull your car over here, sir!' ordered the soldier, pointing to a gravel lay-by at the side of the road.

'Kathleen!' said Michael, with a sigh in his voice as he slowly drove over to the lay-by.

'What right have they to order us about in our own country?'

'Well I think that bloody big gun he's carrying gives him the right. Now they're going to go through all our bloody things.'

As Michael got out of the car the soldier came over to him carrying a wheel brace. 'Here, you'll need that, son, you've got a flat tyre,' said the soldier handing Michael the wheel brace and pointing to the back of the car. 'Thanks,' said Michael, turning to Kathleen. 'We've got a bloody flat tyre.'

After Michael had changed the wheel he was allowed to go without the vehicle being searched, 'See, they're not all bastards.'

'I never said they were, but they shouldn't be in our country telling us what we can and can't do.'

Driving through Derry and across the River Foyle, the heavens opened up and the wipers struggled to keep the windscreen clear. Michael turned on the radio for the midday news. It was the first time since they left Belfast that they had bothered about what was happening in the wider world. The report was the same old depressing story of riots and shootings. Kathleen turned the radio off; as far as she was concerned they were still on honeymoon and the last thing she wanted to hear about was more killings.

As the rain let up, Michael drove into Belfast city centre. There were diversions in operation and many of the roads into the west side of the city were closed by the police and the army. The streets were littered with stones and broken bottles, and sirens echoed in the distance. 'At least we know we're home,' said Kathleen woefully.

When Michael turned into Divis Street, they found themselves in the middle of a pitched battle between the army and a few hundred youths. The rioters were throwing stones and rocks from behind two corporation buses that were in flames. Outnumbered, the soldiers fired CS gas and rubber bullets into the melee.

'Oh God, Michael, get us out of here.'

'I'm trying, but I can't see a fucking thing!'

He tried to reverse back out of the street, but the car stalled. His eyes were stinging with hot tears as the gas engulfed the car. Kathleen was struggling to breathe and began to panic. 'Get us out of here,' she screamed as stones bounced off the car.

Michael finally managed to restart the stalled engine, but he could not get the car into reverse gear. He then carried out a desperate U-turn, only to crash into the back of one of the burning buses. The engine stalled again. 'We better get to hell out of here,' he shouted as Kathleen screamed in terror at the flames lapping against the passenger side of the car.

Michael pulled her from the car just in time. They ran to the corner and watched the flames engulf the car in a fireball. 'We better get away from here,' shouted Michael, pointing to the lines of soldiers advancing up the street. 'Let's go,' he insisted, taking Kathleen by the hand as she stared in a trance at the burning car.

'We've lost all our things. What are we goin' to do?'

'Hell, that doesn't matter now. Let's go before we get arrested!'

Michael instinctively ducked when he heard a whooshing sound pass his head. He suddenly felt Kathleen's hand go limp and he immediately turned to catch her as she fell towards the ground. He took her in his arms, half blinded by the noxious gas. 'Kathleen, are ye all right?' It was then he saw a red mark to the side of her forehead and the plastic bullet that caused it lying on the ground. Through the shouts and screams of the advancing soldiers, he lifted her limp body to his chest and begged God not to take her.

*

Marie put the kettle back on the gas and listened nervously to the news reports on the wireless of the mayhem in the surrounding streets. The plates of ham and cheese sandwiches that she had laid out in the front room were beginning to turn up at the edges. The hall clock dominated the silence with every click of its slow moving hands. Joe played patience, anxiously stealing another look out the front window in the hope of seeing the car turning the corner at the top of the road. Roisin listened with her mother to the escalating violence being reported on the radio.

Marie's fear turned to dread as she listened to the constant high-pitched sound of ambulance sirens in the streets, while

CS gas started to drift up the road from the earlier riots. 'Where's Danny?' she asked as she came back into the living room from the kitchen.

Danny was already on his way down to Divis Street. He was sure that he would find Kathleen and Michael on the other side of the police cordon that was reported to have been deployed around the Lower Falls. The nearer he got to the bottom of the road the more chaos he found. The streets were covered in debris and the air was thick with the toxic fumes. He passed a number of the local lads covered in blood, coming back from the battle.

By the time he reached Divis Street, the riot was over. The road was covered in the remains of the abandoned battlefield. He stepped into a nearby doorway when a convoy of British army Saracens roared past. Turning the corner he walked into a squad of soldiers sweeping the area for rioters. Danny was immediately grabbed by a screaming corporal who pushed him against the metal shutter of a nearby shop.

'I'm just looking for me sister!'

'Fucking shut up and spread your legs, ye Fenian bastard.'

Danny felt the butt of the soldier's rifle pressing into his spine. He was spread-eagle against the metal shutter. He could feel the searching hands of the corporal while another foul-mouthed Scottish soldier shouted abuse into his face. 'What are you, a fucking cockerel?' he mocked, staring at Danny's spiky hair. Danny knew to keep his mouth shut; these soldiers were wearing the maroon cap and badge of the Parachute Regiment.

*

As though in some strange dream, Michael stood in the long hospital corridor while streams of injured people crowded around the accident and emergency waiting area. Every so often the doors would open with a crash and a trolley bed would be wheeled into the chaos while a team of nurses and paramedics frantically worked on the wounded patients. He moved over to the glass panel in the room to where they had wheeled Kathleen a few minutes before. He could feel his heart racing in his chest and he began to feel sick. He took deep breaths to try and clear the nausea when a nurse took him by the arm. 'Is the girl a relative or a friend of yours?'

'Katie, she's my wife. She's pregnant…'

'I'm so sorry, we don't think she is going to pull through … Is she a Catholic?'

'Yes, my God … is she going to die?'

'I think we should get her a priest, she's not going to make … I'm sorry.'

'Can I see her … we only got married a few weeks ago.'

'Of course you can… of course you can,' the nurse said, taking Michael by the arm and leading him to the bed where Kathleen lay with her beautiful pale face, serene and peaceful. Michael gently stroked her hair as the tears ran freely down his face. The life-support machine bleeped with indifference to his pain as the nurse came back with the priest. The priest began to administer the last rites and sprinkle holy water over her still body. The bleeping stopped.

*

Even though the search proved negative, Danny was handed over to the local army unit by the Paras, who were now dealing with sniper fire coming from one of the high-rise flats. While in the back of the army jeep Danny reacted to the barrage of abuse he was getting from some of the pumped up soldiers and punched one of them in the face. The response was immediate and he was kicked and punched in a torrent of blows to his head and body, knocking him unconscious.

'Fuck, Willie! That's enough, you'll fucking kill him,' shouted Harry Mitchell, pulling his two comrades away from their frenzied attack on Danny's battered body. The Saracen suddenly screeched to a halt and the back door was opened by the squad sergeant 'What the fuck are you lot up to?' He shouted. 'How can we hand him over to the police looking like that? Take him somewhere quiet and dump him.'

Barely conscious, Danny was left by the side of the road. He lay on the wet grass verge for hours, unable to get to his feet. Night was falling when a car pulled up. He was helped into the back seat.

He winced in pain every time the car jolted over bumps in the road. He was sure he recognised the face of the driver looking back at him every so often in the mirror. The car pulled up outside the Royal Victoria Hospital. Danny was taken into casualty by two orderlies. He turned to thank the driver, but he was already gone.

Private Mitchell drove back to his barracks in West Belfast before anyone noticed him missing.

Chapter 21

The Volunteer

Kathleen's death caused a public outcry. The army's spokesman put the blame squarely on the shoulders of the rioters, who he insisted put the life of innocent civilians at risk. Few had ever seen Father Cunningham so angry, and he was near to tears as he condemned the British army and its reckless use of plastic bullets. 'They have no right to come to Ireland and kill our children, and then have the audacity to blame everyone else but themselves for their crimes. It gets harder for me to condemn the men from this parish who have resorted to violence against such tyranny … Dear God, we offer up the soul of Kathleen Mary Duffy…'

Hundreds lined the streets as the hearse made its way from the chapel, where she was married only a few weeks earlier, to Milltown Cemetery. The army and the RUC agreed to stay away from the route that the cortège would take, not only as a mark of respect, but to avoid any further unrest that their presence might provoke. Danny was still recovering from his injuries but insisted on following the hearse along with the rest of his family. His hair was now cropped and he wore a suit and tie borrowed from one of his cousins.

After the funeral the family and some close friends returned to the Duffys' cramped house for lunch. After the expense of the wedding, they could not afford to pay for a proper reception. Marie busied herself making tea and sandwiches and tried to be brave for her children, especially for Roisin, who was traumatised by her twin's death. Brendan had returned from Rome as soon as he had heard the awful news. He looked at the white rosary beads he had sent Kathleen, and placed them back on the dressing table beside her wedding photograph. Since he received the news he had prayed for God to give him the strength to comfort his family, but all he wanted to do was break down and cry in his mother's arms. He went out to the backyard to get away from the constant questions about Rome.

'You can pray for a hundred years and God won't make it any better,' said Danny, watching Brendan's obvious internal torment from the back door. 'God doesn't give a damn about anything or she wouldn't be dead.'

'She's with God now and that's all that matters.'

'Aye, right. If he cared, she would be with her husband starting a new life in England, not lying in a grave.'

'Danny, you shouldn't speak like that, you'll condemn your soul to hell.'

'Hell,' Danny sneered. 'We're living in fucking hell.'

Brendan looked at Danny's contemptuous face, knowing there was no point arguing with him. He asked for a cigarette.

'When did you start smoking?'

'I have one now and again,' said Brendan, lighting the cigarette with his own Zippo lighter he bought in Italy. 'I don't have all the answers,' he added, 'but it's better to believe that she's in a better place.'

'But you're not really sure, are you?'

'Who is ever a hundred per cent sure about anything, but it's what I believe and hope, otherwise what is the point to any of our lives.'

'Does there have to be a point?' replied Danny, flicking his cigarette butt towards the back of the yard. 'C'mon Brendan, or should I say Father, it's starting to get a bit chilly out here.'

The next few days were the most difficult. The mutual strength of family unity began to fall apart as a tangible gloom descended on the terraced house. Joe continued drinking every day while Roisin spent most of her time lying in bed crying. Brendan tried to encourage everyone to eat, but failed miserably. He was distressed with his parents constant arguing and name calling; he was desperate to get back to Rome and the sanctuary of the seminary.

Not long after the funeral, Danny knocked on a door in the Ardoyne and waited nervously for someone to answer. He knocked again. He was wondering if he had the right flat number when the door suddenly opened. A heavy-set man in his forties, with at least a week's heavy growth, nodded for him to come in. Danny followed the man along a narrow corridor into a room with blacked out windows. In the flickering glow of candlelight, two serious looking men sat in the corner behind a desk draped in a tricolour. Danny stood to attention with his hands behind his back waiting to be spoken to. After shuffling papers for a few minutes, one of the two men finally spoke with a Donegal accent. 'We don't think you're ready, Duffy. You need a bit of time to get over your sister's death before we can be sure you're joining for the right reasons.'

'You might be a liability for others,' said the other man, whom Danny and everyone else in West Belfast knew as Mickey Flynn.

'I won't be, I promise. I'm ready now.'

'I don't agree,' said Mickey. 'How can you be ready? You probably don't have any idea what you're getting yerself into. This is not about revenge for your sister. This is about putting your own life on the line for the ultimate goal of a united Ireland. Are you willing to kill other human beings who had nothing to do with your sister's death?'

'I understand, but I'm prepared to do what's required.'

'Wait outside until we decide what to do,' said the

Donegal man.

Danny sat in the next room. He lit a cigarette and stared at the crazy patterned wallpaper. It did not take long before the door opened and he was told to go back into the other room. He could feel the sweat trickling down the side of his face as he stood to attention and waited for someone to speak.

'Duffy, we've come to the view that now is not the time for you to make this decision and we've decided to hold your request to become a volunteer for one month. If you're still looking to join us then we'll be happy to welcome you on board,' said Mickey.

'One month? I won't change my mind.'

'We'll see. In the meantime keep quiet about your intentions and stay clear from any trouble. You don't have a criminal record and we want you to keep it that way. So don't be getting involved in any protest marches or street riots. Try and get yerself a driving licence as soon as possible. Here's a number, we'll pay for the lessons. We will be keeping an eye on you,' said Mickey, stubbing out a cigarette on an upturned coffee jar lid.

Danny's heart was still thumping as he walked down the concrete stairwell into the bright daylight. He took a moment to adjust his blurred vision, stopping to light up another cigarette before walking across the road to the bus stop. He felt that he was being watched from one of the many windows in the run-down tower block behind him, but was determined to act as naturally as possible and not be tempted to look back.

Danny was back the following month knocking on the same door for what felt like the second part of a job interview, rather than volunteering for an illegal paramilitary organisation. He was less nervous this time and had not lost his resolve to become a Provo. He even managed to pass his driving test, even though he mounted the pavement during his three point turn, and almost knocked down an old woman at a zebra crossing. His cropped hair had grown and his bruised and cut face was now healed. He stood before the same two men he had met the month before and noticed a green book lying beside Mickey Flynn's packet of cigarettes. It was the IRA Bible, written by some of the most senior members of the organisation while they were prisoners in Long Kesh.

Mickey began the interview with a cough and a puff of cigarette smoke that engulfed the room. 'You're looking a lot better than you did the last time we met.'

'I feel a lot better and I still want to volunteer.'

'I see you've stayed out of trouble and even managed to pass your driving test,' said the other man.

'Yes, I passed first time.'

'Well don't look so bloody pleased with yourself. The driving examiner told me that you were fucking awful,' said Mickey.

'Oh,' Danny sighed, the smile wiped off his face. He was amazed at the time when the examiner passed him and now he knew why.

'Anyway, you have your licence and that's all that matters at the moment. We'll soon have you driving like Stirling Moss. Here, take this book,' added Mickey, handing Danny the green manual.

'I take it you know what it is?' the other man asked.

'Yes,' replied Danny, suddenly realising that he had just joined the IRA.

'Well, so much for secrecy,' said Mickey. 'Read it and memorise every word, but after today never carry it with you in public. If you get caught with this you'll get three years in the Maze. We will be sending you to our training camp in Donegal in two months, so get some cover story ready for your family. You can always tell them you got a job offer in the south. You'll be away for three months and after that we'll assign you to your unit. Have you any questions?'

'No.'

While his family continued to mourn Kathleen's death, Danny spent night after night reading and memorising the contents of the green book, writing notes and even making his own suggestions in the margins. As the weeks passed, life returned to some kind of normality but it would not take much for someone, especially Roisin, to break into a fit of tears that would set everyone else off.

Only Danny managed to hold back the tears, revenge was all that was now on his mind.

Book II

Chapter 22

The Training Camp

In late August, Danny crossed the border into Donegal to begin his training. He had taken the bus to Letterkenny and waited in O'Brien's Bar at the top end of the town for his contact to appear. He had never been in the Republic before and felt a little self conscious about his accent when he ordered a pint of Guinness. There were only a handful of customers in the pub, standing around the bar drinking and smoking. It was midday, and he took a seat by the window with his pint, feeling uneasy that the men at the bar were weighing him up as they whispered amongst themselves in what he took to be Gaelic. Danny lit a cigarette and watched the comings and goings of the townsfolk passing by the window.

'How's about ye, Duffy?'

The coarse voice startled Danny, and he almost spilled his pint as he turned from the window.

'My name's Hughie Dempsey. You're a lot younger than I expected,' said the man, taking a seat opposite and offering Danny his hand.

'Good to meet ye, Mr Dempsey. How did ye know it was me?'

'You're the only one in the bar I haven't had a fight with.'

Dempsey did not say much as he drove along the country roads that twisted and turned through the moors. As they passed a few isolated houses, Danny wondered how anyone could live in such a wilderness. Every so often the car had to slow down to avoid colliding with stray sheep grazing along the edge of the road. 'You've never been to this part of the world before?' Dempsey eventually asked, passing Danny a cigarette and lighting his own.

'No, this is my first time. There's not much here.'

'Well, that's why we're here. There's only a half dozen Garda for this whole parish and you never see them from one day to the next.'

'Have we got much further to go?'

'We'll be there soon enough.'

The conversation dried up again and Danny tried to run some of the salient points of the Green Book through his head, sure that he was going to be quizzed about it. He still had no idea what kind of training he was going to get and imagined it would be mostly learning how to fire a gun and maybe how to make bombs from old alarm clocks. He wanted to ask Dempsey but was afraid he would be criticised for not keeping his mouth shut when he had no real idea who Dempsey was.

'See that mountain there,' said Dempsey. 'That's Errigal; I take it you've heard of it?'

'No.'

'Do they not teach you young fellas anything at school these days? That's the highest mountain in Donegal.'

'It looks more like a volcano.'

'A volcano,' laughed Dempsey. 'Well I guess it does a bit. If it is, it hasn't erupted for a while.'

There was a sudden streak of lightning across the sky followed by a roar of thunder as the heavens opened up and the rain began to splatter off the windscreen. The mountains seemed to disappear in a sheet of grey and Danny became nervous as the visibility in front of them became limited to a few yards. Dempsey seemed unperturbed by the sudden change in the weather and carried on at the same reckless speed. 'This is Dunlewy,' said Dempsey. 'It's not far now,' he added, peering through the mist as he turned down a bumpy dirt track. The car drove for a further couple of miles before pulling up along side a rundown cottage.

Danny followed Dempsey into the cottage, which had just one room. Water was dripping on the stone floor from the leaking thatched roof and there was a fusty smell to the place. There was a cluttered table; a few chairs and what looked like camping equipment stacked in a corner under a plastic sheet. A puddle had formed in a pothole in the middle of the floor and the overflow was running down the uneven flagstones back out under the front door.

'Well, what were you expecting,' Dempsey laughed. 'The Ritz?'

'No, but it would be nice if the roof wasn't leaking all over the place.'

'Don't worry about that! You won't be in here much and believe me, you'll be glad to have the roof over your head when you get it.'

'Where's everyone else?'

'They'll be back in a couple of hours. Make yourself at home, there's a camping stove under that lot,' said Dempsey lifting the plastic sheet to reveal all sorts of bits and pieces under a half dozen tightly rolled sleeping bags. 'You can make yourself some coffee and wait for the others to return. I have to get going.'

'Are there any shops where I can get some ciggies?'

'Not unless you want to walk for a couple of miles in that,' said Dempsey standing at the back door. 'Here, take these, I'll get some on the way home.'

Danny stood at the door and watched the car manoeuvre its way back onto the narrow track and disappear in the thick mist. With Dempsey gone, he decided to try and get the stove working. There was coffee, sugar and a bottle of milk on the window ledge. He did not have to smell the milk to know that it was sour. He pulled the plastic sheet away from the rest of equipment.

'What the fuck are you doing?'

'Nothing, just looking for matches to light the stove,' replied Danny, dropping the plastic sheet and turning to the open doorway where a stocky man in full combat gear stood, holding a rifle. 'Matches! What do you think this is? The fucking boy scouts?' barked the man, with an unmistakable Derry accent. 'I take it you're Duffy.'

'Aye, Danny Duffy.'

'I'm soaking,' shouted another voice, as a half a dozen men pushed their way into the cottage to get out of the foul weather. Once inside, the men began taking off their wet fatigues, drying themselves with grubby towels and sheets of newspapers. The cottage was now like a sauna with the smell of sweat and rising perspiration from the men's muddy bodies. 'How's about you?' asked one of the younger men with a Belfast accent as he pulled on a dry white vest, before kicking his saturated boots into the corner. 'Hear you're from the Falls.'

'Aye, Mill Street, just off the Falls Road.'

'Welcome aboard, the name's Peter Kennedy, from Ballymurphy.'

'Danny Duffy.'

Once the men changed out of their wet gear, the door opened and an older man came in dressed in civilian clothes. He scanned the men, who immediately stopped what they were doing. 'Duffy, come out here a minute, I want to speak to ye!'

Danny squeezed his way out into the fresh air. A glimmer of sunlight appeared through the drenched trees and bushes.

The man nodded for Danny to follow him to the back of the cottage where there was a shabby mobile home standing precariously on building blocks. It was dilapidated, but it had some home comforts that were obviously lacking in the cottage, including a cooker attached to a gas bottle, a small sink and even a portable television. There was another man already sitting in the trailer behind a desk covered in maps and coffee- stained cups. An ashtray sat on the shelf with a week's supply of cigar butts in it. The man behind the desk told Danny to take a seat, and subjected him to a barrage of questions about his family's background. Danny found himself being abruptly corrected or reminded of things he had long since forgotten about. After about ten minutes the questions dried up and his interrogator introduced himself as Conor Sweeney, the chief instructor at the training camp and the other man as Pat Welsh. Danny had to stop himself from offering his hand, and none was offered to him.

'Here take these,' said Pat, handing Danny a rifle and a box of ammunition. 'By the time we're finished with you here, you'll be able to shoot the buttons of a Brit's tunic with that thing.'

'How do you like early starts, Duffy?' asked Sweeney.

'I don't mind.'

That night, after a meagre supper of corned beef and a few boiled potatoes, Danny was given a sleeping bag, which was torn open at the bottom, with a zip that only came halfway up the bag. Most of the foam stuffing was missing and it had a horrible mouldy smell. He decided not to say anything, and rolled it out under the draughty window. He was surprised how early the other men settled down to go to sleep. Although he did not have a watch he guessed it couldn't have been more than nine o'clock when the last candle was blown out. He climbed into the flimsy sleeping bag and lay there as the last of the daylight faded from the room. He found it hard to find a comfortable position and the stone floor was unbearably hard against his bones every time he moved. Wide awake, he listened to the wind howling around the building as water continued to drip through the sodden thatched roof.

The room was now completely dark and he could not see his hand in front of his face. He had never experienced a night so black, and the windows at the front of the cottage offered only more darkness. It was not long before his thoughts turned to Kathleen and Agnes, his beautiful sisters, lying in that graveyard. If not for the snoring and grunts of some of the men lying nearby, he could have been lying in his own grave. He eventually fell into a deep sleep with the rifle and box of ammunition lying beside him.

Chapter 23

Errigal

He woke the next morning with a kick to his ribs and the unnerving figure of Doyle screaming at him. 'Get out of your fucking bed, you lazy bastard!' Danny jumped up and immediately reached for his clothes. He had only one leg in his trousers when he was knocked off his feet with a bundle of fatigues and boots thrown at him by Doyle. 'Get them on, you fucking eejit!' Doyle shouted, kicking Danny's sleeping bag into the corner of the room. 'You're no' signing on the fucking dole this morning.'

The other men were already outside and Danny got dressed, shivering when the damp clothes touched his skin. The boots were at least a size too big for him, but he said nothing, tying the laces as tightly as he could. Once dressed, he tried to see what was going on, but there was only a hint of daylight coming from the dirty windows. He could hear the sound of engines roaring and the crunch of gravel under heavy boots. Doyle threw a rucksack at Danny's feet, and ordered him to get out.

Outside, Sweeney was standing in fatigues beside two mud-smeared vans, shouting orders. Three of the men jumped into the back of one of the vans and Danny followed the other three men into the other. He found himself sitting next to Doyle, who deliberately pushed him into the corner. Sweeney got behind the wheel and crunched the gears into reverse, turning the van onto the dirt track like a rally driver. The van was soon bouncing along the road and the smell of stale sweat and petrol fumes were making Danny feel sick.

The other two men were sitting opposite with their heads bowed down, trying to steal another few minutes of sleep.

The van screeched to a halt, and, as soon as the back doors were opened, Doyle pushed Danny out. Sweeney was looking at a map while his second in command, Pat Welsh, began checking the men's backpacks. Danny had no idea what was in his backpack, but the instructor seemed satisfied and refastened the straps. The men gathered around Sweeney who was checking his watch and noting the time in a notebook. 'Right, men! The sooner you get this over with, the sooner you can get breakfast. Doyle, you keep an eye on Duffy.'

'It'll be a pleasure,' said Doyle, with a menacing grin at Danny.

'The last time you all managed this in less than two and a half hours. Let's see if we can get it nearer the two hour mark,' said Sweeney. 'We'll be back here to pick you up at seven hundred hours.'

Danny was still unsure of what he was supposed to do, but at least he worked out that the time was not far off five o'clock in the morning. The men started to march off in single file across the soft bog. It was still too dark to see more then a few yards at a time. Danny was towards the back of the squad, with only the Derry man following as the backmarker. The ground was saturated and every step was soon a struggle for Danny as the soft, wet peat almost sucked the loose-fitting boots from his feet. He tried his best to keep up with the men in front but his feet were soon heavy and the pain in his legs became unbearable. True to form, Doyle shouted abuse and cajoled him to keep up. Danny tried to blank out the pain by thinking of anything other than the next energy draining step. The other men continued their steady pace and they were soon out of sight, much to the annoyance of Doyle. 'You're a fucking embarrassment, Duffy. IRA? It's the fucking Girl Guides you should have joined. Keep fucking moving!'

After about half an hour or so, Danny could no longer endure the pain in his legs and he fell to his knees in the sodden ground. He could hear Doyle's torrent of abuse but he did not care. Doyle was hoarse by the time Danny forced himself back to his feet and began walking again, his limbs now numb. The dawn was beginning to break and he could just about make out the line of men up ahead. The higher ground was less boggy, moving the pain from the back of his legs to his thighs. The grass and heather gave way to loose stones and the ominous sight of the mountain in front of him began to appear with the increasing daylight. He could now clearly make out the line of men in front as they continued their steady ascent. Doyle had long since given up shouting at him; he was struggling with his own aching legs.

By the time they reached the end of the first stage of the climb, Doyle ordered Danny to take a rest. They were almost halfway up and the last of the night had lifted from the mountain. Danny looked at the view across the valley to the mountains on the other side and the lakes below. He then watched Doyle lighting up a cigarette while pissing down the side of the mountain. He had to resist a strong urge that was compelling him to run at the Derry man and push him over the edge.

The next stage of the climb looked more treacherous with loose scree making each step a potential disaster. The main group had now reached the summit. Danny got up and started the next part of the climb without being ordered to do so by Doyle, who was still smoking the life out of another cigarette. In was not long before Danny could feel the blisters on his feet begin to burst as the wet leather of the boots rubbed against his raw skin. He had now reached the stage where he could trade off the pain in his feet with the pain in his legs as one cancelled the other out for short periods. The higher he got the more determined he was to reach the summit. Every so often, he would stop to watch a stone roll down the mountainside, hoping that they would hit Doyle on the way down. He stopped to let the other men pass who were now descending the mountain, greatly amused at the gap Danny had opened up on Doyle. 'You're doing well,' said Kennedy, patting Danny on the back as he passed.

To his relief the final part of the ascent was probably the easiest part and he finally found himself on the summit. On one side he could see out towards the vastness of the Atlantic and a group of islands whose names were unknown to him. On the other side he could see the road he travelled on only yesterday; winding through the valley all the way back to Letterkenny in the distance. Exhausted, he sat on a flat rock and looked at the clouds drifting overhead. At that moment, he did not care about the instructors or how long it took to get back to the bottom.

'What the fuck are you doing, you fucking idiot!' Doyle shouted as he climbed up the last few rocks to where Danny was sitting, untying his wet bootlaces. 'If you take them off you'll never get them back on again!'

'What do you mean?'

'You're feet will be swollen and the only thing that's keeping them from ballooning is those fucking boots.'

'They're too big for me anyway.'

'Take them off if you want, but I'll no' be carrying you back down!'

Danny was not sure whether this was some kind of wind-up; only a short time ago Doyle acted as if he would have quite happily thrown Danny off the mountain. Nevertheless he began to tighten up his laces just in case. Doyle then took out a cigarette and handed one to Danny, who hesitantly took it, expecting it to be pulled away from his hands at the last minute. He could not help but smile in appreciation and was beginning to think that maybe Doyle's bark was worse that his bite.

'What are you looking at?' Doyle grunted as he took an exaggerated draw from his cigarette and put his lighter back into this tunic pocket. 'I gave you a cigarette. It's up to you to bring your own lighter!'

'You bastard!' shouted Danny throwing the cigarette back at Doyle, who let out an exaggerated laugh, lifting the cigarette and putting it back into the packet.

Danny got up and started to make his way back down the mountain; he was determined to get back down before Doyle and make him look as bad as possible to the instructors and the other men. Doyle did not seem to be in any hurry and lay back to enjoy his cigarette.

Going down was a whole different experience from climbing up, and Danny had to be more careful as the steep gradient propelled him down faster than hc rcally wanted to go. Every so often he could feel the scree move under foot and he had to grip on to the larger rocks to keep his feet. The pain that was in his leg muscles moved to the tendons around his knees,. He could see the other men near the bottom of the mountain trekking back over the bog. They were still moving at a fair pace, trying to break their previous record. Danny was just happy that he was well in front of Doyle.

Soon, with the warm sun rising, Danny's shirt was soaked in sweat under the heavy backpack. He had to stop every so often just to give his knees a rest and to check on how far he had to go. Satisfied with his progress, and with no sign of Doyle behind him, he took a few minutes to catch his breath. The others were only specks in the distance, but he now knew he would make it and began to think about the breakfast that would be waiting for him back at the cottage. He forced himself to quicken the pace.

Desperate to impress, Danny was now virtually running down the last stretch of the descent along a narrow path that cut through the bog. He could hear the other men cheering as he hurried down the last few hundred yards to the gravel lay-by. In spite of the pain burning through his boots and the hunger gnawing at his stomach, he could not help but grin when the other men came forward to congratulate him. He was so weak that he slumped down on the gravel, accepting a bottle of orange juice from one man and a cigarette from another.

The men were in good spirits and were laughing and joking amongst themselves. Danny got to his feet as Sweeney came towards him. 'What happened to Doyle?' demanded Sweeney, searching the side of the mountain with his binoculars.

'I don't know.'

'What the fuck do ye mean ye don't know? Ye were with him. He was in yer unit. When did ye last see him?'

'At the top, he was still there when I started to come down.'

'Yer no' telling me that ye left another volunteer on that fucking mountain. Do ye know if he was injured?'

'No.'

'No, he wasn't injured or no, ye don't know if he was injured?'

'No, he wasn't injured, not when I left him … I'm sorry, I should have gone back and checked.'

'Too right ye should have gone back and checked! And that's exactly what yer going to do!'

The feelings of exhilaration at completing the climb were washed clean from Danny's mind in a deluge of humiliation. He forgot about his aching feet, and prepared mentally to head back up the mountain. Sweeney handed him a bottle of water. 'When yer up there, keep an eye on the van, if I start flashing the headlights then ye can come down, even if ye don't find him. Do ye understand?'

'Yes,' replied Danny, his desperate hunger coming back with a vengeance.

'Take these with ye, just in case ye have a problem seeing

this far,' said Sweeney, handing Danny a pair of binoculars. 'Right, off ye go, you'll get something to eat when ye get back.'

'Why don't I take something for Doyle?' asked Danny, his voice almost pleading for some food to take at least one misery away from his tortured mind.

'No, it's too dangerous to eat up there; it could make him violently sick if he's suffering from exposure or exhaustion. Ye better wait until ye get back down.'

Despite his exhaustion, Danny had no option but to turn and face the mountain again. He began the long climb, scanning the lower slopes for Doyle. He never thought he would be so desperate to see that man again, but there was no sign of him. The wet bog was taking his body to agonies that he had never suffered before, but his determination to prove himself was driving him on, each step a personal battle between his will and the excruciating pain in his leg muscles. As he continued to the first ridge, he began to fear the worst for Doyle, remembering his own nervous steps near the summit and how easy it would be to go cascading down the mountainside into the ravine below.

The skies were not looking very favourable as the clouds began to block out the early morning sun. After nearly an hour, he moved onto the rock stage of the climb; at least now he could take a rest on the dry stone and have a much needed drink of water to restore some of the fluid he could feel running down his aching back. It started to rain, and he turned to check on the vans, hoping to see the headlights flashing, but he could only see halfway down the mountain which was now shrouded in a thick fog.

At the car park Doyle appeared through the deluge with a grin on his face. 'Did he fall for it?' he asked Sweeney, who was scanning the mountain with his binoculars, struggling to see much through the downpour and descending mist.

'Aye, and he's still up there. Ye better get something to

eat and dry yerself off.'

The two-way radio in the van began to give off static, *'Sweeney, are you getting this!? It's HQ here. If the men are not already down get them down A.S.A.P! There's a massive thunderstorm blowing in from the Atlantic and it's heading your way.'*

'They are all down except Duffy … over'

'Well, give him the signal to get back down before he's blown off the fucking thing … copy.'

'Roger!'

The radio fell silent. 'If we can't see him, how is he going to see us?' asked one of the men in the back of the van.

'It's getting bad out there,' said Sweeney, switching the van's headlights on and off in the vain hope that they might penetrate the thick fog that had so quickly engulfed the whole valley.

Soaking wet, Danny clung to the edge of a rock near the summit, he was now convinced that Doyle's broken body was lying somewhere in the vagueness below. He decided there was no way he could get back down the mountain as the storm took hold all around him. He tried his best to shelter from the strong winds behind two huge boulders, his drenched body so numb he could not feel the pain in his legs anymore.

The men were arguing amongst themselves as to what their options were. 'Ye better get yerself in the back and get changed, we're going to have to go up and bring him down,' said Sweeney. 'I think we went too far this time.'

'Ah for fuck's sake, if he can't cope with a bit of fucking rain then what use is he going to be?' groaned Doyle, jumping into the back of the van.

Suddenly, there was a ghostly tap on the steamed up window that made Sweeney reach for his handgun. He cautiously rolled the window down a few inches to see Dempsey standing in the deluge, trying to stop himself from being blown away. 'I've got the stores in the car.'

'Right lads, you heard the man, load up the back of the other van.'

'You look like Captain fuckin' Birdseye in that get up,' said Doyle, putting his own lightweight waterproofs on.

'It does the job,' said Dempsey, who was enjoying the opportunity to stand in the rain as the water simply cascaded off his oilskins. 'What are ye still sitting here for? I can't see you thinking it's a good idea to be going up there today.'

'We've already been up this morning. I sent Duffy back up to test his stamina,' said Sweeney.

'Ah, for Christ's sake he's not still up there in this?'

'I'm afraid so, Dempsey,' said Sweeney, clearly embarrassed about the situation. 'We're waiting for a break in this to go up and get him.'

'Well, you'll have a long wait, the forecast is for this to last all day,' said Dempsey. 'Do you fellas not check the weather before you leave in the morning to go climbing mountains?'

'Ye don't get a choice of what weather yer in when the Brits are chasing you across the country,' snapped Sweeney. 'We have to operate in any weather, we're not delivering groceries in a fisherman's fancy dress outfit,' he spat, getting his dig at Dempsey, whom he saw as a civilian and not a true volunteer.

'I'm just concerned about the young fella. There's no' need to get nasty,' said Dempsey, the rain still bouncing off his waterproofs.

'What are you concerned about, you hardly know him,' said Doyle, always eager to get involved in an argument.

'That lad volunteered a couple of weeks after the Brits

killed his sister with a plastic bloody bullet, and you fucking lot are tryin' to kill him.' said Dempsey, turning back to get into his own car. 'He's also Eugene Tierney's nephew.'

There was a heavy silence in the van for a few minutes as the wipers battled frantically against the torrent of water being thrown at the windscreen. The back of the van was a heady mixture of cigarette smoke and the men's pungent body odour. 'Right, Kennedy get changed, you're going back up with me,' ordered Sweeney, who had already started to pull on his own waterproofs. 'Doyle, I'll take one of the radios and try and keep ye advised as to what's going on. That's if it works in this fucking monsoon.'

By the time the two lead men of the rescue team reached the summit, the wind and rain was virtually blowing horizontally across the face of the mountain. The ground was slippery and they moved tentatively along the edge until they reached a wider section where they could stand without fear of being blown off the ridge. 'Over here,' shouted Kennedy, kneeling over Danny, who was now semi-conscious and shaking violently. Sweeney began to remove Danny's wet clothes and rub his body vigorously with a towel. 'How bad is he?' Kennedy asked, trying to use his own body to shield Danny from the foul weather.

'I think he's got hypothermia. We'll need to get him down quick or we're goin' to lose him!'

'Fucking hell, is there anything I can do?'

'Rub this on his chest, it will help his circulation, and I'll change his wet clothes. If we don't get him dry he'll be dead by the time we get him halfway down this damn mountain.'

'God, I never thought he'd get any where near the top again,' said Kennedy, rubbing the deep heat cream into Danny's chest.

'It's amazing what the human body can endure when it has to.'

‘There’s none of this cream left,’ shouted Kennedy, rubbing the last of it into Danny’s arms.

‘Well, open your jacket and keep him warm with your body,’ shouted Sweeney, battling with the wind as he stretched a waterproof sheet across Danny and Kennedy; using heavy stones to hold it in place. Danny was now spluttering and coughing, which Sweeney took as a good sign, but he still had to get him out of his wet clothes and into dry ones. With the help of Kennedy and the protection of the waterproof shelter he began to change Danny’s clothes for the dry ones he had brought up in his rucksack. Kennedy had already removed Danny’s boots, before Sweeney could stop him. ‘We’ll not get them on again.’

‘Does it matter, he’s no’ fit to walk down anyway. Should we no’ give him some whiskey or something?’

‘No, that’s the last thing you give someone in this condition,’ explained Sweeney, buttoning up the dry shirt, while Kennedy quickly put Danny’s arms into the waterproof jacket.

‘Well, why do those big dogs carry those barrels of brandy around their necks?’

‘God knows, but alcohol accelerates hypothermia … Oh, for fuck’s sake,’ cried Sweeney as he pulled off one of Danny’s socks with some raw skin still attached to it. ‘Kennedy, can ye go into my backpack, and get me some lint bandages… and don’t let them get fucking wet!’

While Sweeney carefully bandaged Danny’s swollen feet, the rain stopped completely, and the wind began to die down as the clouds passed over the mountains to the east and into Northern Ireland. A clear blue sky appeared over the Atlantic and the island of Arranmore reappeared on the cleansed horizon. There’s no rhyme or reason to the weather in this place, thought Sweeney, as he and Kennedy lifted Danny between them. Danny was now conscious and smiled as he saw the rainbow that appeared over the ridge of the mountain. 'Paddy Two Shoes,' he whispered in his stupor.

They began to descend with cautious steps on the slippery scree until they were met by the rest of the men, who took turns carrying Danny down the rest of the way. After nearly three hours hard slog, they reached the bottom of the mountain. All the men were now totally exhausted.

For the next few weeks Danny recovered in Letterkenny Hospital, Dempsey telling the doctor that Danny was his nephew and he had got lost walking in the hills. The story was accepted without question or obvious suspicion by the hospital staff; if they did suspect anything they did not show it. Dempsey had become fond of Danny and easily took to his role as surrogate uncle, paying his 'nephew' regular visits until he was well enough to leave. It was Dempsey who told Danny about the trick that the men had played on him and how it all backfired.

On the day Danny was discharged from the hospital, Dempsey picked him up and drove him back to the cottage. When they arrived, Sweeney was standing at the front door.

'You need to get that exhaust looked at, Dempsey. I could hear ye coming for fucking miles.'

'If you pay for it, I'll get it fixed. Hope you've got the kettle on.'

'You've no time for tea. Take that,' said Sweeney, handing Dempsey a piece of paper and some money.

'Fuck, ye want me to go back into Letterkenny?'

'We must have that stuff today; supplies are running low here.'

'Why don't I just nick into to the shops in Gweedore and get them,' said Dempsey looking at the list.

'I've told ye, Dempsey, we can't buy local. It's too risky.'

'Fuck,' moaned Dempsey, shaking his head and getting back into his car. 'Why did nobody phone this morning when

I *was* in Letterkenny?'

While Dempsey reversed back down the gravel path, Danny stood with his hands in his pockets staring at Sweeney, who he thought was deliberately ignoring him. He wanted an apology, but he did not expect to get one from the likes of Sweeney.

'We are glad to have you back, Duffy. The rest of the men are out training. They'll be back soon. There'll be no more horsing around from the men; you've proved yerself well enough. I've left a sleeping bag and some other things for you. Make yerself some tea. I need to go to Derry for a few days. I'll speak to you later.'

Danny just nodded, but said nothing. He waited for Sweeney to leave before he ventured into the cottage. In the corner he found a brand new sleeping bag and a set of neatly folded fatigues. He picked up an Armalite rifle that was standing against the wall. He as surprised how light it was.

He lit a cigarette and sat beside the window and waited.

After an hour or so, he saw the first of the men appear at the top of the ridge; it was Pat Welsh, at least ten yards in front of the next man, Ownie Coyle; both Donegal men and used to the hills. They looked shattered. Danny saw that the last man over the ridge was Doyle, struggling to keep up. Danny took the pistol and put it in his trouser belt, then lifted the rifle, before hurrying out of the cottage.

He waited at the bottom of the hill behind a cluster of gorse bushes as the men passed one by one on their way back to the cottage. He did not have to wait long before he heard Doyle panting and coughing. Danny suddenly emerged from the bushes and knocked Doyle to the ground with a single blow of the rifle butt. He then put the rifle to the back of the Derry man's head. 'Move and I'll blow yer fucking brains out, ye fat bastard,' he shouted, stamping his heavy boot on Doyle's back to stop him from getting up. 'Duffy, for fuck's sake,' pleaded Doyle, his head starting to clear, and quickly recognising the owner of the threatening voice. 'It was part of the training to make ye go back up again. The same thing happened to me, for fuck's sake.'

'Get up,' said Danny, lifting Doyle's rifle and slinging it over his shoulder.

Doyle slowly got to his feet.

'I was only…'

'Shut tae fuck up! Take that jacket off!' ordered Danny, giving Doyle a push with the butt of the rifle.

The other men were busy changing out of their sodden fatigues and boots, when the door of the cottage abruptly opened with a kick. They instinctively grabbed their rifles and revolvers as Doyle came crashing into the room, falling onto the hard slate floor. 'Ye forgot that fat bastard,' said Danny as the men laughed at Doyle, who lay on the floor with nothing on but his pants and muddy boots.

Chapter 24

The Romper Room

The night was bitterly cold, and the windscreen was continually freezing over with Danny's anxious breathing. The engine was running, but the old car's heating system was broken and the windscreen wipers looked like they were about to stick to the smears of ice crystallizing on the glass. He had been waiting for over ten minutes, looking up every so often at the corrugated windows of a burnt out house. A drunk man staggered across the road, seemingly oblivious to the icy wind blowing through his loose-fitting jacket. Danny kept a close eye on the cars that were passing down the street, but there was no sign of any military activity. He listened on his two-way radio to the coded messages being passed between the barracks in Ballymurphy and the soldiers out on patrol. He could understand most of what was being relayed, noting down any new code to check what it might mean later. He had to keep the side window down to see out properly and pulled the collar of his coat tightly around his neck The cold was unbearable and he tried to get the heater to work again, before giving up and lighting a cigarette, savouring each draw of nicotine before blowing the smoke onto his numb fingers in a vain attempt to keep them warm.

The scattered candles flickered shadows around the walls. Fergal Gallagher threw the butt of his cigarette in the ashes of the fire and looked up at Mickey Flynn.

'How sure are ye that he'll be there tonight?'

‘The information is from a senior member of the UVF. They want him and Burrows taken out as much as we do. Remember, they’ll be armed.’

‘There wouldn’t be much fun in it if they weren’t,’ Fergal sniggered, lifting his revolver from under his sleeping-bag. ‘What’s the new boy’s name?’

‘Danny Duffy, Eugene Tierney’s nephew. He’s a bit green, but I’m told he will be sound.’

‘Eugene’s nephew? Not the fucking boy that was going to become a priest?’

‘No, the younger one.’

‘Does he know what he’s to do tonight?’

‘All he knows is that he’ll be your driver and back-up if needed. I thought I’d let you tell him the details.’

When Fergal got into the passenger seat, Danny rolled up the window and put the car into gear. Fergal wiped the condensation from his side of the window with the sleeve of his jacket. ‘How’s about ye?’ he said. ‘Ye know how to get to the sawmill factory on Selby Road?’

‘Aye.’

‘We’ll head up there and I’ll fill ye in on the way. Do ye smoke?’

‘Aye.’

‘Well, give us one of yer ciggies, I’m sick of smoking roll-ups.’

‘Where’s Mickey?’

‘Don’t worry about him; he’s no use when it comes to anything like this. All talk and no action.’

After a couple of thuds on the dashboard from Fergal, the heater started working and the windows began to clear up. They then drove around the city, avoiding road blocks, before turning back towards the top end of Selby Road, where they waited not far from the entrance to a disused factory. Danny could feel his heart pounding against the heavy metal of his revolver. Fergal sat quietly smoking. The heater struggled to keep the windscreen clear.

Danny could feel every breath rising in his lungs, and was afraid to speak in case Fergal detected the nerves in his voice. He was glad when Fergal turned on the radio, tuning into country hour at the *Grand Ole Opry*, with Johnny Cash and June Carter already halfway through singing ***Jackson***. Despite its grand title, the show was being broadcast from a dingy studio in West Belfast. Danny briefly looked at Fergal, whose eyes were closed as he mouthed the lyrics.

*

The derelict factory hid a sinister secret in its backyard behind the abandoned shelves of warped floorboards and broken wooden sheds covered in ivy. It was an old concrete bomb shelter, built during the Second World War for the factory's workforce. The shelter was now being used by a squad of the UVF and was a notorious 'romper room' to which many unfortunate Catholics were brought for interrogation. In Belfast the word 'interrogation' had long since been accepted as a euphemism for torture and death.

Until now, Jamie Morrison had never attended an interrogation or taken part in the rampant abuse of those unfortunates lifted from the streets by loyalist death squads. Jamie was now collecting intelligence on IRA operations for Major Moorcroft, who in turn was providing protection, allowing the UVF to operate without fear of being arrested by the security forces. Jamie would normally instruct 'Bulldog' Brown to bring back any information that might be useful from the interrogations. Most of the time the victims had next to nothing to divulge, and the interrogation quickly turned into a sadistic orgy of violence. At times even Bulldog had to turn away at the horrors being perpetrated on some captured civilians, who were unlucky enough to be of the wrong religion and in the wrong place at the wrong time.

When Jamie arrived with Bulldog, a naked body was already lying in a pool of its own blood and urine. Boris Kingsley, the leader and main interrogator, was covered in blood. His cousin, 'Ginger' Burrows, was holding the victim's arms as Boris turned to look at Jamie and Bulldog.

'Is he dead?' asked Jamie.

Boris kicked the limp body to see if there was any life left in it to torture. The victim groaned and spurted out a mouthful of blood. 'He's still got plenty of Fenian blood in him yet.'

Jamie shook his head when he saw that the victim was not much older than William. He turned and nodded to Bulldog, who immediately stepped forward and put two bullets into the young man's head.

'What the fuck,' shouted Boris, pointing his bloody knife at Bulldog. 'We weren't fucking finished with him.'

'Calm down, Boris,' said Jamie, trying to impose his authority where any sense of authority did not exist. 'He was as good as dead anyway. You wouldn't have got much more out of him in that state.'

'Fuck, we never got anything out of him anyway,' laughed Boris, wiping a bloody hand down the concrete wall.

'You did this to him for nothing?'

'What do ye mean, for nothing?'

'You're going too fucking far with all this shit. You're supposed to find out what they know, not just butcher them.'

'Fuck you two,' shouted Boris, staring at the revolver in Bulldog's hand, and taking a step towards it.

Jamie nodded to Bulldog that it was time to get out of there.

Once outside, Bulldog put his revolver back down the back of his trousers and heaved a sigh of relief as he lit a cigarette and looked at Jamie, who was still in a state of shock. Jamie knew how brutal their interrogations had become, but he had never seen blood-lust like that before. The campaign of terror being waged against the Catholic community was now beginning to terrorise many within the loyalist paramilitaries themselves; now he knew why. He noticed that his hand was shaking uncontrollably, and wondered if Moorcroft had any idea, or even cared what cruelty was being carried out on behalf of Her Majesty's Government.

'I had to shoot the poor bastard,' said Bulldog, getting into the car. 'There's a limit to everything.'

'Let's get to hell out of here. We don't know what those crazy fuckers will do next,' said Jamie as Bulldog reversed out of the lane onto Selby Road.

*

Danny handed Fergal another cigarette. The streets were quiet and only a few cars passed as they waited, chain-smoking. The radio was still playing old country songs and Fergal tapped his fingers on the dashboard as he stared up the street. He suddenly turned off the radio and wiped the inside of the windscreen. 'That's Kingsley and Burrows coming out now.'

Danny could see two rather undefined figures walking towards them on the other side of the road. He was surprised that Fergal had even noticed them, never mind been able to say who they were. Fergal began to check the barrel of his revolver and issued orders to Danny to drive slowly towards the two figures in the distance. As soon as they were within a couple of hundred feet, Danny put his foot down and drove at speed across the road, bumping the car up onto the pavement.

Fergal immediately jumped out of the passenger's side and began to fire into Burrows, who had only managed to get his gun halfway out of his jacket when the first bullets began to rip into his body. Danny shouted at Fergal to get back in the car when he saw a crowd of men running down the road towards them. Ignoring Danny's pleas, Fergal turned his gun on Kingsley and was about to let him have what was left in the gun's chambers when it jammed. Kingsley, who had frozen in the headlights of the car, saw his chance and turned to run. He only got a few yards when he slipped on the icy pavement. He began to plead for his life. 'Don't shoot me for fuck's sake. I've never hurt anyone in me life!'

When Kingsley tried to get to his feet, Fergal hit him on the side of the head with the butt of his revolver. 'Get out here and shoot the fucker,' he screamed at Danny, while still trying to get his own revolver to fire. 'Shoot the bastard!'

'Fuck!' muttered Danny, reluctantly getting out of the car. He stood over Kingsley, holding his gun with both hands.

'Don't shoot me, son … I've got two little ones at home. You've got the wrong man.'

'Shoot the fucking bastard,' shouted Fergal, before grabbing the revolver from Danny.

Kingsley put his hands to his face. Fergal fired two bullets into his body and one to his head. 'Let's get tae fuck out of here!' he shouted, pulling Danny back towards the car.

Danny got into the driver's seat and put his hand towards the ignition. 'Fuck, fuck!'

'What the fuck's wrong? Get us out of here!' shouted Fergal, firing into the mob of eight heavily-built men charging down the middle of the street towards them. The men stopped, but only for a moment. One of them fired back at the car, before urging the others to follow him.

'Duffy, get us tae fuck out of here!'

'The keys, I can't find the keys,' shouted Danny, frantically searching his pockets, until he saw them lying on the pavement beside Kingsley's body. He got out and grabbed the keys. A brick bounced off the front bonnet as he got back into the driver's seat and started the engine.

Fergal banged the dashboard. 'Move it. Fucking move it!'

Danny drove off the pavement, but immediately lost control and skidded into a parked van. The bumpers became ensnared. He desperately tried to reverse. The wheels slipped on the icy road. A bullet ricocheted off a lamppost, only feet away. Danny put his foot down on the accelerator and rammed the parked van. With Fergal screaming abuse at him and the mob almost upon them, he slammed the gears back into reverse. The bumper broke free just as the driver's window was smashed with a crowbar. Fergal pulled Danny aside and fired, taking half the attacker's head off. With blood splattered over his face, Danny drove into the middle of the road. Bricks and bottles smashed into the back of the car. He put his foot down as far as the accelerator would go. The mob chased after the car, screaming abuse. More shots were fired as Danny turned down the nearest street.

'That was fucking close,' shouted Fergal, lighting up a cigarette and turning to stare at Danny. 'Why didn't ye shoot the fat bastard? If yer a bottle merchant, then yer no use to me, Duffy.'

'No one told me I had to kill anyone. I thought I was only your driver.'

'You're a volunteer … You do what your fucking ordered to do … You better slow down! We don't want to get a pull. If we get stopped, the army will hand us over to those crazy bastards.'

Danny was still trying to take in everything that had happened. He continued along Clifton Street, before heading north along the Crumlin Road towards the Ardoyne.

'I think I might have cracked me fucking kneecap on the car door,' groaned Fergal, as the adrenaline subsided and the pain in his knee became unbearable.

'Will I take ye to the hospital?'

'Are ye fucking daft in the head? That's the first place the Brits will be when they hear what's happened. Only take someone to hospital if they look like they're dying and even then just dump them at the front door and get to hell out of there. Mickey will get someone to look at it tomorrow. Just get me to the house so I can lie down for a while.'

Once back in the Ardoyne, Danny parked the car around the corner from the derelict house. He helped Fergal out of the car and along the lane to the backyard. Fergal groaned every time he put any weight on his left knee. The yard was in darkness.

Once inside, Danny helped Fergal up the stairs. 'I'll go and find an emergency chemist and get ye some painkillers…'

'Never mind the fucking chemist, just stay here. I'll be all right in the morning,' insisted Fergal, slowly getting down and sitting on his sleeping bag.

'How bad is it?'

'It's fucking bad enough. See that tobacco tin over there? Bring it here,' demanded Fergal, lighting a wick that was sticking out of a mountain of multi-coloured wax. 'Duffy, go downstairs and you'll find a kettle under the sink; make us a pot of tea. There's a packet of tea and some sugar in a biscuit tin at the back of the cupboard above the cooker.'

Fergal carefully opened the tin box. He was relieved to see that there was still one primed syringe left. He listened for a moment to Danny rummaging around downstairs, before tying a belt around his thigh and injecting the needle into the side of his leg. After a few seconds he felt a rush of heat invade his body. He withdrew the needle and put the syringe back into its tin. The room began to spin around with the flickering shadows dancing on the walls. He lay back as the heroin began to numb the pain in his knee and the turmoil in his mind.

The following morning, Danny woke in a state of confusion. His body ached after a miserable night sleeping on the floor. He stretched himself and got to his feet, suddenly remembering the three men that Fergal had shot. The thought made his heart race and he picked up the cigarette packet at his feet, quickly throwing it in the corner when he remembered he had smoked the last one the night before. He decided he would have to settle for one of Fergal's roll-ups.

He could barely make out Fergal's face in the scattered light and went over to see if he was awake. For a moment Danny thought Fergal was actually dead, his thin lips looked blue against his ashen grey skin. Fergal then began to cough and splutter before opening his vacant looking eyes. 'Who the hell are you staring at?'

'I was just checking you're still alive,' replied Danny, slightly startled. 'How's the leg?'

'It's killing me. Make me a cup of tea.'

'Have ye any roll-ups left?'

'I left them in the car.'

'But I gave ye your tobacco tin last night.'

'What are ye talking about? I don't have a tobacco tin … oh, that old thing. I keep me money in that,' said Fergal, checking that the tin was still under his sleeping bag. 'So don't let me see ye anywhere near it!'

'All right, but ye don't have to be aggressive.'

‘Who’s being fucking aggressive? Anyway, get me a cup of tea and get the tobacco from the car. I’m dying for a smoke. I still can’t believe you didn’t shoot that fucker last night. If ye weren’t Eugene’s nephew…’

‘I’m sorry. I won’t let you down again.’

‘Ye fucking better not.’

‘I won’t,’ said Danny, picking up the two cups from the floor, before going down the narrow stairs to the dingy kitchenette. While the kettle was coming to the boil he went around the back of the house to get Fergal’s tobacco and cigarette papers. He was shocked at the state of the car. The driver’s windscreen was gone, and the front bumper was completely ripped off. There were at least four bullet holes in the bodywork. It looked like an abandoned wreck. Deciding it was not a good idea to be seen near it in broad daylight; he went to a nearby shop and bought a packet of cigarettes instead.

Fergal was now in excruciating pain, and, after leaving him some cigarettes, Danny went to get Mickey. There had been a thaw during the night and the pavements were now wet instead of icy. He was hungry, unlike Fergal, who seemed to live on fresh air and roll-ups. He hoped Mickey would have something decent to eat.

At Mickey’s safe-house, Danny climbed over the garden fence and chapped the back door. Mickey, spatula in hand, let him in.

‘Where’s Fergal?’

‘Back at the flat, he’s done his knee in. He needs to see a doctor. Can you get one?’

‘Sure, that’s not a problem. How bad is he?’

‘Bad enough, he’s in so much pain he can hardly walk.’

‘You did a good job last night. It’s been on the morning news.’

'You mean, Fergal. He shot the three of them. Who were they anyway?'

'The fat, bald guy was the main target, an evil bastard called Boris Kingsley. He was head of a gang of UVF butchers. The other two were just as bad. They were a bunch of fucking psychos, who didn't care who they murdered. Even the UVF will be celebrating that those fuckers are getting measured for wooden boxes … How did ye get on with Gallagher?'

'I don't think he likes me much. He didn't tell me who these guys were, or that I had to shoot anyone.'

'That's just the way he is … he's the same with everyone … Anyway, I thought you said Fergal shot them?'

'He did, I couldn't do it. Kingsley was lying on the ground pleading for his life. He was going on about his kids and that we had the wrong man. Fergal's gun jammed and he started screaming at me to shoot Kingsley. I just couldn't pull the trigger. Fergal took the gun off me and put three bullets in him.'

'Kingsley's not got fucking kids.'

'Well how was I to know?'

'Never mind Danny, it's not easy to kill someone. Not when they're begging for their life in front of ye.'

'It would have been easier if I knew what kind of bastard he was … That's all I'm saying.'

'Gallagher should have told you, the fucker. He's always been a bit weird, but he's got worse ever since yer uncle was killed.'

'What did he have to do with it?'

'They were on the same operation when they were ambushed by the SAS. I was in the Shamrock Bar a few weeks after it had happened, when big Peter Leeson brought up Eugene getting killed, and all. I don't think he meant anything by it, but Fergal was on the whiskey, and took it all the wrong way. I am sure he thought Leeson was blaming him for leaving Eugene to save his own skin. Anyway, Gallagher went off his head and smashed a pint tumbler into the poor bastard's face, before kicking him unconscious. If the lads in the bar hadn't stopped it, he would have killed him. There was still a big piece glass sticking out of Leeson's forehead when they took him away in the ambulance.'

'Fuck, and that's the guy I've got to work with.'

'He'll be alright once he gets to know you. Being Eugene's nephew will help. Yer uncle was his hero. Anyway, enough said, I'll need to go and get him a doctor. You go back and give him these; they're strong painkillers I use for me back. They might help.'

The smell of bacon turned Danny's gaze towards what was on Mickey's plate. Mickey laughed, 'Ye only have to ask, ye know,' he said, getting up to put a few more rashers onto the hot frying pan and putting the kettle back on the greasy gas stove. 'Do ye want a couple of eggs as well?'

'Aye, if ye don't mind, Mickey. I haven't eaten a thing since yesterday morning, and that was just a bowl of cornflakes.'

The radio was crackling away in the background. Mickey was anxiously waiting for a news update. He helped himself to one of Danny's cigarettes just as the news report confirmed what they already knew; the Provisional IRA claimed responsibility for the three killings.

With a burp and gulp of tea, Danny finished his breakfast and went back with some bacon and bread to make Fergal something to eat. Mickey went to get the doctor.

Danny had completed his first operation as a volunteer, although he wasn't sure he would get to go on another one.

Chapter 25

Gun Running

Mickey Flynn threw another couple of logs of turf on the faltering fire and lit a cigarette. There were three other men in the remote cottage. Cahil Doherty stood by the window, wearing a parka jacket, with a Belgian FN semi-automatic rifle over his shoulder. In his pocket were fresh orders from his own CO in Derry. No one else in the room knew what was in the papers. The two other men in the cottage, Michael Rodgers and Dermot O'Donnell, were members of his unit, and did not even know who they were waiting for. They also had rifles and held them in a relaxed manner, confident that the isolation of the cottage was unknown to the Irish authorities as an IRA safe house. 'What the hell is keeping them?' snapped Doherty, turning away from the window. 'Can ye trust them if they've been stopped?'

'Don't worry, Cahil, they're good lads. They know the score. Relax. They'll be here soon,' said Mickey, getting up from the fire to pour himself a whiskey from a half bottle he had brought along.

'For fuck's sake!' cried Mickey, as Doherty knocked the glass from his hand.

'You're on duty! No drinking.'

'For God's sake, man. I was only having…'

'Quiet!' One of the other men shouted in a broad Donegal accent. 'There's someone coming!'

Mickey sat back down by the fire as the three other men

took up positions at the door and the windows. 'What are they driving?' asked Doherty, in a forced whisper.

'I don't know. They were going to nick a car today.'

'Flynn, come to the window, there's a red van pulling up.'

*

Fergal took his revolver from under the passenger seat. 'I don't like this, keep the engine running.'

'What's up?'

'I don't know, back off a bit.'

The van slowly reversed, its lights slipping down, to rest at the front door of the cottage. The front door suddenly opened. Mickey Flynn appeared and walked nervously towards the van.

'It's Mickey, but I still don't like it,' said Fergal.

'Boys, it's me. What's up?'

Danny rolled down the window as Mickey approached the van. 'Come in, fellas. It's okay; the lads are here.'

Danny got out, while Fergal kept a cautious eye on the open cottage door.

'You weren't followed or anything?'

'No, we didn't see anything,' said Danny.

Fergal was now cautiously looking at the shadows near the cottage windows as he got out of the van, putting the revolver in his coat pocket. 'We got lost for a while. Who's here?'

'Come in, for God's sake!' Doherty shouted when he appeared at the half-open door.

There were no friendly greetings from those inside, who were anxiously standing at their positions. 'You weren't followed, were you?' Doherty asked.

'No! We never seen another soul for miles,' said Fergal.

'Dermott, take the walkie-talkie and drive up to the crossroads. Keep a look out for anything unusual,' ordered Doherty, taking a chair by the fire and gesturing to Danny and Fergal to take a seat. 'Right, lads, you don't know why you're here, but I'm going to tell you in a minute.' Doherty nodded to Mickey and the Donegal man. They went in to the kitchen and began to bring in a half-dozen metal boxes, placing them in the middle of the room.

'What's that?' Fergal asked, as he lit a cigarette from the fire.

'Guns,' Doherty said, grinning with an air of satisfaction as he opened one of the boxes and took out an Armalite AR 15 rifle, and threw it over to Fergal to catch. He then passed a Browning 9mm Automatic pistol to Danny. 'These were smuggled in a few days ago, and we need to get half of them to Derry and the rest to Belfast. That's why you fellas are here; we want you to get them over the border.'

'Christ's sake, man, are ye serious?' Fergal said, still admiring the rifle.

'I'm deadly serious. Flynn has assured us that you two are sound.'

'Sure, sure we are!' said Fergal, putting the rifle down to check out what else was in the boxes.

While Danny and Fergal looked at the cache of weapons, Doherty went on to give details of the plan to get them into the North. By the time he had finished talking; one of his lieutenants had already changed the registration plates on the stolen van.

Mickey had remained quiet throughout the instructions and looked on edge as he watched the weapons being passed around. This was the first time he had been asked to put himself at risk and the strain was starting to show.

The weapons and ammunition were loaded into the back of the van; their weight became obvious on the back tyres. The wind was still whistling through the scrawny trees and out into the moors. 'Do you think the van will make it?' Mickey asked. 'If you get a puncture then…'

'Stop fucking worrying, Flynn. It will make it alright,' said Doherty. 'If there's a problem then you can take a few boxes of ammo.'

'It will be all right,' agreed Fergal. 'If it breaks down we will just nick another van.'

'Right ye better get going,' said Doherty, slapping Fergal on the back. 'Remember, keep yer heads and get these guns through. *Slán go fóill.*'

Danny drove the van along the meandering back roads, towards the border on the outskirts of Derry. He was concentrating on the back of Mickey's old Ford Escort, which was making sure the road up ahead was clear. Fergal lit a cigarette and handed one to Danny. 'Can't be long to go now,' he said, rolling down the window to get some fresh air to clear his head.

'We passed a sign back there; we should be pulling up soon. These roads are murder. Look! He's turning off.'

The van followed the car for about a mile, over a bumpy dirt track, and then slowly up to a two-storey farmhouse in the middle of nowhere.

They stopped a hundred yards from the house and waited for Mickey to check everything was in order. The morning sun was struggling to lift itself over the mountains to the east.

A light came on from one of the upstairs rooms. Mickey stood impatiently at the front door, nervously looking around. They watched the door open. A chubby man, in his late fifties, came out. Mickey waved for them to drive up to the byre at the side of the house.

Danny reversed the van. Inside the byre was an old tractor covered in bird droppings. With the morning light flooding into the byre, panicked hens appeared from every nook and cranny and scattered around the yard in fits of hysteria as the farmer's sheepdog tried to round them up. A cockerel viewed the chaos from the safety of the loft. It crowed its morning call as if to show who was boss. Fergal laughed as he tried to kick one of the fleeing hens.

'Don't be kicking the birds, for fuck's sake,' said the farmer.

'Sorry, boss.'

'Anyway, the name's Brian Kennedy,' said the farmer, sticking out his massive hand.

'Fergal, and this is me right hand man, Danny.' They all shook hands, before getting down to business. Even the hens had calmed down.

The tractor was not as bad as it had first looked. It started after a few roars and a couple of puffs of black diesel fumes, which cleared out the last few hens that were still in hiding. The farmer released the handbrake and the tractor slowly rolled into the yard towards the van. Mickey was already unloading the boxes of ammunition. The tractor had a large metal storage box at the back and once it was alongside the van, they began to fill it with the weapons.

When the job was done, the farmer invited them into the farmhouse for some breakfast. They were surprised and glad to see that there were four plates already on the big kitchen table, with bacon, sausages and eggs. They washed their hands and sat down to eat. The farmer poured the tea and began to tell them of his life farming on the border, and how it was a great place to be when it came to making money. He told with a boastful laugh of how, during the recent foot and mouth outbreak, he managed to get compensation from both the Irish and the British governments for the same cattle. As he said, he was neither a socialist nor a capitalist, but a realist. He then mentioned his wife in hushed whispers as though he was afraid of her. 'She's not one for strangers, but she knows her duty.'

They finished their breakfast with a second cup of strong tea. Suddenly the farmer slumped over his empty plate. The three other men looked at each other. 'What the hell's going on here?' said Fergal, getting to his feet. 'He's not dropped dead on us?'

'No, he's still breathing,' said Mickey, also getting to his feet. 'See if you can wake him up. I don't like this.'

After a few seconds hesitation, Fergal gave the farmer a nudge, but Kennedy simply turned his head to the side and began snoring. 'I think he's in a coma,' said Fergal, turning to look at the other two. 'Can any of ye drive that fucking tractor?'

'He'll be awake in a couple of minutes,' interrupted a coarse female voice, as the door opened and the farmer's wife came in through the kitchen carrying two tin buckets of fresh creamy milk, which she poured into an urn. 'He has a rare sleeping disorder. It only lasts for about five minutes. There's no point trying to wake him until he's able to wake himself,' she added, leaving the kitchen as directly as she had entered it.

'A sleeping disorder,' laughed Fergal. 'How did he get into the Provos?'

'He's not in the Provos,' said Mickey. 'I don't even think he wants a united Ireland, with all his scams.'

'What the hell are ye on about?' demanded Fergal, turning to look at Mickey.

'We pay him to let us smuggle guns through the border. And that's all he's interested in.'

After a few more minutes, the farmer began to grunt and

splutter, moving his head violently. He then sat up as though nothing had happened. 'Right, let's get this stuff over that border before the rest of the country is awake! I'll meet you here,' he said, pointing to a hand drawn map of the local roads, before handing it to Mickey.

When they neared the border checkpoint, Mickey gave the signal for Danny to pull into the side road and to wait for the agreed fifteen minutes before attempting to follow.

Danny and Fergal got out of the van and climbed halfway up a hillock to watch the Escort approach the checkpoint, which was manned by at least a dozen armed soldiers and a couple of RUC officers. The RUC men were there to provide the soldiers with the necessary intelligence on known IRA men. With the exception of a couple of low-ranking officers, the soldiers were nervous looking young men in their late teens and early twenties.

They crouched down among the tangled bracken and thorny gorse bushes, and watched the soldiers order Mickey out of his car. Fergal smiled to himself as he watched them open the boot, before one of the soldiers lifted out a set of golf clubs. 'The fly old bastard, we should have thought of something like that,' he whispered to Danny. The bag was given a cursory examination and put back in to the boot. 'He's getting through,' said Fergal, giving Danny a pat on the back.

After the agreed fifteen minutes had passed, Danny slowly pulled back onto the road and switched on the radio. Fergal was tapping the dashboard to the beat of "Hit Me with Your Rhythm Stick", turning the music up loud as Danny slowed to a stop in front of the barrier.

'Fergal, can ye turn that down?' said Danny, before opening his window to speak to the approaching soldier.

'Ah, leave it,' said Fergal, pulling Danny's hand away from the volume control and continuing to bang his other hand in time with the music. The soldier stood a foot away from the van with his rifle crossed over his arms. He looked unsure of himself; even a little nervous. 'Where are you two heading to?'

'We're going home to Belfast,' replied Danny over the noise of the radio.

One of the RUC officers who had been standing nearby came briskly up behind the soldier. 'Turn that fucking thing down and get out the car!'

'Is there a problem, officer?' asked Danny, before turning off the radio and getting out of the car.

'You as well, get out the car!'

'Ah, get a hold of yerself; I'm getting out,' sneered Fergal. The RUC officer then took a couple of steps back to where his colleague was standing and allowed the soldier to continue with the questioning, while two other soldiers began to search the van. The young corporal then looked carefully at the driving licence Danny produced from his jacket pocket, while another soldier carried out a cursory body search of Fergal. The corporal handed the driving licence to one of the RUC officers, who looked at it briefly before handing it back to Danny, who was now also being searched. 'Where are ye coming from at this time in the morning?' the corporal asked.

'We were at me cousin's wedding in Donegal. We're on our way home,' replied Danny. 'Is this going to take long? I've got me work to go to this morning.'

'Where in Donegal was the wedding?' asked the RUC officer over the soldier's shoulder.

'A place called Gweedore.'

'When was the wedding?'

'The day before last,' replied Danny.

Fergal began to laugh.

'What are you laughing at?' demanded the RUC officer.

'He's still a bit drunk, officer,' explained Danny, with a shrug of his shoulders. 'He's an eejit at the best of times,' he added, with a panicked look towards Fergal.

The other two soldiers had finished searching the van and indicated to the RUC officers that it was clean. Another car pulled up behind the van and the barrier slowly lifted. 'Can we go now, for Christ's sake,' Fergal sneered, opening the passenger door. The corporal, who was in charge of the search turned to the RUC officer who simply nodded his consent. They got back into the van and drove off. Danny turned and looked at Fergal.

'What was that all about?'

'What? We got through didn't we? If they had time to think, then they'd have wondered why we don't have any luggage with us. Who goes to a wedding dressed like this?'

Up ahead, the Escort waited in a lay-by and only pulled onto the road when Mickey saw the van come over the brae in his wing mirror. The two vehicles then turned down a dirt track for a mile or so, before coming to a stop at dung-smeared cattle grates. There was a semi-derelict building a few hundred yards ahead. Mickey got out first and opened the gate, as the three men squelched through a quagmire of mud and dung until they reached the barn. It was only then that they could see the dilapidated yellow and brown tractor tucked up against the lee side of the building. They looked at each other in amazement when they realised that the farmer was fast asleep in the cab. 'He's having a fucking laugh,' said Fergal.

'Get his keys. We'll get the guns loaded and get to hell out of here,' said Mickey, pulling open the tractor door, and removing the bunch of keys dangling from the ignition.

After they loaded all the weapons and ammunition back into the van, Mickey went over to the tractor in a final attempt to wake the farmer. After a few grunts and farts, the farmer began to stir. He took the envelope that Mickey placed in his hand. 'We've already unloaded the stuff,' said Mickey.

Mickey took the lead again and the two vehicles drove back onto the main road into Derry. They drove towards the Bogside.

They continued for another ten minutes before stopping outside lock-ups under a block of flats. 'This must be the Creggan,' said Danny, as he lit a cigarette and passed one to Fergal. They watched Mickey go towards a metal door and pull it open. A man inside signalled for Danny to drive the van straight in.

The lock-up was full of junk; stripped down engines, tyres, and tools. There was just enough space for the car to squeeze in. Mickey pulled the door closed behind them.

Danny and Fergal removed three of the heavy iron boxes from the back of the van. 'That's your lot, make sure you use them wisely,' joked Fergal.

'What about these?' asked the man in a strong Derry accent, trying to open one of the boxes that were still in the back of the van. Fergal stopped him abruptly. 'Those are for Belfast; you've got your share.'

'Fair enough,' replied the man, shrugging his shoulders to show there were no hard feelings, before closing the van door back over. 'Come up and meet the lads and have a cup of tea with us.'

'I don't think we've got enough time,' said Mickey, who wanted to get the whole thing over with as quickly as possible.

'What are ye talking about? Sure we've got enough time,' said Fergal.

The Derry man led them up a concrete stairway, which took them to a central landing on the second floor of what were decanted Council maisonettes. Three of the four doors on the landing were sealed with steel shutters, covered in republican graffiti. Inside the decanted flat, in what was once the living room, sat three men.

'Yer, welcome, Mickey, haven't seen you for ages.'

'No, Martin, too busy trying to get the Brits out. This is Fergal Gallagher and Danny Duffy.'

'Martin Bonner and this is Patsy and Dominic. It's good to meet you lads. Did ye have any problems?'

'No, a piece of piss,' said Fergal, shaking Bonner's hand and nodding to the other men in the room. It was clear to Danny and Fergal that this man was the CO.

Bonner asked one of his men to make a pot of tea and turned to look out of the back window, carefully drawing the shabby curtain aside. 'Look,' he said, pointing to the fields in the distance. 'That's the Republic! So close that you can almost touch it, only you can't because there is a British army observation post on that ridge over there. So we can't even walk from one part of our own country to another without the risk of being shot.'

'We've brought ye plenty of guns, why don't ye take the bastards out tonight,' said Fergal. The other men laughed.

'If only it was that easy,' replied Bonner, as one of his men brought in a rifle and a couple of handguns from the lock-up, passing the Armalite to him. He got up and stood at the window, peering down into the street, deep in thought. He then turned back to Mickey. 'I understand you have another three cases of weapons in the van?'

'Aye,' interrupted Fergal, before Mickey could speak. 'They're for Belfast.'

The CO did not even look at Fergal, but turned to one of his men and spoke in Gaelic. Fergal put his hand inside his jacket pocket, resting it on his revolver.

After a few more minutes, Bonner smiled, before nodding to Patsy to go down and have a look at the other guns. As soon as Fergal realised what was happening, he stood up and pulled out his revolver, pointing it directly at the CO's head. Dominic immediately pointed his revolver at Fergal. Mickey put his own hands up as if to indicate he was not involved. Danny got up and stood beside Fergal, who continued to aim his gun at Bonner's head.

'Those guns are for Belfast. You got yours, and we're leaving with the rest or you're getting a bullet in the fucking head.'

'No need to panic – we're only going to have a look at what's in your van. We put up half the money for this shipment, so all we want is a fair share,' said Bonner. 'So put the gun down. We're not going to start killing each other over nothing.'

'I'm not putting the gun down until you and your cronies allow us to get out of here without any trouble. We've done you a favour by taking those guns through the border. I don't see why you didn't do it yourselves.'

'We'd have done it ourselves, but the border guards know what we all look like.'

'Well, we took the risk for you and we're not going to be mugged for the guns we need to defend our own streets.'

'We can assure you we have no intention of taking the guns, and we have no intention of doing anything to you guys other than thank you for helping to bring the weapons through. Patsy's only gone down to make sure we're not getting any less than what we're due. If the guns are equally divided between us, and the ammunition's the same, then there's no problem and you can go with God's blessing.'

Fergal laughed and turned to Danny. 'He talks like a fucking priest.'

Dominic took a step forward, cocking his revolver. 'Have

you any idea who you're talking to, son?'

'Aye, I'm talking to him. I don't give a fuck who he thinks he is!'

There was a quick shuffling of feet and repositioning as Patsy re-entered the room. 'They've got the same as us.'

Bonner held his hand out to Mickey, and said. 'Your boy is a bit too hot in the head. You better get him back to Belfast before he starts something serious.'

'Right, lads; let's get back down the road. I'm sorry, Martin,' said Mickey. 'I hope there are no hard feelings about this misunderstanding.'

'Don't worry about it. I'd do the same if I were in his shoes. Again, thanks for everything, lads. You've done a good job.'

Mickey led the way back into the lock-up, followed by Danny, with Fergal at the rear, still holding his gun at the ready as he backed down the stairs. No one else left the flat, and as soon as they got downstairs, Mickey opened up the shutter to let the van out. He then jumped into his own car and drove off at speed, before Danny could get the van into gear. 'That was hairy,' said Danny.

'Those cowboys didn't frighten me. I'd have put a bullet in his head as quick as I'd put one in a Brit's head. Fuck him; he wasn't getting our guns!'

*

The drive back to Belfast was uneventful, passing through towns and villages until they could see Belfast in the distance. The further they got from Derry, the fewer tricolours they saw and the more Union Jacks and Red Hand of Ulster flags appeared along the roadside. It was afternoon by the time they drove into the city centre. They continued on to Ballymurphy. This time they knew exactly where they were going and who would be waiting for them.

Once they got to the safe house, they met with local brigade leader, Jack McCrae, and a few of his men. They eagerly checked the cache of weapons. The CO laughed when Fergal told him about the stand-off with the Derry Brigade. He had already received a phone call from Derry, and accepted from Bonner that there was a simple misunderstanding.

Chapter 26

Car Bombs

Declan Murphy was busy searching through drawers and cupboards, taking anything that looked of value. He had been casing the house for hours before he was sure the time was right to make a move. It was a large two-storey town house on the more affluent east side of the river, with easy access through the back garden. He stopped every so often when he thought he heard movement from upstairs. With his flashlight he scanned the various objects of interest, filling his canvas shoulder bag with anything he could sell later for a decent price. He found three First World War medals and a dilapidated looking handgun and put them into his bag. He froze when he heard the sound of floorboards creaking.

'Who's down there?'

Declan was not one for confrontation and he turned off his torch, climbing back out the kitchen window. He scrambled over the fence into the neighbouring garden, forcing his way through a thicket of bushes into an adjacent lane. He ran as fast as he could to get a safe distance between himself and the house.

It was the early hours of the morning and he was a long way from the Ardoyne and the safety of his own lawless streets. He looked back, but there was no-one coming after him. He stopped running.

The roads were quiet and he walked briskly in the direction of the river He could just make out Albert Bridge up ahead. He carried on walking, shifting the heavy bag from one shoulder to the other. Then, just as he got to the start of the bridge he saw a police Land-Rover coming in the opposite direction. He looked away as it passed by. Just when he thought his luck was in, he heard the screech of wheels and the Land Rover coming up behind him.

His heart was racing and, for a second, he thought of throwing the bag into the Lagan. The Land Rover pulled up beside him. There was nowhere to run.

Once in the back of the police vehicle, he was handcuffed by one officer as the other rummaged through the bag. Both officers looked at each other when the gun was discovered.

Declan suddenly realised his folly in taking the gun and quickly admitted the burglary, but pleaded that he only took the gun because it was an antique. The officer in the back of the Land Rover laughed, taunting him. 'You're just a thieving Taig. If it was up to me we would just take ye up to the moors and blow yer Fenian head off.'

The Land Rover eventually arrived outside the police station on Hasting Street. Declan was dragged, screaming and shouting, into the foyer. The sergeant at the bar told him to shut up and behave himself; otherwise he would be going straight to Castlereagh. The mere mention of that infamous place was enough, and Declan stopped his protests immediately.

After being processed, Declan was left to stew in a cell for what seemed like hours. He passed the time reading the protestations of its former occupants scraped into the thick coats of blue paint.

He was running out of graffiti to keep him occupied, when the cell door opened with a clatter of heavy keys. He was taken to one of the interview rooms at the end of the corridor. Once in the dimly lit room, he nervously accepted a cigarette from one of the detectives and took a light from the other. One of the officers lit his own cigarette and took a chair opposite; the other lifted Declan's bag of stolen gear onto the table.

'I told you, I admit it. They're stolen.'

'Oh, we know they're stolen, and we know you stole them. That's not what we're interested in.'

'What then?'

'I think ye know what we're on about, so cut the crap,' said one of the officers, lifting the revolver from the bag.

'So, I nicked that from the house as well. I'm not in the IRA, or anything!'

'Oh, we know that. Even they wouldn't let a lowlife like you join them. You're a thieving Taig, who steals from decent hard working Protestants. What's up with yer own kind; why don't ye break into their houses?'

'They've got nothing tae steal!'

The officer, who was holding the revolver, pulled the cigarette from Declan's lips. 'You fucking Fenian bastard!'

'What did ye do that for? I want tae see my lawyer,' demanded Declan, feeling the torn skin on his top lip.

'Yer lawyer will no' get ye out of this one. Who were ye planning to sell the gun to?'

'Nobody, it's an auld antique.'

'Do ye know how long you'll get for even having this in yer possession? At least ten years!'

'Away tae hell! I only nicked it. It's not like I was going tae use it or anything.'

'Doesn't matter, it's an illegal firearm.'

'I want my lawyer!'

The two detectives laughed at him.

The following morning Declan was released from the police station into the bright sunlight that rose over the massive dockyards in the distance and spread into the back streets of West Belfast. He took a cigarette from the packet given to him that morning by the man who had secured his release, Major Moorcroft, from Military Intelligence. Declan had no intention of using the number the major had given him and threw the piece of paper into the gutter.

*

Marty O'Shea was sitting in a backroom attaching coloured wires to a detonator and delay timer. At his feet was a suitcase packed with high explosives, wrapped in oil-stained brown paper. He was in his mid-fifties, his gaunt, pale face framed with national health spectacles. Wearing a greying goatee beard, he looked every bit the Marxist he espoused to be. He looked up from his work for a moment when he heard a sharp knock at the door. He put everything he was working on under the bed and opened the door.

'Flynn, you're ten minutes late,' he complained, ignoring Fergal and Danny, who followed Mickey into the room.

'We couldn't find the fuckin' place,' countered Fergal.

O'Shea looked at Fergal over his spectacles and smiled. 'If I was easy to find, then I would be in prison by now. Take yer coats off, lads, there's a pot of tea over there.'

Once Mickey, with undue haste, had left, O'Shea pulled the heavy suitcase from under the bed. 'There's about thirty pounds of high explosive in this case and it's to be left in a car as near to the city centre as possible,' he said. 'Fill the tank with petrol to increase the impact. The explosives can be detonated on a half-hour timer to give you a chance to get away and to give the warning to minimise civilian casualties. Remember our aim is to destroy the commercial centre of Belfast, not to kill civilians. Here are the code names you will use when telephoning the police to give the warning; without them they will think it's another hoax call. Any questions?'

'When do we do it?' Fergal asked eagerly.

'I'll prime the explosives tonight, and in the morning you two can load them into the red Granada that's parked in the lane. Best time to drive into the city centre is after the rush hour. Remember to try and put it somewhere near to the main shopping area for maximum effect.'

Fergal and Danny struggled to get to sleep that night as they lay on the wooden floorboards of the flat with the suitcase of high explosives only inches away from them. O'Shea, surrounded by his own ghostly shadows, continued to work through the night with the intensity and precision of a master clockmaker as he fiddled with the timing mechanism to get it as accurate as possible.

It was almost daybreak when Fergal woke and noticed that the old bomb-maker was asleep at his worktable. He quietly slipped out the back door to the outside toilet where he carefully removed a pre-primed syringe from his tobacco tin. He then held it in his mouth as he tied a belt around his upper arm. He began breathing easier when he felt the heroin rushing through his veins.

'Where have you been?' Danny asked, pulling on boots as Fergal came in from the backyard.

'We better wake him up,' said Fergal, ignoring Danny's question, and giving O'Shea a shake.

'What, what time is it?' muttered O'Shea, lifting his head from the table and putting on his spectacles.

'Don't panic, it's still only half eight.'

'Half eight? We better get a move on.'

They loaded the case into the boot of the car and waited for O'Shea to set up the timer. 'Remember when you leave it, trip this switch. That'll set the clock and give you thirty minutes and enough time to phone in the warning. Don't forget; we're not murderers, no matter what the British think.'

Danny tried to hotwire the stolen car, but the engine would not start. Fergal turned and stared at O'Shea, who shrugged his shoulders. 'It was working fine yesterday.'

'Well, it's not working now,' said Danny, getting out of the car and lifting the bonnet to see if he could find out what was wrong with it.

'We'll just have to use the other car,' said Fergal as Danny got back in the driver's seat and unsuccessfully tried to start the engine again.

'Are ye daft, you can't use your own,' said O'Shea.

'It's just another stolen car, for fuck's sake,' said Fergal. 'Why does it matter?'

'Your prints will be all over it. That's why it fucking matters.'

'If we're going to blow it up, there'll be nothing left of it.'

'You can't take a chance with fingerprints. There will be enough bits and pieces left after the blast for them to find your prints. We'll just have to go back in the house and I'll give Flynn a call to get another car over here.'

It was over an hour before the second car arrived, and they drove to the city centre with the thirty pound bomb in the boot. Danny avoided army checkpoints by taking a long diversion around the city, away from the main roads.

*

In the medical faculty of Queen's University, William

Morrison was relieved when he scanned the list of successful candidates and saw his name.

After some boisterous mutual congratulations with a few other successful students, he headed back across town to meet his girlfriend, who was working part-time in Marks and Spencer in the city centre. Sara knew by the smirk on his face that he had passed his anatomy exam. Sara got her coat and handbag, and rushed out to meet him as he stood outside smoking.

'You passed then?' she said, kissing him on the cheek.

'I got sixty-two per cent, not bad.'

'Not bad? It's brilliant. Let's get something to eat. I didn't have any breakfast this morning and I'm starving.'

'Where do you want to go?'

'Somewhere nearby, I've only got half an hour before I have to be back.'

They went to a café just off Union Street for tea and sandwiches. The warm summer sun was shining in through the window as they sat and talked about anything and everything, just enjoying being in each other's company.

'Don't like the look of him,' said Sara as she noticed a man standing across the road. 'Who wears a polo-neck jumper and black leather jacket on a day like this?'

'He looks like a down and out.'

'More like a junkie.'

'Would you like some more tea?' asked the young waitress.

'Yes, please, and I think I'll have another scone,' replied Sara.

'I'll just have some more tea,' said William, holding up his cup.

‘That man’s gone,’ said Sara, looking out to where he had been standing at the corner.

‘Never mind him, do you fancy going to the pictures tonight?’

‘What’s on?’

‘I don’t know, we’ll get a paper.’

‘Oh, I know. *Coal Miner’s Daughter,* I’d love to see that.’

‘Is it no’ a bit cheesy?’

‘Please can we see it? I went to see *Raging Bull* with you last week and I hated it.’

‘Okay, but don’t start crying all the way through it like the last time we watched one of these soppy films.’

A little bell rang as the door opened and another customer came in, followed by a light breeze which carried the smell of recently cut grass into the cafe from the park. The radio behind the counter was playing one of William’s favourite songs. ‘Who’s that?’ He asked, tapping his teaspoon on the table to the beat.

‘Don’t know. Who is it?’

‘It’s Joe Jackson … ***It’s Different For Girls***!’

‘Oh, for goodness sake, is that what yer getting all excited about?’

‘It’s a brilliant song.’

‘It’s all right.’

‘How can ye say it’s all right? It’s brilliant!’

‘Are you finished?’ the waitress asked politely.

‘Yes, thanks very much,’ replied Sara, lifting the empty cups onto the girl’s tray.

*

As they walked away from the car, Fergal noticed two British soldiers on the other side of the road who were searching shoppers' bags outside one of the stores. Danny suddenly realised Fergal was not behind him, but instead was crossing through the traffic towards the soldiers. He watched anxiously as Fergal took a light from one of the soldiers, and began laughing and joking with them as though he had known them all his life. Danny shook his head when Fergal turned and walked nonchalantly back across the road towards him with a grin on his face.

'What was that all about, ye lunatic?'

'I wanted to know what they looked like before I read about them in the paper tomorrow!'

'You're sick! Let's get to fuck out of here before ye get us arrested.'

With the timer primed, they walked up to the corner and crossed the road towards two telephone boxes. Danny rummaged through his jacket for some change and the warning codes. He looked at his watch; there was plenty of time for the street to be cleared and he began to ring the number O'Shea had given him. As the pips began, he put the coins into the slot, but they simply dropped through the hollow-sounding tin box as the line cut off. He tried again, but the phone was obviously broken. He looked anxiously at Fergal who nodded to a young couple in the next kiosk. Fergal knocked on the glass panel to hurry them up with a threatening sneer. The young man made the mistake of sticking his two fingers up at Fergal, who instantly pulled the door open and punched the man in the face, bursting his nose. The girl screamed as Fergal pulled her and her boyfriend from the phone box.

'Now get to fuck,' shouted Fergal.

Danny hurried into the booth and tried to phone again. But the money dropped through. Thinking there must be something up with the shilling he was using, he searched through his pockets for a different coin.

'Leave it!' said Fergal, nodding down the road to the young couple who were standing with the two RUC officers. 'Let's get out of here!'

Danny did not need to be told twice and they both ran across the road and down the nearest lane as they heard a police whistle coming from the other side of the road. After jumping through a few back lanes, they soon lost their pursuers and eventually reached the top of the main road where they heard an almighty explosion. A gust of hot air and thick dust travelled towards them knocking them both onto the ground. There was a moment of surreal quiet before the sound of sirens filled the air. As Danny helped Fergal to his feet, they could see the devastation in the street. A bloody severed hand was lying in the middle of the road, still holding a strap from a shopping bag. Danny, unnerved, stared at the grotesque sight for a moment, with its fingernails neatly varnished. He anxiously looked at his watch; it was still only eleven thirty-five; it wasn't their bomb that went off. 'C'mon, we need to get another telephone,' he shouted at Fergal who was still dazed and unsure what had happened.

They found another phone box and Danny made the call. As he hung up the receiver there was another explosion in the distance; this one further to the west of where they had parked the car. They watched as the city centre skyline became engulfed in smoke.

*

William and Sara rushed from the café into the bright

sunlight. There was a strange calm before they heard the screams from further down the street. The sudden realisation of what was happening stunned them for a moment and they looked at each other wondering which way to run as the hellish sound of human suffering echoed in the distance. They could see terrified people running away from the danger towards them. William took Sara's hand and turned to go back into the café when they were caught in a third explosion.

Sara lay semi-conscious as the noise of the blast turned to a strange empty silence. It seemed like her body was still floating somewhere just above the ground and her limbs were numb to any feeling. She tried to feel for William's hand as her mind began to clear from the shock of the blast. The burning petrol seared her lungs and she began to cough and choke for air. She could feel someone's hands take hold of her body as though lifting her out of a pool of deep water. She gradually got to her feet when the feeling of confusion subsided. Smoke hung like a veil over the wreckage of vehicles strewn across the road and pavement. Through the burning tears in her eyes she could see William lying in the cafe doorway, his pale face almost serene but for the blood running down the side of his head.

One of the first paramedics at the scene had to drag her away from William. She did not even feel the wound she had on her own arm, which was bandaged while she stood in a stupor, watching William being carried into an ambulance.

The security forces sealed off the area as ambulance crews continued to tend the injured with the constant fear of further explosions on their minds. The army bomb disposal teams were stretched to the limit to ensure that the numerous abandoned vehicles in the area were not also laden with more explosives. It was over two hours before police forensic teams were able to enter the streets that took the main impact of the three car bombs. Paramedics were now recovering the remains; bloody disfigured limbs and other unrecognisable body parts that lay scattered amongst the grotesque carnage.

Hungry seagulls were trying to scavenge among the scattered pieces of human flesh, while pop music continued to play in one of the bombed shops – ***Games without Frontiers*** by Peter Gabriel. The smell of scorched flesh along with the burning petrol made most of those dealing with the slaughter physically sick. News was now spreading that there had been further bombings in Derry and Dungannon.

At the hospital's emergency entrance, teams of medics were waiting to deal with the stream of ambulances that queued up outside with the wounded. As soon as the casualties were in the hands of the hospital staff, each ambulance pulled away from the emergency bay and returned to the anarchy of the city centre for more victims. Sara stood by the door as William was lifted carefully on to a waiting trolley and rushed to the operating theatre.

'Are you okay?' asked a young nurse. 'You better come in and I'll have a look at your arm,' she added, taking Sara into the crowed corridor and finding her somewhere to sit while she removed the temporary, blood soaked bandage.

'I need to find out how my fiancé is,' she said, taking little notice of the deep laceration just above her elbow.

'He'll be all right, what's his name?'

'William ...William Morrison,' she replied, still clearly in shock and looking at the wall in front of her in an absent trance. 'I need to find out how he is!'

'Hold on! Just sit there,' said the nurse.

*

Jamie Morrison had left the yard as soon as he was informed that a major IRA offensive was taking place and he was back in his UVF office as the last of the explosions erupted in the distance. He was sure that this was the start of the civil war that had been looming for so long. He tried to imagine what was left of the city centre.

'Boss, they want you over at the club; there's a press conference being arranged,' said Bulldog, standing at the door in full combat gear and carrying a self-loading rifle, over his shoulder.

'Give me a minute,' said Jamie, putting on his leather holster and checking his pistol was fully loaded. 'Where did ye get that?' he asked, on noticing Bulldog's new rifle.

'We got a batch in from Moorcroft this morning. I grabbed this one and stuck my name on it,' said Bulldog, proudly showing Jamie the rifle butt, with 'Bulldog Brown, UVF' engraved on the metal brace with the aid of a pen knife and a shaky hand.

'Are you off yer fucking head?' shouted Jamie. 'Why don't ye advertise yerself as a UVF hit man in the Belfast Telegraph? If the police get their hands on that gun, then every bullet you put into a taig will be traced back to you, ye clown.'

'Hold on, Boss, it no' just me; most of the other guys have put their names…'

'Oh, for fuck's sake! File them off and use the serial numbers to identify them. I thought you lot were getting trained at that army barracks? Do you think the Provos put their names and addresses on their fucking bombs?'

'What would be the point of that?' said Bulldog.

At the press conference, seething with rage, Jamie read out a prepared statement. He was flanked by two senior colleagues, all wearing combat fatigues and balaclavas. Armed men were positioned around the room as the press listened to Jamie, who cleared his throat and continued to read the communiqué in a slow deliberate manner. 'The IRA can no longer expect the loyalist community to sit back and take these attacks on our very existence, without reaping what they have sown. From midnight, the UVF will go on the offensive and take the fight to the Provos in their own backyards.'

'Does this mean civil war?' asked one of the reporters.

'Call it what you like,' replied Jamie as he got up and left the room.

Outside, Bulldog was waiting. His face was contorted with the news he still had to convey. 'Boss, I got a phone call from the hospital a few minutes ago. Your son was caught in the bombing.'

Throwing off his sunglasses and balaclava, Jamie tried to call Liz at home, but the phone simply rang out. He began to fear that she may have also been caught up in the carnage. He took a taxi to the hospital fearing the worst.

Breathing heavily and saturated in sweat, he arrived at the Accident and Emergency department to find Sara sitting in the main corridor, her hair matted with dust and her arm in a sling. He put his hand on her shoulder and brought her out of her deep stupor. 'Where is he?'

'Oh, Mr Morrison, he's in there,' she said, pointing along the corridor. She began to sob.

'Here,' said Jamie, handing her a handkerchief before slowly walking towards the door leading to the intensive care unit. He stopped for a moment and stared through the round glass panel, almost afraid to look at the bed where William lay wired to an array of bleeping machines. He could see the side of William's head was shaved and stitched together with black sutures crudely sticking out from his skull like barbed wire. The lower face was covered with white tape, which held a plastic tube to his mouth. Jamie took a deep breath and went into the room. He stood a few feet from the bed, too afraid to move any closer in case he disturbed the delicate assortment of wires and cables. The door suddenly opened behind him.

'Who said ye could come in here?' demanded a stern looking nurse, carrying some fresh bed linen.

'I'm his father, Mr Morrison. How bad is he?'

'You'll have to speak to the doctor; he'll be along any minute. Could you please take a seat in the corridor while I try and make your son more comfortable, Mr Morrison?'

'Is he going to live?'

'You'll have to speak to the doctor; it's not my place to answer your questions.'

Jamie went back into the corridor, taking another look at William before he closed the door. He turned to see Sara looking towards him with pleading eyes. 'How is he?' she asked, afraid to hear the answer to her own question.

'God knows ... I better phone his mother again.'

Liz was in the middle of cooking a joint of pork, excited that William was bringing Sara home for dinner that evening. The phone rang in the hall.

She steadied herself as she listened to Jamie's stuttering words, before putting the receiver down and rushing upstairs to get changed. She had no time for the tears that were welling up in her eyes; *at least he's still alive. Dear God don't let him die*, she continually mumbled to herself as she rushed back into the kitchen to turn off the pots of potatoes and carrots that were now pumping steam out through their rattling lids. She took out the joint of pork from the oven and left it on the kitchen table half cooked. She then rushed to the front door to wait for the taxi that Jamie had arranged.

Frustrated with each passing minute, she was eventually picked up by Donald Stoat or the Weasel as most people called him. Liz had met him a couple of times before at the lodge and found him to be sycophantically deferential towards her husband in a way that made her feel uncomfortable. 'I appreciate you taking me over to the hospital, Donald,' she said as he opened the door and took off his greasy-looking trilby with his thin bony fingers. 'Not a problem, Mrs Morrison. I'm only happy to be of a service in your hour of need. Have you heard how he is?'

'Yes, he's in a coma…'

'Bastards - excuse my French, Mrs Morrison,' apologised Donald as the car pulled away from the kerb in a stutter. Liz just smiled weakly at him as he looked at her regretfully in his rear view mirror.

Liz cursed the flags and murals that were everywhere as they drove down the Shankill Road. She did not care who planted the bomb, they were all as bad as each other. She was sick to the stomach with the killings. *Please God don't let him die... take me instead.*

The car pulled up outside the main entrance to the hospital and Liz was taken along a maze of corridors by one of the nurses to the intensive care unit. She walked quickly towards Jamie, who was still sitting with Sara in the corridor. He smiled when he saw her and held out his hand, which she reluctantly took as he gave her a hug. She quickly pulled away and turned to speak to Sara. 'Hello, Sara. What happened?'

'Hello, Mrs Morrison. We just came out of the café when there was an explosion. That's all I can remember.'

'How bad is he?'

'I spoke to the doctor,' interrupted Jamie, annoyed at being ignored. 'He may be brain damaged - if he lives.'

'My God,' moaned Liz, pulling her hand away from Jamie. 'Leave me for pity's sake. This is God's punishment for the things you've been up to - and don't think I don't know!'

'For God's sake, woman, will ye keep quiet. I'm only protecting our homes from the animals that planted those damn bombs. He's my son too!'

Liz looked at him with disdain. 'Where is he?'

The staff nurse took Liz over to William's bedside. The sight of his pale white face caused her to stagger slightly as she felt the strength drain from her body. The nurse helped her onto a chair at the side of the bed. She took William's limp hand in her own and began to cry.

Chapter 27

Declan's Trial

Mickey Flynn could smell his own fear as he entered the back room of a terraced house just off the Falls Road. He had received orders earlier that day to attend what was described as 'official disciplinary proceedings'. He was assured in the message that his attendance would be as an observer, since the person who was to be interrogated was not connected to his unit. When he opened the door, it took a moment or two for him to adjust to the dimly lit room. A table lamp cast shadows on the ancient folds of a tricolour hanging behind three men, seated at a table draped in a green cloth. One of the men nodded for him to take a seat at the side of the room. It was only then that he noticed another person sitting opposite with his head covered with a hood and his arms tied behind his back. As Mickey's eyes adjusted, he recognised the man sitting at the centre of the table as Brendan O'Connell, a well-known IRA man from the Strand area of East Belfast. Mickey knew fine well that O'Connell was the chief IRA interrogator of suspected informers, and although he did not recognise the other two men, he was quite sure they were also from the Strand. These men were serious IRA, and Mickey knew his place. He noticed the hooded man nervously shuffling his feet. There was a strong smell of urine coming from the shaking body.

Like a High Court judge, O'Connell whispered to one of his colleagues before the proceedings began. Mickey listened intently as the charges were read over to the accused, who pleaded his innocence through sobs and broken coughs. The allegations were pretty straightforward.

He was accused of being an informer and providing secret information about IRA operations to the security forces. On at least three occasions, units carrying out covert operations were ambushed and a total of seven volunteers had been killed, with four others seriously wounded. He was informed that IRA counter-intelligence had become suspicious of him after he was seen with an undercover British security officer in a bar in Belfast city centre, within days of an operation involving the West Belfast Brigade being foiled by a SAS ambush.

'No ... no ... I was only having a pint when the guy approached me. I didn't tell him anything. I swear on me life.'

'Son, there's no point in denying what we already know!' said O'Connell. 'We've a list here of the number of times ye made contact with the British, and most of those times correspond wi' the discovery of our operations. The evidence speaks for itself. If ye agree that ye were an informer for the British, this might not be as bad for you as ye think.'

'Honest! I didn't tell them anything. I was just giving them false information to stop them arresting me. I didn't tell them about any of the operations!'

'If ye keep lying, we'll still make a judgement on ye based on the evidence we've got already. If ye admit ye were doing it, ye might even be useful to us, but ye have to be honest with us, if we've to trust you in the future.'

'I didn't do anything, honest. I didn't do anything. Jesus, Mary and Joseph, I'm not a grass. You can ask anyone. Ask me cousin, Fergal Gallagher. He knows I'm not a grass.'

Already unnerved, Mickey flinched with the mention of Fergal's name, suddenly realising why he was summoned to attend. He felt the sweat in his own hands as he rubbed his legs nervously, wondering whether he was going to be accused of anything next. He tried to remember the name of Fergal's cousin, who he sometimes saw hanging around the

Shamrock Bar with him, but his mind was blank. The three men began to whisper amongst themselves as though they were about to pass judgement, Mickey looked again at the shivering wreck ... *Declan ... that's it. Declan Murphy.*

It was clear to Mickey that they did not have to use strong-arm tactics as they had already made up their minds that Declan was an informer. All they were looking for was some form of contrition before they killed him. It made it easier on their conscience for what they had to do. He could hear Declan breathing heavily under the hood, his gasps for air becoming more and more erratic as he awaited his fate. The accused suddenly spoke. 'Okay … Okay, I did tell them some things, but I never told them everything. I told them just enough to let them know something was happening. I never told them the times and dates.'

'That's what we want to hear from you, son. There's no point in lying anymore. We're going to take a full statement from ye and you're going to detail all the things ye told the British. The more ye tell us, the better it'll go for ye when we decide what to do with ye.'

Declan began a nervous rant, Mickey moved around nervously on his chair.

Once they had their full confession, Mickey was told to join the tribunal in the other room. Declan was left to ponder his fate.

O'Connell quickly read the statement, shocked at just how much information had been passed to the British army by someone who had no direct involvement in any of the operations. After studying the confession with his two colleagues, O'Connell turned to Mickey. 'These were units and operations that you were in charge of, Flynn. What happened to your security?'

'We knew there was a problem, but I didn't think for a minute that Gallagher was telling all this to his cousin!'

'Do ye think Gallagher is in it with him?'

'No, absolutely no way. Fergal may be a big mouth but he's not a traitor. Sure he was almost killed in the Kyle ambush.'

'That's what I mean. He was the only one that got away.'

'But he's killed more Brits than any other volunteer; they want him more than anyone else. He wouldn't think for a bloody minute that his cousin was working for the British. His family is the most fanatically republican in Belfast. Sure his grandfather died on hunger strike in a British prison.'

'Even so, he's a liability and just as bad as his cousin. We need to bring him in. He's a security risk.'

'I can speak to him. He'll keep his mouth shut in the future.'

'If he shouts his mouth off again, he'll get a bullet in it!' said one of the other men, who until then let O'Connell do all the talking.

As they were talking, they could hear the sobbing from the other room, punctuated by a mixture of prayers and obscenities. O'Connell left Mickey for a moment and went back in to speak to Declan, who insisted his cousin had no idea he was working for the British. O'Connell joined the other men and they agreed amongst themselves that that there could be only one sentence. Mickey wanted to plead some lesser punishment, but he wasn't brave enough and knew these men would see it as a sign of weakness, so he said nothing. After some further discussion, O'Connell ordered Mickey to arrange for the sentence to be carried out. Fergal was to be his cousin's executioner to teach him to keep his mouth shut in future. Mickey shuddered at the thought of having to order Fergal to do such a thing, but could only agree.

Declan lay for hours in the suffocating darkness, not aware that his fate had already been decided. Any information he had given to Moorcroft was generally made up to get a few pounds. On the last occasion he met Moorcroft, the major accused him of being a compulsive liar and a waste of time. Declan knew just being seen with Moorcroft was enough to get him killed, never mind taking money for information, even if that information was false. *How could he prove that now? And if he could, would it make any difference?* He had only given the tribunal what they wanted to hear, hoping it would save him if they thought he was of some value to them. Virtually everything he told them he had heard about after it had happened. Most of the botched IRA operations were reported in the press, and those that were not were still common knowledge in West Belfast.

His interrogators had left him with his hands tied behind his back, his feet bound together with heavy leather belts, but at least they took the hood off. Declan was suffering agonising stomach pains and desperate for the toilet. He was afraid he might wet himself again, or even worse. Gripped with the constant fear of a man on the edge of an abyss, each rattle of a window or creak of a floorboard sent floods of panic through his mind and beads of sweat down his face. His struggle for breath was desperate as the mucus and blood in his nose dried up. He heaved deep breaths, to stop the feeling of sickness rising from his stomach. In his fear he begged God for help.

*

An IRA minder got up and stood at the back door as soon as Mickey led Fergal and Danny into the flat. He was a local man and gave Fergal the key to the upstairs room without hesitation, shaking his head at the thought of what had to be done, but saying nothing. Upstairs, Mickey noticed that the tricolour had been removed from the wall and to his relief the three Strand men had gone. He nodded towards the shivering heap on the floor. Mickey made his excuses and left.

Fergal sat smoking, while staring at his cousin, who was asleep on an old mattress in the corner of the room with his hands and legs still bound. Danny sat down on the floor; placing his head in his hands as Fergal took a quarter-bottle of whiskey from his jacket pocket and took a long hard drink, shivering as the whiskey ran through his body. He thought for a moment of simply going up and shooting Declan in the head while he was still asleep just to get it over with, but stopped himself, taking another drink instead, before handing the bottle to Danny.

Fergal's mind started to wander wildly with the whiskey. He thought about his mother and how she would react if she found out that he had shot her sister's only son.

'Can we not just let him disappear to England?' suggested Danny. 'For Christ's sakes, this is cold-blooded murder!'

'If we don't do it, we'll be facing the same thing,' replied Fergal.

Groaning in his discomfort, Declan began to stir awake on hearing the raised voice, and slowly opened his bloodshot eyes, squinting towards the two men sitting on the other side of the room. At first he thought his interrogators were back, but then he noticed his cousin, staring at him. 'Fergal,' he groaned, hoping for a fleeting second that he may have simply dreamt the whole interrogation in a drunken sleep. Then he realised his hands and feet were tied as he tried to get up. 'Fergal, I didn't tell the Brits anything. They forced me to admit that I grassed you up, but I didn't. I'll do anything. I'll go to America, anywhere. Please just let me go.'

'It's all right, Declan; we're not going to do anything to ye. You're me cousin for fuck's sake. We'll let ye go, but ye can never come back. Ye promise?' insisted Fergal, putting his gun back inside his leather jacket.

'I promise, whatever ye say. I swear … I won't come back.'

‘Ye better not or ye’ll get us both shot.’

‘I’ll go anywhere. I won’t come back. I promise, Fergal.’

‘We’ll take ye over the border tonight and get ye somewhere to stay until we can arrange for ye to get out of Ireland and into America. We’ll need to get ye a false passport.’

‘Thanks, Fergal. I’ll do anything you say.’

Picking up an old rag from the floor, Fergal wiped sweat and tears from Declan’s face, and smiled at him. ‘Don’t worry, it’ll be all right. You’re still me cousin. Is that right, Danny?’

‘Aye, Fergal, if you say so,’ said Danny, moving to the door to check that the minder wasn’t listening to what Fergal was saying. He could hear the radio in the kitchen. He gently closed the door back over. ‘What are we going to tell him?’ he asked, nodding towards the door.

‘We don’t need to tell him anything. They don’t expect us to do it here, do they? So stop worrying!’

‘We’re all goin’ to get shot,’ said Danny, having second thoughts and nervously pacing the room. ‘What the hell are we going to tell O’Connell when he finds out?’

‘We don’t have to tell him anything other than the job was done, and that we dumped him somewhere in the Donegal moors.’

‘All right, Fergal, whatever ye say.’

‘Good. So let’s get out of here.’

Cursing the tight knot, Fergal began to untie Declan’s hands and feet. Danny went to get the van. Fergal picked up the hood from the floor, telling Declan he would have to wear it whilst he is taken down the backstairs to the van. Declan nervously agreed. Fergal gave him a drink of whiskey and lifted him to his feet.

‘Can I see me mother before I go?’

‘For Christ’s sakes, no! Are ye mad? Don’t ye know the risk we’re taking, ye grassing bastard? We’re putting ourselves on the line for ye and you’ll do what you’re fucking told!’

‘Aye, okay, okay, Fergal, I’m sorry.’

Stubbing his cigarette out on the windowsill, Fergal could hear the van pulling up at the backdoor. He took Declan by the arm and helped him downstairs, while Danny spoke to the man in the kitchen. They then took Declan to the van and bundled him into the back. Fergal got into the passenger’s seat as Danny turned on the ignition and slowly drove onto the main road.

It was around nine o’clock, and the roads were quiet. They headed out of Belfast. ‘Are you hungry?’ Fergal asked Declan.

‘Aye, just a wee bit, I haven’t eaten for a couple of days.’

‘We’ll stop and get something to eat when we get near the border. You can take the hood off now.’

Throwing his cigarette end out the window, Danny put on the radio.

‘Where are we going to take him?’

‘I know someone just over the border that’ll look after him for a few days. He’s not in the Provos but he’s a friend of mine,’ replied Fergal.

‘We’ll need to get him some clothes and money. Where are we going to get him a passport?’

‘For Christ’s sakes, stop asking me fucking questions!’ snapped Fergal. ‘I’m trying to think here. We’ll get him sorted that’s all that matters. Just stop asking me questions all the fucking time!’

Turning away, Danny decided the less said at this stage

the better. He began to tune the radio into the local news station as it approached ten-o'clock, but the reception was poor. He gave up and switched it off.

They drove on in silence for another hour before pulling up at a fish and chip shop about a mile from the border. Fergal went for the food and returned with three fish suppers which they ate in silence. When they had finished Danny drove back onto the main road.

They had only gone another couple of miles before Declan complained of stomach pains and that he needed the toilet.

'Why the hell did ye no' do it when we stopped…'

'Sorry, Fergal, but…'

'Shut up! We'll stop in a minute.'

Just before the border, Danny turned into a wooded area off the main road. Fergal then helped Declan out the back of the van and followed him into bushes just off a farm road. Danny tried again to find a decent reception on the radio. He eventually tuned into a station playing country & western music, which he thought would cheer Fergal up. *'And now, one of Country Music's all-time greats, Hank Williams with "Your Cheatin' Heart".'* Tapping his fingers on the dashboard to the music, Danny kept an eye on the cars passing to and from the nearby border. At least there was no sign of any army patrols. *'You'll walk the floor, the way I do. Your cheatin' heart will tell on you…'* A sudden bang echoed like thunder. Danny got out of the van. A second shot, then a third chased the first two into the distance. He could feel his heart tighten in his chest. Then he saw Fergal walking back towards the van with his revolver in his hand. 'Get back in the van, Duffy!'

Danny looked at him in silent shock, before climbing back into the driver's seat. Fergal got in the passenger seat, slamming the door shut.

'What the fuck happened?'

Fergal turned to Danny and stared at him. 'I executed him. So don't say another fucking word.'

Danny turned the car around, heading back onto the main road. Fergal switched the radio off and wiped the splatters of blood from his face. Danny drove on in numbed silence.

*

It took a couple of days before Declan's body was found in the ditch where he fell. The local police saw it as just another sectarian killing. The post-mortem revealed marks on the wrists, which were consistent with being bound with some form of ligature for a considerable time prior to death, while the head wounds left no doubt as to the cause. When the police turned up at his mother's house to inform her that Declan had been murdered, they showed little sympathy, asking her question after question about his associates and possible involvement with the IRA. She told them to get to hell out of her house, screaming obscenities at them as they returned to their Land Rover. She grabbed her coat and ran to her sister's house at the top of the street.

'Where is he?'

'Sinead, what's the matter?'

'Where's Fergal?'

'He's not been near this house for months. What the hell's the matter? Why are ye looking for…?'

'Declan's dead! He's been murdered!'

'Oh my God! What the hell's happened to him?'

'I don't know. He was found with half his head blown off in the woods near the border. They shot my baby in the face!' she screamed. 'They murdered him! They murdered my boy!'

'Who? Who murdered him?'

'The Provos did it!'

'Why would the Provos shoot Declan?'

'The police told me he was an informer. Where's Fergal?'

'I told ye, I don't know where he is. The RUC are lying bastards. Don't believe what they tell ye.'

'Well, they told me he's dead. Shot in the head. Are they lying about that?'

'Come into the kitchen, I'll make ye a cup of tea.'

'He's in the morgue. Are they lying about that?'

'Come on, I'll make ye a nice cup of tea. It will steady your nerves.'

*

Jamie Morrison smiled as he read the confidential RUC report he had just received from one of his old friends from his days in the B-Specials. 'That's him,' said Bulldog, handing Jamie the document with a black and white photograph of Declan attached. 'He was a snitch for Moorcroft.'

'Was it his own that killed him?'

'Ye, it looks that way. Some of the guys at the station are even saying it was his cousin, Fergal Gallagher, that did it.'

'Are they? He's a real nasty piece of work, that bastard. It wouldn't surprise me.'

'The guy was shot in the head three times.'

'Why would the Provos do that? Usually one bullet is enough,' said Jamie, looking again at the picture of Fergal. 'This guy is as crazy as they get. He's the one that shot that rookie soldier in the head on Mill Street.'

'He's killed a lot more according to Moorcroft.'

'I want you to let me know as soon as Moorcroft finds out where he's hiding out. I'm goin' to get this bastard!'

*

Declan's body was released a few days later in a sealed casket; the wounds having disfigured his face beyond recognition. The pathologist had to rely on dental records and a distinctive tattoo for identification. The news spread quickly throughout the backstreets of Belfast that Declan Murphy had been shot by the Provos for being an informer. There would be no IRA funeral or any Republican eulogies for him and, within hours of the news spreading, graffiti appeared opposite his mother's house. *Declan Murphy... Traitor.*

On the morning of the funeral the coffin lay in the front room for a few hours before it was taken to the nearby chapel. Declan's mother received a cheap looking wreath with a card that read, 'Burn in hell you Bastard!' She had assumed it had been sent by someone from a local loyalist paramilitary group, until she saw the Gaelic on the other side of the card. She showed it to her sister, who took the wreath and threw it in the bin at the back of the house before they left for Saint Patrick's.

After the mass, only half a dozen cars followed the coffin, which moved towards its final destination with undue haste. The hearse veered away from the tricolours and other paraphernalia of the IRA plots, and drew up alongside the dry-stone dyke at the back of the cemetery. The grave lay open like a wound in the soil, and a mound of clay lay nearby. Less than a couple of dozen mourners attended at the graveside as the coffin was carried to its final resting place. Father Cunningham followed a few minutes later, after changing from his mass regalia into a simple black suit and dog collar. His two altar boys had refused to attend the graveside after being threatened by the local *Na Fianna Eireann*. He took a moment to look at the turbulent skies overhead, before reading a formal prayer over the coffin while blessing it with holy water. Declan's mother sobbed uncontrollably when her son was lowered into the grave. All eyes, except hers, looked up for a moment as a burst of lightning tore a silver seam through the grey sky, quickly followed by a hollow roar of thunder as the heavens opened up.

Fergal looked on quietly as the drenched mourners scurried away from the graveside to their cars while two old gravediggers began to shovel the wet clay and sods of earth back into the grave. He found it hard to stomach as his mother took her sister away from the graveside to one of the waiting cars. He watched the cortege slowly make its way back out of the cemetery, before turning to Danny. 'Take it up a bit nearer.'

'Do ye think it's a good idea, Fergal?'

'No, but do it anyway.'

'All right,' said Danny as he drove slowly towards the grave with the sleet battering off the windscreen. By the time the car pulled up alongside the grave, the gravediggers had given up and found shelter in a hut nearby. Fergal got out from the passenger side, seemingly immune to the blustery weather. Danny remained in the car to let Fergal confront whatever grief or guilt he had in his increasingly disturbed mind.

Chapter 28

Newry Safe House

Mickey received orders to get Fergal and Danny out of Belfast; the Belfast Command had received intelligence that they were both at the top of the UVF's hit list, and that the British had agreed to hand them over to the UVF for interrogation. At first Fergal refused to leave, until Mickey brought a handwritten order from the Chief of Staff, ordering him out or face a court martial. Arrangements were hastily made to billet them both in a farmhouse just outside the town of Newry, which was close enough to the border for a quick getaway to the Republic. They would only return to Belfast to carry out planned operations.

The safe house was well off the main road, hidden from passing cars by a hedge of hawthorn trees. It was owned by a local man who had emigrated to New Zealand in the early seventies. It was a two-storey whitewashed farmhouse and was being looked after by a neighbour who happened to be a member of the local Newry IRA unit. The house had five rooms and an attached byre which was now in ruins. The amenities were almost non existent and basic comforts amounted to an outside toilet and a well for fresh water. The kitchen was no more that a slate-floored room with a turf burning stove that had not been used in years.

During the first few days, Fergal spent most of his time either maniacally cleaning his revolver, or staring into the fire. He rarely spoke. His nights were a torment to him as he craved the drugs that had for so long confused his dreams in surreal fantasies and masked his inner demons. Danny often lay awake at night listening to his cries of anguish and dread. Danny could bear it no longer and gently woke Fergal from a fit of raving.

'What's the matter?' moaned Fergal, sitting up in an instant and instinctively feeling for his revolver under his pillow.

'You were having a nightmare. You were talking about Declan again?'

'Give me a cigarette.'

Danny gave Fergal a cigarette, and quietly watched the light appear on Fergal's gaunt face as he struck a match off the wall. Fergal took a long draw from the cigarette and turned to stare at Danny.

'What was I saying about Declan?'

'I don't know, you were just shouting his name out and screaming things that I didn't understand. You did the same thing the last couple of nights. I can't get to sleep.'

'I should never have shot him.'

'Then why did you?'

'I intended to get him across the border, but while you were in the car he started thanking me for letting him go. The more he thanked me the more I hated his grovelling face and before I knew what I was doing I shot him in the head. I nearly missed and I blew off the side of his head, I could see his brains, but he was still running around screaming before I put two more bullets into him. That's what I see in my head when I close my eyes every night. We didn't even bury him ... just left him there with half his head scattered in the bushes and his dick still hanging out his trousers. Anyway you know now what kind of bastard I am, so don't ask me about him again,' said Fergal, lying back down on the sweat-stained pillow and staring at the cracks on the ceiling.

Following a couple of weeks of inactivity, they drove

into Newry town together. They had received orders from Belfast that they should meet the Newry unit and provide them with professional support and know-how. A cache of weapons was on its way from the south and the local men had to be trained in using them. Newry was a typical border town with nothing too unusual about it; a variety of shops, a post office, a couple of banks and of course a police station. It was a part of the North that had seen little of the Troubles, and the RUC thought of the local unit of the IRA as a bunch of bungling amateurs.

As Danny drove around town, Fergal seemed to have come out of his depression and had got some of his arrogant humour back as he whistled and embarrassed a couple of pretty girls standing at a zebra crossing. But Danny was more worried about him than ever. He had found discarded needles at the back of the farmhouse, which confirmed a suspicion he had had for weeks. He knew better than to confront Fergal and often watched as he walked across the fields at night to get his weekly deal. At least the drugs seemed to help him sleep better and he was less aggressive during the day. Danny could see the difference in him when the heroin was running low.

They drove to a farmhouse on the outskirts of town where they met the leaders of the Newry unit. The CO was a young farmer named Peter Dailey, who had received orders to kill George Wilson, a local part-time RUC officer, whose movements they had been monitoring over the past couple of weeks. None of the Newry men had killed anyone before, although they had planted a couple of bombs that had failed to go off. Only Dailey had used his handgun and that had resulted in a minor injury to a pursuing RUC officer after one of the failed bomb attempts. His hands were shaking when he explained the detail of the operation to Fergal and Danny. Fergal quickly decided that Dailey was not up to the task, and, without consulting Danny, decided that they should carry out the assassination. The relief on Dailey's face was obvious.

That afternoon, Danny drove back to the farmhouse in silence, he was beginning to see Fergal as nothing more than a ruthless killer, eager for his next victim. If he could kill his cousin, no one was beyond a bullet in the head, not even him.

*

George Wilson was married with two young children and had only been an RUC officer for two years. He was originally from Country Antrim and moved to Newry for the sake of the children. With the lack of recent IRA activity in the area, he took very little precaution in relation to his daily routine, feeling relatively safe in his civilian clothes when off-duty. He had no sense that morning that he had been tailed. He dropped off his wife and children at the marketplace as usual, and agreed to meet them in an hour's time once he had had a pint and placed a few bets in the bookmaker's.

As agreed, Danny and Fergal pulled up a mile or so outside Newry town and met up with Sammy Dailey, the CO's younger brother, who had stolen a Cortina that morning. Danny parked their van off the main road and hot-wired the Cortina. Sammy was told to stay with the van until they got back.

During the drive into Newry, neither Danny nor Fergal said much to each other. They knew what had to be done and they were preparing themselves mentally. Fergal showed no sign of nerves, but that was normal. By the time they reached the centre of the town, it was almost two-thirty. Fergal looked at the photograph of the target, before passing it to Danny. They parked opposite the bookmakers.

They sat in the car for about fifteen minutes, smoking

cigarettes and listening to country music on the radio. Then, just as expected, Wilson came out of the bookmaker's and stood in the bright afternoon sunshine studying his betting slip. Fergal nodded to Danny to drive forward. He took his revolver from the glove compartment. 'Keep the engine running, I won't be long.'

Fergal got out the car and reached for his revolver. Wilson instantly suspected something was wrong when he noticed Fergal walking directly towards him with a smirk on his ghostly, pale face. Before Wilson had time to react, he saw his wife and two children coming out of the butcher's shop. He shouted at them to stay back, before turning to face the stranger, who was now only a few feet away. Fergal took out his revolver. 'This is an IRA operation,' he shouted, before firing two shots, one to Wilson's chest and one to his head. Wilson staggered for a moment before falling to his knees. There were screams from his children as they ran towards their father. Fergal stood and stared at the convulsing body, before firing a third shot into it. He backed off as Wilson's two children screamed at him. He suddenly tripped, falling against a row of railings, dropping the revolver. Danny began tooting his horn frantically. Fergal tried to get to his feet, but the dead officer's wife grabbed him by the jacket and screamed obscenities at him. The more he struggled with her, the tighter she held on to him, pulling his head down towards the ground. He managed to pick up the revolver and fired two bullets into her stomach. She stared into his face, still holding his jacket, before loosening her grip and falling to the ground beside her husband. Danny was pumping the horn frantically and screaming at him to get into the moving car as half a dozen men emerged from the bookmaker's. Fergal fired a shot into the air to warn off the angry faces that were coming towards him, before jumping into the back seat.

In a panic, Danny drove with the back door still open, which battered off a lamppost as he skidded back onto the road. Shots were fired by another off-duty officer who had just arrived on the scene, one of his rounds hitting the back window of the Cortina. Danny drove on at high speed, out of the town and onto the back roads. He looked into his rear-view mirror to check on Fergal, who was slumped in the back seat with blood running down the side of his head. 'Why did ye have to shoot the woman, for Christ's sake?'

That night Fergal woke from one of his nightmares. He got up and sat on the edge of the bed staring at a bottle of whiskey at his feet. There was still a mouthful left and he quickly drank it, throwing the empty bottle into the corner of the room.

The room was a mess with newspapers, dirty plates and clothes lying everywhere. The windows were so dirty that only a faint hint of spring sunlight managed to penetrate into the gloom. He cursed as he looked around for his revolver, which he found under his sweat-soaked pillow. The house was freezing and he spat into the ashes of the fire that had not been lit for days. He could not remember arguing with Danny the night before, but he knew something had happened. He was still wearing the clothes he had fallen asleep in as he struggled downstairs. He staggered to the back door and kicked it open to see that the van was gone. Noticing that Danny's bag and gun were also missing, he began to recall the argument from the night before. 'He's fucked off!' he screamed as he went into a wild rage, kicking and smashing everything he could lay his hands on. 'I'll kill that bastard.'

Danny was not sure what he was doing as he drove back towards Belfast. Fergal's madness was beginning to affect his own sanity. The killing of the woman was the last straw. The only thing he could do now was find Mickey and tell him what had happened.

Once he reached Belfast, Danny drove through the city centre, and then out towards the Ardoyne and into the relative safety of the backstreets where the army and police rarely ventured. He parked the van at the back of the Shamrock and went in to see if Mickey was there.

The barman, Liam Docherty, poured Danny a whiskey. 'Where's Gallagher?'

'He's still down in Newry.'

'Best place for him,' said Liam, who hated Fergal.

'Liam, I've got to find Mickey Flynn,' said Danny, taking a swallow from the glass of Irish. 'Do you know where he is?'

'He's got a new safe house up in Ballymurphy. I don't know the address, but I can get it for you,' said Docherty, topping up Danny's glass of whiskey. 'Is that crazy bastard going to stay down there?'

'God knows. He's lost his mind all together. I need to speak to Mickey about him.'

'I always knew he was a bloody nutcase,' said one of the other men. 'Just have to look at those black eyes and ye know he's not all there.'

'There's Mickey's new address,' said Docherty, replacing the receiver back down and handing Danny a piece of paper with the address on it.

'Thanks, I better get going. If Fergal turns up, don't tell him I was here.'

Still in a rage, Fergal cut across the fields and dykes until he reached the nearest road. He was sweating heavily. After walking for over a mile, a car pulled up. 'Are ye all right there, son?' asked the driver, an elderly man with a Newry accent.

'It's my car...It went of the road a few miles back. I've been walking all morning. You couldn't give me a lift into Newry?'

'Oh, ye poor soul, ye look exhausted,' said the woman passenger, nudging her husband. 'We're going into town ourselves, we'll be glad to give you a lift.'

Mumbling to himself, Fergal climbed into the back seat. The man's smile slipped from his face when he noticed the strong smell of alcohol, but said nothing. The car slowly pulled away from the grass verge as the woman began asking Fergal questions about where he was from and where he was going. After a few strained attempts at polite conversation Fergal had had enough. He pulled out his revolver, held it to the man's head and told him to pull up the car. The woman began screaming hysterically until Fergal screamed back at her to shut up. He ordered the driver out of the car and climbed over into his seat as the woman got out of the passenger's side. Fergal drove off at speed, laughing as he watched the couple in his wing mirror comforting each other at the side of the road.

It was late afternoon by the time he pulled up outside the Shamrock. He banged the back door impatiently. 'Hurry up for fuck's sake.'

'Give me a minute,' said Docherty, struggling to pull back the heavy bolts. 'Oh, it's yourself Fergal. I thought you were still down in Newry with Danny.'

'So he's not been here?'

'Danny? Is he not with you?'

'Would I be asking ye if he was wi' me? He buggered off this morning. Get me a drink, a double,' demanded Fergal, following Docherty into the gloomy bar. 'Is there no-one in?'

'No, a couple of the boys were in a wee while ago, but they're away up home.'

'You don't have a few quid on ye, Docherty? Twenty, or even ten.'

'Business has been bad, Fergal. This place barely pays for itself.'

'You must have something, for God's sake. Even a fiver

will do!'

'I can give you a couple of pounds,' said Docherty looking through his trouser pockets for change.

'That's no use. I need petrol,' shouted Fergal, scattering the coins that Docherty had carefully counted onto the bar. 'There's a till behind ye, what's in that?' Fergal demanded as he downed the whiskey and lit a cigarette.

'Fergal, I can't take it out of that. Seamus will kill me!'

'If ye don't open it up and get me some money, I'll fucking kill ye,' threatened Fergal, putting his hand inside his leather jacket and blowing smoke in Docherty's face.

'Fergal, for God's sake, it's just the float.'

'Open the thing! Ye said there were a few of the lads in earlier. I'll take the float and what they spent and ye can tell that bastard Seamus I'll pay him back when I'm finished getting the Brits out of Ireland.'

'He'll go off his head,' said Docherty, reluctantly opening the ancient-looking till. 'I can give ye about seven pounds?'

Fergal drank the second whiskey and took the money Docherty nervously handed to him. 'This is a dump,' he said as he made his way out the back door. 'No wonder ye don't have any fucking customers.'

After checking a few safe houses, which turned out to be empty, Fergal found the van parked outside an abandoned end-terrace house. Reloading the chambers of his Smith and Wesson, he took a knife from his holdall and went down the alley that led to the back of the house. The back gate was lying open and Mickey was sitting on the steps, outside the kitchen, sunning himself and drinking a can of beer. Mickey was startled when he saw Fergal.

'How are you, Mickey?"

'Aye, well, Fergal, how are things with you?'

'How do ye think they are? You left us in that shithole of a place for three months with no money, and all we got from you was messages telling us we couldn't come back to Belfast. Well I'm here and I'm hungry. What have you got to eat?'

'There's some bacon and bread in the kitchen. You're welcome to it. There was money sent down every week, sure I posted it myself.'

'Thirty pounds for two men to live on all week; how were we supposed to survive on that?'

'I was told there was sixty pounds in the envelopes. I don't know why they would lie about a thing like that.'

'Are you sure you weren't dipping into the money yourself before ye sent it?'

'You know I wouldn't do something like that to you and Danny,' said Mickey, his nervous pleading amusing Fergal.

'I take it Danny's inside, is he?'

'No. Danny is not here. He just stopped here to get some money,' said Mickey.

'What's his van doing lying outside?' asked Fergal, following Mickey into the kitchen.

'He just dumped it there. He didn't want to risk getting stopped. It's easier to avoid the Brits around here if you're on foot. You know that better than anyone.'

'Did you give him any money?'

'Aye, a few pounds. It's all I had.'

'So you've got nothing for me then?'

'No, but I can get you a few quid if you give me a couple of hours. I'll make you a bacon butty and a pot of tea if you like. Then I'll go out and get you some cash.'

'Where're you going to get cash?'

'I'll go round and see the top brass. I'm sure they can come up with a few quid for you. They know what you've been through. They've had a lot to deal with this last wee while.'

'What?'

'The army have imposed a curfew for a couple of weeks and have been raiding houses and arresting people. We've lost a lot of guns and at least sixteen of our lads have been picked up.'

'You could've still got someone to come down and give us some extra money.'

Mickey shrugged his shoulders, his hands shaking as he put the frying-pan on the gas hob. Fergal took a seat in the kitchen and watched Mickey's agitated behaviour. 'What the fuck's up with you?' he finally snapped.

'Ah Fergal, it's been terrible here. The police and army have been giving us such a hard time. My nerves are shot,' said Mickey, as he watched Fergal take his revolver out from inside his jacket pocket and lay it on the blue Formica table. Mickey turned the gas off under the frying-pan by mistake and tried unsuccessfully to light it again. Fergal got up abruptly from his chair and lit the stove with his cigarette lighter, before giving Mickey a long stare. 'You're as nervous as a bag of cats, for Christ's sake … Are ye sure Duffy's no' hiding upstairs?'

'I told ye Fergal, he's no' here,' said Mickey, his hands still shaking, as he put the frying-pan on a high heat and putting a couple of slices of bacon on. 'Fergal, can you look after this and make yourself a pot of tea, while I go round to see if I can get you some money?'

'Aye, but don't be long and get at least fifty quid, if not more.'

'I'll do my best, but I can only get what they give me. I'll be back as soon as I can.'

Chapter 29

The Enemy Within

It was nearly six months since the bombing, but it took only a few days for the reality of William's head injuries to begin to extinguish any hope that Liz had of his recovery. The injuries were so severe that he was destined to remain in a coma unless there was some form of divine intervention. Nevertheless, she travelled to the hospital every day in the hope of the miracle that would bring him back from his unconscious world. She sat by his bed and read him the same stories she once read to him as a child in the hope that they would trigger some reaction. She watched the flickers from under his eyelids and felt that he could sense her presence. William's fiancée, Sara, had only recently stopped visiting after Liz insisted she get on with her own life. Heartbroken, Liz continued her daily visits on her own.

Jamie's reaction was to reap revenge on anyone involved in the bombings, and he spent more and more time in the company of the ruthless men he relied on to satisfy his lust for vengeance. He got little satisfaction when he was informed that two of the IRA car bombers were already dead; victims of an *own goal,* when they were blown up driving a car bomb to the Palace Barracks just outside Belfast. They got off lightly as far as Jamie was concerned.

The intelligence that he received from Major Moorcroft confirmed that both Gallagher and Duffy were two of the suspected car bombers. He ordered his men to concentrate their efforts on finding them, and to immediately bring them to the Shankill - alive if possible.

*

Danny stood in front of three soberly dressed men in a room used as the main HQ of the Northern Command. He had just finished explaining why he had disobeyed orders and come back to Belfast. He then told them, with some hesitation, about Fergal's drug and alcohol abuse. The Brigade commander had already heard reports from Peter Dailey in Newry that Fergal had become a dangerous liability. The killing of the part-time RUC officer's wife had caused such an outcry, even among staunch Republican supporters in Newry that the local IRA unit had to flee to the Republic.

The men listened to Danny, and then conferred among themselves about what to do with Fergal, before he was responsible for some other outrage. They agreed that his state of mind had deteriorated after the execution of his cousin. The merits of putting him in that position were hotly discussed.

After a few minutes of further debate, it was decided that they had to get him to stand down from active service. His mental health was one thing, but the drug-taking was another. They could not make him go to hospital, but they could exile him to the Republic to keep him out of harm's way. Danny did not think that Fergal would take too kindly to being exiled, even to the Republic. One of the other men suggested they should simply have him shot.

A few minutes later, Mickey appeared at the door, his face flushed, as he nervously told those congregated that Fergal was sitting in a safe house in Kilburn Street and was *off his fucking head*. He warned Danny that he thought Fergal was out to kill him. This was enough for those present. Something had to be done about him straight away. They managed to gather some thirty pounds between them and gave it to Mickey, who was told to go back to the house and persuade Fergal to come back to see them on the pretext that they had a special job lined up for him. They would then, by force if necessary, get him over the border and into the Republic. If he refused then there was always another way to put him out of action.

Mickey was not very happy about having to go back, but he had no choice. Apprehensively, he parked outside the terrace house and went around the back to the kitchen door. After anxiously going through the house, he was relieved to find no sign of Fergal. 'Thank fuck', he sighed as he sat down and lit a cigarette.

For the next few nights, Danny slept on a couch in a safe house in the Ardoyne, where he was to lie low until Fergal was found and taken off the street. It was difficult to get a good night's sleep when someone as lethal and brutal as Fergal Gallagher was after you. No-one had seen him for days and his mother's house was being watched around the clock by a team of plain clothes RUC intelligence officers, the IRA, and another couple of tough-looking guys in a pick up truck. The most wanted man in Northern Ireland had vanished.

By the end of the week, it was decided to move Danny to a new safe house. Mickey managed to get the meters rigged so there was a free supply of electricity and gas. Even though the windows were boarded up, Danny taped black plastic bin-liners around the edges so he could use the lamp that Mickey had given him.

'Here are the things you wanted and there're a couple of books to keep you occupied for a few days,' said Mickey as he came into the kitchen with a bag of groceries.

'Have you heard anything more about Fergal?'

'No, the lads have been out looking for him. Don't worry, they'll get him.'

'What are they going to do with him?'

'Shoot the fucker, I hope,' laughed Mickey, half seriously. 'No, I think they just want him out the way before he loses the plot altogether.'

'He shouldn't have been ordered to execute his cousin. I think that's what's messed up his head. He probably wasn't takin' drugs until that happened.'

'Don't kid yourself. He's been takin' drugs for years. Drugs, what does he think he is? A fucking rock star! Here take that,' said Mickey, handing Danny a couple of pounds and two books.

'Have ye got any cigarettes?'

'Here, take them; it's nearly a full packet. I'll come up tomorrow with some more.'

Mickey left, carefully sneaking out the back door and making sure no one was watching. He had parked his car a few blocks away in case he had been followed and took another look up at the windows of the safe house to reassure himself that there was no light seeping through the sides. The streets were quiet as he walked to the car. After a final glance over his shoulder he opened the door and slumped himself down into the cramped driver's seat. The car had been hot-wired and he turned on the ignition with his penknife. It started first time. He was about to drive away when he suddenly felt a hard object press against the back of his head.

'Hello, Mickey, I've been waiting for ages for ye. Where the fuck have ye been?'

'It's yerself, Fergal; ye frightened the life out of me … Put that away, son.'

'Oh, this,' said Fergal, taking the revolver away from Mickey's head. 'Have ye seen that bastard Duffy?'

'No … No … I've no' seen him around. Where have ye been? Why didn't ye wait for me the other day? I managed to get you that money,' rattled Mickey.

'Where is it?'

'I had to give it back when I told them you were gone! They want to talk to ye, son,' said Mickey, trying to control the nerves in his voice. 'They need to speak to you,' he added, noticing for the first time that Fergal's head was shaved bald.

'I know what they want. They want to terminate my contract of employment,' said Fergal with a cackled laugh. 'They might even want to kill me.'

'Don't be daft, son. They just want to talk to you about the new rules of engagement. The whole command structure has changed. The whole set-up's been changed and they need to make sure that everyone is singing from the same hymn sheet. That's why they want to talk to ye, son. You're goin' to be put in charge of your own unit in England.'

'That's not what I've heard,' Fergal sneered, trying to read Mickey's eyes in the yellow glow of the streetlight. 'I've heard that fucker Duffy has told them that I'm a junkie... that's what I've heard.'

'Who the hell would tell you that?'

'It doesn't matter who told me. That's what I've been told. Have ye any money on you?'

'A couple of pounds.'

'Give me it!'

'For Christ's sake, Fergal, it's all...'

'Shut up and give it here. You can get it back from those big shots up in Ballymurphy and tell them until I get some assurance from them that I'm not going to be up before a court martial, I'll just carry on fighting the war as normal. I might even join the INLA.'

'Ye don't want to be talking like that, son.'

'Mickey! Stop calling me son! I'm not your fucking son,' shouted Fergal, putting the money into his jacket pocket. 'And ye can tell Danny not to worry. There're no hard feelings. See ye later, Mickey,' said Fergal, with a grin, slamming the car door closed and covering his bald head with a black woolly tammy.

'Aye, look after yerself!' said Mickey, driving off as soon as the back door closed.

*

Danny boiled a saucepan of water to make a cup of tea while he watched the TV set that Mickey had left him. Life on the run was all about compromise; a mattress on the floor instead of a normal bed, a saucepan instead of a kettle, a cooker with only one hob working, and a black and white TV with constant snow storms of interference were all part of the deal. He poured the boiling water slowly into a big green mug and grabbed a handful of tea biscuits, before settling down on his mattress to watch the second half of the European Cup final match between Nottingham Forest and Hamburg. John Robertson had already scored in the first half and Hamburg was now throwing everything at the Forest goal, which Peter Shilton was blocking with every part of his body.

Danny was just about to dunk his last biscuit into the tea when he was startled by a sudden creaking noise coming from downstairs. He reached for his revolver but couldn't find it under the mattress. His thoughts were confused and he became indecisive as he heard another creak on the floorboards. He began to think he must have left it in the kitchen. Another creak, this time it sounded like someone was now slowly and very carefully climbing the stairs. He left the TV on; it was too late to turn it down. Another creak; this, he guessed, was near the top of the stairs. He put the potato knife he had been using in his back pocket and stood to the side of door. There was another squeak on the floorboards. Danny held his breath.

The door burst open and Fergal rushed into the room. Danny jumped on Fergal from behind, frantically trying to wrestle the gun from his hand. They both fell to the floor. Fergal roared obscenities and struck Danny with the back of his head. Danny plunged the potato knife into Fergal's thigh. Fergal screamed and the revolver flew out of his hand and across the room. Danny tried to disentangle himself as they struggled violently to get to the gun.

In all the commotion, neither of them heard the army vehicles pulling up outside, and by the time they realised what was happening, they were surrounded by half a dozen soldiers from the Parachute Regiment, armed with semi-automatic rifles. Danny dropped the knife and held his hands up. Fergal rolled about the floor in pain.

They were both handcuffed. Once defenceless, they were kicked and punched senseless by two soldiers who had revenge on their minds after seeing two of their mates blown to pieces by a car bomb. One of the Paras was still urinating over Fergal when the RUC arrived at the house with arrest warrants.

'Don't piss on them…we have to take them in,' said the senior RUC officer, as he showed the warrants.

'Too late,' replied one of the soldiers, shaking himself dry. 'Why don't we just put a bullet in their heads now and save everyone a lot of hassle?'

'We have orders to take them to Castlereagh. They're not going to tell us much with bullets in their heads.'

The revolver and knife were picked up off the floor by one of the soldiers and placed inside a plastic bag. The lieutenant in charge of the operation reluctantly handed the productions over to the RUC officers. After a thorough search of the house they found Danny's revolver in the kitchen.

Both Fergal and Danny refused to give their names and were dragged out to the street and then thrown into the back of the waiting RUC Land Rover. Fergal's trouser leg was now saturated with blood and he began to scream for a doctor.

'You can both die in there, for all I care,' shouted one of the officers from the front passenger seat.

'Up the Provos,' shouted Fergal as he struggled to get up from the Land Rover's rough metal floor.

'Shut to fuck up, ye Fenian bastard,' shouted the same officer, spitting through the observation slit into the back of the van.

Fergal began to sing "A Soldier's Song" as the Land Rover turned abruptly around another corner. Danny and Fergal were thrown so close together that Danny could see into the black holes that were once Fergal's eyes.

At the station, the sergeant at the charge bar refused to lock up Fergal when he saw the blood forming a pool at his feet, and ordered the arresting officers to take him to the hospital. After he again refused to give his name and address to the irate police officers, Danny was placed in a holding cell to stew for a while. He knew that he would soon be heading to Castlereagh.

At the safe house, the army tore up the rotten floorboards, and ripped out the interior in a desperate search for more weapons. They tore out so much of the structure of the house that it was beginning to look like it would cave in on itself. Once the house had been stripped back to its bare walls, Major Moorcroft arrived with two other officers from Military Intelligence. The lieutenant turned to salute his superiors and found it difficult to keep the smile from his naturally smug-looking face.

'We had a tip off this was an IRA safe house only an hour ago. Two suspects arrested, sir. They were both carrying weapons and trying to kill each other when we arrived.'

'You should have let them,' said one of the officers.

'Where are they now? I want to speak to them,' demanded Moorcroft.

'In police custody, sir…'

'What! How the hell did that happen? This was a bloody army operation. God damn it!'

'Sorry, Major, they showed up shortly after we arrived with arrest warrants and took the prisoners into custody. They must have got the same tip off.'

'Where did they take them to?'

'The Crumlin Road Station, it's up near…'

'I know where it is, Lieutenant. Did you find anything of interest here?'

'No, sir. I think the place is clean.'

'If you think this is clean, I'd like to see your house!' Moorcroft laughed with his two colleagues.

*

Time was passing slowly as Danny stared at the graffiti scraped on the detention cell walls. It seemed that half the people living in the Falls had spent some time in that cell waiting for whatever lay in store. The light bulb blinked every so often and he wondered if this was the start of the RUC's notorious interrogation tactics.

A clatter of keys at the door made him sit up as the turnkey let an army officer into the cell. There was an air of controlled menace about the man as he stood for a moment and looked at Danny without speaking. Danny turned to stare at the wall concentrating on one name scratched on the thick layers of paint, which he repeated to himself like some ancient Hindu mantra.

'They don't work, son,' said Moorcroft, putting his highly polished boot on the wooden bench next to Danny. 'You see, we train our guys the same techniques, and we know they won't stop someone spilling their guts if they suffer enough pain. Even the fear of pain is sometimes enough for most people. You're only trained this shit to make you think you can deal with your arrest without becoming a grass. You've heard of Castlereagh? Well, I know all you Taigs know all about Castlereagh, because every one of you that ends up there starts talking; maybe not straight away, but eventually. I'm told you won't even give your name. Well that's not a problem, Danny. You joined up with the Provos about eight months ago after your sister Kathleen was killed with a stray plastic bullet. You see, Danny, there's nothing much I need to know about you. You were in the same unit as that mad bastard Fergal Gallagher. We know you two killed the RUC officer and his wife down in Newry. These wooden-tops out there, they don't know that. Just think of the kicking you'll get when they find out. I know you never pulled the trigger, but do you think killing a woman and leaving her two kids orphans really makes up for some stupid bastard firing a plastic bullet in blind panic when a bunch of thugs were throwing stones and petrol bombs at him? Do you think your sister is happy up there in heaven knowing her brother is murdering innocent people in her memory?'

'Leave my sister out of it!'

'Oh, so you do speak. For a minute I thought all that mantra stuff was working. But it doesn't work, does it? You've been staring at that wall but listening to everything I've been saying. You see, Danny, I'm not all that interested in you; it's that psycho Fergal Gallagher I'm interested in. I take it that it was Gallagher you were fighting with before you were arrested ... Back at the mantra again? Well, I'll find out soon enough because he's in hospital under armed guard. The only thing is, the RUC have no idea what a big fish we caught for them. If I got there twenty minutes earlier you would not be here and he would certainly not be in hospital. You would be both squealing like pigs in some grimy torture chamber in the bowels of the Shankill. The thing about some of those lunatics, they don't give a damn whether you talk or not. They do it all for the pleasure of seeing you on the edge of darkness before they pull you back to start it all over again … Still concentrating on that wall, Danny? With those guys your head would he bouncing off the wall just to get them warmed up. Anyway you won't be getting out from the Maze for a long, long time. The gun alone will send you down for at least ten years. Even if there's not enough evidence to get you for the Newry murders, I'm sure they'll find something else to pin on you before they're finished with you at Castlereagh. I know you're not a bad lad, maybe if I was in your shoes and my sister was killed, then I might have done the same thing. All I'm saying is, when you go to court, I can get you a reduced sentence … I'll come and see you nearer the time.'

'Don't bother and close the door on the way out!'

'I've got plenty of time on my side and I'll know where to find you.'

As the steel door closed with a bang, Danny let out a heavy sigh of relief and wiped his sweaty palms on his trousers. He felt like he had held his breath through the whole ordeal. The major was right, the mantra didn't work and he had listened to every word that was said. If he found that hard, how was he going to bear up at Castlereagh when the gloves really came off?

*

Guarded by two armed police officers and handcuffed to a

metal bed frame, Fergal lay in a state of semi-consciousness after an emergency operation on his wounded leg. The stab wound was deep enough to do permanent damage to the ligaments and the pain was excruciating every time he moved. As he slipped in and out of a drug-induced sleep he suddenly found his arms restrained. He struggled to wake himself. 'What the fuck?' he shouted.

'At last we meet, Mr Gallagher,' said Moorcroft, standing at the bottom of the bed, his arms folded. 'Let him go and wait outside, he's not going anywhere,' he added to the two soldiers standing on either side of the bed. 'Tell those two cops at the door that they can go. Mr Gallagher is now in our custody.'

'Who the hell are you?' shouted Fergal, still trying to clear his head.

'That's not your concern. I know all about you and that's all that matters. I spoke to your partner Duffy who was quite happy to make a deal to save his own skin.'

'Piss off. I'm not falling for that old trick. What did you say your name was?'

'I didn't.'

'Duffy is on his way to Castlereagh. He signed a statement before he left.'

'Lies … Fucking lies. Even he wouldn't sign a confession this quick. You'll need to do better than that.'

'He has confessed to his part in the murder of the RUC officer and his wife in Newry and he confirmed that you were the bastard that shot them.'

'If you say so. I'm saying nothing. Now get to hell out of here.'

'I don't think you understand. You're now in my custody.'

'That's fucking illegal.'

'Call it what you like. If you sign a written statement detailing what operations you have been involved in, then we'll hand you back over to the RUC.'

'Fuck off!'

'I know some people in the UVF who would like to meet you. Would you rather speak to them? Even your friends in the IRA will be glad to see the back of you after killing that woman in Newry.'

'You're beginning to bore me.'

'Maybe you'll find this less boring. Are you interested to learn how we know so much about what you've been up to? Are you still proud of killing your cousin, Declan?'

'I'm saying nothing.'

'We know it was you who executed him. The thing is, it wasn't Declan who was giving us the information about your operations. Everything he told us was a pack of lies, but we kept him on the back burner as a potential fall guy. We knew sooner or later you guys would figure out that someone was passing information to us about your unit. Why do you think he was meeting me in the middle of Belfast city centre? We were setting him up to draw the heat from someone more reliable than your lying cousin.'

'You're full of shit.'

'Then you'll not believe me when I tell you it was Mickey Flynn who betrayed you. We dug up some stuff about him interfering with schoolboys in the football team he managed when he was the janitor at Saint … something or other.'

'Why would you tell me this now? You've just signed his death warrant … *If* it's true. What use is he going to be to you then?'

'Don't you worry about that! He stopped giving us anything worthwhile once you blew your cousin's head off. He was more scared of you than us by that time. Maybe once we put you out of your misery, he'll be more amenable.'

'Take a fuck to yerself.'

'Well, enough chat,' said Moorcroft, taking a heavy-duty tape from his pocket and calling in the two soldiers who were standing outside the door. 'Put that on his mouth.'

Fergal struggled violently as the tape was wrapped around his mouth and the morphine drip ripped from his arm. When his head was pulled back, he noticed that one of the 'soldiers' had the letters UVF tattooed just above his wrist. He choked for a breath as the pain returned to the ruptured muscle in his leg. 'There is no way we can get you out of here without causing problems with the RUC, but we'll leave this to keep you company before you find yourself in hell,' said Moorcroft, placing a ticking device under the bed. Still struggling to breathe through the gaps in the tape, Fergal could hear the ticking under his bed as he tried ferociously to break his hands free from the handcuffs. Moorcroft stood at the door for a few seconds to enjoy the moment before throwing the keys to the handcuffs on the floor to add to Fergal's torment. The device ticked away mercilessly.

Moorcroft walked back through the hospital to his Land Rover. He gave a casual salute to the three men waiting there for him. 'We should have put a real bomb under the bed,' said one of his men, removing his army tunic as the driver started up the engine. 'If anyone deserves to die it's that bastard.'

'We don't blow up hospitals, but it will give him a taste of what it's like to think he's about to be blown to pieces,' said Moorcroft, climbing into the front passenger's seat. 'If he's not already shit himself he will when the alarm goes off in a couple of minutes. Let's get out of here.'

Chapter 30

The H-Blocks

Three months after his arrest, Danny stood on trial at the High Court. The charges were read out by the clerk of court. 'You, Daniel Patrick Duffy, have been indicted in the name of Her Majesty's Government on the following charges: membership of an illegal paramilitary organisation, namely the Provisional IRA; possession of an illegal firearm; possession of an offensive weapon, namely a knife; attempted murder of Fergal Gallagher and the reckless endangerment of life to soldiers of Her Majesty's Armed Forces at the time of your arrest. How do you plead?'

'I refuse to recognise the authority of this British court to try an Irishman in Ireland.'

The presiding judges were unmoved by this act of defiance. With no jury to address, they simply ordered the prosecutor to call the first witness for the Crown, and settled down to hear the evidence. Danny turned his head to see his family sitting in the public benches. Marie gasped and put a nervous hand to her mouth when she saw his pale, haunted face. He smiled before being pulled back to face the front by one of the prison officers. Roisin held her mother's hand and squeezed it tightly. Brendan mumbled a few prayers under his breath. Joe looked on with pride.

The three days of brutal interrogation at Castlereagh were enough to force Danny to sign a confession. The charges were serious enough, but at least there was no mention of the Newry killings. Danny had been so badly beaten that it took weeks for him to recover, before he was returned to the Crumlin Road Prison to await his trial.

The confession and the evidence of the RUC officers were enough to seal his fate. Danny had also refused to instruct a lawyer or present any kind of defence, and the Crown case went unchallenged. The trial was over in a matter of hours and he was pulled to his feet for the verdict.

Guilty on all charges!

Marie was told to be prepared for a long sentence, but broke down in tears when he was given a total of sixteen years in prison. As Danny was led away, Brendan and Roisin helped their distraught mother from the court.

After a short journey, the bus stopped outside the Maze Prison. Danny felt overwhelmed by its five metre high concrete walls and watchtowers. The guards dragged him from the prison van and through the massive complex of concrete buildings to the administration section of one of the 'Republican H-Blocks'. He was immediately ordered to undress. Once naked, he was offered the standard prison clothes, which he refused to take. A coarse, grey blanket was thrown at him, and as he bent to pick it up he received a push from behind, knocking him to the ground.

'Get on yer feet! Ye dirty Fenian bastard!'

'Piss off, ye Orange bastard!'

'Get up, ye fucker,' screamed one of the other officers, before brutally punching Danny in the face. Dazed and bleeding from his nose, he was pulled to his feet and dragged down a narrow corridor to the communal showers were he was thrown on to the hard tiles. He lay there as one of the officers turned on the shower. Danny struggled to get to his feet under a deluge of freezing water.

Before he could properly dry himself he was taken to a cell in one of the wings. He sat on the floor, shivering under the coarse blanket, as the whole day's events began playing out in his mind. *Sixteen years!* It seemed like an eternity but, apart from the killing of the woman in Newry, he had no regrets.

The last of the daylight disappeared from the cell, and the human sounds of the prison began to become more apparent. He could make out whispers between other cellmates and the distant sound of a television from the prison officers' rest area. Even so, the wing was strangely quiet in comparison to the Crumlin Road Prison where he had spent the last three months on remand. Now slipping into melancholy, his mind began to wander back to Kathleen's wedding, remembering how happy his family were that day, and how beautiful his sister looked as she walked down the aisle. He turned towards the wall and fell into a deep sleep.

The next morning he awoke to the sound of keys rattling. It took him a few seconds to remember that he was in the Maze. The metal door opened, and a ghostly figure entered, wrapped in a blanket. With his long hair and beard, the man looked biblical, and for a moment Danny thought he was still dreaming. A prisoner officer pushed the frail-looking man further into the cell before closing the metal door. Danny sat up and pulled his blanket around his body.

'How are ye doing, young fella?' said the man, before breaking into a fit of coughing. Danny got to his feet. 'Are ye all right?'

'This will pass in a few minutes,' he wheezed, putting his hand on the cell wall to steady himself.

'Is this your cell?'

'Well, I think it's ours now, young Duffy.'

'How do you know my name?'

'Well, apart from the fact it's on the outside of the cell, the screws told me. I knew yer Uncle Eugene. He was a fine fella. My name's Seamus … Seamus Feeney.'

'Don't let all this hair and beard fool ye,' said Seamus, seeing the concern in Danny's eyes. 'I haven't seen a mirror for a while, but everyone in here looks just as bad. I've been in the hospital wing, pneumonia and other shit.'

The latch at the bottom of the door suddenly opened and two bowls of porridge were pushed into the cell. Seamus picked up the bowls and handed one to Danny. 'Ye better have this before it sets as hard as concrete.'

Danny took the bowl. 'I hate porridge,' he groaned, prodding the oats and milk with a plastic spoon.

'Eat it up, son. It's good for yer bowels and ye need good bowels in this place.'

His stomach empty, Danny tried to force down the porridge, but the slimy texture and the smell of the disinfected cell were making him feel sick. Two mouthfuls were enough and he pushed the bowl away. 'Here, ye have it! I can't eat it.'

With nothing in the cells but themselves, Danny and Seamus soon got to know each other pretty well. Seamus was a talker, and, through bouts of coughing, he told Danny what he had to know to survive being on the blanket. 'How long were ye on hunger strike?' asked Danny, when he realised why Seamus looked so ill.

'Fifty three days. It was called off when we thought we had a deal. But the Brits have gone back on what they promised. You can't trust those bastards.'

After a restless night, Danny woke the next morning to discoverer that his cellmate was not only on the blanket, but a zealous supporter of the dirty protest.

'Probably the right texture for a masterpiece,' said Seamus, putting his hand into the chamber pot to remove his own faeces. He then began to delicately 'paint' the wall with his excrement. Danny held his breath, the smell made him nauseated. When he breathed out again he found himself vomiting into the corner of the cell.

'Ah,' said Seamus. 'You have added a rainbow of colour to my meagre palette.'

It took another week or so before Danny was able to cope with all the conflicting, but generally odious, smells of daily life on the blanket. He was constipated for over five days before he was able to start his own dirty protest. By now Seamus had created his masterpiece, a copy of Salvador Dali's *Christ of Saint John of the Cross*, which he created from memory. 'What do ye think?' he asked, standing back to assess his work after highlighting some areas with a smear of porridge.

'It's shite,' said Danny, before breaking into a fit of laughter at what he could see of Seamus's feigned disappointment under his shrub of wild hair.

'Yes…but it's my shite,' replied Seamus.

As the days dragged on Danny became depressed with the awful state of affairs, and the length of his sentence was now impossible for him to endure. The art that once covered the walls in the cell was now buried under smears of faeces and uneaten food. The stench was unbearable. To add to the appalling conditions, maggots began to emerge from the waste and he watched with revulsion as Seamus collected the wriggling larva from the filth and threw them out the window to the hungry birds that had become accustomed to this new source of prison protein. 'Ach, stop being such a baby, I used to breed these little buggers in jars for fishing on Lough Neagh. I've caught many a good size fish using these beauties.'

'They're disgusting.'

'Ah, they say that beauty is in the eye of the beholder.'

'Aye, and you must be blind. Keep them away from me!'

'You got used to the smell of shit …You'll soon get used to these.'

To Danny's relief the dirty protest was suddenly called off. All the Republican prisoners were taken en masse to the communal showers. New towels and blankets were issued to the men, while teams of industrial cleaners took the opportunity to clean and disinfect the filthy cells.

As Seamus and Danny were taken back to their cells, they had to endure the usual abuse from the more bitter-minded prison officers, 'Look at the soap dodgers. One wash won't stop you stinking of shit!' shouted Dan Carson, a giant of a man, known to his fellow Officers as 'Desperate Dan', due to his uncanny resemblance to the cartoon character in the Dandy comic book. The prisoners had their own name for him: 'Cunt Carson'. Experience had taught the prisoners to ignore the abuse; to react would only result in a beating and achieve nothing. To take the bait in such circumstances was seen as a breach of internal IRA discipline; order had to be maintained, even in prison. Unfortunately Danny had not been at the Maze long enough to learn all the rules. It only took a minor push by one of the officers to set things in motion. 'Get lost, ye dirty Orange bastard,' Danny muttered under his breath before he was grabbed by two prison officers and dragged into the nearby search cell. Dan Carson followed them in. 'Spread yer fucking legs!' shouted Carson, pulling away Danny's blanket. 'Spread them, ye Taig bastard!' screamed another officer as they punched him in the kidneys. Still struggling, Danny was forced to spread his legs. Carson forced his rubber gloved fingers into his back passage. 'What the hell have ye been hiding up yer arse?'

'Yer mother, ye Orange bastard!' Danny shouted as he felt the brutal finger enter his anus.

'Ye cheeky wee bastard!' screamed Carson. 'This will make ye think twice before ye call me a dirty Orange bastard, again,' spat Carson into Danny's ear. Dropping the rubber glove into a waste bin, Carson began beating Danny with his baton before kneeing him in the groin. Danny's scream was so terrifying that hardened men in the cells all along the corridor turned pale at the horror they imagined. Danny was dropped to the tiled floor, his left testicle already turning black as drops of blood dripped from his penis. One of the officers gave Danny a parting kick in the ribs.

*

Dan Carson was already on the IRA's hit list, but the brutal assault on Eugene Tierney's nephew had his name moved to the top. Up until now, the IRA's information on Carson was scant. They did not even know the type of car he was driving. All they knew was that he lived somewhere in the Armagh countryside.

After only two weeks, an unguarded remark by Carson in his local pub, just outside Crossmaglen, was passed to the IRA unit operating in the area. His description was telephoned back to Belfast ... *Big guy, jaw and stubble like Desperate Dan, lives on a farm and drives a Volvo.*

Unaware that the IRA had discovered his remote farmhouse, Carson turned up the radio as one of his favourite songs came on: *Lucille*, by Kenny Rogers. He could just see the kitchen light of the farmhouse up ahead and was wondering what his wife was making for dinner. He pulled up at the cattle grilles and gave his usual cautious look around the hedgerows before getting out of the car. As he unhooked the tie on the metal gate there was a sudden rustle of bushes behind him.

'Keep yer hands on the gate, or yer head will be in that field before the rest of ye,' shouted a distinctive Fermanagh accent. 'If ye move we'll kill ye.'

'Who are ye? What do ye want? I'm just a local farmer,' pleaded Carson, who could see his farmhouse up ahead, so near, but yet so far. He then saw another gunman on the other side of the narrow road moving towards him and he knew he was going to die. 'I've got money in the house … Over three thousand pounds. You can have it…'

'Shut up. We're not here for money.'

It was only a few hours before the evening news confirmed that … *Another member of the prison services, Daniel Carson, has been kidnapped and summarily executed for simply doing his job and serving his community. He left a wife and two young children... He was one of the few Catholics in the province willing to take on such a dangerous job. This brings the total of prison officers killed to twelve since the troubles began…* The news report failed to mention the sadistic abuse that Carson had meted out to defenceless prisoners over the eight years of his distinguished service to the community.

When Danny left the prison hospital and returned to the wing, he was glad to see that his cellmate had not restarted his dirty protest. He was also glad to hear that Seamus had been turned down for inclusion on the next hunger strike.

'Are ye all right?' Seamus asked. 'You still look a bit sore.'

'I'm fine,' said Danny, wrapping the blanket around himself and rolling a cigarette. 'I'm just still a bit tender, that's all.'

'Well, he's roasting in hell now.'

'He got what he deserved. I still can't believe he was a Catholic.'

'They got him to dig his own grave. He was crying like a baby and begging for his miserable life.'

'To hell with him,' was all Danny could say as the painful throbbing began again in his swollen testicle.

'There was something warped about that man,' said Seamus. 'He'd married a Protestant woman from

Carrickfergus and brought his kids up as Protestants. They say that turncoats are often the worst; they've got more to prove than most. Anyway that's done and dusted now. The screws are all shitting themselves and keeping a low profile. They don't want to be the next to get a bullet in the head.'

Chapter 31

Hunger Strike

On the 28th of February 1981, Bobby Sands ate his last food, an orange, which he complained was bitter to the taste. The irony was not lost on him. He was just over a week away from his twenty-seventh birthday.

Sinn Fein marked the start of his fast with a rally in West Belfast. The prisoners' demands were read to the thousands of supporters who attended. '*We have asserted that we are political prisoners and everything about our country, our interrogation, trials and prison conditions show that we are politically motivated and not motivated by selfish reasons and selfish ends. As further demonstration of our selflessness and the justice of our cause, a number of our comrades, beginning today with Bobby Sands, will hunger strike to the death unless the British government abandons its criminalization policy and meets our demands.*'

Tiny crystal radios were smuggled into the Maze to keep the prisoners aware of the media reaction to the strike. Seamus was trusted with one and ordered to relay news reports to the rest of the men by various methods including shouting out anything of interest in Gaelic. He was in the furthest cell from the prison administration centre, and would have plenty of time to hide the radio when the prison officers entered the wing. While Seamus was tuned into news bulletins, Danny would sit by the door listening for any guards entering the corridor.

One night as Seamus listened to the radio it was obvious to him that the media and general public were treating the news of a second hunger strike with bemusement. The British newspapers went further and ridiculed the very idea as a nonsensical attempt to get the IRA's flagging fortunes back on track. Margaret Thatcher was no more willing to compromise than she had been before. *'The government will not surrender control of what goes on in the prisons to a particular group of prisoners. It will not concede the demand for political status, or recognise that murder and violence are less culpable because they are claimed to be committed for political motives.'*

On the 15th of March, Francis Hughes, from Bellaghy, County Derry, became the second man to go on hunger strike.

The British government continued to play down the hunger strike as another distraction by the IRA from the daily killings for which they were responsible. But the unexpected death of Frank Maguire, the MP for Fermanagh and South Tyrone, gave the hunger strike a twist of fate that put the spotlight of the world on the prisoners' struggle. The prisoners agreed with the outside leadership that Bobby Sands should stand for the vacant Westminster seat. It was clear that such a move would be a major coup for the cause and it was felt that if Sands was elected, the British government would not let a member of its own parliament starve to death. Once the decision was made, other potential nationalist candidates withdrew from the by-election to give Sands a clear run against the only remaining candidate, Harry West of the Official Unionist Party.

On the day of the count, Seamus was frantically trying to tune into the radio to get the election results. Wrapped in his blanket, Danny stood guard at the door. The radio whistled wildly as it struggled to pick up a signal.

'I can't get the damn thing to stay in tune. Wonder what time it is?' moaned Seamus, trying everything he could think of to get the radio to work properly.

'There's a lot of noise coming from the Circle,' said

Danny. 'The screws must be watching it on TV.'

At that moment a roar went up and echoed down the corridor of the wing and into each cell like a passing ill wind. 'Damn it, he must have lost,' said Seamus, giving up on the radio. There was another cheer from the Circle and the distant sound of periodic clapping. Then a few seconds later an agonising hush was heard that seemed to be at odds with what went before.

'Put it away,' shouted Danny in a whisper. 'There's a screw coming.'

'Damn it,' said Seamus, quickly sliding the radio back into its hiding place. They sat on their respective mattresses and listened to the guard's progress along the row of cells. He pulled one of the observation covers open. 'You're all very quiet today for some reason. Don't tell me he's dead already!'

'Piss off,' was the response he got from whichever cell he was peering into.

'Now don't be like that. Well, I'm away back to watch the Hurricane beat Davis. It's a pity you lot don't have a telly; it's a great game,' he shouted, as he slammed the observation slit closed.

So that was the noise from the Circle, thought Danny. 'Seamus, they've been cheering the snooker,' he explained. 'The results can't be in yet. Try and see if you can pick up something.'

Seamus retrieved the radio and retuned into Radio Ulster as a political discussion between various guests was interrupted and the programme suddenly switched to the live count in Enniskillen. After a few agonising minutes, the returning officer announced; *Bobby Sands, Anti-H-Block, Political Prisoner, 30,492 votes...Harry West, Official Unionist Party, 29,046 votes. Bobby Sands is duly elected the MP for the constituency of Fermanagh and South Tyrone.*

Seamus could not contain himself and shouted in Gaelic that Sands had won the election. The rest of the wing erupted in cheers in spite of their CO's orders to take the news in silence. The prison officers came running to find out what was happening, but the prisoners went back to their silent ways as Seamus quickly put the radio back up his backside.

The election of Bobby Sands to Parliament sent shock waves of horror through the British government and the loyalist community in the province. News reporters from all over the world soon descended on the rural town of Enniskillen. The win had been a major triumph for the prisoners, and it was now generally believed that the British government, despite Mrs Thatcher's intransigence, would seek a settlement. Bobby Sands was overjoyed, if not a bit bemused that he was now a member of the British parliament, an institution he would have been happier to blow up than sit in.

Sticking to the timetable, on the 22nd of March, two more prisoners joined the hunger strike, Raymond McCreesh, from Camlough, County Armagh, along with the INLA's commanding officer, Patsy O'Hara, from Derry.

Despite his upbeat mood after being elected, Bobby Sands' health deteriorated and he was transferred to the prison hospital. He was soon joined by Frank Hughes. Food was still placed on the tables at the foot of their beds, but they had grown used to the cravings and were simply amused at the variety of dishes that appeared and disappeared every day. One of the priests who attended at the hospital was enraged at the plates of hot food being replaced at every meal time; *Even the devil did not tempt Christ during his forty day fast in the wilderness with plates of lamb chops.*

As the weeks passed the mood in the prison became sombre as no concessions were forthcoming from the British government.

'How many days is that now?' Danny asked, watching Seamus score another mark on the wall.

‘That’s forty-six. He must be getting quite ill.’

‘They won’t let him die,’ said Danny. ‘Not now he’s an MP!’

‘I wouldn’t bet on it. They let others die in the past. Bobby won’t give in unless he gets us political status, you can bet his life on that!’ Seamus shook his head as he realised what he had said and pulled the blanket over his face to try and get some sleep.

The wing had become quiet over the last few days, and the prison staff retreated to the Circle, emerging only when they had to carry out routine duties. After the earlier excitement and euphoria of the election, a deep depression hung over the Republican part of the prison. The language coming out of number 10 Downing Street was as defiant as ever and the lack of progress was making the unthinkable thinkable. Maybe Sands would have to die to bring the whole thing to a head.

As the days slipped by, the tension grew and attempts by the Irish government to get the British to compromise fell on deaf ears. The Catholic Church made similar pleadings, although it took the view that starving oneself to death was suicide and therefore a sin against God. Many ordinary priests in Ireland viewed such self-sacrifice as akin to Christ’s death on the cross, and declined to condemn the hunger strike from the pulpit. In the end it was decided that the men would receive the sacraments if they so wished. The fear for many in the country was the possibility of civil war if Sands was allowed to die and both sides began to prepare for the worst.

By the end of April the news from the hospital wing was not good and Sands could no longer speak to or even see his visitors. It was clear to those who stood around his bed that he was fading fast. His skin became thin, almost translucent. The smell of death now permeated the room. The prison warders had stopped leaving the trays of food at the bottom of the bed. The end was close at hand and on the 5th of May

1981, after sixty-six days without food, he slipped into a coma and shortly thereafter died.

The news travelled around the H-Blocks like a miasma of disbelief, grown men turning away to shed tears that severe beatings failed to produce.

The security forces were put on high alert as the mood in the streets turned to anger and violence. Riots erupted across the North and beyond. The news that so many feared was echoed through the streets of West Belfast with the deafening sound of dustbin lids banging on the cobbled streets. Cars were hijacked and set on fire, while stones and petrol bombs rained down on the RUC and army as they tried to intervene.

The only place that seemed to escape the whirlwind was the Maze Prison itself. The prisoners became subdued by the news, while prison staff kept a low profile to avoid any confrontation. In the quiet of the evening, Danny mouthed his favourite Sands poem, *Weeping Winds*, while Seamus said the Rosary in a monotone whisper, beating his chest with his fists and swearing at the end of each amen. 'The bastards let him die!'

*

Marie sat quietly, staring into the past as the last of the daylight drifted from the room. Her shoulders were hunched and the streaks of grey were beginning to take over her unkempt hair. Her eyes were now permanently glazed over with sadness and the endless prescriptions of Diazepam. The only noise in the room was the constant ticking of the wall clock above the fireplace. She lit a white candle and placed it on a Formica table where she tended a shrine of photographs of her children, lifting Kathleen's wedding photograph which took pride of place in the centre of the table. Once she would have cried at the very thought of Kathleen, but her pain had become frozen inside her and she put the photo back down on the table just behind the candle. Alongside was a picture of Roisin, wearing her bridesmaid dress proudly holding on to Brendan in his white novice cassock. She smiled sadly at the photograph; neither of them had been back to Belfast since Danny's trial. Brendan had returned to Rome, while Roisin had moved to a teaching job in Glasgow. Marie then looked at Danny's cheeky grin in his school photograph. The news of Bobby Sands' death made her fearful for him, and she went down on her knees to pray that he would not be tempted to go on the hunger strike.

Chapter 32

Ramsey's Return

From all around the world the condolences came in for the Sands family while the condemnations mounted against the British government. Even the 'Iron Lady' was shaken by the outpouring of anti-British feeling that was being reported as far and wide as Russia, India, Iran, and of course in the many countries where the descendants of the Irish diaspora had found a home. But, despite the obvious bad feelings caused by her obduracy, Mrs Thatcher was, at least in public, not for turning.

In the heart of Warwickshire, Ramsey enjoyed the freedom his retirement had brought him. He had sold his London flat and moved to the country. With the last of the day's sunshine on his back, he was walking through the rose garden when he heard the sound of a car crunching slowly through the loose gravel at the front of the house. Placing his secateurs and a handful of cuttings into a wheelbarrow, he walked to the front of the house to see whoever was impatiently ringing the doorbell.

'Good afternoon, can I help you?'

'We're looking for Captain Ramsey.'

'Well you have found him, although I have not been called Captain Ramsey for some time. How can I help you?' he asked, shaking hands with the two immaculately dressed gentlemen, before inviting them into the house.

'We have been asked to speak to you on behalf of the government, but anything we say must be subject to the utmost secrecy,' said the older looking of the two men, who then introduced himself as Harvey Jones.

'Your years of experience in Northern Ireland have not gone unnoticed.'

'Oh, a knighthood, that's nice,' mocked Ramsey.

'Well, not quite. That's not why we are here.'

'Would you like a drink?'

'I'll take a brandy,' said Jones, 'unfortunately Reynolds is driving.'

'I'm sure one brandy won't cause you to run off the road,' said Ramsey, pouring himself a large gin.

'If you don't mind, I'll have a scotch,' said Reynolds, 'on the rocks.'

The three men took a seat in the conservatory at the back of the house. Ramsey knew as soon as he saw the two men at the door that they were from Whitehall. Since leaving the Foreign Office, he had heard nothing from his former employers other than one minor enquiry about his pension.

'It's a very lovely place you have here,' said Jones, sipping his brandy.

'Yes, thank you ...Why don't you tell me why you're here?'

'We have been asked to offer you an opportunity to help your country in a matter of national importance. You will no doubt be aware of the escalating violence in Northern Ireland since the death of Bobby Sands. The government fears that further deaths will damage our reputation abroad and may even lead to civil war in Ireland.'

'Maybe civil war is the answer. Perhaps we should simply withdraw all British forces and let them sort it out themselves.'

'Well, perhaps,' said Jones, looking over to Reynolds for

a moment. 'Do you want to explain things, George?'

'I'm sure I don't have to tell you that in spite of what you hear in the media, there are clandestine negotiations taking place between representatives of Her Majesty's Government and the Provisional IRA. Those negotiating have reached a stalemate. Your name was mentioned by one of the IRA leaders and they have asked for you to act as a go-between during these discussions.'

'Why me? There must be umpteen civil servants with the necessary experience to do this work. Why would I give up this to go back to Belfast? Surely you could get a younger man to do your bidding.'

'The IRA has made it clear that they don't trust those who they have been negotiating with, and have, for some reason, asked for you to be involved.'

'What's in it for me?'

'You'll be doing it for your government and country.'

'That's not good enough any more. I gave over forty-five years service to my country, and my own government blackmailed me into doing its dirty work,' said Ramsey, well aware that both men would have gone through his file thoroughly before they set out that morning.

'Mrs Thatcher has personally asked that you take over as lead negotiator and report back directly to her. You will receive a full grade one salary and expenses. The situation is critical now that two others are on the verge of death. This country's standing in the rest of the world is being undermined by the day.'

'I will do it,' said Ramsey, 'but only if I receive a knighthood when it's all over!'

'That's not in our gift, but we'll pass your demand on to those who have the necessary influence in that department,' said Jones, placing his empty glass on the wicker table.

*

Lost in thought, Danny was staring through the wire mesh window out to the bleak walls and the fading daylight. All he could hear was the constant cawing of crows above the wind whistling through the razor wire. He had received a letter from his mother that morning. She was angry that he continued to refuse to have visits, while she knew fine well that other prisoners on the blanket were seeing their families. She complained bitterly that he had not replied to her last letter and that not being able to visit him was depressing her and the rest of the family. Danny read the letter time and time again before finally letting Seamus read it. Seamus struggled to read the tiny handwriting and had to guess what some of the words were, but he got the gist of it. 'Well?'

'Is there any reason why I can't take visits?'

'No, none whatsoever, we need people to take visits to get things smuggled in and out of the wing. The wearing of the prison uniform for visits is not a breach of the protest, it's part of it.'

'Then why do you never take visits?'

'I made up my mind to do my time this way. It's easier for me. Visits just upset me and make the time seem longer ... I also intend to join this hunger strike.'

'What? You're not well enough. You won't last a week.'

'My health is much better since the strike started, and, anyway, I'll bide my time. The longer this goes on the more likely they'll have a mass strike just to bring it to a head. Anyway, that's for another time. It might never come to that. I think ye should write back to your mother and put yerself down for a visit.'

*

It was after midnight when Joe, full drunk, climbed the stairs to the bedroom. Marie watched him fall down on his knees at the bottom of the bed. 'You don't think God told that soldier to fire at poor Kathleen just because you stopped going to mass,' she taunted, sitting up to look at Joe mumbling incoherent prayers into his hands. Joe did not respond and continued with his contrition until he eventfully lay on the floor and fell into a drunken sleep.

The following morning a letter from Danny arrived with two visitor passes. After reading the letter again, Marie got herself dressed. She was determined to catch the ten o'clock bus to the Maze. She looked at the wall clock again and brushed her hair in the hall mirror, before nervously counting the change in her purse. She looked more like her old self as she fixed her blouse and put on another daub of lipstick.

'You'd think you were going out to see yer fancy man,' said Joe, who was still half drunk.

'I'm going to visit Danny this morning. Ye better get back to your bed before you fall down those stairs. If you weren't still drunk ye could be going with me. I better go, there's the taxi outside.'

The taxi took her into the centre of Belfast where she joined the queue of prisoners' families waiting for the bus. It was a sunny morning, and the rush hour was beginning to subside when the bus pulled up at the terminal.

The journey was uneventful and she spent her time praying to herself and watching the countryside pass by. Once at the Maze, the stark walls and the disdainful looks from some of the prison officers made her feel uncomfortable as she was ushered through administration into the waiting rooms, where her visitor's pass and identification were scrutinised. She had nothing to hide, unlike some of the other visitors, but the rigorous body search and the manner in which she was treated left her feeling angry and violated.

Danny was already sitting at a table at the far side of the visiting hall. He looked dwarfed in his oversized prison clothes, raising his hand to wave when he saw his mother in the group of visitors coming into the room. There was no other chair at the table until a guard brought one over. 'There, no one expects you to stand during a visit. We're not that bad,' he said with a smile.

Marie smiled back then took Danny's hand. 'How are ye, son? Ye look awfully pale.'

'Don't be crying, Mammy. You'll have me crying next. The screws would love that!'

'I'm glad ye came off the blanket, son…'

'What are ye talking about? I'm still on it.'

'But what are ye wearing that for? Is that not a…?'

'Aye, we have to wear it to get a visit. But it doesn't mean I'll be wearing it after ye leave. It's the only time we are able to wear it and still maintain the protest. It's a compromise we had to make.'

'You're not … I don't know how to say it…'

'No, the dirty protest stopped when the strike started. The cells have all been cleaned and we take showers…'

'Good, at least that's one thing. I brought ye some cigarettes and a few things, but they said ye couldn't have them. They took them off me at the gate.'

'We're still no' allowed anything, but make sure ye get them back when ye leave. I don't want to think that some screw will be smoking them tonight. Are ye still working in the shop?'

'No,' she laughed. 'Your lot blew it up last month.'

'Keep the noise down!' barked one of the prison officers.

'And don't be touching with your hands! If I see ye doing it again, I'll stop the visit.'

Marie pulled her hands away and clasped them in front of herself. They talked about the rest of the family and how well Brendan was doing in Rome. 'Roisin writes home every week and asks about you,' said Marie. 'Until now I've not had much to tell her since your trial. You never write, son.'

'I don't know what to write.'

Marie continued with a barrage of questions that managed to get no more than laconic noises until she finally came to the point. 'Now tell me that you will not let them put you on that hunger strike.'

'They don't put you on it, ye volunteer.'

'Well, promise me you won't volunteer. I don't give a damn about all this protesting. What will it get you? It'll not get the Brits out. It'll only cause more sufferings, and for what? You're my son and I don't want you dying for Ireland or anything else,' she pleaded, taking hold of his hand tightly. 'Promise me…'

'Right, that's enough. I told you!' shouted the guard standing at the door. 'Visit over!'

Ushered out of the hall, Marie began to cry and plead with the officers as she was taken back into the administration area and subjected to a further humiliating search.

Danny was taken into the search cell and ordered to strip. His hands began to shake as he tried to unbutton his shirt, with the memory of the last time he was put over the mirror for an internal search. He could feel the officer's aggressive breathing on his back as he dropped the shirt to the floor and began to unbutton his trousers.

'Hurry up, for fuck's sake.'

Still holding on to the waistband of his trousers, he refused to let go, and stood shivering in the cold room. The two officers looked at each other in bemusement. 'You must have something pretty special up yer arse if you're not prepared to let us see it. Now drop yer trousers or we'll rip them off ye,' shouted the more aggressive of the two, grabbing Danny by the arm. A struggle ensued. Danny continued to refuse to let go of his trousers as the officers screamed abuse at him. Just as Danny's grip was beginning to weaken, the cell door opened abruptly.

'Stop! Let him go!' He's not to be strip-searched! Orders from the governor! Leave him alone. He is under my jurisdiction.'

'What the hell are ye on about? He was seen touching hands with his visitor and he must have something to hide the way he's hanging on to those bloody trousers.'

'He's got a medical exemption signed by the governor,' said the intervening officer, showing a letter with the governor's signature on it. He is only to be searched by medical staff, and that will happen back at the wing ... Put your shirt back on, son.'

When Danny got back to his cell, Seamus told him the news that Frank Hughes had died. That evening, prayers were said. Danny lay under his blanket as the murmured words were repeated through the various Stations of the Cross. He listened while Seamus took one of the stations, kneeling on the floor in front of the steel door. The loose electric wire was still buzzing outside and the late evening sunshine was fading with every whispered prayer. Danny did not want to think of the hunger strike or the death of Francis Hughes, someone he had never even met before. He tried to remember the Stations of the Cross, and he visualised all the paintings on the road to the crucifixion around Saint Patrick's Chapel. He recalled the many Sundays he sat in mass, bored to distraction, looking at the paintings to pass the time. He could only remember eight, but the one that remained in his head as he tried to get to sleep was Jesus nailed to the cross with the blood dripping from the crown of thorns. Danny fell asleep, dreaming he was being nailed to his own cross.

*

In his pinstriped suit and Oxford tie, Ramsey returned to Northern Ireland, his sense of duty restored. He found the early morning papers dominated by the death of two more hunger strikers, Raymond McCreesh and Patsy O'Hara, who both died within hours of one another after sixty-one days without food. Many of the families were now becoming desperate for a settlement; anything that would save their own sons from following the others into a martyr's grave. Ramsey had a feeling of admiration for these men, who were prepared to die for what they believed in.

In order to regain the confidence of those negotiating on behalf of the prisoners, Ramsey made it his priority to find out as much as he could about the four prisoners who had already died, and, more importantly, those replacing them on the strike. He already knew much about Bobby Sands, who had become the symbol of the hunger strike around the world. The others he was less informed about and requested the men's MI5 files to be on his desk when he arrived at Stormont Castle that afternoon. Now in his late sixties, Ramsey had retained the energy of a man half his age, and he was determined to work tirelessly to save further loss of life in spite of Mrs Thatcher's intransigence. During his retirement he had finished the first draft of his memoirs, and he saw the hunger strike as an opportunity to be involved in something that had a real sense of history.

Following a brief meeting with the Secretary of State for Northern Ireland, Humphrey Atkins, Ramsey locked himself in his new office overlooking the lush grounds of the castle and perused the MI5 files that were already sitting on his desk when he arrived.

After reading the files of those already dead he turned to those still on the hunger strike. All the buff folders had a black and white photograph of the prisoner stapled to the front cover, and he studied each one for a moment before opening the file. He felt some hope when he read the file of Brendan McLaughlin who had been taken off the hunger strike after only thirteen days, after suffering internal bleeding from a perforated ulcer. It was clear to him that the IRA did not want the prisoners to die simply for the sake of dying. He then studied the files of the four prisoners who were next in line to starve to death.

Joe McDonnell's fast was further on than the others and Ramsey reckoned he had only a few weeks to live unless he could reach a settlement with the prisoners soon. The more Ramsey read about these men, the more he was convinced that they would not come off the strike unless they were granted the political status they demanded. The next file he read did nothing to change his mind. Some of the pictures were faded as though the men had died already and he was looking at their ghosts.

Desperate not to waste any more precious time, Ramsey spent the next few days and nights making calls to Whitehall and to Sinn Fein officials, to see how far apart the two sides were in coming to a compromise that would bring the hunger strike to an end. He believed that both sides wanted a settlement before there were any more deaths: his only concern was Sinn Fein's insistence that it was up to the prisoners to accept or reject what was offered. The Sinn Fein leadership made it clear that they could not order the men off the strike. Ramsey felt he had no option but to meet the prisoners face to face, and he agreed with his contact in Sinn Fein to a clandestine meeting with the hunger strikers and their representatives in the prison hospital. After another couple of calls to Whitehall, he was informed that he would be able to attend the Maze the following morning. A prison van, driven by a MI5 agent, would collect him and the Sinn

Fein negotiator at 5am.

It was still early, but the austere walls of the Maze Prison could be seen in the distance, with their rolls of razor wire and silhouetted watchtowers, against the haunting moonlit sky. Ramsey and the Sinn Fein negotiator were taken directly to the hospital wing.

Ramsey was not prepared for what he saw and the sight of the emaciated men and the smell of vomit in the room almost made him throw up. Joe McDonnell was in obvious pain and near to death. Martin Hurson was much worse looking than Kieran Doherty and Kevin Lynch, who both started their fasts before him. The other two men in the room were well enough to be out of bed and were sitting in their pyjamas at the side of McDonnell's bed.

As he looked around, Ramsey was surprised to see the plates of food still lying on trays at the side of the beds and ordered the male nurse to take them away. He took a seat near to McDonnell's bed to make sure the dying man could hear what was being said. The other men listened quietly without entering into any discussion. Ramsey soon learned not to mention Mrs Thatcher's name a second time, when it drew looks of hate and muttered curses from a few of the otherwise stoical men. It was only after he had said his piece and looked around for a response that he noticed a Catholic priest and another man in prison clothes entering the room. Ramsey recognised the other man from his files. It was the wing OC, Brendan McFarlane. He turned back to the men and found it impossible to detect any emotion from their gaunt faces.

'The men will think about what you've offered and get back to you tomorrow,' said McFarlane.

Hoping for an answer now, Ramsey turned back to the other men who were nodding in agreement with each other, 'We'll give you an answer tomorrow,' said Lynch as he took a long draw from his rolled cigarette and coughed out the smoke.

'What about him?' Ramsey asked, nodding towards McDonnell's bed. 'Will he last until tomorrow?'

There was a rasping whisper from McDonnell's bed. 'Don't worry about me. I'll hang on as long as it takes.'

Chapter 33

Radio Waves

When a request for further volunteers was circulated, Seamus thought his time had come. He made his request to the commanding officer co-ordinating the strike to have his name placed on the list. He was told he would be considered so long as he was medically fit. Danny pretended to be pleased for him, but he was hoping that he was only being put on the list as a last resort and the strike would be over long before Seamus was ever called to make such a sacrifice.

After a recent clamp down in security, the burden of having to conceal the crystal radio had to be shared between Seamus and Danny. The men running the strike had access to their own radio, but due to the precarious temperament of the crystal sets, they were constantly having difficulty catching a signal, and part or whole of a news bulletin could be missed. Danny was soon as proficient as Seamus at getting the radio to tune into Radio Ulster. If anything of importance was reported, then whoever was listening to the programme would relay the salient points to the other, who would then note them down as best they could onto a cigarette paper. The volume of the set was so low that they had to practically stick it into their ears, but once lodged properly the clarity at times could be quite remarkable. One night, after lights-out, the radio failed again. After numerous attempts to get a signal, Seamus gave up and handed the set to Danny. 'Don't wake me up unless ye hear something worthwhile.'

'Like what?'

'Like Thatcher dropping dead.'

Desperate to hear some outside voices, Danny continued to try and get a signal. He held the wire aerial in every possible position and moved the set here, there and everywhere to get some response. He heard the rattle of keys down the other end of the corridor and then the clatter of the iron grilles being opened and locked. Seamus groaned in his sleep, but did not wake up. It was rare for a cell search at this time of night and Danny simply put the radio under his plastic mattress where he kept the letters from his mother. He listened as the grilles opened again and one of the prison officers began his patrol. It was Murdock, whistling the tune from the Addams Family, the only one he seemed to know. None of the other officers walked as slowly as he did, or spent so much time peering into each cell. Danny covered himself and pretended to be sleeping, listening to the opening and closing of the observation slits as Murdock made his painfully slow progress along the wing. He was well known as a non-abusive screw by the inmates, and would often make a friendly comment, but tonight most of the prisoners were either asleep, or pretending to be, as he whistled on to the next cell. Some of the prisoners were sure that his nonchalant whistles had a benevolent purpose as it obviously acted as a warning for them to put away any contraband before he reached their cell. Maybe he just wanted a quiet life, but it was surprising that the other officers did not see it as compromising the whole point of a random cell check.

Danny faced the wall in the hope that Murdock would carry on his whistling way, and he could get the radio back out and try again to get a reception. He listened as the observation slit opened, imagining Murdock looking through the spy-hole like a Cyclops, before the flap closed the mythological eye with a clunk.

Seamus was now lying on his back snoring loudly, dreaming about the endless green fields and fleeting blues skies of his lost childhood. Danny gave him a dig in the ribs to get him to turn onto his side, which usually had the effect of reducing the snoring to grunts and heavy breathing, but Seamus did not respond and continued to snore just as loudly. Outside the window the loose electric wire began to hum as another surge of electricity came over from the generator. It reminded Danny of an old James Cagney film, when the prison lights dipped as the lever was pulled down to switch on the electric chair. He tried to remember the name of the film when, over Seamus's constant snoring, he heard the grilles being closed at the other end of the wing. He gave Seamus another push to get him to stop snoring, but it only changed his tumult to a more annoying, neighing snore. Frustrated, Danny began kicking the soles of Seamus's feet, calling to him in a strained whisper to turn on his side. After another few grunts Seamus finally turned back to face the wall.

With Seamus now sleeping quietly, Danny heard the faint crackles and whistles of the radio coming from the plastic mattress. It was warm to the touch, and as he fiddled with it there was a glow of energy that seemed to be coming from the buzzing cable outside the window. He touched the pipe beside his bed with the earth wire and the radio immediately tuned into a station. He could clearly hear a disc jockey. He took it away from his ear, surprised at how loud it had become. Wrapping the radio in the corner of his blanket to keep the volume down, he listened to the apocalyptic lyrics of a song he had never heard before: "Ghost Town". The reception improved with every surge from the electric cable still buzzing outside the window. After a few more songs, he realised that he was tuned into the John Peel Show. For the first time he had somehow managed to get BBC Radio 1, and it sounded as clear as a bell. He was about to wake Seamus up to tell him when the familiar pips started. *'This is the BBC News at eleven o' clock. Under tight security in Northern Ireland, The Prime Minister, Mrs Thatcher, was at Stormont Castle today where she gave a press conference, blaming the IRA's leadership for the recent deaths of hunger strikers. She condemned them for the loss of life, saying that they were totally responsible for the situation when they 'persuaded, coerced or ordered' the hunger strikers to starve to death. Mrs Thatcher went on to say that the IRA may have played their last card...'* The station then played Mrs Thatcher's interview with a local Belfast reporter, recorded shortly after the official press conference. *'The fact is that the people of Northern Ireland, the leaders of all religious communities and people almost everywhere have rejected violence. Violence is practised by people who cannot persuade and therefore have to resort to fear and intimidation. I believe the community has rejected that and the Provisional IRA knows that.'*

From under his blanket Danny cursed Thatcher. He had come to hate her condescending voice and blamed her personally for the deaths of the four hunger strikers. He could visualise her as she spoke and could not believe she had the gall to come to the Six Counties and attack the IRA about ordering the hunger strikers to die against their will! 'Sure the Hunger Strikers are the IRA,' he muttered to himself. 'That bitch should have to get a passport to come to Ireland ... the Tory cow.'

'...Now more of today's other news. Two men, believed to be IRA gunmen, were shot and killed in Londonderry. Both men were armed and, it's believed, about to carry out an IRA operation when they were confronted by the security forces and killed in a shoot out...'

Danny was not sure whether this report was so important that he had to wake up Seamus, who was still sleeping soundly. If he was still snoring he would have, but now Seamus was quiet, he decided to tell him in the morning and went back under his blanket to listen to the radio as it hummed and whistled in his ear.

The next morning Seamus woke up at the first hint of light creeping into the cell. He sat on the chamber-pot and tried to relieve himself of the pains in his stomach. He was constipated as usual and to take his mind off the task he picked up the Bible and began to look for the same thing he had been looking for the last couple of weeks; the words that Bobby Sands was supposed to have said at the start of his fast: *'Greater love than this hath no man than that he lay down his life for his friends.'*

He flicked through the Bible, stopping at random pages, looking for the elusive phrase that had now become such an inspiration to many of the men on the wing. But, as before, he could not find the passage, and was beginning to wonder if the Bibles the authorities had put in all the cells were corrupted Protestant Bibles, and that Bobby had somehow managed to get a Catholic version from one of the priests.

As usual, he got distracted from his quest and began to read a parable in the New Testament about Jesus turning water into wine at the wedding feast of Cana. He had heard the story read out in mass many times before, but this was the first time he had seen it written down. As he was reading, he was aware of a constant buzzing noise he first thought was the loose electric wire outside the window, but then he was sure he could make out a tune of some kind. He listened to hear if it was coming from one of the other cells or maybe from the screws in the Circle. He slowly and painfully relieved himself of his burden and cleaned himself as best he could. The music was becoming more audible and he was sure he had heard the tune before. He then looked at Danny who had just turned in his sleep, which gave the radio more freedom to crackle Tom Jones singing "The Green, Green Grass of Home".

He woke Danny abruptly and held the radio before the latter's eyes. The radio was still playing and Danny's face looked confused. 'Tom Jones?'

'I'm not asking you to guess who is fucking singing. Why the hell did ye have it on all night listening to music?'

'Sorry, Seamus, I fell asleep after getting tuned into Radio 1 and the eleven o'clock news…'

'All right, but don't do it again!' said Seamus who found it difficult to be angry with Danny for any length of time.

'You could've been caught with it. Think of the bloody carry on that would have caused,' he said, putting the radio back into its condom sheath. 'I've been given this because they trust me and I told them that you were sound. So don't be making a fool or a liar out of me by being an idiot and getting caught listening to fucking music.'

'Sorry, Seamus, I just fell asleep after the news, that's all,' replied Danny.

'Did ye hear anything worthwhile?'

'Aye, there was a report that Thatcher was in Belfast yesterday and making all kind of talk about...'

'So old 'Tin knickers' was in Belfast, was she?' interrupted Seamus, noting down the observation with zeal. 'What did she say?'

'Not much.'

'What do ye mean, not much? She must have been here for some reason.'

'I can't remember. She was just doing some shopping in Marks and Spencer and ranting on about the IRA forcing the prisoners to go on hunger strikes. That's about the gist of it. If it was important I would've woke ye up. Anyway it's the news for Christ's sake, it's not like I'm tuning into MI5 and getting something secret. The guys outside will have listened to it anyway.'

'That's not the point! It's to keep the guys in here who have to do the negotiations informed. Knowledge is power and ignorance is ... bullshit.'

'I thought ignorance was supposed to be bliss?'

'Ye know what I mean, smart arse.'

'Oh, I nearly forgot, two of our lads were killed in Derry after a shoot-out with the Brits.'

'Well, how could ye forget that? They're probably

somebody in here's brother or friend. What if it had been your brother?'

'Ok, I'm sorry, Seamus. Stop giving me a hard time, I've just woke up. The other guys must have picked this up anyway, on the other radio.'

'Did they give the names?'

'Mm … no.'

'No, or can't ye remember?'

'No, they didn't. They just called them suspected IRA terrorists or something like that.'

By now, the rest of the wing was slowly coming to life. Heavy keys were rattling in locks, metal doors banging and orders being shouted at prisoners who were already slopping out their chamber-pots. The dirty protest may have been suspended but the blanket protest continued and the prisoners filed out to empty their pots and take a shower before breakfast. The prisoners took the opportunity of the communal showers to pass on messages and news about the men still on the strike. Everyone in the wing was soon aware that Joe McDonnell was only days from death.

With four men already dead, Jamie Morrison was now sure he would lose the lodge sweepstake. He never even thought that one of them would go the whole way, never mind four, which was the number he picked from the bowl he and other committee members passed around at the start of the hunger strike. It wasn't losing the bet or the death of another Republican prisoner that worried him, but the publicity the IRA were getting around the world. They now seemed to have a moral high ground that the loyalist prisoners could only look up to, some with quiet admiration as their own talk of a hunger strike for the same political status came to nothing. Jamie took his copy of the Belfast Telegraph he was reading and made his way to the lodge where he had arranged to meet Bulldog Brown.

'What do ye think, Jamie?' asked Bulldog, placing a pint in front of his boss.

'About what?'

'About McDonnell, do ye think he'll last much longer?'

'Does it matter? They've already got four fucking martyrs, while our lot look like they're putting on weight.'

'You don't expect our guys to go on hunger strike?'

'Why not, if we don't and they win political status, then we will be classed as criminals while the IRA will be seen as freedom fighters. We need to do something.'

'If the British government gives in and grants political status to the IRA, then they will have to grant it to both sides.'

'Then we'll be indebted to the IRA and be seen by others as not having their commitment ... anyway, any word about that bastard Gallagher?'

'He's still in the mental hospital, he might never get out.'

'But can we get someone in to get him?'

'We're tryin', but that place is more secure than the Maze. He's also under twenty-four hour armed guard.'

'I always knew that bastard was a psycho, but now he's a certified nutter.'

'Another pint, Jamie?'

'No, I better not. I have to go up and see William this afternoon with Liz.'

'How is he?'

'He's in a fucking coma, how do ye think he is?'

Chapter 34

Morto

Brendan had spent the morning in prayer. He was becoming increasingly anxious that Danny had not responded to any of his letters. He was now convinced that his brother was planning to join the hunger strike. Even with the beauty and solemnity around him, his mind was always troubled. The loss of Kathleen on top of Agnes was a devastating blow to all the family and Brendan said endless prayers to ease his feelings of grief and sadness. He managed to get a recent copy of the Belfast Telegraph and was dismayed when he read that some of the families felt their men were simply being sacrificed and that the IRA was ordering them to fast to their death for political reasons.

After prayers, Brendan walked around the Eternal City. He had seen most of the main tourist attractions by now; the Colosseum, the Pantheon and, of course, the overwhelming magnificence of Saint Peter's Basilica. To his surprise, he was drawn more to the pre-Christian period, and the lives of the Emperors, than to the Popes. He found the Roman Forum the most interesting part of the city and had difficulty believing he was walking on the same marble footpaths that Julius Caesar had once walked on some two thousand years before. By midday the sun was getting too strong, and he returned to the coolness of his room to continue his studies.

That evening, in the quiet of his room, Brendan lit a candle and went down on his knees to pray for all those who suffered in the world. He then prayed for the souls of his dead sisters. He listened as the Angelus bells rang in the nearby church and he blessed himself before undressing for bed; he had to be up early to assist Father Grasso with preparations for the Papal mass.

He awoke with the sun rising over the rooftops. It was a beautiful day. He smiled when he saw that his roommate was already up and away to the canteen for breakfast; no one liked their food like Father Simon. Brendan blessed himself and began to say his morning prayers as the church bells were chiming in the distance. The door opened abruptly. Father Simon, breathing heavily, rushed into the room. 'Brendan, another hunger striker has died! It has just been on the radio.'

'Did they say which one,' asked Brendan, blessing himself and kissing the crucifix on his rosary beads.

'Joseph McDonnell … God forgive Margaret Thatcher, if he can find it in his heart.'

'Kneel with me, Father Simon … We will pray for both their souls.'

'I'm not praying for hers,' said Father Simon.

'It's our *duty* to find forgiveness.'

*

Worn out by his relentless attempts to reach a settlement, Ramsey felt a pain in his chest when he read of Joe McDonnell's death in the morning papers. He had made an offer, only days earlier, that he was sure would bring the hunger strike to an end. The prisoners would get most of their demands, with the exception of conferring political status. They would be allowed to wear their own clothes, normal visiting rights would be restored along with most of the men's lost remission; prison work would be restricted to general maintenance duties and further education; they would have the right to free assembly within the confines of the normal recreational periods. That there would be no recognition of any special political status was nothing but semantics to Ramsey. He could not understand how a man could die for something that seemed to him to be so trivial in the whole scheme of things. He was also beginning to think that maybe martyrdom was what this was all about and the demand for political status was just a red herring. He looked through the files on his desk; Joe McDonnell's photograph had acquired a strange other-worldly look to it.

*

Liz took a sponge from a bowl on the bedside cabinet and began to press it gently around William's face to keep the skin moist. Even though the monitors continued to bleep and flicker, William's condition had not improved. The doctors were now suggesting switching off the life support machine, but Liz refused to give her consent. Every day she continued to sit by his bedside and pray for a miracle. Sometimes she talked to William as though he was listening to every word, often reading him stories she had read to him as a child.

Today was his birthday. She opened the cards, reading each one in turn. There was one from Sara; it was heartbreaking. Liz touched the words where the ink was smudged with what she knew were Sara's tears. Liz read it to William, but found each sentence difficult to say without crying.

Once she had read all the cards, she opened a box on her lap containing a birthday cake, and began to place candles on it. She paused for a moment when she put the last candle on the cake. *Can it really be twenty years?* Her mind then slipped back to the maternity ward. She could feel the scar on her stomach were she was stitched.

'I'm sorry, I couldn't get away any earlier,' said a voice that snapped Liz out of her trance.

'Oh, Irene … you're here now, that's all that matters.'

'Where's Jamie?'

'Do ye need to ask?'

'But it's William's birthday … Men … they're selfish bastards the lot of them.'

'It's not his fault. He can't bear to see William like this. I prefer it when he isn't here. I told him to go to the lodge and that I might meet him there later tonight.'

'When was the last time you were in the lodge? It must over twenty years ago.'

'Something like that.'

'And I don't think you will be going there tonight either.'

'No, probably not, this is where I belong,' said Liz, wetting William's lips with the damp sponge.

'But it's not fair on you.'

'Nothing is fair, that's the point. If life was fair then William would be sitting talking to me now … If life was fair then all those young men wouldn't be starving themselves to death just to have a decent life for their families…'

'Liz, you can't be serious. It's those murdering bastards that put yer son in here!'

'Was it? Are they the only ones to blame for all this killing? I don't know what Jamie gets up to when he's out all night. But I know he's up to no good. There's blood on his hands, and some other mother will be suffering as much as I suffer because of his hatred … if only he knew.'

'Knew what?'

Liz paused and turned to look at William. She was tempted to tell Irene everything.

'Liz? Knew what?'

'An eye for an eye will only leave us all blind… here, can you take this along to the nurses, I'm sure they wouldn't mind a bit of cake with their tea.'

That night, twenty four-year old Martin Hurson from County Tyrone, was deteriorating fast after only forty-six days into his fast. He was unable to hold down water and was now suffering from dehydration and violent convolutions. He was given the last rites in the hospital wing of the Maze Prison.

*

The news of Joe McDonnell's death was still fresh in Brendan's mind when he received a letter from his mother telling him that Danny was thinking of putting his name forward to join the hunger strike. He read the letter again as the taxi drove through the noisy rush hour traffic on the way to the airport. He rolled down the window to get some fresh air and asked the driver to turn on the radio. He was now able to understand enough Italian to pick up the gist of what was said and asked the driver if there had been any news that morning about the hunger strike in Ireland. The driver had not heard anything, but then gestured his disgust, calling Mrs Thatcher a murderer, before switching on the radio.

Brendan wiped the sweat from his forehead and loosened his collar. It was a long drive to Fiumicino Airport, and the heat in the back of the taxi was stifling. He lost himself marvelling at the beautiful façades of the city's buildings as the taxi jockeyed for position in the manic traffic. He was suddenly startled out of his contemplation when the taxi driver lost his cool, and began to curse and toot his horn impatiently at a car in front. *'Mi scusi, Padre, mi scusi,'* the taxi driver pleaded sheepishly when he remembered the occupation of his passenger.

Now out of the city, the roads were less congested and the taxi picked up speed. Brendan made the most of the cooler air that was blowing in through the windows. He smiled when the driver began to hum along to Iva Zanicchi singing "Un Fiume Amaro" as they neared the airport.

Brendan watched the planes coming in to land, his fear of flying playing on his mind. The sky was a blanket of solid blue, and the sun was reflecting beams of light off the wings of the planes as they landed or lifted into the simmering heat. The taxi went under a subway before emerging at the main building, a chaotic place that always felt intimidating to Brendan. He checked his ticket and confirmed with the driver that it was terminal one he was going to. The taxi came to an abrupt stop. *'Terminale di uno.'*

He paid the driver, who was reluctant to accept the tip offered, but finally took the few silver coins with a respectful doff of his cap. He then placed Brendan's suitcase on the pavement and banged the car boot door closed. *'Arrivederci, Padre!'*

The airport was busy and Brendan looked around to get his bearings. He picked up his heavy case and began to walk towards the entrance clearly marked Departures in English and Italian.

'Padre, Padre,' shouted the taxi driver, half in and half out of the front seat of his cab, and gesticulating to Brendan, who walked slowly back towards him. 'Morto, Morto,' repeated the taxi driver, pointing at the radio and wiping his sweating forehead with his handkerchief. *'Morto, Padre.'*

'Momento, signore,' pleaded Brendan, who was able to understand enough from the radio to know that Martin Hurson had died during the night. The driver cursed the British, before banging the dashboard of his taxi and driving

off. Brendan wondered how long it would be before he heard the same news about Danny.

*

Brendan entered the front room to an embrace of relief from his mother. She was so glad to have him home. Roisin gave her brother an awkward handshake and was at a loss to say anything. He smiled and gave her a kiss on her cheek, 'I'm still your brother,' he said with a laugh. She gave him a hug and said, 'Well, don't expect me to call ye father.'

'How are ye, Dad?' asked Brendan as Joe got up from his chair and wiped his hand on his trousers before taking his son's hand. 'I'm fine, son. We're glad yer home. Here, have me seat.'

'No, Dad, I'm fed up sitting. I've been on the plane for hours. You sit down. I'll give mother a hand in the kitchen.'

'Ah, don't be daft, that's women's work. Roisin, go and help yer mother so I can talk to me son.'

'Women's work!' snapped Roisin. 'Ye wouldn't know what work was if it came up and bit ye on the arse … Oh sorry, Brendan.'

'Don't be silly, I've heard of an arse before. Sure I've got one meself.'

'Sit down,' insisted Joe, offering his seat again as Roisin went into the kitchen.

'Thanks, Dad,' said Brendan, feeling awkward as he sat down on the worn-out chair. His father took a seat opposite and looked long and hard at his son as though he was about to interrogate him about whether or not he had actually seen God in the Vatican.

'Yer looking well, son, we've missed you here … with Danny talking about going on hunger strike, and all.'

'Well, I'm here to speak to him. He has no right going on a hunger strike. It's a sin against God and his family.'

'Good, I think he'll listen to you all right, being a priest now and all,' said Joe rather absent-mindedly as he looked towards the door and listened to the voices talking away in the kitchen. 'I don't like asking ye, son, but you wouldn't have a few pounds on ye? I've a terrible thirst. Yer mother doesn't understand. It will only be a loan until I get me dole money … for all that is.'

'Here, it's not a loan, it's a gift. But I don't want ye getting roaring drunk and upsetting Mammy,' said Brendan, handing his father two ten pound notes.

'Thank ye son … yer a good boy. We're all proud of ye,' said Joe, sheepishly putting the money into his pocket and getting up to put his jacket and cap on. 'Now don't be telling yer mother. You know what she's like; she doesn't understand a man's thirst.'

'Dad, should ye not stay and have your dinner first?'

'No, if I stay for that I won't get out at all. Give me a couple of minutes before ye let her know I'm away. I don't want yer mother out screaming after me again. There's only so much shame a man can take in his own street.'

*

Seamus was finally told that he was not physically well enough to go on the strike. The last thing that the leadership wanted was for someone to die of complications after only a few weeks without food. It would be an unacceptable situation and one that would give the British media more ammunition to accuse the IRA of ordering the men to their deaths for their own motives, and not for the prisoners' rights. Seamus reluctantly agreed.

When Danny eventually made up his mind and put his name forward, Seamus went off his head. 'Why didn't ye speak to me first?' he demanded.

'What's up? I thought ye'd be glad.'

'You don't go on a hunger strike to make me feel glad. You're too young, for Christ's sake!'

'What age do ye need to be to die for yer country? I'm going on it and that's my choice.'

'We'll see about that! You have no idea what it takes to starve yerself for sixty days knowing you're going to die at the end of it. Have ye even thought about it?'

'Of course I have!'

'Have ye thought about what it's going to be like for yer poor mother, when the priest is throwing holy water over yer skin and bones, and yer family's pleading for you to come off the fast, and ye want to, but ye can't, because you'll let everyone down, including the men that went before ye. How are ye going to cope with that? This is no fucking game.'

'I can do it!'

'But why do ye want to do it?'

'To get political status and help free my country from the Brits ... Why did you want to do it?'

Seamus sat silently for a moment, pulling his blanket around him and looking lost for an answer. He could have said he wanted to die for his country like Danny, but was that why he wanted to go on a gruelling fast for sixty days or more and starve himself to death? Did he want to be a martyr for the sake of being a martyr? Was his life not worth living in prison with more than twenty years of misery ahead of him? He had never thought of it before. Was it the idea of sacrificing himself so that others may live better lives? He did not know. Or was it because he could not forget the day his fiancée threw her engagement ring in the Lagan and called him a murdering bastard when she found out he was in the IRA. He could not blame her; after all, her younger brother lost a leg when an IRA car bomb blew up half a dozen shops in the heart of Belfast only a few weeks earlier. Seamus did not say anything else and lay down while Danny defiantly waited for an answer. There was none.

The hunger strike was dragging on with no end in sight and the families, with the help of Father Denis Faul, a prominent Catholic priest, were now openly protesting to Sinn Fein about the futility of further loss of life.

The British government continued the line that they did not negotiate with terrorists and murderers, however, in the shadows Ramsey made fresh proposals. The brinkmanship continued as proposals and counter-proposals, with pedantic hair-splitting passed between the protagonists. For a moment, Ramsey believed the nightmare was coming to an end when Paddy Quinn was taken off the hunger strike by his family. However, Quinn himself was distraught when he regained consciousness and discovered that his mother had intervened to save his life. When she asked him, if he was not glad to be alive, his reply said it all. 'I don't know if I am or not.'

This false dawn quickly passed and the deaths continued with the loss of Lynch and Doherty within hours of one another. With his mind constantly tormented by the ghostly faces of the hunger strikers, Ramsey was now questioning his own sanity.

*

With an added sense of urgency, it was agreed that Brendan and Roisin would go to the Maze together. Brendan decided to attend without the clerical collar, in spite of his mother's pleas that it might make a difference. Roisin thought Brendan was right; Danny was never too taken by religion and it might provoke him. They laughed about how he used to carry on during the short time he was an altar boy. 'He was always a bit of a pagan, like his father,' said Marie, nodding disdainfully towards Joe who was sitting by the fireplace, sleeping off another afternoon session.

'Shut up, I can hear ye. I'm not that fucking drunk. At least Danny is a man, not a poof like that other one with the rosary beads…'

'Shut up, shut up!' screamed Roisin, attacking her father with a barrage of punches as Brendan pulled her off. 'Yer an old bitter drunk,' she shouted. 'Ye just want Danny to be a martyr so ye can think yer a big man with all yer old cronies and cadge drink off people!' She began to cry as Brendan took her into the kitchen and made her a cup of tea. 'Let him say what he wants, it doesn't matter. Who takes any notice of him these days, anyway?'

'Ye'll not get another meal in this house,' said Marie. 'I'm finished wi' ye. And I don't want ye any where near Danny either. How could ye say such a thing to Brendan? God forgive ye, Joe Duffy, for I won't. I see ye stopped going on yer knees for poor Kathleen; the devil must be back in ye with that old whiskey ye love so much.'

'Tiocfaidh ár lá,' roared Joe, as Marie slammed the living room door closed on him.

Danny was already sitting at a table in the visiting room when Brendan and Roisin nervously made their way through the rows of tables and chairs. There was an awkward exchange of smiles before they took their seats. 'How are ye, Danny?' asked Brendan, saddened to see him looking so wretched.

'Fine, yer looking well yerself; got a tan and all.'

'I'm fine; ye can't help getting a tan in Rome.'

'And how are you, Roisin?'

'I'm grand, Danny, just grand, so I am.'

'Still no' got a boyfriend?'

'Maybe I have, or maybe I haven't.'

'How have they been treating you?' asked Brendan.

'Couldn't be better ... that's why we're on hunger strike.'

'I didn't mean...'

'That's all right. You look like a real priest now,' said Danny. 'All ye need now is a collar.'

'I am a real priest now; sure ye know I was ordained before I went to Rome. I've got the collar in me pocket. You're looking like ye lost some weight?'

'Well, it's hard to eat much when there are men starving themselves to death in here.'

'But ye don't have to join them,' interrupted Roisin.

'I don't want to argue about it again. It's my decision.'

'That's typical of you. You don't think about anyone else. What about Mammy? How do ye think she feels?' Roisin pleaded in an angry whisper.

'You know it's a mortal sin to kill yerself,' said Brendan.

'Don't start that with me. It's more of a sin for me to watch others die and not to have the courage to join them. This is a war we're fighting and people die in wars.'

'Aye, but they don't kill themselves,' said Roisin, her voice breaking as tears began to roll down her cheeks. 'Why did ye have to put yer name forward?'

'I brought you rosary beads from Rome,' said Brendan, 'but they told me I couldn't give you them. I will ask one of the prison chaplains to give them to you. Are ye still saying yer prayers?'

'Jesus, Brendan, I'm yer brother. Don't speak to me like yer the fucking Pope!'

'Danny, for God's sake,' said Roisin.

'No, he's right. I didn't come here as a priest. I came as your brother to try and persuade you not to go through with this. But you seem to have yer mind made up.'

'I have, and I won't change my mind even if yer telling me I'll go to hell. I'm already in fucking hell.'

'Don't say that,' pleaded Roisin, wiping her tears again.

'If ye don't support me, I'm going to have to stop taking visits.'

'We will support you, Danny,' said Brendan. 'Even though I don't agree with what you're doing, I respect your honesty in doing it. But you will have to accept how much pain this is going to cause the rest of us. We have already lost Agnes and Katie, and none of us want to lose you. But we can't stop you.'

When he got back to the cell Danny sat quietly on his mattress; the visit left him emotionally spent. He was not afraid to die, but he was terrified of failing to see it through and letting the others down. The idea of dying was almost like an escape from the prison his mind was in, and he longed for the peace it would bring. As he lay with his thoughts he could hear the wind whistling through the endless coils of razor wire along the high concrete walls. *Maybe if I believed in God, like Brendan, I would have the strength to do this?*

Chapter 35

The Hunger

Looking for an outlet for her anger, Marie joined the anti H-Block protest to find out for herself what was happening from relatives who had sons, either on the strike or waiting to join it. The news that Thomas McElwee was on the verge of death caused another flurry of meetings between the families, politicians and priests; all demanding an end to the strike. The Catholic Church called for the IRA to put an end to the senseless loss of life, and the Irish government sent representatives to the prison in the hope of persuading the men to accept what was on offer from the British government.

Marie was heartened by the number of mothers who were determined to take their sons off the strike as soon as they became unconscious. They had been assured by Sinn Fein that the IRA leadership would not interfere with their decision, and it would be a matter for each family to decide whether or not to intervene.

Rushing home that evening, with her mood lifted, she wrote another letter to Danny begging him to hold off his fast until at least another month, and, if he was still determined to go on the strike, she would support him. Marie knew she could never support him starving to death. All she wanted now was to delay matters in the hope that others would bring the strike to an end before he put his life at risk.

She awoke early the next morning, eager to get to the Sinn Fein offices to have her letter delivered to Danny as soon as possible. It was a miserable looking morning outside, but she was still in high spirits as she dressed and went downstairs to find Joe sleeping in the front room. Marie decided there was not much point in waking him up and starting a row. She could barely speak to him these days without losing her temper. Quickly brushing her hair, she put on her coat and hurried along the street to the Sinn Fein office.

Scattered at the corner of the road was all the usual debris of the previous night's rioting, and she had to be careful not to trip over the broken stones and shattered glass strewn across the road and pavement. There were two burnt out cars still smouldering on the other side of the road, and she could make out where some of the petrol bombs had landed from the fire stains and broken glass embedded into the scorched tarmac. She turned into Clonard Street, amazed to see the gable end of the terraced houses covered in a twenty foot mural of Bobby Sands. It sent a shiver down her spine and she hurried across the road.

When she got to the Sinn Fein office, she spoke to the receptionist, giving her Danny's details and prison number. The girl took the carefully folded letter and placed it in a wooden box with others destined for the Maze that afternoon. The receptionist then handed Marie a brown envelope containing a letter from Danny, which she immediately opened. Her eyes strained to read the tiny handwriting and she moved over to the window to get some more light onto the crumpled cigarette paper. Her heart almost stopped as she read the words again. *'I started the hunger strike yesterday, don't worry about me'.* She could hear the phone ringing in the background as her mind became wild with panicked thoughts. She tried to catch her breath.

'Are you all right, Mrs Duffy?' asked the receptionist, placing the phone on the receiver.

'Yes, I'm okay,' said Marie, steadying herself for a moment. 'When was this letter sent, there's no date on it?'

'It's hard to say. Even if the men date them it might be weeks after they are written before they get a chance to smuggle them out.'

‘My God, weeks? Is Gerry Adams here?’

‘No, there’s no one here, they’re all at the prison; Thomas McElwee is in a bad way…’

‘My God, is there no end to this nightmare?’

*

The following day, tired and drawn, Ramsey stood before the bathroom mirror and wondered how he had become such an old-looking man. He had slept badly the night before; afraid his latest attempt to reach a settlement had come to nothing. He lifted his copy of the London Times from the hall table on his way into the dining room. The headlines were predicting the imminent death of McElwee. He could not eat his breakfast without thinking of the gaunt men he had met in prison, with their thin skin stretched across fragile bones. He moved the food around his plate and watched the sun rise above the trees, filling the room with bright, warm sunshine. He pushed the plate away and lit a cigarette. There was a knock on the door.

‘Come in.’

‘Mr Atkins wishes to see you, sir.’

‘Tell him I’ll be along in a few minutes … Carol, has there been any news from the prison?’

‘No sir, I’ve not heard anything.’

After a few anxious draws on his cigarette, Ramsey followed her into the corridor to the Secretary of State’s office on the second floor. Atkins was pacing around the room, dictating a letter to his secretary who was scribbling shorthand onto her notepad. ‘Come in, Ramsey … Nancy, I will finish the letter to Mrs Thatcher later.’

'I can come back,' suggested Ramsey.

'No, come in. The prime minister prefers letters to telephone calls unless the matter is urgent. I think she just likes to correct my bad grammar. Has there been any progress?'

'No, not really. We offered very near to what they are looking for, but I don't think they'll trust any deal, unless Mrs Thatcher makes the offer on television herself.'

'Well, that's not going to happen. I received a telephone call this morning that the fella … what's his name, Mc … something, is at death's door?'

'McElwee, it's all over the papers.'

'That's a strange name. Anyway, he's in a bad way, and may not last very long. He's got a few days at most. I just don't understand these people. Is there nothing that will get them to call off this bloody hunger strike before we have another death; not to mention all the trouble that will follow it?'

'Political status … Give them that and the strike will stop…'

'Impossible! That's out of the question. The prime minister will not give in to conceding political status. It's out of the question.'

The door suddenly opened. 'The governor is on line two, sir,' said Nancy, her face expressing her concern.

The Secretary of State lifted the phone and listened without saying anything. He placed the phone back down and turned to Ramsey. 'That's another one dead!'

As with the others, the province erupted in an explosion of violence with the news of Thomas McElwee's death. Riots continued from dusk to dawn and the IRA stepped up its bombing campaign. Ramsey watched the mayhem unfold over the next few days on the evening news reports. The calls for calm from moderate politicians on both sides went unheeded. He was worn out and now regretted coming out of retirement; even a knighthood would not make up for the psychological damage dealing with the hunger strike had inflicted on him, but he had to see it through to the bitter end, even if it killed him.

*

Marie had waited all morning to see Father Cunningham, who was busy conducting two christenings, after saying morning mass. Mrs Mooney, the parish housekeeper, knew the Duffy family well and handed Marie a cup of tea while she waited in the chapel house. They sat and chatted about how well Brendan was doing with his studies in Rome, and how it would be nice to have him back as the local parish priest after Father McFadden's retirement next year. Mrs Mooney poured Marie another cup of tea just as Father Cunningham came in with his usual jovial smile. 'We've not had much of a summer at all this year … Morning, Mrs Duffy.'

'Good morning, Father.'

'Are ye here to see me? Or is it just a chat with Bridget?' he asked, placing a crucifix in a drawer along with the white cassock and purple sash he wore for the christenings.

'Oh, she's here to speak to you, Father,' said Mrs Mooney, lifting the china pot to pour the priest's tea, with his usual two heaped spoonfuls of sugar. 'She's been here all morning waiting for you. I'll take this tray away and leave you both in peace.'

'You can leave a few of those, Mrs Mooney,' the priest said, lifting the plate of scones from the tray and putting them back on the coffee table.

'Now what's the matter?' Father Cunningham asked,

stirring his tea. 'Is it Danny?'

'Yes, Father, he's on the hunger strike. He won't see me unless I support him. I can't support him, Father. I can't stand by and watch him starve himself.'

'Now, Marie, I'm doing all I can to persuade him and the others that the time has come to bring this to an end and accept what's been offered. I spoke to Danny yesterday…'

'You saw Danny yesterday?' asked Marie, her tears frozen in her eyes. 'How is he, Father?'

'He's fine; he's not even been transferred to the hospital yet. There are others who are in much worse shape than him. Poor Michael Devine is one of them. He's my priority now.'

'When did Danny stop eating?'

'This is his third week. I promise I will do everything in my power to stop this hunger strike. I can't think of any reason for further loss of life. It will not make any difference to what they end up settling for.'

'Father, I need to see him. He refused to see me in case I make a scene and embarrass him in front of the other prisoners. Tell him I won't. I need to speak to him.' She broken down in tears as Father Cunningham put his hand on her shoulder.

'I'll speak to him tomorrow. He'll see you … I promise. Now go home and say a few prayers for those who have already died and I'll do what I can for those still alive.'

'Thank you, Father.'

*

Danny had only agreed to see his family after Father Cunningham gave his word that they would not try and take him off the hunger strike, and that they would support his decision, even if it meant letting him die. Marie made it clear to Father Cunningham in confession afterwards that she had lied to him and would never stand by and let Danny die. The priest confessed right back to her that he knew she had lied and that he also lied to Danny about not intervening when he became unconscious… 'There are lies and lies in this world; some are for the greater good. Say an Our Father and three Hail Marys … and I'll do the same.'

After an early morning bout of coughing and dry stomach wrenching Danny sat up in his bed trying to catch his breath. His mouth was unbearably dehydrated. He gasped as he sipped from a glass of tepid water. This had become his only source of pleasure; all other bodily functions offered him nothing but pain. As he took the glass away from his dry, cracked lips he noticed for the first time someone standing at the door. He had been on hunger strike now for nearly four weeks and his eyesight had become blurred and it was difficult for him to focus.

'How are ye, son?'

'I'm fine, Mammy. Who's that with ye?' he asked, his eyes squinting at a figure standing at the bottom of the bed.

'It's me … Brendan.'

'Your brother's come all the way from Rome to see you again,' said Marie, gently taking Danny's bony hand in her own. 'Are ye sure you want to go through with this, son?'

'Mammy, I don't want ye coming here if you're going to try and get me to come off…'

'She's your mother, what do ye expect her to do?' Brendan said, with an uncharacteristic anger in his voice that was only mitigated by the lump in his throat. 'We promised that we'd support you, and we will, but that doesn't mean we can't hope that you'll change yer mind and come off this strike. What else do ye have to prove to the world?'

'We're not doing it to prove anything other than we're not common criminals, and that we should have the same rights as any other soldier who fights for his country's freedom,' said Danny, before being overtaken by a bout of convulsions and throwing up a thick green bile into a bucket at the side of the bed.

'Oh, son, there,' said Marie, anxiously rubbing Danny's back. 'Bring it up.'

'Mammy! You're hurting me back,' moaned Danny, through a splutter of coughs and groans.

'Jesus, Mary and Joseph,' gasped Marie, recoiling from the putrid smell from the bucket, which was splattered with bile and blood. Turning away she noticed the plate of food sitting on a tray and quickly became nauseated and light-headed. 'I have to go,' she said in a daze. 'I can't take much more of this! Brendan, will ye give me a hand.'

Brendan helped his mother into the corridor where she sat down in a state of shock and bewilderment. One of the male nurses gave her a glass of water.

'You stay here for a few minutes. I'm going in to speak to him,' said Brendan, with an air of authority that brought a weak smile from his mother's pallid lips.

Recovered from his attack of sickness, Danny sat back on the pillow propped up against the metal bedstead as his brother handed him a handkerchief to wipe his mouth. Brendan brought out a prayer card from his wallet and handed it to Danny.

'I know you're not one for prayers but keep this with you; it might be a comfort. I see you have at least started reading the scriptures,' added Brendan, picking up the leather bound Bible from the bedside table.

'I'm not reading it. Father Cunningham left it there last week.'

'Mammy tells me that you stopped going to mass after

Kathleen's funeral. You know it's a sin…'

'I don't believe in all that stuff anymore…'

'Starving yourself to death is an even greater sin and if you don't repent you'll go to hell ...'

'And you'll go to heaven, no doubt? I don't want you preaching to me, Brendan. You're a priest. That's your choice. Will your heaven be heaven, if you know your brother is suffering in hell for eternity?'

'You don't have to suffer in hell, you can repent. It's never too late … I brought this from Rome, it was blessed by the Pope,' said Brendan, handing Danny a silver crucifix.

'How's Mammy?' Danny asked, putting the crucifix into his pyjama pocket without looking at it.

'She'll be okay. It's one thing putting yourself through this, I can forgive you for that. It's what you're putting Mammy through. If you…'

'Brendan, please go! You know that I can't come off this even if I wanted to…So please go and tell Mammy that it's better that she doesn't come to see me like this.'

'You think it's that easy? Have you any idea how hard it is for her to know that ye don't want to see her? There are other families now determined to take their men off as soon as they become unconscious. Do ye think we'll be any different? This hunger strike has achieved all it's going to achieve. We'll not stand by and let you commit suicide for nothing.'

'What's da saying about it?'

'When he's sober, not very much, but he sings yer praises when he's drunk, which Mammy tells me is nearly every night.'

'Why is he no' here?'

'Mammy doesn't want him to encourage you. He might

want a dead Irish hero in the family, but none of the rest of us wants one. They'll make a big deal about you for a couple of months and then you'll be forgotten like the rest. Mammy will be the one that has to tend your grave. Has she not buried enough of her children without you adding to her misery?'

'I'm no' doing this to make Mammy suffer…'

'It doesn't matter why yer doing it. She'll be the one who suffers the most and will go on suffering when the world's media has moved on to something else.'

'If yer going to take me off when I'm unconscious, what's the big deal?'

'Ye might be brain damaged by then.'

'Can ye pass me that bucket?' Danny asked as another fit of sickness raked up more mucus and blood from his chest. When he sat back to recover his composure, his pyjama top lay open and Brendan noticed the raw sores and lesions on his thin yellow skin. Brendan's anger at his brother was subdued for a moment with a feeling of admiration at his Christ-like determination to endure what was a horrendous way for anyone to die. He kneeled by the bedside and began to pray.

Chapter 36

Tiocfaidh ár lá

Staying at his parents' house was difficult for Brendan; his mother's neurotic behaviour and his father's constant drinking were depressing him. He was glad that Roisin was coming home from Glasgow for a few days.

He met her at the harbour. They decided to go into the city centre for lunch. The streets were busy despite the constant threat of IRA bombs. Brendan wore a suit he bought in Rome; he had decided not to dress as a priest while in Belfast in case it provoked trouble. He kept his collar in his pocket. Roisin was desperate to find out about Danny and how her mother was coping.

'Will we get a pot of tea?' asked Brendan as they took a seat in a corner café.

'No, I'll have a coffee,' said Roisin, putting her small suitcase on the floor under the table. 'Do ye think he'll go through with it?'

'If he has to, yes, but that doesn't mean we can't stop him when the time comes. One of the families took their lad off yesterday. Most of the other mothers have vowed to do the same. Mammy won't let him die.'

'It's over six weeks now, he must be very ill. Even if he stops, it could do permanent damage to him the longer he's on it,' said Roisin.

'That's why we have to persuade the others, who are further on than him, to come off. When he sees that there's no shame in stopping then maybe he'll come off himself. If we've to wait until he's unconscious before we can intervene, it may be too late by then.'

'How does he look?'

'Not good. His body and face are very thin and his eyes are almost blank when he looks at ye. He still throws up, but there is nothing in his stomach but acid and water. I've been up twice in the last week and ye can see the deterioration in just a few days. I was there when poor Mickey Devine died, God rest his soul. It's dire. How many more will die before someone calls this bloody thing off?'

'I pray for him every day. Poor Mammy, how can he put her through this?'

'I don't know, only he can answer that. Anyway how are ye getting on in Glasgow?'

'It's great. I like me job and I get on well wi' the girl I share the flat wi'. She's a great laugh and Celtic mad. I went to Parkhead wi' her a couple of weeks ago. They got beat two-one; I think I jinxed the team. Anyway I don't like football that much; it reminds me of what's going on over here and I don't want reminded … How's Daddy?'

'When he's no' drunk and arguing with Mammy, he's normally sleeping. I haven't spoken to him much. I don't think he'll ever get over Kathleen getting killed. Mammy says he prays like a condemned man one minute and curses God to hell the next.'

'It wasn't his fault.'

'No, but for some reason he thinks it is.'

'Can't ye speak to him?'

'Don't ye think I've tried? He doesn't want to listen to me or anyone else. Sometimes I think he just likes wallowing in his own misery.'

'You don't sound like a priest sometimes.'

'Sometimes I don't feel like one.'

The waitress brought them over two cups of coffee and a plate of tuna and cucumber sandwiches. They continued to chat and laugh about things that they remembered from their childhood. The wind was picking up outside and blowing through the silver birch trees in the park across the road. Roisin was glad she wore her new coat, and tucked her scarf inside the collar when the wind caused a draught at the door.

'What's your school like?'

'It's absolutely massive. It's the biggest secondary school in Glasgow. I love it.'

'That's good.'

'It's great being able to walk about the shops not having to worry if a bomb might go off at anytime. And no one cares if yer a Catholic or Protestant the way they do here.'

'But it's a Catholic school?'

'Of course, but it's not like here.'

'Are ye still going to mass?'

'Of course I am,' she lied. 'How are ye enjoying Rome?'

'Fine, it's a beautiful city, but I don't think that being a scholar in Rome is really what I want to do with my life. So I have asked to be placed at a parish in Dublin where one of the priests is retiring in a few months time. I think I will be more useful there.'

'Would ye like anything else?' the waitress asked, lifting the empty plates from the table.

'No thanks, could we have the bill please?' asked Roisin, opening her purse and counting out some change.

'No, I'll get it,' said Brendan.

'No, ye will not,' insisted Roisin, handing the waitress a crisp new five pound note from her purse.

When they left the café, the wind and rain blew hard against their backs, almost pushing them along the street. Brendan held on to Roisin's arm tightly as they ran across the road. When they got to the top of the street they were battered by a cross wind at the corner. The rain became torrential. 'Welcome back to sunny Belfast,' said Brendan, still holding on to his sister.

'I've got a brolly in my … Oh my case! I've left it in the café.'

'I'll go back and get it, you wait at that bus shelter; there's no point both of us getting soaked to the skin. Brendan rushed back to the café, his coat blowing around him like a battered sail in a roaring sea, the rain running down his face and neck. Cars were now throwing up waves of water as they carelessly splashed through the puddles. He looked up ahead and saw that there was a commotion across the road from the café.

'That's the fella there,' shouted a woman in an accusing tone.

Brendan suddenly realised the reason for the commotion. He walked towards the agitated crowd. 'It's all right, my sister left her suitcase in the café,' he said as two men walked up to meet him.

'Where's your sister now?' One of the men demanded as he roughly took Brendan's arm.

'It's okay; she's waiting for me at the bus stop. She forgot it that's all,' insisted Brendan, struggling to free himself, as the older looking man took hold of his other arm.

'Well you can go in and bring it out. We thought it was a bloody bomb and now the army are on their way!'

The two men pushed Brendan towards the front door of the café as he heard the sound of police sirens getting closer. He was beginning to feel a sense of panic and quickly opened the latch on the café door. He picked up Roisin's small suitcase from under the table and went back outside as the first police cars began to pull up on the other side of the road. A heavily-armed army Land Rover screeched to a halt, as police and soldiers took up position behind their vehicles, and screamed at him to put the case down and get on the ground. He carefully placed the case on the pavement and raised his hands as instructed, slowly getting down on his knees, before lying face down on the road. There were further orders being screamed through the deluge, but he could not make them out. He suddenly felt a hand grabbing him by the collar of his coat and then another as he was dragged to his feet and pulled across the road. Every time he tried to speak he was screamed at to shut up as two British soldiers pushed him up against the railings of the park and searched through his clothes.

'He said it was his sister's suitcase,' shouted the waitress, who had come over to the two soldiers. 'There was a girl ... I don't think he would have came back for it if there was a bomb in it.'

'Right, everyone, get back!' shouted a stony faced lieutenant as he ordered his men to widen the cordon around the street. 'Make sure that there's no one still in those buildings, sergeant.'

'What's in the suitcase?' The lieutenant demanded. 'It might save us blowing it up.'

'For God's sake it's my sister's suitcase; she's just back from Glasgow for the weekend. I'm a Catholic priest!'

'You don't look like any priest I've ever seen,' said the lieutenant as he opened the side of Brendan's jacket with its expensive looking Italian label. 'Take him into the jeep at the back; we'll question him later.'

Two soldiers dragged Brendan behind the police cordon. He could see a bomb disposal team operating their remote control robot from behind their heavily armoured Land

Rover. They had managed to get the suitcase off the ground and take it towards the park gate. Brendan could hear the lieutenant screaming orders to clear everyone away from the park area as the robot continued to carry the suitcase further into the park.

Drenched, Brendan sat in the back of an army jeep wondering how this could have happened when there was an explosion which shook the jeep to one side. He recoiled on the hard wooden seat and looked at the two soldiers who were guarding him, in disbelief. His mind was confused with the sudden shock of hearing the bang. *Was Roisin carrying a bomb in that suitcase? No...never...Why would she have let him go back for it? It didn't make sense. It was all insane. Was she in the IRA? Why would she let him go back for the case? Was he going mad?* Just as Brendan was beginning to doubt his own sanity, the lieutenant appeared at the back of the jeep. 'Your sister was a foolish girl leaving that case in the café. She'll have to buy herself a new wardrobe for her stupidity, Father Duffy,' said the lieutenant handing back the documents that the soldiers had taken from Brendan during the search.

'The explosion?' said Brendan; still not sure of what had happened.

'Oh, that. We had to carry out a controlled explosion, if there had been any explosives in the case then we would have heard something a bit louder than that. Your sister's standing with one of my men. You can tell her not too be so stupid in the future. We can't take any chances, you understand?'

'Yes, I understand. Can we go?'

'You're free to go. Here give me your hand,' said the lieutenant, helping Brendan down from the back of the Land Rover.

Roisin was standing on the other side of the police cordon looking bewildered at the pieces of her clothes that were caught in the branches of a tree. 'Are you all right?' she asked as Brendan walked towards her with the lieutenant.

'I'm fine.'

Marie was busy cooking dinner in the kitchen, anxiously clock watching when the doorbell rang. She dried her hands on a tea towel and rushed to open the door.

'My God, you're both drenched. Come in and get yourselves dried before ye catch yer death. I'll put a fire on in the front room. Give me your coats and I'll hang them up before they're ruined.'

'It's ruined already,' groaned Roisin, handing her mother the wet coat.

'It's a lovely coat. Where did ye buy it?'

'I got it in Fraser's store in Buchanan Street. It was nearly thirty pounds.'

'Thirty pounds? You must be earning plenty.'

'It took me nearly two months to save up for it.'

'Is Daddy in?' Roisin asked as she followed Brendan into the kitchen.

'No, he's down that bloody pub again,' said Marie. 'No wonder they call it the Glue Pot, he's stuck in it every bloody night! Oh sorry, son, I didn't mean to swear in front of ye.'

'That's all right, Mammy, I'm only a priest, not a saint. You'd think he'd stay in when he knew Roisin was arriving,' said Brendan, still trying to flatten out the creases in his trousers. 'Will he be back for dinner?'

'Your guess is as good as mine; he comes and goes as he pleases. I've given up talking to him. He doesn't listen to me anymore.'

'How does he get the money to drink all the time?' asked Roisin, vigorously drying her long curly hair.

‘God knows, but those Republican dives are cheap drinking dens and he gets drunk on fresh air these days. At least when he comes home he usually just falls asleep in front of the fire until the morning … I bought some lamb chops for dinner, is that all right?’

‘That sounds grand, Mammy, but don’t make me too much; I’m on a diet,’ said Roisin, who had already lost at least a stone since she moved to Glasgow.

‘You must have a boyfriend over there if you’re dieting at your age.’

‘Oh, stop it, Mammy, I’ve not. There’s nothing wrong in trying to look good. Anyway do you like me suit?’ she asked, proud of her new outfit with its military style jacket and fashionable shoulder pads.

‘It very Dynasty,’ said Marie. ‘That must have cost a pretty penny.’

‘Let’s put it this way: it took longer than the coat to save up for.’

‘Dinner will be ready in about half an hour. It’ll give ye time to change out of those wet things and get them hanging up before they start to dry out. Roisin, your room’s all ready for ye. Poor Brendan has given it up to sleep on the sofa … Roisin, where’s your things?’

‘She left her suitcase at the ferry terminal in Stranraer,’ lied Brendan. ‘We phoned over. They’ll hold on to it until she picks it up tomorrow.’

‘Thanks, Father,’ whispered Roisin, giving Brendan a peck on the cheek as she passed him to go upstairs to get changed.

While Marie was plating out the dinner, the front door opened and Joe staggered into the hall, singing and muttering an old rebel song under his breath. He was soaked through and struggled to get his wet jacket off.

'There's your drunken father now. He must have smelt the chops from the pub,' said Marie as she poured hot gravy over Roisin's lamb cutlets. 'No, stay where ye are,' she added when Roisin motioned to get up and greet him. 'He might just go straight upstairs to his bed.'

'Tiocfaidh ár lá,' shouted Joe, staggering into the kitchen.

'Why don't you shut up and welcome your daughter, you old bloody drunkard?' scolded Marie, putting the frying-pan back on the gas and angrily throwing on two more chops in the sizzling hot lard.

'Hello, Daddy,' said Roisin.

'Good to have ye home ... *Tiocfaidh ár lá,'* he shouted as he tried to light a crumpled cigarette.

'Sit down, before ye bloody fall down,' snapped Marie.

With a desperate sigh, Brendan moved to let his father sit at the table, while Roisin continued to eat her dinner before any arguing started.

The fierce autumnal winds were still blowing outside and the room smelt damp with the wet clothes drying on hangers around the house. Joe tried to look sober as he took a deep draw from his cigarette, dropping a long line of ash onto the kitchen table. 'And how's yerself?' he finally asked with a hiccup.

'I'm okay. It's Danny I'm worried about,' said Roisin, before noticing her mother shaking her head.

'Don't get him started, for God's sake.'

'Danny, that's my boy...*Tiocfaidh ár lá!'*

'What are ye on about, Daddy?'

'Our time will come; it's what Bobby Sands said before he went on the hunger strike,' said Brendan, getting up from the table. 'Mammy, I'm not really hungry, I'll heat it up later.

I'm going over to see Father Cunningham. He's got some Latin books for me.'

'You'd be better learning the Gaelic than that old stuff,' slurred Joe as Marie looked at him with disdain.

'Here, eat this up and shut up,' she said angrily, putting a plate of burnt chops and mashed potatoes in front of him.

'It seems like a sin for us to be eating when poor Danny's…'

'Joe, will ye keep quiet about Danny. If it's such a sin for ye then don't bloody eat it!' barked Marie, her earlier happiness at having Roisin back home now ruined by the husband she could barely look at.

'Mammy, I'm going upstairs for a sleep; I'm dead beat,' said Roisin, getting up from the table when she heard Brendan closing the front door behind him. She went to the room she had once shared with her sisters and brothers. It was now redecorated in Laura Ashley style wallpaper and soft furnishings Marie got cheap from the market. The single beds were gone and a double bed was made up in similar bedding to the floral curtains. She was surprised to see that the picture of Pope John XXIII was replaced with a colourful framed print of a harlequin with a sad face and a solitary tear frozen on his chalk white face. Curious, she looked into her parents' room, which now had two single beds, but the gloomy holy pictures and statues were still there and she noticed that Pope John had found his way into their room.

Early the next morning, Marie woke the whole house in a state of near hysteria. She had just heard on the radio that another hunger striker, Matt Devlin, had been taken off by his family and it looked like there was a strong possibility that the strike would be called off. Brendan and Roisin got dressed quickly and joined their mother downstairs in the kitchen. Joe lifted his head for a moment, and then went back to sleep, soon snoring and shouting out random curses.

Unable to conceal her excitement, Marie made a pot of

tea, her face bright and happy. She could not stop smiling as she told them what was said on the morning news. Roisin placed some bread under the grill, with tears running down her cheeks. Brendan blessed himself and said a decade of the rosary, with his mother getting on her knees beside him. Once the prayers were over, they sat in silence, waiting for the next news bulletin.

It soon became clear from the next report that the earlier announcement was over-optimistic in its rhetoric. The newsreader confirmed that the other hunger strikers continued to refuse the offer made by the British government to settle the strike. A gloom descended on the Duffy house once more.

Now almost blind and hard of hearing, Danny had difficulty, at times, determining whether he was awake or in a deep hypnotic sleep. Ghostly shapes passed in his blurred vision and strange noises rattled in his ears like passing trains in the distance. Confused by a mixture of hallucinations and reality, he smiled at the haunted images. His life was ebbing away. His body was now covered with so many blistering sores and lesions that the nurses had to routinely turn him to administer antiseptic creams to the raw festering wounds.

Holding on to Brendan's arm tightly, Roisin recoiled in horror when she saw Danny's emaciated body shrouded under a thin white sheet, like an old man's corpse in a morgue. Her eyes lowered to his clasped bony hands weakly holding the child's white confirmation rosary beads placed there by their mother.

'Can ye hear me, son?' pleaded Marie. 'It's Mammy. I'm here with yer father, Brendan and Roisin...They're talking about calling off the hunger strike, son. Laurence McKeown's family took him off yesterday. Can ye hear me?'

'I think he's unconscious, Mammy,' said Roisin, coming forward and taking Danny's hand to feel his faint pulse.

'Kathleen?' said Danny in a strange whispered trance. 'Is that you, Kathleen?'

'No, Danny … It's me … Roisin,' she said, the tears running down her cheeks onto his gaunt face.

'Maybe we should get the doctor,' said Brendan, suddenly afraid that he might have to administer his own brother with the last rites.

Joe stood at the back in silence, his mouth dry and his head pounding. He wanted to say something but the words were not there and he searched his pockets for a cigarette. A doctor came in and immediately opened Danny's loose pyjama top and checked his heartbeat.

'Is he all right, doctor?' Marie asked, her hand nervously hovering over her dry lips.

'He's drifting in and out of consciousness, but his heart is still strong. You should do the right thing and take him off now, before there is any permanent damage to his mind and body.'

'No, no …You promised, Mammy … No,' Danny coughed and spluttered, lifting his head up from the pillow, before falling back into a state of near comatose.

'How long has he got, doctor?' Brendan asked.

'He's been on the strike fifty-one…'

'Fifty-two days,' interrupted Marie.

'Fifty-two days,' continued the doctor. 'He could last another couple of weeks at most, but in this condition he could go any time, there's no way of knowing. It's as much down to him and his will to live, as it is down to anything else. My advice is to take him off soon. But that's a matter for you. I can't force feed him, or give any medical treatment without his consent, which, as you have just heard, he still refuses to give, but as soon as he becomes unconscious then you must take him off as soon as possible. I've seen enough young men starve to death in here.'

Brendan opened his briefcase when the doctor left. He placed a purple sash around his neck as his mother and sister embraced each other, their words inaudible in their deep sobs of despair. Marie was already on her knees praying. Joe just stood back and smoked another cigarette and said nothing.

Book III

Chapter 37

The Great Escape

Marie was just getting ready to go to morning mass when she received a message delivered by a young fella, who had run all the way from the Sinn Fein Office on the Falls Road. Her hands were shaking as she read the note: *A car will be with you in one hour's time, Daniel is gravely ill.*

'What's wrong, mother?' asked Brendan, when she came back into the front room, ashen faced.

'Wake your sister, we have to go to the prison, yer brother is dying … Don't wake yer father, I don't want him there.'

They were met by one of the prison doctors, who cautioned them before going in to see Danny. 'He is still conscious, but only just. He could die at any moment. I strongly advise you to stop this now, before it's too late.'

'I want to see him,' said Marie, slowly pushing the door open. 'Oh, my God…'

Danny was in a delirium, his eyes rolling wildly in his head as he muttered incoherently to himself. He was so gaunt that his skeleton was visible through his skin. Roisin turned away and began crying, she could not bear to look at him. Brendan took her back out to the corridor as their mother stood at the bottom of Danny's bed in a trance.

'Mrs Duffy, he doesn't have much time,' said the doctor.

'What will happen if we take him off now … will he be normal?'

'There's a chance that he may have suffered some brain damage, it's hard to say.'

'Mother, for God's sake, what are ye waiting for,' shouted Brendan as he came back into the room.

'Mrs Duffy!' urged the doctor.

Marie went towards Danny and kissed him on the forehead. 'I am sorry, son. I know ye will forever hate me for this, but I can't let you die.'

That was all the doctor had to hear. He immediately attached a drip to Danny's arm and called for assistance. Brendan put his arm around his mother and took her out to the corridor.

*

When Humphrey Atkins was replaced by Jim Prior, Ramsey took the initiative and persuaded the new Secretary of State to visit the prisoners in the Maze. The minister was appalled at the men's suffering, and immediately gave Ramsey the green light to offer the hunger strikers most of what they demanded. Prior could not, however, agree to the use of the term: *political status*. Thatcher had made that very clear to him on his appointment, although that was in effect what he was offering. Ramsey now saw the opportunity to finally reach a settlement without further loss of life. He retuned to his office and faxed the new proposals to Sinn Fein. He waited impatiently, pacing the room until the phone rang.

When Ramsey hung up, he broke down and wept, repeating the words in his mind again and again … *They've accepted the terms!!*

'Jim Prior is on his way to see you, sir … are you okay?'

'Carol, please knock in future before barging in … Sorry … I'm fine, just give me a minute,' said Ramsey, wiping his face with his handkerchief and getting up to look out the window at the autumnal trees. 'I'm just glad it's over.'

*

Danny had fasted for fifty-four days before the doctors intervened. His condition was so bad that he was immediately transferred to the Royal Victoria Hospital, where he gradually recovered from the ordeal with no long-lasting damage to his health. When he was out of danger he was taken to Musgrave Park Hospital to convalesce, before being returned to the Maze a few weeks after the hunger strike was brought to an end.

The men on the wing stopped what they were doing and clapped and cheered him as he was led back to his cell in the new clothes that his mother had brought in for him to wear. The wing was strange and familiar to him at the same time; prisoners who spent years confined to filthy cells, naked with wild looking long hair and beards, were now standing around the corridors chatting and smoking, wearing their own clothes. The beards and long hair were gone and the place seemed more like a community centre than the brutal prison he remembered. The cell door was lying open and Seamus was sitting up in bed reading Tolstoy's *War and Peace*, and smoking a Marlboro cigarette. The cell was pristine clean and there were pictures on the walls where there was once only human excrement. A radio sat on the window ledge beside a small, spiky cactus plant.

'I heard all the commotion,' said Seamus, looking up from his book with a smile on his face, 'I thought it must be Danny boy coming back.'

'So you decided to just lie in your bloody bed,' said Danny, feigning annoyance.

'I would have got up but…' he said, lifting his leg slowly from under the sheets. 'I twisted it coming down the steps in the showers.'

'Well, it's good to see that ye stopped wiping yer arse on the walls,' said Danny, throwing him a packet of cigarettes, 'Me ma brought me in forty this morning.'

'Yer a sound lad,' said Seamus catching the packet in one hand and quickly putting it under his pillow.

'What's that yer reading? I thought you couldn't read.'

'It's War and Peace, ye cheeky bastard. I've decided to get an education.'

'What's it been like in here since the strike stopped?'

'Sound; the screws are just glad it's all over. They pretty much leave us now to get on with it. It's a pity that it took the lives of ten men for them to let us live like human beings.'

'Do ye think it was all worth it?'

'Is anything worth all those dead men? The only real thing to come out of it as far as I can see is that Sinn Fein are now contesting elections and winning. That would never have happened without Bobby and the others doing what they did … And you of course.'

'That's not why we went on hunger strike.'

'Maybe not, Danny, but we got what we were looking for. This is something none of us thought would happen. It might just be that things will change quicker if we start to get our own people elected.'

'If they don't take the seats that they win, what's the point?'

'It shows the British and the rest of the world that we have a mandate for change in Northern Ireland. That's the important thing.'

'Maybe yer right, Seamus, but that'll not happen overnight.'

*

Over the next two years time passed slowly in the Maze. The world's media had long since moved on. Danny knew that would soon change when he received his orders from the wing OC.

Early one morning, Seamus looked up from the book he was reading to see Danny standing at the cell door, counting under his breath, 'Twenty-one, twenty-two, twenty three…'

'What the hell are ye up to?'

'Damn it, Seamus, ye made me lose count!'

'What are ye up to?' repeated Seamus, with a serious tone to his voice that demanded an answer.

'I can't tell ye.' said Danny, sitting down on his bed to roll a cigarette.

'You won't tell yer own cellmate!'

'Seamus, I can't. Not yet.'

'Well to hell wi' you!'

Seamus lay back down on his bed. He knew fine well what Danny was doing but he wasn't sure why. He pretended he was no longer interested and continued reading his book, *Rights of Man* by Thomas Paine, as Danny blew anxious smoke rings towards the ceiling. Seamus started to read out a passage from the book, as much to annoy Danny as anything else. *'No man should be accused, arrested, or held in confinement, except in cases determined by law, and according to the forms which it has prescribed. All who promote, solicit, execute or cause it to be executed arbitrarily ought to be punished...'*

'Danny, listen to this,' said Seamus, suddenly appreciating the content of what he had just read. 'No man should...'

Danny shrugged his shoulders at Seamus. He got up to look out the cell window towards the heather covered fields in the distance. He could smell the honeysuckle that was wrapped around the hedgerows and longed to be able to walk through the fields with the sun on his back. 'The birds will be missing their maggots,' he said as he stubbed out the cigarette and sat back down on his bed again with a sigh. Frustrated, Danny looked at Seamus, who was ignoring him and reading with the intensity of an academic studying for a philosophy exam. 'I'll have to do that all again tomorrow because of you,' he complained, hoping that Seamus would stop reading for a while.

'Do what? Count how long it takes the screws to walk along the corridor from the grilles?' said Seamus, with a knowing grin. 'Usually three minutes at most, unless it's Murdock. He takes nearly four minutes.'

'How the hell do ye know that?'

'It helps me to get to sleep at night. I hear them open the grilles and listen to every step until they turn back and clatter their keys to reopen the gate. I sometimes count how long it takes, better than counting sheep. It's okay so long as they don't stop and talk to anyone; then it's knackered!'

'I know it seems a bit stupid. I think they just asked me to do this to keep me occupied,' said Danny, rolling another cigarette.

'Who?' asked Seamus, sitting up and putting down his book.

'I can't tell ye, they'll go off their heads.'

'Well, that could only be Bernie and Gerry. What are they

up to?'

'If I tell ye, don't mention it to anyone,' whispered Danny, pushing the door closed with his foot. 'We are planning to break out of here.'

'Oh fuck, and just when I was getting used to the quiet life.'

By the end of the following week, two handguns were smuggled into the wing. Danny was given his orders and passed a lock-back knife to help him overcome Murdoch when he reached the final cell during his routine early-morning rounds. Seamus was amazed that the whole thing was going ahead. 'How can we get men out of this place, for Christ's sake? It's the most secure prison in Europe!'

'Never ye mind. If you want to stay behind, then that's up to you.'

'I can't go anyway. Gerry told me I was only going to be a burden on the others. They should have let me go on the hunger strike, I'm finished anyway…'

'I'm sorry, Seamus, Gerry's right. Even if we got you out, you would hardly last five minutes with your lungs.'

'You can always help.'

'How?'

'When I grab Murdock, you can help me get him into a cell before he starts shouting his head off.'

'Okay, but I'll end up with another ten years on my sentence.'

'What does that matter? You'll be an old man when ye get out of here anyway. What difference will it make?'

'Thanks,' said Seamus, lying back on his bed and staring at the ceiling, curses wheezing from his chest. He was waiting for the right moment to ask Danny if he would look out for his nephew, Tony Feeney, or Curly, as everyone, even the prison guards, called him. He was only nineteen years old, but nearly thirteen stone with a mop of long curly red hair. Curly was serving a fifteen year sentence for possession of explosives and conspiracy to cause explosions, after being arrested on his first operation, a botched attempt to blow up a police station.

'Yer having a laugh,' said Danny, when Seamus put the proposition to him. 'That fat lump couldn't run the length of himself. He'll get me caught.'

'He's my brother's boy, for God's sake. Just keep an eye on him for me. Is that too much to ask ye?'

'All right,' said Danny, 'but he better not get me caught. You tell him to follow me and do as I say. If he gives me any cheek then he's on his own. But if he gets me caught…'

When the morning of the planned breakout arrived, there was a nervous tension in the air. Danny stood by the door and watched the other prisoners carrying out the menial tasks that were key to getting into the secure administration centre. They had to get into the operations room before any of the officers had a chance to react and set off the alarms. He watched one of the prisoners carrying a tray of tea towards the grilles at the bottom of the corridor. The gate opened and the prisoners exchanged some light-hearted banter with Murdock, who then began his slow walk along the wing, stopping briefly at each cell. Murdock managed to get halfway along, when he decided to speak to one of the prisoners about the previous night's football. Danny watched anxiously, his hand in his pocket tightly gripping the handle of the knife, hoping he would not have to use it. He could hear Seamus breathing heavily behind him, his chest wheezing more than usual. He felt his own heart pounding as he mentally urged Murdock to get a move on. After the prisoner made an excuse to break off the conversation, Murdock continued his slow walk. Danny suddenly heard a commotion further along the corridor and the sound of a metal tray dropping on the concrete floor. Murdock turned to see what was happening. Danny ran towards him with the knife in his hand. He grabbed the officer around the neck, placing the sharp blade under his chin. 'Keep yer mouth shut and ye won't get hurt. This is an IRA operation!'

Murdock was in such a state of shock that he could not have called out even if he wanted to. Seamus and two other prisoners ran to Danny's aid and bundled the frightened man into an empty cell. There was a shot that echoed around the wing that startled everyone. Then orders were shouted at the top of the corridor by one of the other prisoners to the officer in the control centre. Seamus grabbed Danny's arm and they looked at each other, anxiously waiting for the sirens to sound. There were more shouts as another prisoner appeared at the grilles with a set of keys and opened the gate into the wing.

'Remember, Danny, look after Curly for me!'

'Don't worry. Get back in the cell and I'll lock ye in.'

The overpowered prison officers were bundled into the empty cells and stripped to their underwear, while some of the prisoners dressed in their uniforms to execute the next stage of the escape. Danny saw Curly standing outside one of the cells and grabbed him by the arm. 'Stay close to me, and do what I tell ye.'

More orders were being shouted out in Gaelic as the escapees followed the main leaders out into the side yard where a delivery van had already been hijacked by one of the other prisoners. Curly followed Danny and about thirty others into the back of the van. They sat in the darkness as it made its way to the front gatehouse.

The van stopped after a few minutes and some of the men, wearing the prison officers' uniforms, got out of the van and ran towards the gatehouse. The shutter was pulled down again and the rest of the prisoners were left in the back, waiting anxiously for the van to start moving again.

'I don't like it,' said Curly. 'It's taking too long.'

'I know, something's wrong,' said Danny, now wondering just how much longer his prison sentence was going to be.

The back shutter was suddenly pulled up. 'It's every man for himself!' shouted one of the prisoners as the sirens began wailing all around. The men poured out of the van into the pandemonium of guards fighting with prisoners. Danny ran towards the main gate, which was lying wide open. When he reached the outer barrier he heard Curly shouting for help. He turned to see him on the ground wrestling with one of the prison officers. Danny ran back and kicked the guard full force in the face, before dragging Curly to his feet.

Once through the main gate, they ran across the road towards the open fields. Danny could already feel the burning in his throat and the tightness in his muscles as he leapt over a stone dyke and ran towards the woods in the distance. When he crossed the field, he looked back to see Curly and three other escapees following close behind. Most of the other prisoners were running in small groups in different directions, although some had already been captured by prison guards. He could see army vehicles pulling up on the roadway, and soldiers climbing over the stone dyke at the bottom of the field, screaming orders to each other as they joined the chaos.

Danny shouted at Curly to hurry, before jumping over another dyke, finally reaching the cover of the trees and gorse bushes. Trying to catch his breath, he suddenly heard the sound of rotor blades overhead. He looked back to see Curly trying to keep up with the other two prisoners who were now well ahead of him as they jumped the dyke and ran into the woods without stopping. For a moment Danny felt the urge to follow them, but he could not take his eyes off Curly, who was puffing and panting, near exhaustion. *If only I hadn't promised Seamus to look after him.*

A Land Rover got itself stuck in the mud at the bottom of the field. The soldiers got out, and began running after the fleeing prisoners. For a moment Danny feared that they would start firing. Curly stopped for a breather in the open field. 'Curly, get over here! Hurry up for fuck's sake or you'll get us both caught.'

Curly finally reached the dyke, and dragged himself over before falling at Danny's feet. 'I'm knackered … I can't run … another step. I need to rest for a while.'

'Get up! The Brits are heading this way. It will be dark soon and ye can rest then,' shouted Danny, pulling Curly to his feet.

They forced their way through the thick bracken and ferns until they reached a path that took them deep into the woods. Danny had no energy left to shout at Curly and had to keep slowing down to let him catch up. The dense trees eventually opened up to more fields. They stayed close to the hedgerows that offered at least some cover, before continuing to struggle through the countryside for hours until they reached the banks of a stream. Totally exhausted, they threw themselves on the moss around a storm-felled tree to rest for a while. The last of the daylight was beginning to fade.

Their rest was transient, and it was not long before they heard the sound of voices calling behind them. Again, Danny had to pull Curly to his feet, threatening to leave him behind if he did not get a move on. They waded across the shallow water in constant fear of a bullet in the back. Curly dragged himself onto the other bank.

'I can't go any further…'

'Get up.'

'Just leave me.'

'If you don't get moving you'll be back in prison tonight…now get fucking up!'

Curly forced himself back onto his feet and staggered

after Danny, their clothes and boots now soaking wet. They were too weak to run, and had to walk mile after mile in virtual darkness until they reached an isolated farm, where they took shelter in the barn. Drained, Curly collapsed onto a pile of straw and began to remove his wet boots.

'Leave then on, stupid, or your feet will swell up and ye won't get them back on again!'

'But me feet are raw.'

'So are mine, so do as yer told, or I'll stick that pitch fork up yer arse … We'll have to get moving again soon.'

'I can't walk any further.'

'Stop fucking moaning … I'm going to see if there's a car up at the house we can nick.'

With Curly still trying to control his erratic breathing, Danny crept up to the window of the farmhouse. He could see an old man sitting in front of the fire smoking a pipe and reading a newspaper. Danny pulled back from the window when an elderly woman entered the room with plates and cutlery, and began to set the table. He then walked around to the side of the house where there was an old battered looking car covered in mud. He could not believe his luck when he looked through the window to see the keys in the ignition.

They were soon driving through the quiet country lanes on their way to the border. Danny knew he could only risk driving on the back roads for so long before they would eventually run into an army road block, but he was prepared to take a risk and at least put some miles on the clock before ditching the car. Curly was hoping in his mind that they could drive all the way to Dublin and he switched on the radio just as the evening news came on… *This is the six-o'clock news. The government is reeling today from what is reported to be the largest prison breakout in British history. Shortly after 2.30 pm this afternoon, IRA prisoners in the Maze Prison seized control of their wing by taking a number of prison officers hostage at gunpoint. One officer who attempted to prevent the escape was shot in the head; his condition is critical. A number of other officers were also wounded during the breakout, one stabbed three times in the chest, when he attempted to raise the alarm, another was shot in the leg while chasing two prisoners who had failed to reached the outer fence. The other prisoners made good their escape by hijacking cars or running into the open fields. The army and RUC immediately threw a cordon of vehicle checkpoints in strategic positions across Northern Ireland. Mrs Thatcher has made a statement while on a visit to Canada, saying 'It is the gravest breakout in our present history, and there must be a very deep inquiry'.*

'Fuck her. Did it say how many got out?' asked Danny, handing Curly a cigarette from a packet he found in the car. 'No … Why was that car flashing its lights at you?'

'I don't know, they might be warning us there's a road block up ahead,' said Danny, slowing down and throwing his cigarette out the window, before turning onto a dirt track, where he ditched the car. They began to hike across the fields again, both now struggling with burst blisters and raw wet skin. It took a few painful miles before they got into their stride again, keeping the North Star at their backs.

Moorcroft was in constant radio contact with his men on the ground, as the helicopter swooped low over the countryside, its searchlight scanning the fields below. Every so often he would fire into clumps of trees and bushes to ferret out any escapees who might be hiding in them. Killing a few IRA men in the process was of no consequence to him. Low on fuel, the pilot signalled to him that they had to return to base. The Puma made a final sweep across the fields before turning back as Moorcroft radioed his men to continue the search.

Once the helicopter landed, he received a radio message about a stolen car found a few hundred yards from an RUC check-point in Armagh. He took a fresh magazine of bullets, and jumped into his Land Rover with three of his men and two tracker dogs. He gave orders to *shoot to kill*.

Chapter 38

On the Border

The raw dawn crept over the hills and the low-lying fields around the border. Danny, without waking from his deep sleep, instinctively wiped away a couple of annoying insects that strayed onto his face, while Curly turned uncomfortably in his bed of crushed ferns and dead pine needles.

Danny's dreams were enchanted with the smell of burning turf, which flurried up the hillside from the scattering of cottages and farmhouses below. He could almost touch the yellow flames as they danced around his fingers while the echoed voice of his mother welcomed him home. In his mind he took a strangely long cigarette from the breast pocket of his green tunic and lit it with the bright red blaze from a piece of wood he had lifted from the hearth. He had to keep getting up to close the window, which blew open constantly, taking away the warmth he felt from the illusory fire.

'Danny, wake up! Wake up!' Curly repeated, shaking Danny out of his heavy sleep and away from the warmth of his mother's fire. 'Listen!' whispered Curly as Danny groaned at the miserable reality of his damp clothes and aching body. 'Can ye hear it?'

'No, what the hell is it? I can't hear anything.'

'Listen,' urged Curly.

Suddenly awake to the danger, Danny could now make out the sound of helicopter rotors. Curly was tightly holding on to Danny's jacket as they both looked up through the canopy of trees to occasionally catch a glimpse of the helicopter as it roared above them, shining its searchlight into the thicket of trees. Thankfully for them, there were still enough leaves on most of the trees and shrubs to give them cover. They lay still in the undergrowth, their hearts beating intensely, almost in rhythm with the roar of the Puma's engines.

Curly slowly released his grip on Danny's jacket as the searchlight lifted and the slapping sound of the rotors blades began to drift off.

'They may be looking for somewhere to land!' Curly said, scurrying to a gap to watch the helicopter descend the hillside towards the town on the other side of the river. Danny crawled up beside him in time to watch it make a sweeping turn and head back over the fields, fading into the grey skies as the dawn began to break in earnest.

'Thank God,' said Curly, rummaging through his jacket pockets for a cigarette. 'We'll have to get out of here before they come back. But how will we get across the border in broad daylight?'

'See that farmhouse down there?'

'Aye,' replied Curly, looking down at the farmhouse and adjacent barn, with its rusty red corrugated roof.

'We'll have to take a chance and hope they're friendly. Most of the people living on the border will be Republicans.'

'What if they're not?'

'That's the chance we'll have to take. They might be able to help us get over the border.'

With the helicopter gone, they lay in a tangled nest of bracken and observed the farm as the morning sun lifted the last of the night from the surrounding fields. After taking a long draw, Danny passed Curly the cigarette as if it were some sacred gift to be cherished before its fleeting magic was gone. Each draw was savoured as they watched the lights come on in the upstairs windows of the farmhouse. Before long, smoke scattered from the two chimneystacks.

A young woman came out of the house with a metal bucket and scurried across the backyard to a stack of turf. They watched her fill the bucket. The wind blew her hair about wildly. She then wiped her hands on her apron before turning back towards the house. Danny passed the last of the cigarette back to Curly. They watched as a dozen or so black and white cows emerged from the dilapidated barn, followed by an old man waving a stick in the air, goading the reluctant cattle into a field at the back of the farm. The herd of Friesians were soon trotting along a muddy path away from the farmhouse and into open fields further up the hillside.

'What do ye think?' Curly asked.

'We have to take a chance. We won't last long in these wet clothes. They must be Republicans.'

'What if they're not?'

'Then we're in trouble.'

'Look, there's the girl again,' said Curly as they watched her come out of the back door and throw a basin of water into the yard.

'We better do something soon, before the old fella gets back,' said Danny. 'I'll go down first. When I give you the signal you come down, but not before. If I don't come back out the house after a couple of minutes then get to hell out of here.'

'Why don't I come with ye?'

'Just do what I tell ye. There's no point the two of us getting caught! We still don't know who's in there.'

Danny got to his feet and put the knife in his trouser belt. 'Don't worry. We'll be eating breakfast soon.' After scanning the horizon, he kicked his way through the mangled undergrowth of ferns and brambles, descending into the fields towards the farmhouse. At the bottom of the field, he climbed over a dry stone dyke, and stealthily made his way along the hedgerow towards the farmyard.

The wind began to toss the long grasses and heather around. Curly was shivering uncontrollably with a mixture of fear and cold. He looked over to where he had last seen the farmer, who had now disappeared behind some trees near the river. When he turned back, Danny was already in the farmhouse.

Still shivering, Curly nervously watched the back of the farmhouse, as he scraped dried mud embedded under his nails with the end of a broken twig.

With no sign of Danny, Curly could wait no longer and began to make his way down the field, climbing over the dry stone dyke and running into the farmyard. As he walked through the puddles of mud and cow dung, the back door suddenly opened and Danny appeared holding the knife.

'I told ye to wait!'

'I thought something happened to you!'

'Well, something did happen.'

Curly stared into the house to see the girl lying on the kitchen floor with a blood-stained kitchen knife lying nearby.

'Did ye have to kill her?'

'It was her that stabbed me,' groaned Danny as Curly noticed the blood dripping onto the floor from Danny's arm. 'I punched her when she stuck that thing into my arm. I think she may have hit her head when she fell. Go over and see if she's all right. There's no-one else in the house.'

Curly cautiously walked over to the girl, who was beginning to come around. He picked up the knife and quickly stepped back. 'Why did she do that?'

'God knows. She did it anyway. See if she's all right.'

'Get yer hands off me!' the girl screamed.

'She's not as sweet as she looks,' laughed Danny,

removing his heavy wet jacket to take a look at his bloody arm. 'You bitch! Ye could have done me some serious damage if I didn't have this jacket on. Sit on that chair and don't move from it until we're out of here or ye'll get this in ye,' ordered Danny, gesticulating with the lock-back knife.

The girl sneered at Danny. She got to her feet and grabbed the back of the chair, lifting it away from the kitchen table, before banging it back down on the uneven flagstone floor. She sat herself down with the same deliberate disdain, folding her arms and staring at Danny with eyes wild with scorn. 'What the hell are ye doing in my house?' she demanded, pushing her hair away from her eyes.

'I told ye,' said Danny, taking a seat opposite. 'This is an IRA operation and ye'll have nothing to worry about if ye just sit there and keep yer mouth shut until we decide what we're doing.'

'Typical IRA! Ye don't even know what the hell yer doing. Well I'm not scared of ye… You're some of the ones that broke out of the prison.'

'Aye, and what of it?' said Curly, wiping the blood stained potato knife on his jacket sleeve and trying to sound as tough as Danny.

'Listen to him! Isn't he the hard man?' sneered the girl, with a mock laugh in her voice.

'Yer a bit of a hard ticket yerself,' said Danny, still dabbing the wound on his arm with a tea-towel. 'Who's the old fella that took the cows out this morning?'

'You leave him alone; that's me grandfather,' she replied, somewhat hesitantly.

'When will he be back?' asked Danny, sensing a weakness in her voice for the first time.

'He'll be back in shortly for his breakfast … He's an old man,' she added with a plea in her voice.

'We're not murderers. We won't do him any harm. We want to get out of here as much as you want to get rid of us. If ye give us yer word that ye won't do anything daft, we'll be gone before he gets back. Curly, go and see if ye can get us any dry clothes to wear.'

'I won't do anything if ye get to hell out of here as quick as ye came. I don't want any trouble,' she said. 'Just take what you want and leave.'

'Yer right! You won't do anything. You won't get a chance to stab me again,' said Danny, lifting his own knife from the table. 'Why don't ye make us something to eat and we'll be out of here before ye know it … Is there a car here?'

'No, it's in the garage getting fixed.'

'Shit! Have ye any money in the house?'

'There are a few pounds in change in that jar on the table. Take it, if it gets ye out of here.'

Desperate to get out of his wet jeans, Curly went into one of the bedrooms at the top of the stairs to look for clothes. The wooden floorboards creaked. He moved over to a large chest of drawers crammed with old pictures in heavy metal frames. There were piles of coins and odd keys in between the family photographs and an ancient-looking carriage clock buried behind the clutter. He looked at the photographs to see if he could see the girl, but they seemed to be from another era. He opened the first drawer that was stuffed with woollen jumpers, which he threw onto the bed, separating anything he thought, would be of any use to him or Danny.

Downstairs, Danny had managed to pull the laceration on his arm together with some sticky tape to help it seal with the blood that was already congealing around the wound. The girl was now more compliant, but he kept a careful eye on her as she placed slices of bacon on a large frying pan. 'We don't have any coffee, only tea.'

'That will do fine,' he said. 'Hope you've got some eggs

to go with that bacon?'

'Well, it is a farm.'

'Where's yer family?' he asked, pulling his sleeve down.

'I told you, he's out in the fields with the cattle.'

'Aye, but where's yer parents?'

'What's it to you?' she snapped back, angrily cracking an egg into the spitting frying-pan.

'They don't live here, I take it?'

'No.'

'So you're not expecting anyone else this morning?'

'No, no-one.'

'There's yer breakfast,' she said, almost dropping the plate on the table in front of Danny. 'Ye better tell yer partner in crime to come down. I wouldn't like it to get cold on him,' she added sarcastically.

Before Danny got a chance to shout, Curly was already clambering down the stairs with his arms full of clothing. He dropped most of the clothes on the kitchen floor, still holding a grey-blue uniform by the clothes-hanger.

'Put that back!' shouted the girl as she tried to grab it from Curly's hand. 'It's me father's!'

'Give her it,' ordered Danny.

The girl grabbed the uniform and ran upstairs. Curly placed a revolver on the table in front of Danny. 'I found this as well. Her father must be in the RUC.'

'Go up and see what she's up to,' said Danny, lifting the revolver from the table, 'and see if there's any ammo for this thing.'

Curly went back up the stairs, each step creaking under his muddy boots. He felt a sense of trepidation and curiosity in equal measure as he peered into the first room. Then he heard sobbing coming from one of the other rooms further along the hall. The door was ajar and he could see the girl sitting on the edge of the bed, with the uniform tight in her arms as she pressed her sobs against the back of the jacket. The room was bright and softly decorated in contrast to the austerity of her grandfather's room. She was startled from her thoughts when Curly slowly opened the heavy wooden door.

'Are ye all right? I didn't mean to make ye cry.'

'Well, you shouldn't have killed him, then.'

'I haven't killed anyone.'

'It might not have been you, but you're IRA and they killed him. He wasn't even in uniform when they shot him. He was out buying my birthday present,' she said, crying again.

'I'm sorry. When did it happen?'

'How can you be sorry? Is that not what you're all about? Killing people! Your friend downstairs has killed. I can see it in his eyes. And he'll kill again, and so will you.'

'Where's your mother?'

'My mother died when I was a baby, I never knew her.'

'I'm sorry.'

She got up and put the uniform over the back of a chair and turned to look out the window, 'You better go downstairs and have your breakfast.'

Danny was already changing out of his wet clothes and trying to find something that would fit him from the pile of clothing on the floor. Nothing seemed to fit, so he eventually settled for a baggy pair of black trousers, which he turned up at the bottom and took up the slack in the waist with a thick leather belt. He tried on a heavy check shirt, which was as voluminous as the trousers. He noticed Curly standing grinning at him.

'I don't know what you think is so funny, you better get upstairs and try on that uniform.'

'Go to hell. I'm not wearing the uniform. It's the girl's father's uniform.'

'What are ye on about? It will get us across the border.'

'I'm not wearing it.'

Danny was staring at Curly in disbelief, when their stand off was interrupted by the sound of someone cleaning their boots at the back door. Danny quickly took up a position behind the door, nodding to Curly to go upstairs and get the girl. Curly threw the bundle of clothes into the corner and moved into the hall as he listened to the girl coming down the stairs. The back door opened and Danny held his breath. He then heard the gruff voice of the farmer. 'Rose! Come out a minute!'

With the knife in his hand, Danny held the door open with the handle as he peered through a crack in one of the panels. He could see the farmer, shotgun in hand, cautiously peering towards the kitchen window. Danny was now sweating under the heavy shirt and pullover, which obviously belonged to the heavyset farmer who had the upper hand with what was almost certainly a loaded shotgun against an unloaded revolver and a knife.

'Rose, come out will ye!' shouted the farmer, moving slowly away from the door.

'Don't move. This is an IRA operation, stay where you are and drop the shotgun!'

'Run, run,' shouted Rose, before Curly could muffle her screams.

The farmer turned and began to run through the muddy yard towards the barn. 'Stop or I will shoot!' shouted Danny as he stepped out into the backyard and pointed the unloaded revolver in the direction of the fleeing farmer, who then slipped in the mud with the shotgun falling from his hand.

'You have nothing to worry about. We will be out of here in a few minutes,' said Danny as he picked up the shotgun to his overwhelming relief.

'Grandpa!' shouted Rose, running from the farmhouse, and splashing mud in every direction. 'Grandpa!'

'He's okay,' said Danny. 'Help him up.'

'Grandpa, are ye all right?'

'I'm all right, I slipped, that's all.'

'Curly!'

Curly walked over towards the barn, rather shame-faced, holding his hand that bore Rose's fresh teeth marks. Danny handed him the empty revolver and shook his head at him. 'I'm out here catching this old fella and you're away getting love bites.'

'Ah piss off, will ye?' said Curly, snatching the empty revolver from Danny's outstretched hand. 'I held her as long as I could; sure, she stabbed you quickly enough!'

'You're a couple of cowboys, that's what you are,' said Rose, still struggling to help her grandfather to his feet.

'Shut up!' shouted Danny, 'listen!'

'Choppers!' said Curly, looking at the dots in the horizon heading towards them.

'Get to your fucking feet,' shouted Danny, pushing Rose away and grabbing the farmer by the arm. 'Curly, get a hold of her and if she bites you this time, bite her back!'

Danny pulled the barn door open, pushing the old man onto some bales of hay as Curly struggled with Rose, who seemed to have all her old fight back. They listened as the helicopters roared overhead for a few moments before moving on. Danny smiled at Curly, who was still struggling with the girl.

Chapter 39

The Hunt

In the Operation Headquarters, the walls were covered with ordnance survey maps, with the border enlarged to a detailed scale, peppered with pins and red felt-tipped pen marks. Colonel Burke was the officer in charge of army operations in the South Armagh area, and was determined to stop any IRA prisoners getting over the border. The opposite wall was set aside for the immediate crisis. Black and white photographs of all the prison escapees dominated the room. Already a number of the faces had Colonel Burke's felt tip across them, confirming they had been captured and returned to the Maze Prison.

The colonel was sure that most of the escapees were still in the area and likely in safe houses waiting for the border controls to relax. The number of soldiers under his command had tripled since the prison breakout.

'What have you got there, captain?'

'It's a balaclava which was recovered by one of the dogs last night just before we called off the search.'

'*Hunt*, Cuthbert. You *search* for your lost keys and you *hunt* your enemy. Remember that, my good man.'

'Yes, sir. This is where the car was recovered,' said the captain, circling the general area on the map with his cane.

'So even if they continued all night, it's unlikely that they would have made the border by sun up.'

'I agree, sir. The nearest town to the border from where

they were heading is Middletown,' said the captain, tapping the town's significance on the map with the tip of his finger.

'How many do you reckon are heading that way?'

'Two or three, maybe four. We're not sure.'

'Do we know who any of them are?' asked the colonel, turning to the wall with the photos of IRA escapees. 'Would any of those fellows be in this little batch?' he added, pointing to a group of eight faces, all high up the IRA hierarchy, and seen as the masterminds behind the mass breakout.

'Could be, we're just not sure. All we know is the car was stolen from a farm and dumped in a field, where it was found a few hours later by local RUC officers.'

'What about fingerprints?'

'We have sent off the prints found in the car to the RUC forensic unit. They still haven't got back to us.'

'Well, chase that up, I like to know who we are dealing with.'

'Yes, sir.'

'What are we doing in the meantime?'

'I've sent out the Pumas to have another look at the area, and to direct the ground forces to likely hideouts. They'll not get through, sir.'

'Well make sure they don't. I don't want to be reading about their great escape again in *The Times* tomorrow. If you trace these men, I don't want the regulars to engage them unless absolutely necessary. Major Moorcroft and his SAS unit are on standby; they don't mess about with unnecessary niceties, and if the quarry is not immediately submissive they will soon make them ex-IRA men.'

*

Danny was sitting with the shotgun over his arm, watching the minutes pass slowly on the kitchen clock. He had run out of ideas, and was simply waiting for nightfall to try and make it over the fields into the Republic.

In the corner, the farmer was quietly slurping from a bowl of chicken soup that his granddaughter had made. She had cleaned him up and he was sitting like a big docile bear, tearing at lumps of bread with his great big hands and dipping them into his thick broth. Rose ladled out another bowl of soup for Curly, before placing a begrudged bowl before Danny. It was still only midday.

'What's the nearest town called?' asked Danny, looking at a map that Curly had found when he was looking for ammunition.

'Middletown,' said the old man, before taking another slurp of his soup.

'So Monaghan is the nearest town in the Republic,' said Danny, trying to gauge the distances on the map. 'How far do ye reckon?'

'Don't be telling him, grandpa, let him find out for himself.'

'It's about six, maybe seven miles along the A3.'

'Grandpa!'

'Ah, Rose, what does it matter so long as they leave us in peace…Aah…Aah.'

'Grandpa, what's wrong?'

'Get my tablets, it's my angina. Aah…'

'Go with her, Curly' ordered Danny, as Rose rushed into the front sitting-room.

'I'll be all right in a minute,' said the old man. 'It comes and goes…Thanks, Rose,' he said, turning to take the little pink tablets and a glass of water in his shaking hands.

As Danny watched the farmer's discomfort subside, a new plan was emerging in his mind that might get them over the border. 'That's it. That's it,' he repeated.

'What is it?' asked Curly.

'There's no phone in this house, is there?' Danny asked the farmer.

'No, there's never been a phone in the house.'

'So what would happen if he really had a heart attack?'

'There's a public phone just down the road before ye go into town,' said Rose, lifting the empty soup bowls and placing them in the sink. 'Why would you be worried about him having a heart attack?'

'I'm not,' replied Danny coldly. 'Where is the nearest hospital?'

'That would be in Armagh, about ten miles back up the A3,' said the farmer, seemingly recovered from his mild angina attack. 'Or even Monaghan over the border.'

'If you do as we say we'll be gone in a couple of hours.'

'We're not helping you. Why should we?' said Rose defiantly, moving over to stand beside her grandfather.

'Well, if we end up staying here any longer the army is going to come sooner or later and this place will be riddled with bullets, because they're not taking me back alive. You don't have to help us, you just have to do what yer told and no one gets hurt.'

'What do you want us to do?' asked the farmer, taking his granddaughter's hand in his own to reassure her.

'I want the girl to phone an ambulance and tell them you've had a heart attack. Curly will go with her, and if there's any funny business... well, I don't need to tell you what will happen.'

'And what if I refuse?' said Rose.

'Then we're staying put and you and your granddad have to take your chances. Like I said, the SAS will not be too concerned if they take us alive or dead. And if that results in a couple of civilians taking a few bullets, do ye think they'll give a fuck? They'll probably blame us for shooting you anyway.'

'Do as he says, Rose,' pleaded her grandfather, who did not seem to have any of his granddaughter's defiant spirit.

'Your grandfather will stay here with me and you'll come back as soon as you make the call.'

'What are ye planning to do, highjack the ambulance?' Rose asked, an uncontrolled smile appearing on her lips. 'You're a pair of cowboys all right.'

'Well, if you don't want this to turn into the gunfight at the OK Corral, you better get yer coat and get up to that phone and make the call… and take Wyatt Earp with you.'

*

The heavy passenger door of Major Moorcroft's jeep slammed behind him as he walked briskly over to a group of camouflaged soldiers, who had been taking observations from a makeshift canvas hide.

'Any joy, lads?'

'No, sir. We've seen plenty of rabbits but nothing much else,' said the captain in charge of the observation post. 'The farms and outhouses to the west have already been searched and cleared, and Captain Travers has radioed to confirm that his platoon has moved over the River Cor into the town of Middletown. It's the main market town in the district and there are a number of farms in the area. If they're still on this side of the border then we'll get them, sir.'

'Well, keep your eyes peeled.'

'Major! We've caught two of them,' the soldier monitoring the radio inside the hide shouted. 'One of them has been shot.'

'Good, good,' said Moorcroft, satisfied that his tactics were bearing fruit. 'Do we have any names?'

'They've refused to give their names and have been taken into police custody for interrogation.'

'I'm sure the RUC will kick their names out of them,' said one of the other officers.

'As soon as you get their names I want them radioed to me instantly! I don't want that idiot Travers doing anything until my unit gets there, do ye hear?'

'Yes, sir!' replied the captain, saluting his superior as the major turned back to his vehicle.

'Who does he think he is?' said the lieutenant.

'An SAS major!' replied the captain.

*

Curly squeezed into the phone box to listen to Rose making the emergency call. When she put the receiver back down, she pushed him back out into the street. 'Let me out! I've done yer dirty work for ye.'

'Hold on, will ye?' shouted Curly, who could hardly keep up with her as she rushed over the stony road back towards the farm. Every step Curly took caused him pain. His feet were still raw, and covered with fresh blisters and cuts that his ill-fitting boots gnawed at. Despite his aching feet, he managed to catch up with Rose by the time she reached the farm. He grabbed her arm to show that he was still in charge.

She shrugged his hand away and opened the back door to the kitchen. 'Where is he? Where's me grandfather?' she demanded, staring at Danny who was fully dressed, with his parka jacket ominously zipped up to his neck and holding the shotgun directly at Rose. 'He's all right. He's in the living-room.'

'Get out my way,' shouted Rose, pushing past Danny.

Still holding the shotgun, Danny followed her into the front room where her grandfather was gagged and tied to a chair. There was another chair nearby with rope already tied to the frame and waiting for its occupant. 'You know we have to do it. We can't take any risks,' said Danny as Rose turned back towards him. 'You're not going to kill us?'

'No, we're soldiers not murderers … If we were going to kill you, why would we need to tie you both up? I will phone the local police as soon as we get over the border.'

'It's all right, grandpa, they'll be gone soon,' she said, taking off her coat and folding it neatly onto a nearby table. She then sat down without another word.

Danny tied her to the chair, securing the knotted handkerchief around her mouth. He took a long look at her; those angry eyes looking straight through him, with the same scornful defiance she had when she stuck the knife in his arm. 'I promise, I'll phone the police as soon as we're over the border.' He switched off the light.

*

Tired of seeing nothing but sheep and cows, Captain Travers lit a cigarette, passing his binoculars to Private Mitchell. The news that the two men who had been arrested earlier were low ranking IRA men had taken some of the shine off the operation. The last radio message ordered the search to continue until all the remaining buildings in the area had been cleared.

While one of his men held an umbrella overhead, Captain Travers spread an ordnance survey map across the bonnet of his Land Rover. He circled the area which had still to be searched around Middletown. Apart from the town itself there were at least twenty buildings in the area that were still to be cleared. The distant church spire of the town gave the soldiers their only real bearing as to where they were in relation to the scattered houses and barns. Travers gave his men the order to get ready to move out.

'Captain, I just got a message through that there's something suspicious happening at one of the farms just outside the town. One of the neighbours noticed a scruffy stranger hanging about the farm. The farm's called Grange Farm,' said the radio operator.

'Which farm would that be?' asked Travers rhetorically as he checked the red circled co-ordinates with the various properties on a separate list taken from the voters roll. 'That must be it down there,' he said, pointing through the sheets of grey rain.

'Right, men!' screamed the platoon sergeant. 'We're going to give this farm a visit.'

*

Danny was sitting in the kitchen rubbing his swollen hand and bruised knuckles. He had already changed into the ambulance driver's uniform, which the driver did not give up without a fight.

'I think ye broke his jaw,' said Curly as he came back into the kitchen having made sure that the ambulance men were securely locked in the cellar underneath the house.

'Hurry up and get that on,' said Danny, throwing the other ambulance uniform at Curly's feet. 'We'll be in Dublin before the pubs close.'

*

Toying with the tip of his moustache, Moorcroft listened to the radio report from Captain Travers, which seemed promising. He ordered his SAS unit to the farmhouse. The *shoot to kill* order was given.

Captain Travers and his men took up positions around the farmhouse and out- buildings. Their orders were clear – they were not to do anything until the SAS unit arrived unless the suspects tried to make a break for it. The rain was now lashing down and visibility was minimal. The platoon's marksmen were ordered to take positions behind the stone dyke, which surrounded most of the farmhouse and various outbuildings.

'What the hell is that at the back of the house?' asked Travers.

'It looks like an ambulance, sir.'

'An ambulance, corporal, are ye sure?'

'Yes sir, it's an ambulance. There's someone coming out the house.'

Travers watched as the grey silhouettes of two men appeared. The internal lights came on for the first time and he could make out that one of the men was wearing what looked like a duffel coat, while the other had on a parka jacket. 'This all looks a bit fishy to me. You two men come with me, the rest of you keep yer heads down.'

His hand still throbbing, Danny jumped into the driver's seat beside Curly, who was looking forward to a fish supper when they got to Dublin. Before Danny got a chance to turn on the engine, there was a rapid chap at the driver's window. Danny put his left hand under his parka to find the revolver and slowly lowered the window down.

'God, ye gave me a fright there,' he said, hiding the nerves in his voice, and his Belfast accent.

'What's happened here?' asked Travers, his two colleagues standing behind him with their rifles at the ready. 'Why are ye wearing that thing?'

'Well for god's sake, it's pissing down; it's only me parka,' said Danny, pulling it open to make sure the soldiers could see the ambulance uniform underneath. 'We're taking an old fella to the hospital in Armagh,' continued Danny, as Travers looked past him to where Curly was sitting.

'We have to get going,' said Danny. 'We have to get to the hospital before he has another turn. He's in a fair amount of pain. It's a suspected heart attack.'

'Should someone not be in the back with the patient?' asked Travers.

'There's a nurse with him.'

'Is there anyone else in the house?'

'No, his granddaughter was here, but has gone to pick up her brother and they're going to meet us up at the hospital.'

Curly could feel the sweat running down from his armpits, afraid the captain was about to ask him something. He knew he did not have the confidence to speak with any authority or even hide his strong Belfast accent the way Danny could.

'We have to be going,' insisted Danny, impatiently turning on the engine and the windscreen wipers. 'You wouldn't happen to know the Man. United score last night, would ye?'

'Um … no,' replied Travers, rather embarrassed at his lack of knowledge about football, before turning to his two men, who both shrugged their shoulders.

‘I’ll find out when I get home. Now, don’t be catching yer death in that rain,’ said Danny, turning on the headlights and slowly reversing the ambulance, before manoeuvring down the muddy path onto the road.

‘Thank God,’ exhaled Curly as the ambulance drove through the waterlogged road towards the town. ‘Where did ye get the accent?’

‘I stayed in Newry for a few months and that’s how they speak down there.’

By the time they approached the border, Curly managed to find and operate the klaxons, and as they cautiously approached the checkpoint, the soldiers slowly opened the barrier and waved them through. Danny tooted his horn in feigned appreciation.

‘You’re a chancer, Duffy. Uncle Seamus was right about you.’

‘I’ll take that as a compliment.’

In the meantime, Captain Travers had withdrawn back over the stone dyke to await the arrival of Major Moorcroft and his SAS unit. He was still asking if anybody knew the Manchester United score.

Chapter 40

Dublin

Once over the border they drove as far as Monaghan, where they changed into their own damp clothes and dumped the ambulance in a country lane. They walked a couple of miles across country before thumbing a lift to Dublin. When they arrived in Parnell Square, Danny phoned the local Sinn Fein office.

An hour later they were met by Francis O'Malley, a strange little man, who wore a black Trilby hat and a pair of black-rimmed spectacles. He drove them across town to a boarding house just south of the Liffey, in the Ranelagh district of Dublin. The car pulled up outside a row of Edwardian terraced houses. O'Malley nodded towards one of the doors, before handing Danny a fistful of Irish banknotes and a rucksack containing clean clothes. 'The landlady is expecting ye both, and mind, yer here looking for building work.'

'Do you have any cigarettes?' asked Danny taking the rucksack.

'Here take these, that all I've got,' said O'Malley, handing Danny a packet of tobacco and some roll-up papers.

'Thanks, you will remember to phone the RUC about those people we left in the farmhouse,' said Danny, getting out of the car with Curly.

'Of course ... Phone me if you have any problems,' said O'Malley, doffing his hat and driving off as though he was glad to be rid of them.

The front door was opened by a cheery, middle-aged woman, who greeted them in a thick Dublin accent. 'Come in the pair of you. My name's Mary Kelly, I've been expecting the pair of ye.'

They followed the landlady upstairs, past the first landing to a narrow corridor at the top of the house, where she showed them into a sparsely furnished room; with two single beds, separated by a huge chest of drawers. 'The bathroom's at the end of the hall. There's plenty of hot water, and you'll no doubt want to clean up before you come down for some dinner.'

Curly, was so tired that he did not have the strength to get undressed before lying on top of his bed in his wet clothes and immediately falling asleep. Danny lit a cigarette and looked out at the street below. He watched the occasional car passing until he finished his smoke. He decided to have bath.

As soon as he got into the bathtub, he could feel the weight of sleep closing his eyelids as his mind surrendered to the warm steam of carbolic soap. He felt himself slip further down the tub and into the warm soapy water. They had made it!

*

'Are you no' finished yet?' shouted Curly, knocking the bathroom door. 'Have ye fallen asleep in there? I need the fucking toilet!'

'I'll be out in a minute,' replied Danny, waking from his stupor. The contrast between the warm water and the cold air exaggerated his body's shivering as he got out of the bath and briskly dried himself. He then wrapped the damp towel around his waist and opened the door.

‘About time, you’ve been in there for ages,’ moaned Curly, pushing past Danny.

‘I thought you were sleeping, Curly.’

Danny went back to the bedroom and searched through the rucksack to see what O’Malley had left them to change into. He was not happy with what he found. Most of the clothes were mismatched and old fashioned. He picked out the best ones, folding what remained back into the rucksack. He went back to the bathroom and knocked on the door. ‘Curly! I’ve left the rucksack outside with dry clothes in it.’

‘Danny, you’ve used all the fucking hot water,’ shouted Curly over the noise of the water spurting from the taps.

‘Well, ye should have got in first, and stop fucking swearing!’

Danny lay back on his bed and rolled a cigarette. He smiled when he heard Curly in the hall, lifting the rucksack. The bedroom door suddenly opened and Curly entered in a strop, wearing a baggy pair of brown corduroys and holding the other clothes neatly folded in his hands. ‘They’re having a laugh,’ he said, throwing down the multi-coloured tank top and floral printed shirt on the floor.

‘They’re worse than the ones the Brits tried to make us wear in jail,’ laughed Danny.

‘How come your gear’s all right?’

‘Mine are shit as well.’

‘But they’re not as bad as these fucking things. If I get arrested in these, I’ll be a fucking laughing stock.’

‘Curly, they’re not that bad,’ Danny lied, trying to control his laughter. ‘We’ll buy new gear tomorrow. At least they’re clean and dry,’ he added, desperate to see Curly in his hippy clothes.

Curly had little option, it was either the hideously, colourful dry clothes or the wet, dirty ones now lying on the bathroom floor. He took a cigarette from Danny, who tried to talk up the quality of the brown corduroys, with their extravagant flared bottoms. 'They're not that bad. My cousin had a pair of Oxford Bags like them.'

'But they're not Oxford Bags,' moaned Curly. 'They're just baggy old *Cords*. 'I'm not wearing these stupid things!'

'Your dinner is nearly ready, boys,' proclaimed Mrs Kelly, opening the bedroom door and poking her head in. 'I'm sure you lads will want something to eat. Can I come in?'

'Come in, Mrs Kelly,' replied Danny.

'I hope you're hungry,' she said. 'I've had building workers in here before and they were great eaters. I hate making food and it not getting eaten.'

'We're starving, missus, you don't have to worry about us on that score,' said Danny.

'Five minutes,' she proclaimed.

The smell of steak and kidney pie overcame Curly's dress sense and he reluctantly put on the shirt and tank top, before tying a heavy, leather belt around the waist of his trousers.

'Remember Curly, if anyone asks, we're here looking for building work,' said Danny as he flicked the cigarette butt out the window.

'Shit, I look like Donny Osmond, with this daft gear on,' moaned Curly.

'Don't flatter yerself; ye look more like Jimmy Osmond.'

'Piss off,' sulked Curly, before reluctantly following Danny down the narrow stairs.

*

Saint Jude's was a parish church on the extreme north side of Dublin in the shadow of the sprawling Ballymun housing estate. The area was dominated by seven high rise concrete blocks, built in the mid-sixties, each named in memory of the signatories to the 1916 Proclamation of Independence. Ballymun was now one of the worst areas in the city for violence and drug-dealing. Brendan had become well known in the parish after taking over from Father Hume, the elderly priest who had worn himself out dealing with the acute deprivation of his parishioners. Brendan was quick to involve himself in local housing groups, fighting for better living conditions. He was well aware that Danny was on the run, and probably somewhere in the Republic. He kept him in his prayers, hoping he would not return to a life of violence.

After morning mass, he went into the chapel house to get changed, folding his cassock-alb into the bottom drawer of his dresser with his other vestments. He had arranged to meet a local councillor to discuss ways of stopping the drug dealers on the estate making life hell for everyone.

'Father, there's a fella at the door wanting to have a word with you,' said Mrs Reilly, Brendan's elderly housekeeper. 'I don't like the look of him.'

'I don't have time. Ask him to come back this afternoon. And you shouldn't judge a book by its cover, Mrs Reilly.'

'Hello, Father Duffy,' said Danny, who had followed the housekeeper into the house and was standing behind her at the door.

'Mrs Reilly, could you go and make a pot of tea.'

'Father, remember you have a meeting with Councillor Kean in half an hour.'

'Yes, of course. Can you phone the councillor and tell him I'll be there in an hour's time.'

'Excuse me,' said the housekeeper, turning to pass Danny at the door.

Once Mrs Reilly had left, Brendan smiled and embraced Danny. 'Thank God you're safe. I've been worried about you.'

'I'm fine, you're looking well … how's Mammy been?'

'She phoned this morning to see if I had heard anything about you. She's sick with worry … Where are ye staying?'

'I'm staying in a boarding house, for now, but I may have to get out of the country altogether. I thought I'd come and see ye, while I still have the chance.'

'I'm glad ye did, Danny, and I hope ye do get out of the country … It's not safe in Dublin. Where will ye go?'

'I don't know, America maybe.'

The door opened and Mrs Reilly returned with a tray laden with crockery that looked too heavy for her to carry. Brendan took the tray and placed it on the table.

'Will that be all, Father?'

'Thank you, Mrs Reilly. You can head off home, now.'

'I'll see you in the morning, Father … and don't forget your meeting with Councillor Kean,' she stressed, before making her way to the front door to get her hat and coat.

'I won't. God bless you, Mrs Reilly.'

'I better go,' said Danny.

'You've only just got here. Stay and have a cup of tea with me.'

'You go to your meeting, Brendan. I just came by to let ye know I'm okay. If I'm found here I will only get ye into trouble. Tell Mammy I'm fine. I'll write to her and Roisin once I'm out of Ireland. Goodbye Brendan.'

'Goodbye Danny, and write to me as well.'

'I will.'

The following night, Danny and Curly were in a pub down beside the Liffey getting drunk for a second night in a row. In the far end of the pub a band was playing. Danny ordered another two whiskies and a couple of packets of crisps for Curly, who was regretting not having any dinner before they went out. The next song was a bit more subdued than the last, an old Irish love song called "Sally Gardens". Danny remembered one of the prisoners singing it at the time of the hunger strike. The haunting melody and the whiskey were starting to make him feel depressed. He thought about all those who had died. He went back to the bar for another whiskey before Curly had even touched his drink.

Thankfully, Curly was more interested in listening to the band than talking. It gave Danny time to think; his mind was on the hunger strike again. He cursed Thatcher as the whiskey burned its way down his throat. He ordered another drink. Curly gave up trying to keep up with him.

Near the end of the night the band began to play a song that they both knew better than anyone in the bar as the old gravel voice of the singer began to sing "Back Home in Derry". After the first few lines, Danny tried singing along; he was now so drunk that he was shouting the words out of tune. Heads began to turn towards him with looks of admonition. Curly pulled Danny's sleeve and gave a contrite wave to the barman who had stopped serving and was now staring at Danny.

'Why don't ye keep quiet,' said one of the men at the bar. 'Don't you know who wrote this song?'

'Why don't ye shut up!' roared Danny.

'That's it!' the barman shouted. 'You two, out!'

'And who's going to put us out?'

'Danny, for God's sake, let's go,' pleaded Curly, holding a submissive hand up to the big strapping barman. 'We're leaving.'

'Sit down, Curly. We'll leave when I've heard the end of this song,' ordered Danny, standing up face to face with the barman, who backed off as Danny began singing again in defiance of him. The band could see what was happening and skipped the last verse, rattling through the chorus in double quick time. Danny pushed past the barman and staggered to the front door. He stopped for a minute and stared at the ancient looking singer for a moment. 'There's only one man that can sing that song and he's dead... *Tiocfaidh ár lá!'*

Curly could feel the push from a number of hands as he squeezed himself out the front door after Danny, who began shouting the chorus of the song again, before throwing up at the side of the road. The madness seemed to leave him as quick as it came on. 'Are ye all right? We better get out of here,' said Curly, watching a Garda car passing slowly on the other side of the road.

'I'm all right, give me a minute. See if ye can flag down a taxi.'

*

Moorcroft was glad to have Captain Armstrong along with him, a seasoned SAS man who had been previously posted to 'bandit country' in County Armagh's border region. Both men, although working for Military Intelligence, were on a hastily contrived leave of absence, and their covert operations were subject to special rules of engagement. Their orders were unambiguous: track down and kill, if necessary, any escapees from the Maze hiding out in the Republic. If caught in the process they would be disowned by the British government as rogue officers acting on their own initiative.

'What number is it,' asked Moorcroft, turning the car into Albany Street.

'Number twenty-two ... there it is,' said Armstrong, pointing to a house on the right hand side of the road. Can we trust that O'Malley character?'

'He's been giving us information for years. He hasn't let us down yet,' said Moorcroft, parking the car, before turning on the overhead light to look through a brown envelope containing papers and photographs. He passed one of the files to Armstrong.

'He doesn't look old enough to be in the IRA,' said Armstrong, studying the black and white photograph of Curly that was stapled to one of the files.

'That was probably taken a few years ago, he's nineteen,' said Moorcroft. 'He's small fry. It's Duffy I want. He's a serious Provo. He was the driver in Newry when Gallagher shot the policeman and his wife...'

'Duffy looks it,' replied Armstrong, staring at Danny's prison photograph and scanning the list of classified information about him.

'He's getting the full treatment, that bastard. No warnings mind! He never gave any warnings when he was operating with Gallagher.'

'Do ye think they're armed?'

'Well as far as I'm concerned it won't make any difference. They won't get a chance to use them!' Moorcroft said, patting the revolver, in his coat pocket. 'Look, there's someone at the door.'

They watched Mrs Kelly standing on the top step of the house, wiping her hands with a tea towel. She looked up and down the street before going back into the house, shaking her head.

'How do we do this?'

'We wait until they're in the street and take them out then. You take Feeney and I'll take Duffy.'

*

Danny and Curly walked along the riverfront as the wind blew across the Liffey. After a while it began to rain hard. Curly tried in vain to hail a taxi, but none would stop when they saw Danny staggering along the pavement. They had been walking against the icy wind for nearly twenty minutes before their luck changed. They gratefully clambered in to the warmth of a private hire cab.

'Where to?'

'Albany Street,' said Curly.

'Oh, I know where that is. Are ye boys from Belfast?'

'Aye,' said Curly, when Danny did not answer. 'We're down looking for building work.'

'Ah, sure there's plenty about. Have ye tried the new shopping centre being built in town?'

'No … not yet, we'll give it a try tomorrow,' said Curly.

'It's a terrible night to be caught out in that …you're lucky I was planning to head home meself. How are ye both liking Dublin?' asked the driver, but no-one answered him this time; his passengers were both too tired to pay him any more attention. He drove on in silence until he finally turned onto Albany Street.

'What's number did ye say?'

'Drive on!'

'What?'

'Just drive on,' repeated Danny, suddenly alert.

Curly looked at Danny's serious expression and then back at the windows of the boarding house. There was a light on in the front lounge window, but the rest of the house was in darkness. He looked at Danny again but did not say anything. Danny told the driver to pull up at end of the road, and paid the fare. They both got out of the taxi with the rain still hammering off the road.

'What the hell's wrong?' asked Curly, scurrying along the pavement after Danny.

'You didn't see the car we passed outside the boarding house... the blue Cortina?'

'No.'

'There were two plain clothes RUC sitting in it.'

'How do ye know they were RUC?' asked Curly, sceptical about Danny's skills of observation, when only a few minutes earlier he looked like he was about to fall into the Liffey.

'Trust me! The car had Armagh plates,' he said, going down a short flight of stairs of a nearby basement garden. They took shelter under the stairway leading to the flat above. Danny lit a cigarette and handed one to Curly, who was still thinking that Danny may be getting a bit paranoid with all the whiskey he had been drinking recently.

'What are we going to do now?' Curly asked, shivering out a long breath of air and smoke. 'What about our stuff?'

'What stuff? We're wearing it.'

Danny looked down the street, but he could not see the Cortina for other parked vehicles. He then carefully moved over to the bay windows, peering into the basement flat. There was no sign of life. He clambered back over the shrubs and scattering of mouldy plant pots to the front door, before hesitantly tapping the brass knocker.

'What the hell are ye doing?'

'If anyone answers we'll tell them we're lost,' he whispered, rattling the ornate doorknocker again. Curly watched anxiously for the lights to suddenly come on, but nothing happened. He then grabbed Danny's arm before he could try again as a car passed slowly on the street above them. They waited until it drove on before Danny rattled the letterbox again. Still there was no sound from behind the closed storm doors. Danny suddenly pulled Curly into the frame of the doorway, when he heard a sash window open above them. They could see the shadow of someone looking out over the front garden, before they heard the window bang closed again.

'Why don't we go back and see if that car is still there?' suggested Curly, trying to stop his teeth chittering and desperate to get to a warm bed. Danny ignored the suggestion and clambered back towards the window, pulling overgrown clematis from the wall and almost losing his footing on the slimy undergrowth. All the windows were locked tight and he returned to the shelter of the overhanging concrete staircase, where Curly was now shivering uncontrollably. 'I can't get them to open,' said Danny, pressing his weight against the storm doors.

'Are you all right?' Danny asked when he turned to see Curly bent double and trying to catch his breath.

'No, I don't feel well.'

'Wait here, I'll be back in a minute,' said Danny, cautiously climbing back up to the pavement. There was a young couple, walking under an umbrella on the other side of the road, more interested in each other than what Danny might be up to. A strong wind was blowing down the street and he turned up his jacket collar, before crossing over the road to follow directly behind the two young lovers. He walked back to the boarding house to see if the suspicious car was still there. He saw the Cortina with the Armagh registration plates. He hurried past, stealing a look into the steamed up windows. He saw two men lying back in their seats. They were asleep. Danny walked on quickly.

The wind was getting wild. He walked down an alleyway and climbed over a six-foot wall into the back gardens. He found a narrow path behind a cluster of shrubs and made his way to the back of the basement flat.

Satisfied that there was no one in the flat he forced the back door open. It did not take much for the rotten door frame to yield. The state of the kitchen reassured him that the flat had not been occupied for some time.

When he opened the front door he found Curly lying under the stairs.

Chapter 41

Paddy Two-Shoes

Liz laid fresh flowers and lifted the wet, decaying leaves from the grave. She then wiped the oval picture of William that was embedded in the marble headstone. Even after nearly two years, she had still not come to terms with his death and felt her life meaningless without him. She tried not to think about the terrible day when she agreed with Jamie to have the life-support machine switched off. She was well aware by that time that William was not coming back, and she was just prolonging her own suffering, and maybe even William's by refusing to let him go. She decided if God wanted him so much then she would no longer stand in the doctors' way.

Once the decision was made, she felt a great weight lift from her shoulders, although holding William's hand as the doctor switched the life-support off was beyond agony. He struggled to breathe for a short time on his own, but quickly lost the fight and quietly slipped away. Liz simply kissed him on the forehead and said goodbye, leaving Jamie, who was sobbing uncontrollably, to do the same. She reassured herself that it was over, and he was now at peace in heaven where she would see him again one day, when her own time came.

Once she had cleared all the dead leaves, Liz made her way back down the road, where she took the bus back home. She did not mind that Jamie found it too difficult, even after all this time, to go to the grave. It was only a fifteen minute bus journey, and she preferred to be on her own, able to talk to William without anyone thinking she had gone mad.

When she got home, Jamie had already left for the lodge. She noticed that his tea was still warm and his newspaper was lying open at an article about the H-Block escapees. She looked at the pictures of those still on the run, and her heart skipped a beat. She stared in disbelief at a face that could have been Jamie twenty years earlier. Danny Duffy: the child she carried in her womb for nine months, a dangerous terrorist. She began to feel faint and had to sit down for a moment to collect her thoughts. She wondered if Jamie saw *himself* in the picture. Was that why he left in such a hurry without letting her know he was going out? Now that William had been dead for over two years, should she tell him about his *real* son?

*

Danny had spent the night trying to keep Curly warm, but he knew that his friend was seriously ill and getting worse. He had found some blankets in a cupboard and took Curly's wet clothes off, before wrapping him in the dry blankets. There was a portable gas fire in the hall, which he moved into the front room, where Curly lay shivering violently on the sofa. Even with the gas fire on full, it struggled to heat the draughty room. All night Danny was in a dilemma: the weaker Curly became, the more he struggled with the prospect of having to take him to the hospital.

Daylight began to fill the room. Curly was asleep, his chest wheezing with every breath and his face as white and gaunt as any corpse. Danny put another blanket over him, before leaving through the back door and over the garden wall.

It was still too early to expect anyone to be in the Sinn Fein Office, so he telephoned the number that O'Malley gave him. It took a while for the phone to answer. Danny explained that Curly was ill and needed a doctor. There was a long pause. 'Are ye still there, O'Malley!?'

'Yes, how bad is he?'

'He's bad enough … ye need to get a doctor over here. Don't send him to the boarding house, it's being watched. The doctor will have to meet me here …' Danny looked around for some kind of landmark. 'I'll be waiting at the phone box opposite the Bank of Ireland on Woodville Street.

After making the call, Danny sat on a nearby wall and lit a cigarette. He watched a milk float passing down the street as a few lights came on in the apartments opposite. He was hoping that the doctor would be able to give Curly something that would clear up whatever was wrong with him. A hospital was the last resort, and would almost certainly mean Curly being arrested and extradited back to the North.

Danny became impatient; it was now over an hour since he made the call to O'Malley. Smoking his last cigarette, he noticed that a corner shop was now open on the opposite side of the road. He made his way over.

The shopkeeper was busy cutting the string tied around a bundle of morning newspapers, before sorting them out into piles for the arrival of the paperboys. He got off his knees when he heard his first customer of the day coming into the shop.

'Good morning. It looks like it might be a decent day after all that rain last night,' said the shopkeeper, before going behind the counter to serve Danny. 'What can I get ye.'

'A packet of Carroll's and a box of matches,' said Danny, who then noticed the headline on one of the newspapers lying on the on the floor. *Another two Maze escapees arrested.*

'Is that all?'

'I'll take a paper as well.'

'Help yerself, I haven't had a chance to sort them yet.'

Danny picked up the *Irish Times*, paid thc shopkeeper and left.

He was about to cross back over to the phone box when he saw the blue Cortina passing slowly down the street, before pulling up just beyond the phone box. He took out his revolver and went back into the shop.

'If you do as I say, ye won't get hurt!'

'Take what ye want,' urged the terrified shopkeeper when he saw the gun pointing at him.

'I'm not going to rob ye, for fuck's sake. Is there a back way out of here?'

'Yes, there's a fire exit,' said the shopkeeper, indicating behind the counter.

Danny ran through the car park at the back of the shop and down the nearest street. He only stopped running when he was sure he was well away from the shop. 'That bastard O'Malley,' he muttered to himself. He made his way through the unfamiliar streets until he reached a main road where he flagged down at taxi. 'Where are ye going, young fella.'

'Saint Jude's in Ballymun.'

*

As soon as Brendan saw Curly, he knew that he was seriously ill. 'I think he may have bronchial pneumonia. You have to call an ambulance immediately. If you don't then he will die, and if you won't do it, then I will.'

'I know, but ...'

'Don't worry, I'll phone and tell them he's my cousin. The police don't have to get involved, it's not like it's a bullet wound or anything. You'll just have to find somewhere else to stay. Whose house is this anyway?' Brendan asked, putting his coat back on and pulling the blankets back over Curly, who was still struggling to breathe. 'It's obviously not a boarding house.'

'It's just an empty house. We had been staying in a boarding house at the top of the road until last night. We were going back, but there was a suspicious looking car parked outside. It had Armagh plates. I thought at first it was RUC special branch, but they may even be UVF.'

'I don't think you should stay here in the meantime, just in case one of the ambulance crew recognises you from the papers. I know you're in the Republic, but you can't take any risks.'

'You don't have to tell me that … I'm sorry, Brendan, for getting you involved.'

'No you're not. You're never sorry for any thing you do.'

Brendan took a note of the address from one of the letters lying behind the front door before climbing the short flight of steps up to the pavement. The street was quiet, but, as he walked on, he heard a car come along the road. He watched it pass down the street, turning right at the bottom of the road. He began to take deep breaths to steady his nerves, and rehearsed what he was going to say when he made the call to the hospital.

It was nearly twenty minutes before the ambulance arrived. With no sign of the blue Cortina, Danny watched from across the street as the ambulance pulled up outside the flat. Brendan came out of the house and hurried the two ambulance men, who followed him down the stairs to the basement flat. Some of the neighbours were standing about pointing and talking amongst themselves. Danny listened to what they were saying. Curly was carried out on a stretcher, and carefully put into the back of the ambulance.

'That must be poor Mrs McGuire's son they're taking away,' said one elderly woman to her friend, who was nodding in agreement. 'I thought he went back to England after her funeral.'

'He must be in a bad way, with the priest there and all,' said the other woman, still shaking her head. 'God help him.'

Danny stepped back onto the pavement, satisfied with what he had heard. He watched Brendan get into the back of the ambulance. Gradually the neighbours dispersed now that the drama was over. Danny lit a cigarette when the ambulance sped down the street.

He walked towards the city centre, where he found a quiet pub near to St Stephen's Green. He bought a pint. He tried to phone the Sinn Fein office, but all he got each time was an engaged tone. He finished his pint and left the bar. He walked along Dawson Street, not sure where he was going. He carried on walking along the main road until he could see O'Connell Bridge up ahead.

Crossing the busy bridge, he glanced briefly at the murky waters of the Liffey, before walking into the wide spread that was O'Connell Street. A group of Japanese tourists were taking pictures of the most substantial building in the street, the General Post Office where Patrick Pearse read the Proclamation of Irish Independence. Danny put his finger in one of the many bullets holes that were still evident on the front of the building and its columns. He was about to go into the post office, when he noticed two *gardai* officers at the entrance. He hesitated, and turned away, walking briskly towards O'Connell Bridge. It began to rain.

With nowhere else to go, he walked back to the basement flat. Miserable and freezing, he laid his wet clothes around the gas fire. He dried himself with some towels he found in an airing cupboard and wrapped a couple of blankets around himself. He could not afford to end up like Curly.

Worn out, he quickly fell into a deep sleep. He did not hear the blue Cortina pulling up on the other side of the road.

Danny's mind conjured up vague dreams that made no sense until he found himself sitting on a rocky outcrop overlooking Belfast. He could see all the way down the Shankill, draped in the colours of the Union. He watched the bands of the Orange Order marching down the middle of the road playing "The Sash". They continued all the way to the Lagan, which was shrouded in a nebulous, grey fog that gradually swallowed them up until all he could hear was the pounding beat of the Lambeg drum. He then looked towards the terraced streets of the Falls, where he could see a solitary tricolour moving slowly down the middle of Mill Street. It was followed by a procession of ghostly figures.

'Watching your own funeral, son,' said a voice that drifted to him on the wind.

Danny turned to see an old man sitting nearby. 'Who the hell are you?'

'It doesn't matter who I am, it's who *you* are that's important.'

'I know who I'm, but who are you, old man?'

'You came looking for me once, when you were a young boy.'

'Paddy Two-Shoes?' laughed Danny. 'Are ye going to tell me that's a shillelagh ye have there?'

'No, it's a stick. A shillelagh is the thing they sell in souvenir shops to gullible tourists. And the name's not Paddy Two-Shoes. That's a silly name your father made up. Why would anyone be called Paddy Two-Shoes, haven't we all got two shoes?'

'He made you up as well, you're not real. Go away and

stop annoying me.'

'If I'm not real, then why are ye taking to me?'

'Leave me alone, old man,' said Danny looking back down at the funeral procession that was also making its way towards the Lagan.

'That's the future becoming the past,' said the old man as the fog swallowed up the coffin and the hundreds that followed it into the Lagan.

Danny turned to speak, but the old man was gone, all he could see was the gorse blowing wildly in the wind. The fog from the Lagan began to drift up the mountainside. It quickly engulfed him. He struggled to breathe as he tried to free himself from the dream.

He woke with a start and felt a sudden draught as if there was an evil presence in the room. With his eyes now wide open, he thought he could hear someone breathing. He hoped he was imagining things. A plume of smoke slowly passed above his head. He tried to remember where he had left the revolver, but couldn't think straight.

'You're a noisy sleeper, Duffy! Who the fuck is Paddy Two-Shoes?'

With the morning light blinding him, Danny turned and saw Fergal Gallagher sitting in the chair opposite, smoking. He thought for a second that he was seeing things as his eyes adjusted to the bright light. 'What the fuck are ye doing here? I thought they locked ye up in that asylum for life,' said Danny, sitting up and pulling the blanket around his body, desperately feeling for the revolver under the pillow.

I broke out of that place months ago. It was a piece of piss. At least it got me off the smack and let me get my head sorted. I've got the green light from Northern Command. It was them that sent me to find you … I'm sorry, Danny, but I have some bad news … your Dad was killed the other day.'

'What? Me dad, killed! Fuck, what happened?'

'We think it was the UVF that picked him up. He got a bullet to the head. At least they didn't torture him.'

'So that makes it alright?'

'I'm just saying, it could have been worse.'

'Do ye know who did it?'

'We think it was Morrison that ordered it. He gives the orders for most of these killings. But he's a hard man to get near. He lives in the heart of the Shankill and when he goes anywhere he's always surrounded by bodyguards. But we'll get him one of these days. When he least expects it.'

'The bastards! But why did they kill me da?'

'Because they couldn't get you; they're probably trying to draw you out.'

'When's the funeral?'

'I'm not sure. I don't think they've released the body yet … but ye can't go to the funeral. The Brits will be expecting you to turn up.'

'How did you find me?'

'You should be glad I did,' Fergal replied, his voice slightly smug as he threw two buff files onto Danny's lap. 'The two fuckers that had them are lying in their car with bullets in their heads…'

'Shit…' was all Danny could think to say, looking at the photographs of Curly and himself on the front of the files. 'The blue Cortina?'

'The very one, so you've not been totally blind.'

'I noticed it a few times parked up the road. It had Armagh plates. RUC special branch?'

'No, SAS. That bastard Moorcroft was one of them. I think he shit himself before I put a bullet in his head. They were watching the boarding house…'

‘Fuck.’

‘I’m heading back to Belfast today before the *gardai* find their car. Ye can come with me if ye want, but ye definitely can’t stay here. If I could find ye, then the police can find ye easily enough.’

‘You seem to know everything. Do you know that Curly ended up with pneumonia and is in hospital?’

‘He’s fine, he’ll be out in a couple of days and we’ll get him up to Sligo. He’s got family there who’ll look after him.’

‘What about me? What am I supposed to do?’

‘If you don’t want to go back to Belfast, you can go to America if you want. I can get ye an Irish passport. Whatever ye do, ye can’t stay here. We’ve got a few safe houses ye can use down in Cork until you decide if you want to go to the States or not. If they find you in Dublin they’ll pin these two stiffs on ye, for sure,’ said Fergal, sounding nothing like the man Danny had grown to fear and hate.

‘Thanks Fergal - are we alright?’

‘We’re grand; I was a bit fucked up … that’s all behind us. So ye can stop looking for your gun. You left it in the kitchen, ye dozy bastard,’ said Fergal, taking Danny’s revolver from his coat pocket. ‘Here, and don’t be so fucking careless with it. If those two SAS fuckers found ye before I found them, then ye’d be going to yer own funeral.’

‘What now?’

‘We better get out of here,’ replied Fergal, stubbing his cigarette end into the threadbare carpet, before nodding towards the noise outside the window.

Danny went to the window and watched as a police car sped up the street with its blue lights flashing and siren screaming. There was already an ambulance parked beside the Cortina and another police car came down the road from the other direction. One officer began tying tape around lampposts to cordon off the area. He could see stretchers coming out of the ambulance as one senior officer stopped the paramedics from taking the bodies from the car. He watched as a scene of crime officer lifted items from the car and placed them in clear plastic bags. The crowd grew larger as another two police cars pulled up.

Chapter 42

Waiting in Vain

An icy wind blew through the streets as hundreds of mourners gathered around the corner house on Mill Street. Under pressure from Joe's family, Marie relented and allowed the coffin to be draped in the tricolour. Along with Brendan, Joe's two brothers and three of his cousins carried the casket out to the waiting hearse. The crowd in the street cheered and clapped, with a few shouting abuse at an army helicopter circling overhead.

Marie and Roisin were led by a local Sinn Fein councillor to the waiting cars. Flowers and wreaths were placed into the hearse, while Marie took a seat in the back of one of the cars along with Roisin. The crowd continued to swell as the cortège turned down towards the Falls Road.

At the steps of the chapel, the tricolour was removed on the insistence of Father Cunningham. It was folded neatly and handed to Marie along with a black beret and a pair of black gloves. Marie immediately handed them to Roisin. She knew that the funeral was being used as an IRA publicity stunt and that there was little she could do about it.

The family and other mourners settled down in their seats inside the crowded chapel. Father Cunningham, once more, condemned the men of violence from the pulpit. Some of the mourners walked out when he blamed the Provisional IRA as much as the loyalist paramilitaries for turning the back streets of Belfast into murder alleys. Marie sat stone-faced during the sermon as it echoed through loudspeakers, and out to the crowds in the nearby streets. Her mind drifted back to when she first met Joe at a Saint Patrick's Day dance. She found it hard to recall much of that night, but the bump on her stomach a few months later led to a hurried marriage that neither of them was ready for. Joe was handsome then, and full of energy and ideas that made his eyes light up when he spoke. Marie could not see the man she had married, in the old, bitter drunk that he finally became. She turned to look at the coffin and the picture of Joe that Roisin picked from Kathleen's wedding album; one of the few times in his life that he wore a decent suit. He was smiling, the proud father. It was a good picture.

She wondered if the ten shillings she gave to Father McFadden, all those years ago, to pray for Joe's soul would help get him into heaven. Now a little more cynical, Marie was pretty sure that the ten shillings never saw the inside of any chapel donation box. The noise of kneeling boards banging on the floor brought Marie out of her thoughts. She got down on her knees and prayed.

Brendan was first to take Holy Communion, before putting on a white cassock and helping Father Cunningham deal with the hundreds who queued along the side aisles waiting to take the sacrament.

Once the mass was over, Father Cunningham descended from the altar to offer his condolences to the Duffy family, before they followed the coffin out of the chapel.

Outside the coffin was once more draped in the tricolour, before being placed back into the hearse for Joe's final journey to Milltown Cemetery.

At the graveside the coffin was gently lowered on top of two smaller ones with only a few inches of earth between them. There was an unnerving sound when the weight of Joe's coffin seemed to crush what was below it. Father Cunningham began to read. 'In the name of the Father, we commit the body of Joseph Patrick Duffy to the peace of the grave … From dust we came, and to dust we shall return. Jesus Christ is the resurrection and the life. Give him O'

Lord your peace and let your eternal light shine upon him. Amen.'

Marie jumped with fright when a sudden volley of rifle fire blasted into the sky, echoing like a ricochet around the graveyard; another volley, and then another. If only they had shown him this much respect when he was alive, then maybe he would not have ended up the sad drunk he had become, she angrily thought to herself. The tears began to run down her pale face with every thud of hard clay that was shovelled onto the coffin. She looked back over to the wall where the four men in balaclavas and combat fatigues had made their defiant salute. There was no one there.

When the family got home, Marie put Joe's memorial card on the table in the living room with all the other photographs of the family. Roisin was worried about her mother, who rarely ate, and spent most of her time in bed or on her knees. Roisin made the mistake in telling her mother that Danny was one of the four men who fired the volley of shots at the funeral.

'And how do ye know that?' she demanded.

'I saw him take off the balaclava when a few of the lads led him away.'

'If he's in Belfast, why has he not come to see his mother?'

'He can't,' said Brendan, shaking his head at Roisin. 'He's probably on his way back over the border by now. He can't come here. He's one of the most wanted men in Ireland. The army have this house under constant surveillance.'

'He'll be here soon. I better get something nice in for his dinner.'

'Mammy, he won't be coming home,' said Brendan, becoming frustrated.

'Why would he not come home? Sure he could come in the back door, who's going to know? Roisin, you'll have to sleep with me, so Brendan and Danny can take your room.'

‘Mammy … He’s not coming home,’ repeated Brendan, taking her in his arms.

The following week, still fretting about her mother’s state of mind, Roisin returned to her teaching job in Glasgow. Brendan stayed on a few days longer, and tried his best to find out what he could about Danny, but no one he contacted in Sinn Fein was able or willing to give him any information.

On the morning Brendan left for Dublin, Marie took out her rosary beads and prayed on her knees for hours. She then sat for the rest of the day in the kitchen waiting for Danny. She continued this ritual everyday, but her prayers were never answered. Only two weeks after Joe’s funeral, her sister, Theresa, found Marie slumped over the kitchen table, the rosary beads still in her cold hands.

Chapter 43

A Few Years Later

Following a minor stroke, Jamie Morrison took early retirement from the shipyards and gave up his UVF role to a younger man. Jamie recovered his health during a six month period of convalescence, during which time he gradually turned the backyard into a beautiful garden. Once he felt more like his old self again, he decided to take up politics and was duly selected to run as a Progressive Unionist candidate in the forthcoming council elections. Liz tried to dissuade him at first, fearful that the stress would bring on another, more serious, stroke. However, Jamie's mind was made up, and there was nothing she could say that would change it. She eventually relented and even became his secretary, canvassing just as hard as anyone to get him elected.

In spite of all their hard work, Jamie failed to win a seat on the council. Liz now hoped he would try and enjoy his retirement, but she soon discovered that Jamie was as determined as ever to get into politics.

'I think I'll give Paisley a call,' he said one day after reading about the DUP's gains in the opinion polls. 'I'd have a better chance of getting elected with them the next time.'

'Jamie, can you not just leave it for awhile. You don't want to end up in hospital again. This time ye might not be so lucky … Why don't we go on holiday for a couple of weeks, see how you feel about it when you get back.'

'Holiday? Where?' he responded with very little

enthusiasm.

'We could go to Tenerife. It's still warm there at this time of year. Irene was there last January and she loved it.'

'Well, maybe yer right … Anyway, I think I'll go out and plant some of those tulip bulbs before we get a frost and the soil becomes impossible to dig.'

After watching television for awhile, Liz put the kettle on and shouted out to Jamie to come in before it got dark. He just waved at her and carried on pottering around the garden. She left a cup of tea for him on the window sill, before rushing back indoors as the bitter November wind sliced through her thin blouse. She closed the door with a bang and shivered before going back into the house. She noticed the picture of William was lying face down in the hall. She picked it up and stared at it, trying to remember how old he would have been when the picture was taken. Her thoughts were wiped away when she heard three loud bangs. She hurried to the back door. She saw Jamie lying face down in the fish pond. She ran up the path and kneeled down, pulling him from the blood red water. As she lifted the top of his body, a piece of brain dropped into the pond with a splash; the goldfish immediately began to feed on it. She then heard the screech of car wheels turning in the cul-de-sac at the back of the house. She rushed to the garden gate and into the street. The car passed slowly. The passenger rolled down the window, and sneered at her. '*Tiocfaidh ár lá!,* missus.'

Liz made to grab him, but the car screeched away.

When questioned later by the police, Liz was asked to look through pictures of known IRA gunmen. The two detectives noticed her hesitation when she was shown Danny Duffy's photograph.

'Is that one of them?'

Liz looked at the photograph again, and then shook her head. 'No, that's not him … I didn't get a good look at them.'

Epilogue

Belfast Herald

10th April 1998

The political deal which aimed to form the lasting settlement following the 1994 paramilitary ceasefires in Northern Ireland, known as the Good Friday Agreement, was signed today by the British Prime Minister, Tony Blair and the Irish Taoiseach, Bertie Ahern, along with all the main Northern Ireland political parties, with the exception of the Democratic Unionists.

The plans are for a Northern Ireland Assembly, to be set up with a power-sharing executive and new cross-border institutions, involving the Irish Republic and a body linking devolved assemblies across the UK with Westminster and Dublin. The Irish Republic has also rescinded its constitutional claim to the six counties which form Northern Ireland.

A copy of the Agreement was posted to every household in the province and the Irish Republic and put to referendums in May, which gave substantial support for the Agreement, by 74% and 94% respectively. The lower amount of support in Northern Ireland was attributed to a significant number of sceptical Unionist voters.

The document opens with the words: We, the participants in the multi-party negotiations, believe that the agreement we have negotiated offers a truly historic opportunity for a new beginning, and believe the best way to honour those who died or have been injured, and their families, was to make a fresh start. The participants reaffirm their total and absolute commitment to exclusively democratic and peaceful means of resolving differences on political issues, and their opposition to any use or threat of force. The participants acknowledge that it would be wrong to make any change in the status of Northern Ireland save with the consent of a majority of its people. There will be changes made to British law and the Irish constitution, from which their territorial claim over Northern Ireland is removed. The Agreement will establish the operation of a democratically elected power-sharing assembly in Northern Ireland, including safeguards for cross-community participation, such as the allocation of Committee Chairs, Ministers and Committee membership in proportion to party strengths. A North and South Ministerial Council are to bring together those with executive responsibilities in Northern Ireland and the Irish government on matters of mutual interest. A British-Irish Council is to be set up to promote the harmonious and mutually beneficial development of the totality of relationships among the peoples of these islands.

The participants affirm their commitment to the mutual respect, the civil rights and the religious liberties of everyone in the community. Measures will include the establishment of a new Northern Ireland Human Rights Commission and the incorporation of the European Convention on Human Rights into Northern Ireland law.

The decommissioning of paramilitary weapons requires the participants to use any influence they may have to achieve decommissioning of all arms 'within two years following endorsement in referendums North and South of the agreement and in the context of the implementation of the overall settlement.

The British government is committed to as early a return as possible to normal security arrangements in Northern Ireland. The independent Patten Commission will look at the issue of policing, as well as a parallel commission looking into criminal justice in Northern Ireland. There would also be provisions put into place for the early release of paramilitary prisoners, as long as the organizations to which they are linked maintain a complete and unequivocal ceasefire.

The parties acknowledge the substantial differences between them but declare they will work to ensure the success of the Agreement. Over the last thirty years Northern Ireland's Troubles have left a deep and profoundly regrettable legacy of suffering.

Today, in the High Court in Belfast, a retired midwife pled guilty to the deliberate switching of two hundred and thirty new born babies over a period of nearly thirty years, while she was a maternity nurse in various hospitals throughout Northern Ireland. The authorities believe there could be hundreds more cases where victims have failed to come forward for the DNA testing programme set up by the Northern Ireland Health Service. The nurse has been called the most hated women in Northern Ireland and has been held in protective custody since her arrest. The motives for her actions are unknown. Her defence barrister Allan Stafford QC gave details of his client's tragic childhood as a possible explanation for her grave crimes. She was born out of wedlock in 1928 in Sligo to her unmarried fifteen year old Catholic mother who was forced to give the child up for adoption by her family and the local parish priest. For her sins, her mother was then sent to the Magdalene Asylum, where she hanged herself after only a few weeks, while the child was adopted by Mr and Mrs Chambers, a Protestant couple who were unable to have their own children. The

Chambers family later moved from the Free State to Carrickfergus in the North and brought up young Bridget as their own, only telling her of the adoption when she was sixteen. It is believed that the sudden realisation that she was adopted may have triggered a neurosis which led to further psychiatric problems during her life. The resentment she felt when she realised she was not the biological child of her adoptive parents seems to have manifested itself in the criminal charges to which she has now pled guilty.

The Lord Justice, Andrew Copeland QC, told the frail looking accused that she had caused untold pain and sufferings to hundreds of families around the country, for what he saw as nothing more than wicked and spiteful criminal behaviour, based on a warped sense of injustice for her own unfortunate childhood. The judge deferred sentence for a further three weeks to have her further psychiatrically assessed under the Mental Health Act...

Some other books from Ringwood Publishing

All titles are available from the Ringwood website (including first edition signed copies) and from usual outlets.
Also available in Kindle, Kobo and Nook.
www.ringwoodpublishing.com

Ringwood Publishing, 24 Duncan Avenue, Glasgow, G14 9HN

mail@ringwoodpublishing.com

Dark Loch

Charles P Sharkey

Dark Loch is an epic tale of the effects of the First World War on the lives of the residents of a small Scottish rural community. A crucial central strand is the long-running romance between tenant crofter Callum Macnair and Caitriona Dunbar, the beautiful daughter of the local Laird.

The story is initially set in the fictional village of Glenfay on the banks of Loch Fay on the west coast of Scotland. The main characters are the tenant crofters who work the land leased to them by the laird, Lord Charles Dunbar, and his family. The crofters live a harsh existence in harmony with the land and the changing seasons, unaware of the devastating war that is soon to engulf the continent of Europe.

The book vividly and dramatically explores the impact of that war on all the main characters and how their lives are drastically altered forever

Between Two Bridges

Brian McHugh

In New York, 1933, Prohibition is coming to an end, but not everyone is celebrating. A few astute businessmen realise that by legally importing liquor before the Volstead Act is repealed, they can net themselves a small fortune. Charlie McKenna, an Irishman who spent time in Glasgow during the Great War, is sent to complete the deal with Denholm Distillers in their St Enoch Square office.

Fast-forward to present-day Glasgow. Still reeling from the murder of their friend, three old friends are once again knocked off-course by the resurfacing of a battered diary. It soon leads them back into their investigation of Julie's grandfather, Charlie McKenna. More troubling tales of war, gold and gangsters soon begin to surface.

Between Two Bridges is a fast-paced adventure with a well-researched historical setting.

ISBN: 978-1-901514-35-3 £9.99

Torn Edges

Brian McHugh

When a gold coin very similar to a family heirloom is found at the scene of a Glasgow murder, a search is begun that takes the McKenna family, assisted by their Librarian friend Liam, through their own family history right back to the tumultuous days of the Irish Civil War.

Parallel to this unravelling of the family involvement of this period, Torn Edges author Brian McHugh has interwoven the remarkable story of the actual participation of two of the McKenna family, Charlie and Pat, across both sides of the conflict in the desperate days of 1922 Ireland.

Torn Edges is both entertaining and well-written, and will be of considerable interest to all in both Scottish and Irish communities.

ISBN: 978-1-901514-05-6 £9.99

Scotball

Stephen O'Donnell

Peter Fitzpatrick returns home to Kirkintilloch with his Czech wife after five years in Prague. Resuming his previous career in banking and financial service, he feels unfulfilled. His application to host a television programme discussing the hot topics relating to Scottish football eventually finds favour. 'The Scottish Football Debate', or 'Scotball' is born.

Scotball is a searing examination of the current state of Scottish football and the various social, political and economic forces that combine to strangle its integrity and potential.

ISBN: 978-1-901514-13-1 £9.99

Paradise Road

Stephen O'Donnell

Paradise Road is the story of Kevin McGarry, who through a combination of injury and disillusionment is forced to abandon any thoughts of playing football professionally. Instead he settles for following his favourite team, Glasgow Celtic, whilst trying to eke out a living as a joiner. It considers the role of young working-class men in our post-industrial society.

ISBN: 978-1-901514-07-0 £9.99